Praise for *Where the Wandering Ends*

"Love, hope, courage, and survival thread their way through this magically crafted story combining history and mythology. This story stays with me—the love and sacrifice of mothers, promises made by children, unbearable loss, and dreams cast aside but never forgotten."

—HEATHER MORRIS, *NEW YORK TIMES* BESTSELLING AUTHOR
OF *THE TATTOOIST OF AUSCHWITZ* AND *THE THREE SISTERS*

"From maestro winds to fried smelt, from Mother Nyx to the Ionian Sea, and from ouzo to olive trees, this book hums with the tantalizing spirit of Greece. Leaning into 20th century Greek history—including a pivotal storyline including Britain's Prince Philip, and his mother, Princess Alice of Greece—author Yvette Manessis Corporon, herself a first-generation Greek-American, takes us past the Second World War, through the bloody civil war of the late 1940s, and through the difficult years in the conflict's aftermath, all through the eyes of a few families from the island of Corfu whose lives intersect through the years. A sweeping, multigenerational story of love, loss and sacrifice, Where the Wandering Ends is a beautiful journey through time in a war-ravaged, picturesque land of royalty, ruin, and hope."

—KRISTIN HARMEL, *NEW YORK TIMES* BESTSELLING
AUTHOR OF *THE FOREST OF VANISHING STARS*

"Set on the romantic island of Corfu, *Where the Wandering Ends* is a powerful, emotional tale of recent history, showing the disruption of lives during the Greek Civil War, not only to the simple Corfiots but also to the Greek royal family who called Corfu their home."

—RHYS BOWEN, *NEW YORK TIMES* BESTSELLING AUTHOR OF THE
ROYAL SPYNESS AND MOLLY MURPHY HISTORICAL MYSTERIES
AND INTERNATIONAL BESTSELLER *THE VENICE SKETCHBOOK*

"In her latest novel, *Where the Wandering Ends*, Yvette Manessis Corporon takes readers to the Greek isle of Corfu, a stunning locale where the sun-drenched cliffs meet the shimmering blue of the Ionian Sea. There, a sweeping family saga unfolds over multiple generations, filled with war, love, loss, and ultimately redemption. Corporon tells a transportive story filled with pathos and longing, a tale of homecoming, woven with beautiful threads from history, mythology, and the indelible truths and wisdom of the human heart."

—ALLISON PATAKI, *NEW YORK TIMES* BESTSELLING AUTHOR
OF *THE MAGNIFICENT LIVES OF MAJORIE POST*

"A soul-stirring tale of love, loss, friendship, family, and fate set amid the ravages of war, *Where the Wandering Ends* is especially relevant today. Yvette Manessis Corporon writes with grace and crystalline clarity about what matters most: the transcendent resilience of the human spirit."

—CHRISTOPHER ANDERSEN, #1 *NEW YORK TIMES* BESTSELLING AUTHOR

"Emotive, transportive, and gorgeously rendered, this novel plumbs the depths of how we find our way back from great heartache and loss. Heartbreaking one moment and utterly life-affirming the next, *Where the Wandering Ends* will open your eyes to a moment in history that should not be forgotten."

—SUSAN MEISSNER, *USA TODAY* BESTSELLING
AUTHOR OF *THE NATURE OF FRAGILE THINGS*

"Yvette Corporon takes her place among the best of historical fiction with this evocative, sometimes mystical, novel. Filled with characters you'll come to love, hard-won faith, dreams lost and found, and settings that will take your breath, this story follows the complex and winding ways that life endures in the aftermath of war. From the hillsides of Corfu to the streets of NYC, *Where the Wandering Ends* is a sensitive celebration of unconditional love."

—KIMBERLY BROCK, BESTSELLING AUTHOR OF
THE LOST BOOK OF ELEANOR DARE

"A vibrant tale of family, love and loss, and the hope of new beginnings. Corporon's research is impeccable as she lays Greece's rich and storied history before readers, providing the perfect backdrop for her multigenerational story. *Where the Wandering Ends* truly brings readers to the heart of Greece in a story that is as sweeping as a saga and yet as intimate as a mother's love. I enjoyed it immensely."

—KATHERINE REAY, BESTSELLING AUTHOR OF *THE
LONDON HOUSE* AND *THE PRINTED LETTER BOOKSHOP*

"Yvette Corporon's *Where the Wandering Ends* is a lush, lyrical treasure of historical fiction centering on the island of Corfu in the late 1940s, whose people, recovering from the horrors of World War II are now thrust into greater uncertainty as Greek civil war looms. Masterfully using the tension of time and circumstance, Corporon crafts an unforgettable novel that, at its heart, is a story about the complexities of people and how, even in the midst of chaos and fear, love shines through."

—JOY CALLAWAY, INTERNATIONAL BESTSELLING AUTHOR OF
THE GRAND DESIGN AND *THE FIFTH AVENUE ARTISTS SOCIETY*

"Told in lush, masterful prose, *Where the Wandering Ends* transports the reader to Corfu, Greece, during the Greek Civil War and spins a mesmerizing story of loss, love, and hope. Perfect for lovers of historical fiction who are eager to explore a little-known area of twentieth-century history."

—ANITA ABRIEL, INTERNATIONAL BESTSELLING
AUTHOR OF *THE LIGHT AFTER THE WAR*

Praise for *Something Beautiful Happened*

"Part thriller, part history, this meticulously researched memoir tells a searing story of human kindness in brutal times."

—NICHOLAS GAGE, BESTSELLING AUTHOR OF *ELENI*

"This beautifully written story will light the way through life's darkest moments, proving that kindness is the most powerful force of all."

—ROMA DOWNEY, ACTOR, PRODUCER, AND
PRESIDENT OF LIGHTWORKERS MEDIA

"This heartwarming story has so many amazing twists, turns, and beautiful invisible thread connections which proves how there is more goodness and love in our world than evil."

—LAURA SCHROFF, #1 *NEW YORK TIMES* AND INTERNATIONAL
BESTSELLING AUTHOR OF *AN INVISIBLE THREAD*

"As heartwarming as it is moving and thought-provoking, *Something Beautiful Happened* is part evocative and touching personal memoir, part insightful and uncompromising factual accounting, lending critical perspective on the ongoing fight against intolerance."

—KIMBERLY MCCREIGHT, *NEW YORK TIMES* BESTSELLING
AUTHOR OF *RECONSTRUCTING AMELIA* AND *THE OUTLIERS*

"*Something Beautiful Happened* is both an engrossing peek into a little-known chapter of World War II and one family's harrowing tale of finding the lost pieces of its own history. With impeccable research and rich detail, Yvette Manessis Corporon deftly intertwines these narratives to create a powerful and unforgettable memoir. I will be thinking about these characters for a long time to come."

—KAREN ABBOTT, *NEW YORK TIMES* BESTSELLING
AUTHOR OF *LIAR, TEMPTRESS, SOLDIER, SPY*

Praise for *When the Cypress Whispers*

"*When the Cypress Whispers* is a rich, emotionally nuanced story about a woman's deeply held connection to her family and her past. With an evocative setting and finely drawn characters, Corporon creates a beautiful world you won't soon forget."

—EMILY GIFFIN, *NEW YORK TIMES* BESTSELLING AUTHOR

"*When The Cypress Whispers* is an unforgettable book about what it truly means to love and be loved . . . Yvette has taken the myths, history, and culture of our homeland and crafted a deeply moving story that will stay with you long after you've finished the last page."

—MARIA MENOUNOS

"The power of family tradition and heritage is compassionately explored in Corporon's debut about Daphne, a Greek-American woman who, having lost her husband and the father of her daughter, Evie, in a car accident in the US, tries to rebuild the pieces of her life in Greece . . . Corporon can tell a good tale, and her love for her Greek heritage permeates the story."

—*PUBLISHERS WEEKLY*

"Though Daphne's journey is the emotional center of the book, the real star is the island of Erikousa, from the sun-baked patios to the spitting widows who meet every ferry. There is just enough humor to balance the heartache, and a dash of history adds depth. Readers will be transported."

—*BOOKLIST*

"Sun-drenched, evocative, and a wee bit magical, *When the Cypress Whispers* is both a perfect beach read and a compelling portrait of a family of strong women."

—*SHELF AWARENESS*

Where the
Wandering
Ends

ALSO BY YVETTE MANESSIS CORPORON

When the Cypress Whispers
Something Beautiful Happened

Where the Wandering Ends

A NOVEL

YVETTE MANESSIS CORPORON

HARPER MUSE

Where the Wandering Ends

Copyright © 2022 Yvette Manessis Corporon

Published by Harper Muse, an imprint of HarperCollins Focus LLC.

Interior design by Emily Ghattas

Republished with permission of Princeton University Press, from *C.P. Cavafy: Collected Poems.– Revised Edition*, "Ithaka," C. P. Cavafy, 1992; permission conveyed through Copyright Clearance Center, Inc.

Any internet addresses (websites, blogs, etc.) in this book are offered as a resource. They are not intended in any way to be or imply an endorsement by HarperCollins Focus LLC, nor does HarperCollins Focus LLC vouch for the content of these sites for the life of this book.

ISBN: 978-1-4002-3881-1 (ITPE)

Library of Congress Cataloging-in-Publication Data

Names: Corporon, Yvette Manessis, author.
Title: Where the wandering ends : a novel / Yvette Manessis Corporon.
Description: [Nashville] : Harper Muse, [2022] | Summary: "Two young friends are separated by unspeakable tragedy during the Greek Civil War, haunted by a vow to return to one another and their home on the island of Corfu where queens, villagers, and goddesses come together to prove there is no force more powerful than the magic of a mother's love"-- Provided by publisher.
Identifiers: LCCN 2021061624 (print) | LCCN 2021061625 (ebook) | ISBN 9781400236077 (hardcover) | ISBN 9781400236084 (epub) | ISBN 9781400236091
Subjects: LCGFT: Novels.
Classification: LCC PS3603.O7713 W49 2022 (print) | LCC PS3603.O7713 (ebook) | DDC 813/.6--dc23
LC record available at https://lccn.loc.gov/2021061624
LC ebook record available at https://lccn.loc.gov/2021061625

Printed in the United States of America

22 23 24 25 26 LSC 5 4 3 2 1

For my mother, Kiki
And for my children, Christiana and Nico

What you leave behind is not what is engraved in stone monuments, but what is woven into the lives of others.

—PERICLES

Part One

One

Corfu
September 1946

Somewhere in the distance she could hear Mama's voice calling her, but Katerina willed her away, if only for a little while longer.

She was happy here, swinging back and forth under the shade of this beautiful old olive tree. Up and down she swung, soaring higher and higher and then floating back again. She could see the entire island from up here, the ancient gnarled and knotted olive tree groves, the weathered old church, the cemetery overcrowded with stones and loved ones long gone, and even Clotho's pristine house tucked into the hillside with her lush garden overlooking the sea. And as she soared higher, Katerina gazed beyond the jagged cypress-covered cliffs, across the azure Ionian Sea, to the distant horizon where fishing boats bobbed, silhouetted against the sun, and dolphins swam and jumped in unison.

The silk ribbons adorning her hair tickled her face each time she lifted back up toward the sky, and her white silk dress filled with air like a balloon each time the swing brought her back down. And then a smile unfurled across her face as she spotted her. The golden woman had come to her again.

She saw her in the distance, across the hillside, walking toward Katerina's swing. Her hair flowed free and loose behind her, lifting and lilting up and down like a sail, expertly catching the maestro winds. Katerina squinted her eyes as she leaned in as far as the swing would allow, but still she could not quite make out the woman's face. Even so, the golden woman's smile radiated light as pure and bright as the midday sun. Katerina felt so full of love for this woman, yet she did not know who she was or why she came to visit. How could that be?

Katerina continued to swing higher and higher as she watched the woman walk toward her, closer and closer. Once more her body tilted up toward the sun. She leaned her head back, as far as it would go, and felt the wonder of weightlessness as her hair floated behind her.

She soared higher, pushing the boundaries between heaven and earth, but she knew the woman would not let anything happen to her. The woman was closer now. Close enough for Katerina to smell her sweet scent, the perfume of the village itself: roses and wisteria and rosemary and basil, fermented on the breeze.

The woman was almost there; Katerina could almost see her face through the haze of light. Katerina reached out her hand, imploring her to come closer.

Please, she thought, knowing the woman could read her innermost thoughts, a silent understanding between them. She mouthed the word as she released the swing to go to her. "Please . . ."

"Katerina."

Katerina opened her eyes. Her mother, Maria, was smiling above her. "Were you dreaming? You were smiling. It must have been a good dream."

Katerina rubbed her eyes and sat up on the cot, tucked into the corner below the icons of the Virgin Mary and Saint Spyridon that were affixed to the wall with black nails. Crosses made from dried palms were tucked between the icons and the wall, replaced yearly after the Palm Sunday service. The older palms were burned every year after church, as it would be a sin to simply throw them away.

She changed from her yellowed and threadbare nightshirt to a plain brown wool dress, handed down from her cousin Calliope, that buttoned from her throat to past her knees and itched despite the undershirt and slip she wore beneath. Katerina walked out to the terrace where Mama had breakfast waiting on the table in the shade of the grape arbor that dripped with green orbs. The grapes filled the air with their sweet aroma. A symphony of buzzing bees darted about. Through the morning mist, she could see the shoreline of Albania to the east and the silhouette of the tiny island of Erikousa to the north. Katerina nibbled on the crust of yesterday's bread drizzled with just a hint of honey and sipped from a cup of goat's milk, which was still warm. She tried her best to keep her head straight and not wince as Mama brushed and plaited her hair.

"I have to tell Baba what Calliope said yesterday. She's so mean, Mama. Why is she so mean?"

"Children often mimic what they see at home, Katerina. Calliope's mother is not a kind woman. I hate to speak ill of your father's sister, but Thea Sofia is a vicious gossip and she puts her nose where it does not belong. It doesn't make it right, but Calliope is behaving the way she sees her mother behave. Just steer as clear of her as you can," Mama said.

"The way you do, Mama?"

Mama said nothing. She just kept plaiting Katerina's hair.

With her straight, sharp nose, fair hair, and green eyes, Mama looked nothing like the other dark and sturdy mothers in the village. Mama had come to Corfu twelve years earlier as an anxious young bride after meeting Baba at a cousin's wedding on her family's island of Tinos. After a few bottles of wine and an intense negotiation by their fathers over the restaurant's finest ouzo, it was decided by the end of that first night that Mama and Baba would be married. Mama, just sixteen, and Baba, twenty, had never met before that day. The wedding took place in a small village church with only a handful of family members in attendance. Mama's wedding day had been the last time she had seen her own family or stepped foot on Tinos.

With no dowry to speak of and no mother to send her off with words of comfort or advice, all the young bride brought with her to Corfu were her memories and a few trinkets: faded photos, yellowed linens, and her parents' wedding crowns all kept locked away in her mother's old keepsake chest.

Katerina loved to sit with Mama and look through all of the treasures in that chest. Each time they did, Mama would place the crowns on Katerina's head and smile, her eyes misting over as she promised to take Katerina to her beloved island of Tinos to visit the magnificent church of the Virgin Mary, the Panagia of Tinos.

"We'll go to Tinos together one day," Mama always promised. "And Panagia will bless you, Katerina. She will bless and protect you like she does all of the virtuous girls who pray to her."

Katerina couldn't wait for the day that she could go and pray to Panagia in Tinos. She knew exactly what she would pray for and hoped the Virgin would be kind enough to make her beautiful, too, just like her mother.

Katerina especially loved when Mama told her the story of how the church came to be. Katerina sat in awe each time Mama explained how Panagia herself visited an old, pious nun in her dream. Panagia spoke to the nun, telling her where the villagers should dig to find her buried icon. Not long after that, the wooden icon was found in that very spot. Katerina hoped that one day she, too, might be visited by Panagia and told where to find buried treasure. She would like that very much.

As much as she loved hearing stories about her mother's island, Katerina often wondered why they had never been back to visit and why none of their relatives came to visit on Corfu. She wondered, too, if her mother was lonely with no one to keep her company all day but the kittens, the chickens, and the family's stubborn skinny goat. Mama never joined the other mothers who met sometimes to clean the cemetery, mill their olives together, or pick chamomile and oregano from the mountainside.

Katerina had asked a handful of times if her mother had a best friend, if she might come visit, and if she had a daughter for Katerina to play with. But each time, Mama always found another chore for Katerina, insisting she urgently needed water from the fresh spring or the floor needed to be swept or kindling gathered. So Katerina had simply stopped asking. She never lost hope, though, that the day would come when she would learn at last all of the secrets her mother kept guarded and locked away as tightly as the items in the keepsake chest.

Each night Katerina prayed before bed, down on her knees, back straight with hands clasped, just the way Mama had taught her. Each night she asked the Virgin Panagia to help her grow as big as her obnoxious cousin Calliope, who called Katerina a baby and declared herself practically a full-blown woman. Katerina also prayed for their chickens to lay more eggs, for her father to catch more fish, and for their tired old goat to produce more milk. She prayed that soon they would make the trip across the sea to Tinos.

Her prayers had yet to be answered, but Katerina had learned to be patient. With so much suffering all around them, she knew God was probably busy answering the prayers of other, perhaps needier children. Night after night, as her knees bled on the floor, scabs cracking open like eggshells, she promised herself that she would be patient with God as she awaited her turn. But deep down Katerina hoped he would hurry up already. She was growing quite tired of being small and hungry with ugly, scabbed knees.

"What will you study today?" Mama asked Katerina as she finished the plait, fastening the end with a piece of black yarn.

"Mr. Andonis said we'll continue along with Odysseus and his travels. I'm so excited. I love the part when he comes home and no one knows it's him. Only the dog," she said, using her sleeve to wipe the milk from her lip.

"As you should be, my love. Pay close attention," Mama said. "Remember, you are the first girl in our family to be taught to read and write. Each day you leave this house, you take me with you. Through your eyes, it is as if I am learning too, as if I am sitting beside you in your classroom."

8

YVETTE MANESSIS CORPORON

Like all of the other daughters, wives, and mothers before her, Mama was never sent to school. Educations, like opinions, were thought unnecessary for those born to serve others. But Mr. Andonis, the new schoolteacher, had changed all that. When he arrived in their tiny village just five years earlier, he brought with him a passion for the classics and an intolerance for ignorance, as well as the fervent belief that even provincial girls deserved an education.

"Yes, I promise to pay close attention," Katerina replied as she devoured the bread and finished the last sip of milk. "Where is Baba? He promised to walk me to school today."

Mama did not answer.

Katerina watched as Mama walked over to the washbasin where Baba's work clothes were soaking. Silently, Mama bent over the basin, scrubbing and pounding his shirt into the soapy water.

Two

Corfu

September 1946

Laki stood at the water's edge and looked out across the bay to the horizon. No stars were visible in the sky, the first light of the new day just now beginning to cut through the darkness. Only the silver moon could be seen against the black.

Laki looked down on the stiff body of the man and exhaled before flipping the corpse and rummaging through his pockets. From the wet billfold he pulled out a few *drachmas*. He whispered a word of thanks, grateful for the light of the moon and for the glassy sea, which reflected shimmering moonlight across the beach. He glanced up and down the shoreline again, squinting into the darkness to make sure he was indeed alone. Certain no one was watching, he stuffed the wet bills into his own pocket before shifting the man to his other side to search for more.

He knew what he held in his fingers even before he pulled the wet paper from the man's pocket. He had done this many times and could predict what he would find with one glance at a dead man's face. This was a young man, clean-shaven with a square jaw, jet-black hair, and a thin band of gold on his finger. He had been handsome and strong and loved. But that was before his boat had been blown out of the brilliant blue waters between Albania and Corfu.

Laki thought for a moment of the woman's face that would soon greet him on this waterlogged photograph. He thought of the face that would soon be streaked with tears and of the body that would be shrouded in black upon hearing of her young husband's death. He said a silent prayer, asking God to give this woman strength, allowing her a few final moments of anonymity, of blissful ignorance before he glanced upon her face and branded her a widow.

Laki slipped the photo out of the man's pocket and held it up to his face. He sucked in his breath and let out a soft moan. Shaking his head, he said another prayer, this one for the beautiful little girl who sat on her mother's knee in the photo. She was no more than ten, just like his precious Katerina. The girl smiling back at him from the photo had shiny black hair like her father and the piercing black eyes and bee-stung lips of her mother. He looked closer at the photo and noticed the serene smile on the woman's face and then her hands, one wrapped around her daughter's tiny waist and the other resting on her own swollen belly. He was not a man who cried easily, or ever. But his eyes filled with tears as he looked down at this man and the family he had left behind.

"Senseless," he said out loud as if there were anyone to hear him. "Senseless." Louder this time. "Barbarians."

Greek killing Greek. Cousin killing cousin. Brother killing brother. After so many years of war, oppression, and Italian and then German occupation, Laki never would have imagined that his own people would turn against each other the way they had. The newspapers called it an impending civil war, but he called it something else: cannibalism.

He bent down once again and returned the photo to the man's pocket. When he heard that a boat belonging to the Communist Greek People's Liberation Navy had been blown out of the water by government firepower, he knew what would happen next. He knew the fish would be scared away once again, making it even more difficult for the villagers to feed their families. He also knew the tide would bring the dead men's bodies to rest here, in this pristine cove, just as it had the Italian soldiers years before when their ship was destroyed by German grenades in these very waters.

He shook his head as he thought of those men massacred by the Nazis. The Italians had been good to Laki and all of the villagers throughout the occupation, even trading squares of chocolate for octopuses and lobsters. He smiled thinking of the times he presented Katerina with the sweet treats. How she would squeal and sigh as the dark squares dissolved on her tongue. Those young Italian boys had boarded boats after the long occupation thinking they were finally homebound, waving to the villagers as they sailed away. In reality, the Italians were deceived and murdered, their boats bombarded with gunfire and grenades from the very soldiers who had assured them safe passage. Instead of returning to the arms of their loved ones, their lifeless bodies came to rest here on this beach, with Laki rummaging through their pockets hoping to find some way to feed his family.

Now, as he stood over the body of this young man, he realized he could not continue, even though he knew more bodies had washed up and there were more pockets to rummage farther down the beach. He knew it was time to leave this cove and head home before the sunrise could reveal his secret. He was a poor man with nothing to his name but his old family home, a torn and tangled fishing net, and a small garden plot. It was barely enough for them to survive on. But unlike the dead man at his feet, he had the luxury of walking through the door where Maria would have a meal waiting for him and kissing the cheek of beautiful Katerina, whose giggles echoed on the breeze like an angelic chorus. He knew in his heart that as difficult as things were, at least for now, they were the lucky ones.

Thousands were dying from famine all across Greece, but living in their tiny seaside village meant that at least there would always be fish to eat. Fishing might be difficult for a while after the mines planted just off the coast of Albania were detonated, or when the government managed to identify and destroy a Communist navy boat, but Laki knew that eventually, as always, the fish would be back. No, it wasn't the famine that worried him most. It was the increasing violence and waves of terror that had started in the remote northern villages and now had begun to spread south, closer to Corfu and even to Athens.

Laki had seen the newspapers and heard the radio reports. Entire villages burned to the ground. Innocent civilians—shepherds, farmers, fishermen—tortured, slaughtered, often in front of their families. Lifeless bodies hanging from olive trees, heads impaled on sticks in village squares as a warning to others. Old women, mothers, and young girls assaulted and raped. He prayed every day that the madness would end. He prayed that his own village and family would remain safe.

Initially it had appeared as if the danger was confined to the north, to those poor, unfortunate villages bordering Albania and Bulgaria. But then the news came from Athens. Protests, Communists and monarchists fighting in the streets, civilians gunned down, bodies littering Syntagma Square. In villages like theirs, people were used to hardship, to going without. But hearing that the cultured and educated people of Athens were living without electricity and gas; that people were starving, being murdered, dying by the thousands; that was more than he could fathom.

He also knew for certain that the threat was moving closer. This body at his feet proved it. He had heard rumors that the Communist navy had commanded units in the southern Ionian islands of Lefkada and Zakynthos, but had never wanted to believe that they could take root here on Corfu. Not on Corfu.

He was a poor man with barely an elementary education, but even so, there was a pride that came along with being born a Corfiot, one that had nothing to do with schooling or money or valuables. Laki felt it, infused with the island's rich history each time he visited Corfu Town and walked beneath the expansive arches, grand café-lined squares, and elegant esplanades. This was a place where even the poorest of men strived to be better and appreciated the art and beauty surrounding them and the magnificence

of their island and her storied past. He was never one for political arguments, unlike the other men who clustered around the radio at the *kafenio*,
shouting over one another. In the past it was enough to be Greek, Corfiot,
united against a common foreign enemy. But now it seemed the enemy was
among them, of their own, and often hiding in plain sight.

Laki believed in civility and hard work. Only once had he raised his
voice in anger during a political discussion. He could not sit silently when
Panos, the left-leaning former schoolteacher, argued that the monarchist
citizens of Corfu were brainwashed in their support of the royal family
and tone-deaf to the plight of the poor Greek citizens. The tone and tenor
of the conversation quickly rose along with the volume of their voices.
What began as a heated debate ended with an overturned kafenio table
and an ill-timed, ill-advised punch thrown by an old fisherman at the
teacher. But while other men in the village argued that a man with such
extreme political beliefs had no business teaching children, Laki—though
he disagreed with the teacher's political views—argued that he was a good
teacher and deserved to keep his job as long as he kept his political views
out of the classroom and away from the children. In the end, Panos was
forced out, issuing a warning to the villagers as he stormed away from the
schoolhouse and his only source of income: "Mark my word, King George
will never return from exile. Open your eyes and minds. The monarchy
will never be restored. It's time for the people to take our country back from
these false idols."

Laki often thought of that day, the teacher spitting at the villagers as
he walked past, then tipping his hat toward Laki when they crossed paths.
His words often echoed in Laki's ear as he played the rhetoric over again
and again in his mind. Despite the passionate arguments on both sides,
Laki kept coming to the very same conclusion. He had always supported
the monarchy, nationalistic pride swelling in his chest when the king and
his family were here on Corfu, enjoying their time in the summer palace of
Mon Repos. But truly, what difference did it make to him if King George
returned from exile? After King George was driven out of the country by

the German invasion in 1941, Greece was now set to vote on whether he should be restored to power. While Laki was steadfast in his support of the monarchy, he also knew that even if the king returned, it was not as if Laki would ever be invited to the palace for dinner.

And what of the Communists? They had been the heroes, the ones who led the resistance and fought so valiantly against the Germans during the occupation . . . initially. But those slaughtered innocents who voiced their support of the monarchy or refused to stand publicly with the Communists proved that even the noblest of causes could quickly turn to bloodlust when personal vendettas drove politics and inhumanity was masqueraded as ideology.

And Laki knew that regardless of who claimed to be the salvation of Greece, the sea would always be the sea, and the earth and sky the same as well, no matter what the newspapers or radio said. He had lived off the land and sea his entire life, just as his parents had, and their parents before them. These were the things that mattered to him, the things God provided that could not be controlled by guns or violence or rhetoric.

He was a poor, uneducated man, but his faith was strong. Laki believed that in some way, by some miracle, they would survive this horrendous war and everything would be all right again. Even a man with empty pockets could be full of hope. When all else had been stripped away, sometimes that was all he had left to sustain him.

Laki took one last look at the dead man's body before beginning his walk home. The amber light of dawn now reflected on the sea's surface and the gold band on the man's finger.

"Please forgive me," he whispered. Then he reached down and pulled the wedding band from the man's finger.

Laki dug his hands deep into his pockets and started toward home. Last night as he tucked Katerina into bed, Laki promised he would walk her to school in the morning. In these lean and difficult times, Laki's word was all he had to offer his little girl. And Laki would move heaven and earth to keep it.

Three

Corfu

September 1946

"Marco, Stefano," Yianna shouted again as she climbed the rocky path leading to the house. With one hand she lifted the hem of her skirt, stepping gingerly over the collapsed portion of the stone wall between the garden and the patio, careful not to crack the precious eggs that she cradled in her apron with her other hand.

"Marco, Stefano. Come on. Your father will be back any moment. Get up. You'll be late for school."

It was not yet seven o'clock and Yianna had climbed up and down the hillside a half dozen times already, including two trips down to the freshwater spring, which meant two trips back up the steep and craggy terrain hauling the filled water jugs. Usually this was Marco and Stefano's job. But with the threat of the approaching maestro winds, Aleko had left the house long before sunrise this morning, hoping to lift his nets before the glassy sea turned choppy and whitecapped. With Aleko gone and no one there to simultaneously tease and accuse her of coddling them, Yianna had not been able to resist the urge to let her boys sleep in.

It was hard to tell sometimes which of her sons hated fetching water more. While Marco was more vocal in his complaints, Stefano had learned that bemoaning his chores only served to delay the inevitable. And with that her eldest son had come to the realization that no matter how hot or heavy the dreaded trip to the spring was, it simply served him best to suffer in silence. Marco, on the other hand, loved to moan and complain and occasionally throw himself to the ground in protest. In those instances, Yianna would simply hand him the empty jugs with strict instructions to strip naked and wash himself in the cold-water spring before stepping foot in the house again. It didn't matter that the floor of their home was dirt itself. Yianna, like all of the village mothers, understood that embarrassment is often a mother's most effective way of making a point.

With a laugh and a slap of his calloused hands across the backs of the boys' heads, Aleko often liked to remind Yianna that boys were like mules, stubborn and stupid, whose only redeeming quality was the ability to carry heavy loads up the mountain. It was not that she completely disagreed, but in these difficult times it was so rare that she could treat the boys to something special. Luxuries like a bit of sugar or a sturdy new pair of shoes existed only in a well-intentioned mother's dreams. Knowing this, she made certain to savor each of life's unexpected gifts, however small. An extra hour of sleep was the only escape she could provide her children right now.

It was the least she could do for her boys, she reasoned. They had both made such a fuss over her birthday the night before, singing to her at the top of their lungs. And then with a broad smile on his sun-kissed face, Stefano had asked her to lean in, to remove the white kerchief covering her hair, and to bend down toward him just a little bit closer. Her eldest son's gesture, as sweet as the scent emanating from his hands, overwhelmed her. From behind his back, Stefano presented her with a crown of gardenias, a simple yet exquisite wreath woven from her favorite flowers. He placed the crown on her head and smiled, his white teeth gleaming against the deep olive of his skin. "Happy birthday to the most wonderful mother in the village."

She narrowed her eyes at him.

"All right, all right. I stand corrected." Stefano laughed. "Happy birthday to the best mother in all of Greece."

Yianna nodded her head and lifted her chin high. "Now that's better."

"Happy birthday to the best mother in the whole wide world," Marco shouted, stretching his arms as wide as he could, and then he turned and stuck out his tongue at his brother.

Stefano shook his head and laughed. "You win."

"Happy birthday, Mama, from the winner," Marco declared as he threw himself into her arms.

Yianna wrapped one arm around his waist as the other flew to her head to keep the flowers from tumbling. She savored each and every hug from Marco, who at ten was nearing the age when she knew his unbridled and bountiful hugs would soon become yet another precious memory of better times long in the past. At twelve, Stefano rarely allowed her to hug him anymore, except for the rare occasion when the need for a mother's assurance outweighed his desire to be a man.

"Happy birthday, my love," Aleko added from the doorway where he was rolling a cigarette between his fingers. He smiled at her in that mischievous way of his. Salt and sweat stained the black fisherman's cap tilted on his head, black eyes twinkling beneath his dark lashes. It was what she had first noticed about him, those eyes and those lashes. She would never forget the way he unabashedly stared at her that Easter Sunday as the parishioners all shouted and sang "Christ Has Risen" while hoisting their candles in the air at midnight to celebrate Christ's emergence from the tomb. She had felt his eyes on her, burning into her as if he had stepped too close to her with the light of the resurrection.

She stood there smiling at her sons and husband, wearing a stained apron over a faded black ankle-length skirt, a frayed brown cardigan sweater, and a glorious crown of gardenias on her head. The tears fell from her cheek, leaving tiny watermarks on the dirt beneath her feet.

"See, Mama, even if you don't live in a palace anymore, you can still wear a crown," Marco added. She knew he intended his words to bring another smile to her face, and so she forced one, even as she felt the familiar wave of melancholy pull her under.

Yes, she had lived in a palace once, a grand royal palace among princes and princesses, with even a young prince as her playmate. She had no true memories of that time, only hazy, fractured images, but her mother, Vasiliki, had told her the stories again and again. And Yianna in turn had recited the stories over and over again to her husband and sons until they, too, were well versed in how their family's fate and fortune had turned.

It was a lifetime ago when Yianna's mother had served as a maid to Princess Alice, the wife of Prince Andrew, the fourth son of King George I. Yianna's mother lived and worked with the princess's family in the royal palace of Mon Repos, just forty kilometers away on the outskirts of Corfu Town. It might as well have been a million miles and lifetimes ago.

Some of Yianna's earliest memories were of the nights she sat curled in her mother's lap right here on this patio as the fireflies danced around them and the sky above faded from blue to black. And each night Yianna would listen as her mother recalled the stories of her life working as a maid in Mon Repos and her unlikely friendship with Princess Alice. When Yianna was born in the servants' quarters above the cellar, Alice had welcomed her to Mon Repos, where she was raised beside Alice's only son, Prince Philip. Just shy of three years old when Philip was born, at first Yianna thought the tiny prince was her very own living and breathing doll. And then, when Philip grew to babble his first words and toddle his first steps, Yianna was always beside her little playmate, roaming the cavernous halls and bucolic gardens of Mon Repos under Vasiliki's watchful eye.

Those idyllic years abruptly came to an end when Alice and her family were exiled from Greece after her husband, Prince Andrew, was blamed for the disastrous outcome of the Greco-Turkish War in 1922. But Princess

Alice was so moved by Vasiliki's love and loyalty that she made a promise to her loyal maid.

"I will never forget your kindness and how you loved my family, Vasiliki. I will return to Greece one day. This is my home. You have helped make it my home. And your family will always find a home with mine."

With the royal family forced into exile and Mon Repos shuttered, Vasiliki had no choice but to return with her husband and Yianna to the village where generations of her family had been born and raised. Perched on the verdant cliffs of northeastern Corfu overlooking the Ionian Sea, with the shores of Albania in the distance, Pelekito was a place where families were as deeply rooted and entwined as the ancient olive trees that canopied her landscape.

And while Yianna's earliest memories were of her mother telling her of Princess Alice's promise, reciting her words each evening like a prayer, they were Yianna's final memories of her mother as well. Vasiliki went to her grave still waiting for Alice's return, insisting she would somehow, someday fulfill her vow.

And now, in this tiny home bursting with generations of memories, both joyous and heartbreaking, Yianna and Aleko were raising their own children. But it wasn't just the old house, garden, and little plot of land that Yianna inherited from her mother. She, too, never gave up hope that Princess Alice might one day return to keep her promise and that she might be reunited with Philip, the prince who had been her first friend.

As the years went on, the details of her mother's stories faded into soft focus, as if it were all a dream. But while the minutiae slipped away, muddied with the passing years, Yianna never could allow herself to completely lose hope, however difficult it was at times. She often found herself staring out across the sea, wondering if her family's luck had sailed away from Corfu that night along with the tiny prince.

There were times Yianna would laugh and smile and warn her husband and sons that they just might wake up one day to find her gone, returned to Mon Repos where she rightfully belonged. And then there were days that it was difficult to joke or smile at all, when the reality of what was and the longing for what might have been consumed her.

She pushed those thoughts away. Not today. Even when she cursed her fate at times, Yianna always thanked God that at least she had been born on Corfu, a fertile green island, unlike the barren, arid earth of so many other islands and villages. Between her garden and the fish Aleko caught daily, Yianna went to bed each night knowing that despite all of life's hardships, at least her children would never starve.

"Boys, come on. I let you sleep in. It's time to get up for school," she yelled into the house. Yianna glanced at the gardenia crown, now hanging on the wall beside the plastic crowns she and Aleko had worn on their wedding day as the priest led them three times around the altar. Even from several feet away in the outdoor kitchen, she could still smell their perfume carried on the breeze.

She grabbed a handful of twigs from the pile next to the outdoor stove and lit a match, setting the kindling ablaze. With her paring knife, she cut up two small potatoes that she had dug up from the garden the day before and fried the potatoes in olive oil. When the potatoes were crisp on the outside and tender in the center, she removed them from the fire and cracked four eggs into the sizzling pan. The smell of the fire mixed with the eggs wafted through the door and into the house. The boys sprang up from the thin mattress they shared on the floor, just as she knew they would.

"Mama. Are you sure?" Stefano looked from the frying pan to his mother.

She nodded and smiled.

"But how?" Marco asked.

"Don't worry." Yianna waved their concern away with the back of her hand. Just yesterday she had spotted the boys listening from the garden as she and Aleko discussed in hushed and worried tones why one of their two hens had stopped laying eggs.

"Don't worry. I took a little walk today and happened to pass the mayor's house."

"You didn't!" both boys shouted in unison, picturing their mother stealing eggs from the mayor.

With its imposing iron gate, freshly stuccoed exterior, ornate wooden doors, and vast garden, the mayor's house was the envy of all the villagers and by far the nicest home for miles around. And while the mayor took great pride in maintaining his home to perfection, the mayor's mother, Thea Olga, took even greater pride in protecting it from trespassers. Thea Olga was a bent old woman with a habit of leaning out the house's windows and throwing rocks at children who dared cross her property. Despite her gnarled fingers and cataracts, the old woman's aim was legendarily precise.

"I merely borrowed them." Yianna smiled as she plated the eggs and potatoes. The eggs' edges were brown and crisped and the orange yolks were slightly soft, just the way the boys liked them. "I'll replace them when that lazy hen of ours decides to earn her keep. Come on, finish your breakfast. Don't be late for school."

She leaned against the doorframe and watched as the boys inhaled their breakfast, then pulled water from the well to wash their hands and faces. They dressed, bounding back to their mother for a kiss. As Marco stood before her, she bent down to tighten the fishing line that was tied around the sole and leather of his shoes. The shoes had served Stefano well and, for a while, Marco too. But now it seemed the old shoes had nothing left to give and were well beyond help from even the fishing line. Marco scratched his head as he looked up at his mother and smiled. She smiled back at him, tweaking his nose.

Stefano waved a final goodbye and grabbed his leather school bag, which his grandmother had brought back to the village when she returned from Mon Repos, claiming it once held the schoolbooks of the royal children. Stefano had laid claim to the bag, draping it proudly across his shoulder each day as he left for school. Yianna would never speak the words out loud, but she knew Stefano's prized bag held nothing more than a crudely fashioned slingshot, a dulled pencil nub, and just for today, a single book. It was a tattered and frayed copy of the *Odyssey* borrowed overnight from Mr. Andonis, the schoolteacher.

Yianna knew what this bag and this borrowed book meant to her son. It was as if she could somehow see deep inside her elder child, to his heart and most private thoughts. She knew he longed to be a schoolteacher himself one day with piles and piles of books to devour and teach. She understood that draping the leather strap across his chest each morning made Stefano feel like a proper scholar, even if he did not own a single book of his own.

Each week she would dip a soft cloth into a bit of olive oil before rubbing and polishing the bag to shined perfection. As she handed him the bag each morning, Yianna made sure to encourage Stefano's dreams and passions, even as she tamped down her own. In her elder son, Yianna saw the truest reflection of herself.

While she prayed that Stefano might somehow, someday achieve his dreams, it was her younger son, Marco, for whom she worried most. Sweet, precocious, yet innocent Marco. Well-intentioned and loving, like a puppy stumbling over his own paws. As troublesome as it was to think Stefano might not one day see his dreams of scholarly success come true, at least he had a dream. Marco, she feared, had none.

"Let the boy be," Aleko insisted again and again. And each time he did, Yianna would nod and force a smile, avoiding unnecessary confrontation. But internally Yianna's emotions churned like the current. She wanted more for her sons, things that existed beyond the land and sea. Yianna wanted a life for them measured by more than the weight of one's fishing nets.

Once the boys left for school, Yianna set about her chores. Today she would pull down and wash her mother's linens as she did each month without fail. She went from window to window and door to door, gathering the curtains and lace cloths and runners that Alice and Vasiliki had crocheted together over the years and that Alice gifted to Vasiliki in their final hours together. The delicate patterns that now covered every surface of the tiny stone house had once made their home among the grand windows and marble foyers and finery of Mon Repos. Yianna soaked them

first in soapy water drawn from the fresh spring, massaging the fabric ever
so gently with her fingertips. She was always careful not to wring them,
lest they lose their shape; the delicate rosettes, silken scalloped edges, and
weblike patterns were so magnificent that they made her think they could
have been woven at the hands of Arachne and Athena during their famed
competition. Yianna stood over them, sometimes for hours upon hours as
they dried in the sun, keeping watch, shooing away any birds or insects
that dared come too close before hanging them again in the windows and
doorframes among the dirt and stones and rotting wood.

Four

Corfu

September 1946

"So tell me. What did you dream?" Mama asked.

But before Katerina could answer, he swooped in from behind, grabbing her by the waist and tossing her into the air. It wasn't nearly as high as the swing in her dream, but it was just as exciting nonetheless.

"Baba," she cried.

Baba hugged her. Katerina let out a little squeal, like a kitten grasped too tightly in a child's hand.

"I thought you had forgotten," she said. "When I woke up and saw you weren't here, I thought you had forgotten."

"I made a promise to my girl." Baba glanced at Mama as he spoke. "I promised you that I would walk you to school. So here I am."

"But where have you been?" Katerina asked.

"I had some work to do in the village early this morning. But I came back, just as I said I would. Have I ever broken my promise to you, Katerina?"

"No."

"And I never will. Do you love me, Katerina?"

"Of course I do," she said as she wrapped her arms around his neck. The scruff of his beard scratched her cheek, but she just held tighter.

"Then you must have faith in me, because I love you too. I love you more than you can ever imagine, even more than all of the numbers Mr. Andonis could ever possibly teach you." He laughed as he unwrapped her arms from his neck and placed her on the garden wall beside a glorious rosebush blanketed with deep red flowers. Mama stood in the doorway watching them.

"I want you to think of love like a flower, Katerina. A rose," he continued, tracing his fingers along a single perfect rose. "Look at this beautiful flower, so rich in color and so fragrant and so very beautiful. But this flower, this beautiful rose, can't grow without the soil. This precious flower needs soil to keep her rooted and to thrive, the foundation upon which she grows. That's exactly the way it is with love and faith. For love to exist, between a parent and child, between adults, even between friends, for any type of love to grow and thrive, it must be rooted in faith. There can be no love without faith in one another, without trust. Do you understand?"

"Yes, Baba. I do." She nodded her head up and down.

"Good. Because I love you, Katerina. I love you with all of my heart. When I give you my word, you can trust that I will never lie to you, my sweet girl. And in turn, you must have faith in me," he said as he plucked the rose and handed it to her. "Come on. I'll walk you to school like I promised to. And I know exactly the story I'm going to tell you as we walk."

Katerina ran to the doorway to kiss her mother goodbye.

"Remember, pay close attention. I want to hear every detail tonight," Mama said.

Katerina skipped back to Baba and grabbed her father's hand.

∞

Maria watched as Katerina and Laki walked together out of the gate and toward the schoolyard, Katerina's dark braids bouncing down her back with each step, Laki's tanned arm wrapped around her tiny waist. As they faded from sight, Maria wondered what might have been had her own father kept his promises. She sometimes wondered how life might have been different if she had not lost her mother so young and if she had grown up with the reassurance of an arm wrapped protectively around her.

"There can be no love without faith in one another, without trust."

She had once had both love and faith in her life. Maria had known a mother's love so beautiful and pure that it was difficult to believe sometimes that it had actually existed. But then in a single moment, her childhood and her faith were shattered, stripped away. She had often wondered in the years that followed if her ability to love had been lost that night as well. And for the longest time she believed it so. But then ten years ago, after the tears and the blood and the screams, in the moment the midwife at last placed Katerina, crying and slick into her arms, she knew that despite it all, a piece of her heart had remained intact.

Maria wondered if perhaps one day, with the passing of time, the pain and the memories might dull. Perhaps one day she might discover another small portion of her heart that had survived as well, waiting for the right moment to release her from her promise. But as quickly as the thought entered her mind, she willed it away. She had trained herself to sweep these considerations from her thoughts like cobwebs from the rafters.

Five

Corfu
September 1946

"All right then, Orpheus and Eurydice," Baba began as they walked. "Once there was a lute player named Orpheus. He was so talented that even the gods would stop what they were doing to listen to him play. Even the wildest beasts were tamed when Orpheus's beautiful music danced in the air. Orpheus fell in love with a beautiful girl named Eurydice, and they were married one day in a field filled with wildflowers and friends.

"Well, on their wedding day, as Orpheus played his lute and Eurydice danced with the nymphs, a poisonous snake slithered up through the grass and bit her. Orpheus's beautiful bride died instantly. He was devastated and decided that he would go to the underworld himself and plead with King Hades and Queen Persephone to allow Eurydice to return to him. Orpheus walked all the way down through the gates of hell, past bloodthirsty Cerberus, and even through Tartarus, where the wicked and the damned suffer in eternity. Finally, he reached the dark palace where Hades and Persephone were waiting for him seated on golden thrones. Orpheus pleaded with them to allow Eurydice to return with him to the land of the living. He said he was a poor man and could offer them no gold or jewels. Instead, he said, he would offer the king and queen the only thing he had of any value at all: his music. Only after he played his lute, a song so beautiful it brought Queen Persephone to tears, did Hades agree.

"Hades said Eurydice and Orpheus could return together to the world of the living, but on one condition. Orpheus was to walk back to earth through hell, past the gates of Tartarus and bloodthirsty Cerberus. He said Eurydice would follow behind silently, but Orpheus was never to look back to her. If he did, she would be sent back to the underworld and lost to him forever.

"Orpheus did as he was told, looking straight ahead. He walked back up toward the sun hearing Eurydice's faint footsteps behind him. And then, as they were nearly at the place where the land of the dead gives way to the land of the living, Eurydice's footsteps became fainter and fainter, until he could hear them no more. Fearing he had been tricked, Orpheus turned to make sure Eurydice was still behind him. As he did, he caught one last glimpse of his beautiful bride before she was transformed into a shade before his very eyes and returned to the underworld forever."

Baba stopped as the story ended. He bent down, until he was eye to eye with Katerina. "Do you understand, Katerina? To love someone, to have faith in them, is to continue forward, knowing in your heart that they will always be there to follow behind. No matter how silent their footsteps, no matter how lonely you feel at times."

Katerina squeezed her father's hand and smiled at him.

"Good," he said as he smiled and patted her bottom. "Now off you go."

Katerina squeezed his hand one last time before dropping it and running toward Marco, who was waiting for her at the entrance of the old schoolhouse that sat at the edge of the ancient olive tree grove between the churchyard and the sea.

Six

Corfu
September 1946

Andonis wore slacks and a jacket and a freshly pressed button-down shirt. His black hair was shaved at the nape and longer on top, slicked back with a drop of Brylcreem that he purchased on his monthly trip to Corfu Town for supplies and a coffee with friends. He stood in front of the classroom staring out at his students. It wasn't a holiday, or even a Sunday; the schoolteacher dressed like this every day. For Andonis, every day in his classroom with his beloved books and his students, every day he was able to share his love of literature and learning with these children, was an occasion worthy of dressing in his Sunday best.

He had stumbled upon the job opening by chance, reading about the vacancy in the Corfu newspaper as he sipped coffee at a café along the Liston promenade, watching in wonder as the world went by. He was newly arrived in Corfu and loved to sit for hours, nursing his coffee and taking in the beauty and elegance of the island. After falling so quickly and completely in love with the island's cosmopolitan center, he never imagined that he would make a mountain village his home again. But Pelekito, just an hour bus ride outside of the city center, was nothing like the drab, gray village of his youth, where misery was communal and joy was seemingly rationed along with the bread and milk and wheat. On Corfu, even the poorest villagers had a joy about them, an appreciation of life and a smile at the ready, all illuminated by that magical Corfiot light.

He could not believe his luck when the mayor told him the job was his, showing him the modest apartment adjacent to the school that would serve as his home. As he stepped outside and took in the view, the lush hills and cypresses dotting the landscape and blue Ionian in the distance, he thought he was dreaming. The mayor assured him this was in fact his new reality, placing his hand on his shoulder, explaining that the previous teacher had been relieved of his duties for his extreme political views.

"Do you have extreme political views?" the mayor asked.

"Only that I would be extremely honored to teach the children of this beautiful village," he replied.

They celebrated with a toast at the kafenio and Andonis had been proud to call Pelekito home ever since. It was the best of both worlds, quiet and peaceful, just an hour bus ride from the amenities and culture of Corfu Town. He loved this village and his new life here. But above all, he loved his students.

They had been studying the *Odyssey* for several weeks now, and a melancholy feeling had set in as they neared the end. Teaching Homer's epic poem was always a favorite lesson; he never tired of sharing and explaining the story of Odysseus and his travels to his students. Others might have argued that the lesson was better suited for older students, but Andonis disagreed, priding himself on finding ways to teach the story so all of the children could relate to Homer's masterpiece. He knew that every child and adult, no matter how young or old, could find value, honor, and life lessons along with each step and stop of Odysseus's journey home.

Stefano had returned the book to him that morning, as promised. Andonis's mind raced with the possibilities, smiling to himself as he ran through the titles of the books he would lend the young man. It made him happy to think that this bright, inquisitive child could know the pleasure of losing himself in a book beyond the confines of this stuffy classroom, without the distractions of pretty girls and disruptive boys. He knew what it was to dream of being anywhere but where you were. He knew the value of an escape. He wanted to give that gift to Stefano, to all of his students. A borrowed book was all he had to offer. For now, it would have to suffice.

He held the *Odyssey* in his hands, tattered and dog-eared, the bindings struggling to hold on and the pages beginning to fall out. It was his prized possession, the only copy of the *Odyssey* that he owned, given to him by his mother when he was just a child. It was as if the memories of his mother were etched on every page along with Homer's lyrical words.

As always, money had been tight, but his mother, a seamstress, had taken in extra work and saved for months to present her son with a copy of his beloved *Odyssey* for his birthday. There were no bookstores in the small village where they lived, and he learned later that his mother had told his father that she was helping a sick neighbor and secretly boarded a bus for the two-hour trip to Athens so she could purchase a copy from the closest bookstore and surprise him with his birthday gift.

As he lay in his bed at night counting the minutes until his birthday, he'd heard the thud and the crash of glass on the floor from the room next to his. He'd heard his father yelling and then his mother's muffled scream. She'd never meant for his father to find out, to learn that she was taking in extra work and saving the money to buy her son a book, the one thing she knew he wanted. It was supposed to be a secret.

But then the knock at the door had come, and Andonis's father answered it, already three ouzos in. The neighbor handed him his shirts and said how heartwarming it was to see a mother work so hard to buy a birthday gift for her son. Then his father bid the neighbor good night and closed the door by slamming Mama against it.

The next morning his mother had turned her face away as she handed him the wrapped treasure. He feigned ignorance, pretending not to see. But he knew why her eye was black and also what caused the cut on her upper lip, which left a trace of blood on his cheek as she kissed him and wished him a happy birthday.

Andonis held this birthday gift with both hands and leaned against his desk. He cleared his throat, fingering the soft, rounded edges of the book's once sharp and angular spine. He then pushed his round glasses up on his nose, ran his fingers through his hair, and began to speak. He looked across the room at the fourteen students seated before him, a mixture of boys and girls ranging from age seven to seventeen. A mixture of interest, intelligence, and attention.

"And so, when Odysseus finally comes back to Ithaka, he can't reveal himself right away. Why? Because no one is to be trusted. He has heard the rumors, but he knows he can't depend on them. He has to see this with his own eyes. So when he returns to the castle, he disguises himself in the robes of a beggar and says he has news of Odysseus for Penelope. He tells Penelope that her husband is well and nearby. And Penelope, overjoyed at the news, tells the old beggar of a dream she had. She tells him she dreamed of twenty geese and of a giant eagle that swooped down and killed them all. Now, Homer tells us that the eagle is Odysseus, but he never makes clear who the geese represent. Who are the twenty geese of Penelope? Are they the suitors? Is this a premonition of Odysseus killing the men who vie for the hand of his wife, or do the twenty geese represent the number of years he has been away? Does this mean that Penelope's waiting is over? I want you to think about this tonight. What do you think Homer is telling us? And we will discuss tomorrow. Have a good afternoon, children."

The children darted out of the schoolroom as soon as the words were out of his mouth. Stefano and Marco lingered behind. It was Stefano's turn to wash down the board with water gathered from the well behind the church. Andonis always admired the way the Scarapolis brothers stayed to help one another when it was their turn to tidy the classroom. He made a mental note to mention this to their mother the next time he saw her. Of the girls, only Katerina stayed behind in her seat. Andonis sat at his desk, carefully turning the fragile pages of his book and planning his lesson for the next day.

"But what does it mean?" Katerina asked as she stood and approached the teacher.

"What does what mean?" He looked up and smiled as Katerina approached his desk.

"Odysseus comes back, he kills the suitors, and Penelope's wait is over. Can the dream mean both of those things?"

"Oh, Katerina, what a mind you have. So inquisitive and astute. You know, in other parts of the world, young girls like you go on to university. Maybe one day you will too."

Katerina smiled.

"Only Homer can know for sure what the dream means. There are as many opinions as there are people who have read of Odysseus's travels. I think like anything in this life, it is our responsibility to decide where we put our faith and in what to believe. What you think is just as important as anyone else's thoughts. No one's opinion weighs heavier than your own. No one's."

Andonis stood and walked to the front of his desk and leaned against it. "There are many different ideas as to what Homer means. We would be here for days dissecting them all. Would you like to know what I think, in my humble opinion?"

Katerina smiled and nodded her head.

"I think the dream is true, a prophecy. I think the number twenty is significant, as that is the number of years Penelope waited loyally for Odysseus to return home. And I think the dead geese represent all the years that she waited, that Homer is telling us loyalty is never in vain. That honor and virtue are ultimately rewarded, however difficult the road back home."

Katerina absorbed his words the way a wilting flower in dry soil soaks up the rain. His words seemed to lift her, fill her up, and bring out her smile and the brightness in her wide, eager eyes.

The teacher watched the transformation, the effect his words had on this intelligent, beautiful young girl who was so eager for knowledge. He knew she never would have been given the chance to learn had he not insisted that the girls of the village be educated when he arrived here five years ago.

This is why I'm here.

The events of these past few months had been quite unexpected. He was a jumble of thoughts and emotions and, yes, even fear. *Everything is going to be all right,* he told himself again, as he had so often recently. But it was getting harder and harder for Andonis to believe his own words, just as it was getting harder and harder to deny the truth.

Seven

As Katerina stepped out of the classroom and into the dry afternoon heat, the musty scent of old schoolbooks; dry, rotting wood; and overheated adolescents gave way to a perfume of honeysuckle, rosemary, wild thyme, and the faintest hint of an outdoor cooking fire. She had stayed behind to speak with Mr. Andonis and hoped Calliope would have given up already. But Calliope, stubborn as an old mule and yet not nearly as smart, pounced the moment she saw Katerina emerging from the schoolhouse.

"It's not true. Not a word of it," Katerina insisted. She crossed her arms tightly to her chest as she stomped away from Calliope.

The barrage had begun during playtime, when Katerina wanted nothing more than to sit with Marco and plan their next secret adventure together. But Calliope had seen them whispering behind the school gate and swooped in to begin her attack.

"It's true. She's a witch. I know it. Everyone knows it. You're just too dumb to see it," Calliope taunted as she jabbed her finger into Katerina's arm. Katerina did her best to ignore Calliope, walking faster now until she was almost out of breath.

Once they rounded the corner, past the schoolyard gate, Katerina stopped, savoring the shade of the ancient olive tree. With her sturdy and stocky trunk, knotted brown bark, and canopy of branches dripping with waxy verdant leaves, the tree always seemed to Katerina like a kindly old grandmother, a *yia-yia* extending her arms out and beckoning the island's children to the respite of her shade.

"I'm telling you, it's not true," Katerina insisted again.

"Yes, it is," Calliope shot back. "Shut up and listen to Agathe. She knows the whole story. Her mother told her, and every word of it is true." Calliope picked up a handful of dirt and gravel and threw it at Katerina. She then turned her attention to Agathe, a skinny cousin who had inherited Calliope's hand-me-down dresses as well as her penchant for gossip.

Agathe looked from Katerina to Calliope. She did as she was told and went on with her story.

"For three days Niko went down to the port to collect his nets just as the sun rose on the horizon, and for three days Niko found his boat tied with an unfamiliar knot. Each day he untied the knot and set out to pull in his catch. And each of those days his nets were empty. Nothing. His own family went hungry even as he watched the other fishermen pull in enough fish to feed an entire wedding party. So on the third night Niko decided to spend the night keeping watch on his boat to find out who was to blame. Just after the sun set, he climbed below and waited. And finally, in the middle of the night, when only owls and demons are awake, he heard her. He saw her clear as day at the helm of his boat. But before he could say a word, she raised her arms up and commanded the boat across the sea. Niko said the boat flew faster than an airplane across the sky. Across the sea and across the globe. A trip that should have taken days took mere moments. And then the boat stopped, and she got out."

"First of all, that is impossible. And second of all, you can't be certain it was her," Katerina protested.

"But it was," Calliope insisted, turning and poking her finger into Agathe's chest. "Tell my stupid cousin who it was."

Agathe stopped and turned to face Katerina. "It was Marlena."

"See, I told you it was Marlena," Calliope said, now waving her index finger in Katerina's face. "Now tell her what you told me, where the boat landed. Tell her where they were."

"Af-ri-ca," Agathe replied, whispering the answer while slowly and deliberately enunciating each syllable. "The boat flew to Africa. When it finally stopped, Marlena got out and walked away from the boat and the sea and went deep into the forest. Knowing no one would believe his story, Niko jumped out of the boat and plucked a flower from a plant he saw growing at the edge of the forest. It was unlike any flower he had ever seen before, surely nothing anyone had ever seen on Corfu. The flower was a deep purple, almost black, with large, sturdy petals that ended in a point as sharp as a needle. The smell was like a hundred bottles of perfume all packed into a single petal. Niko knew this magical flower was his proof of what had happened and where he had been. He hid again, clutching the flower to his chest as Marlena commanded the boat once more across the sea and back to Corfu.

"The next day was Sunday. Niko woke early and dressed in his best clothes, even polishing his shoes with a cloth dipped in his wife's finest olive oil. He waited in the back of the church and watched as Marlena stood with her baby daughter and husband. At the end of the service, as the priest was handing out the blessed bread, Niko walked to the front of the altar and announced to the congregation what happened. He told them where he had been and who Marlena really was, what she really was. That she was a witch. No one believed him, of course, until he pulled from his pocket this strange flower. Instantly the church filled with its sweet, intoxicating scent. Marlena didn't say a word. My grandmother swears she saw a single tear run down Marlena's face before she handed baby Clotho to her husband, turned, and walked out the church door, never to be seen again."

"She just disappeared? People don't just disappear," Katerina protested, kicking at the dirt, which enveloped the girls in a dust cloud.

Calliope's eyes narrowed as her mouth drew into a light line. Katerina took that as her cue to quickly walk away from the girls and their silly gossip and stories.

"She didn't disappear. She flew home. To Africa. And she's not people. She's a witch. Just like her daughter. Just like Clotho," Calliope shouted.

Katerina hurried away from the girls, even faster now, not even stopping to pick a cluster of plump blackberries she spotted, tempting her from a roadside bush.

"That's why she lives alone. That's why she could never find a husband and never had any children. That's why there have been no fish lately. She scared them away, just like her mother did. We'll all starve to death because Clotho frightened the fish away," Calliope shouted, a torrent of words streaming out of her mouth like a fast-flowing river. Deliberate. Unstoppable.

"My mother warned me never to be alone with her, that she drinks the blood of children," Agathe added.

"Stay away from her if you know what's good for you," Calliope yelled, then Agathe and Calliope raced down the dirt path toward home, their braids trailing and bouncing behind them.

Katerina stopped and turned, watching as the girls skipped away. She waited until they were farther down the path, closer to the olive oil mill. When she could no longer see or hear them, she clutched her schoolbooks tighter to her chest and began to run back toward the olive tree grove. He was already waiting for her by the time she reached the yia-yia tree.

"Are you ready?" Marco asked Katerina just as Stefano emerged from the schoolhouse.

"Tell Mama I'll be home later," Marco shouted to his brother.

Stefano waved as he slung his book bag on his shoulder and began the long walk back home.

Katerina smiled at Marco and started running, even before the words escaped her lips. "Race you."

They ran across the olive grove, careful not to stumble on the large protruding roots and tarps that lined the ground to catch the fallen olives. As fast as their legs could carry them, they raced past the tiny port, past the café where the men sat, nursing their afternoon coffees while listening to the latest news on the impending civil war and arguing over the righteous path for Greece.

They continued down the path, past the curve to the spot in the road just in front of the mayor's front gate. Marco stopped.

"Should we take the shortcut?" he asked.

Katerina stared up at the house. As they stood there, the front door flew open. It was Stamati, the mayor's son, who was about a year older than Katerina and Marco and spent more time being punished by Mr. Andonis than he did learning his lessons. He ran out the door and bounded out the gate, not bothering to close either behind him.

"What are you staring at?" he muttered as he brushed past them.

Katerina and Marco said nothing. They just stepped aside to let him pass.

"I don't understand it," Katerina said, shaking her head.

"What?"

"Why is he always such a jerk? And Thea Olga, why is she always so mean and so unhappy? If I lived here I would be so happy all the time. I just know my mama and baba would be so happy, too, if this was our home. Look at it. They have everything they could ever want or ask for. Why isn't it enough?"

"Do you ever think about what it would be like to live here?" he asked.

"I do."

"You do?"

"Yes, I do. I think we would all be happy here. Wouldn't you?"

But before Marco had the chance to answer, Thea Olga poked her head out of the door that Stamati had left open. Katerina and Marco ducked behind the gate to hide from her.

"That boy will never learn. Look at him, leaving the door open, letting in all the mosquitoes and flies. I'll fix him and fix him good," she muttered as she closed the door.

Marco looked to Katerina and nodded. It was a calculated risk, but one they were willing to take. Marco and Katerina knew they could race across the mayor's garden before Thea Olga could hobble back from the front door to her perch at the back window.

Katerina and Marco ran as fast as they could across the garden and up the steep, rocky trail to the top of the mountain. Finally standing on the plateau, they looked out across the horizon. The sky was crystal blue and clear, a perfect mirror reflection of the glassy sea below.

Shielding her eyes from the sun, Katerina looked down toward the bottom of the mountain and smiled when she spotted the house tucked into the hillside like the mountain had grown around it, like it was God's plan all along.

It was a small, one-room house, like most on the island. But unlike the other homes whose drab surroundings spoke to the state of their haggard owners' lives—mothers too busy chasing children and cobbling together meals to pull weeds or plant flowers, fathers too busy mending fishing nets and arguing over politics to whitewash cracked and yellowed stucco, villagers too busy wondering how they would survive these gray days of wartime to infuse any color into their homes or their lives—this home was none of those things. The brilliant whitewash of the walls and floor was a perfect canvas for the rainbow explosion of colors growing around it. Deep blood reds, pale ethereal pinks, robin's-egg blues, and fiery orange blossoms crowded the garden and grew abundantly in the glazed pots and earth-filled cans that adorned every corner and every crevice of the patio. This was a house alive in color. This was a house alive.

Katerina and Marco burst through the gate woven from bamboo fronds and into the garden. They heard her, whispering and singing softly, even before they saw her. She was exactly where they knew she would be. Clad in her mother's apron, she held pruning shears in her hand and wore her father's faded fisherman's cap low on her forehead to shield her face from the sun. She walked among the massive rosebushes, earthy tomato vines, and her prized fig tree, chatting with her beloved plants and flowers, coaxing them to grow big, fragrant, and vibrant, speaking to them as lovingly as if they were her own children.

"There you are," she said as she spotted the children racing toward her. "I knew you would come today."

Red-faced and winded, Katerina and Marco gasped and struggled to catch their breath.

"We had to come," Katerina blurted out. "I couldn't wait to get here, to see you, to tell you. I had the most interesting dream last night."

"Well, you must tell me all about it then." She handed each of the children a plump purple fig before walking into the house. Marco sucked on his finger where the fruit's sweet sap had dripped. He then peeled back the fig's purple velvet skin before breaking open the fruit and savoring each bite. He loved the way the tiny seeds cracked and popped in his mouth, an explosion of flavor and texture. Without hesitation, Katerina handed her fig to Marco.

The woman returned outside to the children clutching a faded and worn leather-bound book in one hand and a tray of figs in the other. She rubbed her hand in circles on the leather cover. "Come, let's see what this dream of yours means." She tilted back her cap, tucked her long black hair behind her ears, licked her index finger, and flipped through the yellowed pages of her book.

Katerina, Marco, and Clotho sat right there, in the shade of an olive tree that afternoon, snacking on perfectly ripe figs and consulting Marlena's old dream diary to discover the meaning of Katerina's dream.

Eight

Corfu
September 1946

Katerina and Marco went down the mountain toward home, their bellies filled with Clotho's impossibly sweet figs and their minds with her words.

"A dream can be a mirror. Sometimes it is something to hold up and look into, to help you examine what's behind you or to better examine yourself. Sometimes, in the black of night, dreams help us see what we often overlook in the light of day," Clotho told her. *"This woman you see in your dreams is watching over you."*

"But why do I dream about her again and again?"

"Because she is always with you."

"But why won't she answer me when I speak to her?"

"Some conversations are beyond words."

"Who is she?"

"I'm not sure. But we will find out in time."

Marco and Katerina walked slowly in silence, each wrapped up in their own thoughts. They savored their afternoons with Clotho, and it wasn't just for the treats that grew in her garden. Sure, some of the villagers whispered about her, insisting there was dark magic in her blood and in the very air surrounding her house. But the children didn't believe that silly talk. The only magic they had witnessed was how the plants and flowers seemed to respond to Clotho's voice. How she charmed and coaxed them to grow, even after the seasons had changed and the other gardens in the village had grown barren and dry.

To the children, it seemed Clotho's magic was in how she infused beauty in everything she touched. Her crochet needles produced elaborate and delicate patterns quickly and effortlessly, just as her garden produced the most perfect flowers and fruits. Despite their differences in age—Clotho was nearing thirty and Katerina and Marco were both ten—in Clotho, Katerina and Marco felt they had found their only true friend, besides each other.

Calliope didn't see it that way. She insisted it was creepy and odd that Clotho lived by herself and didn't have a husband or any children of her own. Katerina insisted it was creepy that Calliope let Michale kiss her behind the freshwater spring.

Katerina had asked Clotho about it once. And once had been enough.

"Why don't you have children?"

"Because I don't have a husband."

"Why don't you have a husband?"

"Because I'm not married."

"Why aren't you married?"

"Because I don't have a husband."

It was as simple as that. What Katerina didn't understand was why others couldn't see the perfection of Clotho's explanation.

The children parted as they approached the old mill, clutching the gifts that Clotho had folded into their hands as they said their goodbyes. Each of them held a small jar of honey, harvested from the bees in Clotho's garden. She had tucked a small extra gift under Marco's arm, a cluster of white roses meant for his mother, Yianna.

"See you tomorrow," Marco shouted as he began the steep climb home.

"Bye," Katerina called as she continued down the road that cut straight through town and toward her house.

Katerina skipped along the road, stopping now and again to pick up a rock and toss it into the sea. She smiled as rock after rock sailed past the road, over the beach, and landed in the sea with a splash. She was getting bigger and stronger. This proved it. Just a few months ago, try as she might, none of her rocks ever made it past the sandy slope of the beach.

She beamed and continued skipping as she replayed Mr. Andonis's morning lesson in her head. She couldn't wait to share with her mother stories of Odysseus's travels and the monsters and murderers he met on his prolonged trip back home to Ithaka.

She heard the raised voices just as she approached the bend in the road that led to the center of town. She never intended to stop and listen. She had planned on going straight home, but the urgency in their voices made her curious. She was used to the loud voices, the bombastic pronouncements and pontification of the men attempting to outdo each other, talking over one another to get their point heard, whether the talk was about politics, fishing, or the weather. But immediately she knew something was different. While some of the men continued to shout, others spoke in barely a whisper. Even at ten years old, Katerina understood that hushed words often scream with importance.

"Thirteen policemen. God-fearing Greek Orthodox men, fathers, husbands, countrymen, and patriots. Murdered. The entire police station of Litochoro burned and destroyed, with many of the officers still in it. Burned alive," one man said.

"I thought they were driven back. That they finally learned their lesson," another man added.

"It doesn't seem that way." Katerina recognized the mayor's voice. "The partisans have been hiding in the mountains. Despite what you might have heard, or what you'd like to think, they have not disbanded. They have been waiting, training, gaining resources and funding from their Communist comrades. It sounds as if they are now emboldened and fortified. And I'm afraid this is the beginning."

"Don't you think that maybe they're right?" a man asked. "Maybe it's time for a change. I mean, look at us here on Corfu. Why is it the wealthy get wealthier and we, the Greeks on whose backs this country was built, the small villages, find it harder and harder to feed our children? How can Communism be any worse than what we have now? Maybe Greece has had its fill of the monarchy."

"You think so?" Mr. Andonis replied, his voice rising with emotion. "Let's not forget that if it were not for the monarchy, you would not be able to call yourself a Greek. Have you forgotten your history or, as some have conveniently done, rewritten the past to suit yourself? It's only because of the monarchy, for the enthronement of King George I, that Britain gifted the Ionian islands, including your beloved Corfu, to Greece. So don't tell me that we owe nothing to the monarchy and then tell me how proud you are to call yourself a Greek. One would not exist without the other."

The men paused for a moment to take in the teacher's history lesson.

"How have we come to this?" Katerina's baba was now speaking.

"It is more than just opposing ideologies we have to fear. It's not as simple as Communist versus monarchist," Mr. Andonis added. "I had a letter from my sister, who lives with her husband and children in Karditsa. She saw with her own eyes what this dangerous atmosphere can breed. She told me that a neighbor was murdered, his home burned to the ground by government soldiers. And for nothing but the power of greed and rumor. It was a blood feud. A family dispute, cousins who had not spoken in years over a piece of property. One cousin bitter because the other inherited the more fertile plot of land. Shepherds arguing over grass, a piece of land where goats eat and defecate. And so, to gain revenge, this man told the government soldiers that his cousin had helped the partisans by giving a soldier food and something to drink. It was a lie. But the police burned his home to the ground and hung the man from a tree in the center of town, leaving his body there to rot as a warning to others. Families ruined, all over petty jealousy. These are dangerous times we are living in. In more ways than just one."

"Come on. That can't be true. With no proof at all," the mayor said, huffing dramatically.

"It is true. Every word of it," Mr. Andonis replied. "Rumor and jealousy are just as dangerous as guns in this climate."

"But that's barbaric," the mayor insisted. His sentiments were echoed by several more of the men who grunted their disbelief. "These are men, not animals."

"It's shocking what civilized men will do to save themselves or further their agenda."

"Impossible." The mayor pulled worry beads from his pocket, twirling them around on his fingers.

"Quite possible, I'm afraid. Look at what happened in Athens. Look at what happened to Eleni Papadaki." Mr. Andonis's voice cracked as he said her name.

"What does one have to do with the other?" the mayor asked, his tone confirming just how absurd he found the schoolteacher's argument.

"She was set up by another actress. It was a lie, pure and simple," Mr. Andonis replied.

"There was nothing simple about it," an older fisherman challenged. "Eleni Papadaki was a Nazi collaborator."

"She was nothing of the sort." Mr. Andonis's voice was raised now as well. "Eleni Papadaki was a victim of jealousy. An older actress jealous of a younger, more talented actress. She found a way to get rid of her rival once and for all. Falsely accused of helping the Germans, convicted without a trial. Raped, then hacked to death with an ax, her skin ripped from her body . . . Do you really need me to go on?"

"I heard that when she was brought in for questioning, she arrived in a fur coat and red lipstick," another man added.

The men all silently contemplated this for a moment. No one could remember the last time they saw a woman wearing red lipstick, let alone a fur coat.

"A beautiful young woman brutally murdered. For what? For nothing. Jealousy. Lies. All around us, lives are being extinguished without a thought, as if blowing out a candle, as if they were nothing," Mr. Andonis continued. "This is what we've come to. This is what we have been reduced to . . ." His voice trailed off.

"Animals." Katerina recognized Baba's voice again.

"No," Mr. Andonis sighed. "Animals kill to survive. This is something very different, I'm afraid."

Katerina pressed her back up against the wall of the café. Surely she had misunderstood. They must be talking about a film or even a play. Of course they were. She recognized the name Eleni Papadaki. Mr. Andonis had spoken about her in class during a lesson on the ancient playwrights. She remembered how he had held up a yellowed newspaper, showing the actress onstage dressed as Clytemnestra in *Electra*. His eyes took on a faraway look as he stood before the students and described what it was like to sit in an open-air theater at dusk as Greece's finest actors stepped back in time, personifying the greatest characters in literature. He'd said he wished that the children would one day have the opportunity to see such a performance for themselves. Surely he must be speaking about another one of Eleni Papadaki's performances. The fur coat and red lips were her costume, just like that beautiful draped toga in the newspaper photo when she played Clytemnestra. Surely that's what the men were talking about, Katerina attempted to convince herself as she felt the tingling in her eyes give way to tears. The alternative was too horrifying to even consider.

Just then, Laki came around the corner. "Well now, look what I've found. A little stray kitten roaming the port." He bent down and kissed the tip of her nose. "And please tell me, little one, what you are doing back here hiding? Or perhaps I'd be better off not knowing."

She leaned her body forward and wrapped her arms around him. "It's just a story, right, Baba?" she asked. "What Mr. Andonis said happened to that actress. It was just a story, wasn't it? Like a role in a play or something you see at the cinema . . . a story . . ."

He held Katerina tighter.

She lifted her head and looked at him. "It can't be true, can it, Baba?"

Baba kissed her forehead, then lifted her to his shoulders and headed toward home.

Because, after all, it's not really a lie if the words are never spoken out loud.

Nine

Corfu
October 1946

"There you are," Yianna said as Marco walked through the gate. She was standing in the outdoor kitchen, scrubbing potatoes with the well water that she had pulled up earlier in the day. Yianna looked up at the sky, noting the sun had begun her lazy descent over Corfu's lush western hills, then out over the open sea of the Ionian where she would come to rest behind the cliffs of Erikousa silhouetted in the distance. Yianna had merely an hour before daylight would fade to black, and she was woefully behind on her tasks. She scrubbed faster as she watched Marco chase frogs around the patio and then race into the outhouse, slamming the door behind him.

She thought about asking him to help with the dinner preparations but then laughed out loud, although in truth she didn't find the situation truly funny. Amused exasperation was a more accurate way to describe her feelings. Several months back Yianna had done just that, asked Marco to wash the vegetables and help get dinner on the table. He reluctantly agreed, and she went to the cellar to get a jug of olive oil. When she returned to the outdoor kitchen, she found Marco smiling proudly over the freshly washed produce. It wasn't until she reached for the water jug to fill the dinner glasses that she realized Marco had used up their entire supply of fresh water instead of the well water for the task. An hour's trip up and down the mountain, down the drain in an instant.

From that day on, Yianna resigned herself to managing all of the dinner tasks herself. It was just easier this way. She often wondered if this was what her mischievous younger son intended all along.

Yianna laid all of the vegetables on the table, surveying the afternoon's haul as Marco emerged from the outhouse. Four blood-red tomatoes, three vibrant green zucchini, a small head of cabbage, and five golden potatoes, all harvested that morning from her garden.

"Hello, Mama," Marco shouted, tossing a bag on the floor.

Yianna stepped away from the vegetables to get a closer look at what he had thrown on the ground. She noticed the bag move and recoiled a bit. She then leaned in closer and watched as two frogs escaped from the sack and hopped away to the safety of the garden. Yianna shook her head and laughed. Boys. She was surrounded by boys. So many times throughout the years Yianna had prayed for God to grant her a daughter. She loved her sons beyond measure, but always wondered what life would be like if she had been blessed with a daughter as well. She knew as well as any woman in Greece that mothers lose their sons to their wives eventually. But every mother knows that a daughter will never leave her side. She wondered which of her sons would step up to care for her when the time came.

Yianna walked back to the table and her dinner preparations. She lifted a tomato to her nose and inhaled. She could never get enough of the tomato's deep, earthy scent. She dreaded this time of year, when the season was coming to a close and soon the vine would stop producing its sweet fruit. Although it was still warm for an October afternoon, Yianna shivered a bit, thinking of the impending winter months. She prayed Aleko would at last be able to haul in enough fish to sell at the market in Corfu Town this week. She didn't want to imagine another winter without a proper stove to warm the house and could not fathom how Marco would manage another season without a new pair of shoes.

She dried her hands on her apron and looked across the sea to Albania in the distance. It was so close, just twelve kilometers. From her yard she could see its sandy beaches and green cliffs. Yianna often found herself staring out over the sea and wondering what life was like just across the narrow channel that separated the two countries. She squinted and looked closer, wondering why she never spotted a soul on the beach and then wondering if swimming or sunbathing was even allowed in Communist countries. *Probably not*, she thought.

While it was still considered immodest for women here in the village to wear swimsuits and sunbathe, Yianna had seen the photos in the European ladies' magazines that Clotho often brought back from town.

Yianna and Clotho were old childhood friends. They had grown up in the village but felt very much like outsiders, a fact that bonded them as children and cemented their friendship as adults. It seemed that every happy memory of Yianna's life happened with Clotho standing beside her. When the other girls of the village gossiped and laughed at the idea that Yianna, one of the poorest girls in the village, had once lived among royalty, Clotho had always stood up for her. Clotho was quite young when she discovered that rumors of witchcraft in her lineage could be used to her advantage. She was not above threatening to curse and cast a spell on anyone who dared say harmful things about her one and only friend.

Together Yianna and Clotho had pored over countless magazine images of glamorous women in sleek swimsuits, elegant sunhats, and crimson-tinted lips sipping champagne and lounging on umbrellaed sunbeds. Aleko had told her that small tourist hotels had begun popping up along Corfu's southern coast and that a wealthy Frenchman was scouting the island for seaside property to open something called Club Mediterranee along the beach in Ipsos. A place where people did nothing all day but lie in the sun. *Imagine that*, Yianna thought.

The world was changing around them, but time still seemed to stand still here in Pelekito. Yianna wondered what it was to feel the sun on her bare skin and lie still on the sand, enjoying the warmth of an afternoon as the sea lapped rhythmically at her feet. But those luxuries were reserved for women born of a different time and place. And though Yianna still dreamed of returning to the grandeur of life at Mon Repos one day, while she was here in Pelekito, she was always mindful of keeping her place.

Like the other women in the village, Yianna had not gone to school. She knew nothing of politics or economics and had never studied history. But she was educated in ways beyond letters and numbers. Yianna was fluent in reading the faces of the ones she loved and had seen the change in Aleko's face these past few weeks. She noticed as his eyes grew darker and the lines on his forehead and around his eyes etched deeper. Each night after the boys were asleep, she asked Aleko to share with her what he had heard from the radio and the other men in town. At first he was hesitant, not wanting to give her more reason to worry, but eventually he began to open up a bit, to share with her details of what the men in the village discussed. It wasn't long before she wondered if it might have been better not to have asked at all.

Yianna had celebrated, along with every family in town and all across Corfu, and Greece as well, when the Germans at last surrendered. She, like all of her fellow Greeks, thought the dark days were behind them. But now, as the rest of Europe reveled in post-war peace, it felt as if Greece was spiraling toward something unprecedented. She could sense the stress in Aleko's body, the way he tensed up when he spoke of the devastation along the northern border. He was not one to cry much, or ever, but she felt the wetness of his cheek on hers as she held him and he spoke of mothers who refused to join the partisans, who had babies and would not put down their children to pick up a gun. He told her how these mothers were made to watch as their babies were shot on the spot, then had guns thrust into their hands. Aleko told her of parents who drove their children from their own homes, sending them out into the mountains with nothing more than a corner of bread. They would rather their children died in the wild, on Greek soil, than at the hands of the barbaric partisans.

It is not supposed to be like this, she found herself thinking again and again as she listened to him each night. He spoke as if whispering the words in the darkness somehow unburdened him. She would carry the weight for both of them if she could. But Yianna also knew there was little she could do beyond envelop her husband and children in love. That was her one and only role in life, her one and only contribution.

It's not supposed to be like this. Yianna felt as if she had been defined by these words her entire life. As if peace and joy were stalked by circumstance and tragedy, the way feral cats at the port taunted and toyed with mice before administering their fatal pounce. She had seen glimmers of hope several times in her life. Of peace, of opportunities to further her family. She never anticipated or expected that she would again be surrounded by the finery and abundance of her early childhood; just perhaps enough to live on without the constant worry. There had been flickers of that possibility, and then, like the explosive light of a shooting star bursting and streaking across the sky, her hopes always faded away again to nothing.

"Hey!" Marco shouted. "What happened to my frogs?" He ran in circles in search of the escaped amphibians.

Yianna smiled as she watched him. She thanked God for her young, silly son, grateful for the light and levity and love that he brought to her life.

"What's going on? What did you lose?" Aleko asked as he walked in through the gate carrying a basket of fish, Stefano beside him.

"How did my men do today?" Yianna asked as she stirred the vegetables in the pan.

"We did all right," Aleko said as he placed the basket on the floor. She walked over and peeked in. There were at least a dozen fish—mullet, sea bream, octopuses, and a few sea urchins. Enough to keep the family fed, but not nearly enough for Aleko to sell at the market.

Yianna plucked the fish from the basket and went to work preparing them for dinner. She ran her knife up and down each side of the fish, making sure to remove the scales, then she slid the knife from one side of the belly to the other, emptying the guts into a bucket at her feet. She used the well water to rinse the fish before dousing it in olive oil and dried oregano and stuffing the cavity with lemons slices, garlic, and freshly cut thyme. She grilled the fish over the open flame alongside the pan of roasted vegetables.

She called her boys to the table. They ate outside, under the lemon tree, as the sun began to set behind the silhouette of Erikousa in the distance.

"How was school today?" she asked.

"Fine," Marco replied as he shoved another bite of fish into his mouth.

"Good," Stefano said, helping himself to another portion. "We finished the *Odyssey*. Mr. Andonis is helping me map Odysseus's journey. I'm going to sail his route one day, from Ermones on the western coast. Did you know that's supposed to be the real location of the Phaeacians' palace? They were master seamen, and if it wasn't for their help, Odysseus might never have made it home. So I guess that proves they were from Corfu, right, Baba?" Stefano laughed. His father slapped his back in agreement.

"I'm going to retrace every stop along the way, every single place Homer wrote about on Odysseus's road back home to Ithaka," Stefano announced.

"That sounds wonderful," Yianna said, placing her fork down beside her plate as she gazed at her son. The gold and orange sky reflected in his eyes like fire.

"And so, when I become a teacher one day, like Mr. Andonis, I can tell my students what Odysseus's journey really looked like and tell them I was there." He waved his fork in the air for emphasis before stabbing a potato. Stefano's teeth scraped the metal as he placed the potato in his mouth.

"That sounds so exciting, and you will be the best teacher to ever grace the inside of a classroom." Yianna beamed as Marco rolled his eyes. "What an adventure you'll have." She grabbed a lemon from the tree and sliced it in half before squeezing the juice on the fish.

"We started Cavafy's poem 'Ithaka' today," Stefano said as he reached across the table, stealing a potato off of Marco's plate. Marco then leaned across the table himself, arm flailing back and forth in an effort to hit his older brother. Stefano expertly dodged and weaved away from Marco, who grew increasingly red-faced and frustrated with each missed punch. Yianna shook her head at the pair and stifled a laugh as she took a potato from her own plate and placed it on Marco's. Stefano never missed a beat, continuing with his report of the day's events.

"Mr. Andonis said all the students my age will have a chance to recite it for the class. We can choose which part we want to perform."

"Which will you pick?" Yianna asked.

"I like the first part when he talks about the monsters."

"Tell me," she said. "Let me hear you." She motioned for him to stand up. Stefano looked to his father.

"You don't need my permission. Go ahead, do as your mother asked." Aleko leaned back in his chair and began to roll a cigarette. Marco fidgeted in his seat as his brother stood.

Stefano raised his hands to his hair, slicking it back dramatically. He straightened his collar and smiled, pretending to adjust a bow tie. He then looked from his parents to his brother and across the horizon, as if he were center stage of a storied amphitheater. And then he spoke.

> "As you set out for Ithaka
> hope your voyage is a long one,
> full of adventure, full of discovery.
> Laistrygonians and Cyclops,
> angry Poseidon—don't be afraid of them:
> you'll never find things like that on your way
> as long as you keep your thoughts raised high,
> as long as a rare excitement
> stirs your spirit and your body.
> Laistrygonians and Cyclops,
> wild Poseidon—you won't encounter them
> unless you bring them along inside your soul,
> unless your soul sets them up in front of you.
> Hope your voyage is a long one.

May there be many summer mornings when,

with what pleasure, what joy,

you come into harbors seen for the first time;

may you stop at Phoenician trading stations

to buy fine things,

mother of pearl and coral, amber and ebony,

sensual perfume of every kind—

as many sensual perfumes as you can;

and may you visit many Egyptian cities

to gather stories of knowledge from their scholars.

Keep Ithaka always in your mind.

Arriving there is what you're destined for.

But do not hurry the journey at all.

Better if it lasts for years,

so you are old by the time you reach the island,

wealthy with all you've gained on the way,

not expecting Ithaka to make you rich.

Ithaka gave you the marvelous journey.

Without her you wouldn't have set out.

She has nothing left to give you now.

And if you find her poor, Ithaka won't have fooled you.

Wise as you will have become, so full of experience,

you will have understood by then what these Ithakas

      mean."

As he finished speaking, Stefano took a deep, dramatic bow, waving his hands as if thanking the adoring crowd at the back of a theater. He turned to his mother and took another deep bow before falling into his chair.

"Bravo!" Yianna shouted and clapped. "Bravo. That was beautiful. Marco, what about you? What are you learning in school these days?"

Marco picked at the fish bones on his plate and ignored his mother's question. "Oh, I almost forgot to tell you," he said. "I saw Clotho today, and she said she's going to come by and see you tomorrow. That she has something special for you."

Yianna knew exactly what he was doing, changing the subject so she would not be upset with him. It amazed her sometimes, how two boys from the same parents, raised in the same household and so close in age, could be so very different.

"I'm so glad. It's been so long." And she was glad. It had been quite a while since she had seen her friend. Most of the women of the village, even those who rarely left their homes, were guaranteed at least a weekly visit at church. But Clotho did not attend church. She was very much a woman of faith, but chose instead to pray privately at home. She had explained this to Yianna years ago, saying she felt no need to return to the location of her family's ruin.

Aleko stood up from the table and walked out to the edge of the terrace. The sky had turned from red-tinged and golden to gray as the light faded. He lifted his head and surveyed the horizon. Heavy, low clouds had moved in from Italy across the Adriatic and were now blanketing the northern point of Corfu from Agios Stefanos all the way to Kassiopi. He ran his fingers through his hair and inhaled the sea air.

"There is a maestro coming. This one will last for days." He shook his head. "I have to get out early and drop both sets of nets if there's any hope of making any sales this week."

Stefano nodded his head, understanding what this meant.

"I'm sorry, son. I hate to take you from school. I really do, especially after that impressive performance you just gave," he said with a wink. "But I need your help tomorrow. We'll get twice the work done. I just need you for one day and then you can perform the entire 'Ithaka' to your heart's content. After tomorrow the weather will be too choppy for anyone to head out onto the water for days." Aleko placed his hand, tanned and strong, on his son's shoulder. "If we sell enough fish, I'll take some time off and we can sail together on Odysseus's travels." He winked at Yianna and then whispered in Stefano's ear, "Let's keep an eye out for those nymphs, shall we?"

Yianna feigned exasperation, tossing a napkin at her husband. He ducked out of the way and smiled broader.

"I'll come, Baba. Let me help you," Marco pleaded.

Aleko smiled and shook his head. "No. You go to school. Let that teacher try to get some sense into you. Lord knows the rest of us don't stand a chance at doing so. Besides, I'm not so convinced you're a Phaeacian. Last time you came with me, you spent the day vomiting over the side of the boat. I can't have that tomorrow. The fish are supposed to feed us, not the other way around." He tousled Marco's hair.

"Of course, Baba," Stefano replied. "Mr. Andonis said we'll take turns reciting the poem all week. I have plenty of time to dazzle them. We'll haul in so many fish that we won't know what to do with all the money we'll make."

Aleko laughed. "Well, of course we will. We'll buy your mother a proper crown."

Yianna couldn't help herself this time. A laugh that sounded more like a snort escaped her lips. This dissolved everyone into laughter.

She cleared the table and carried the dishes to the basin. Yianna scrubbed the plates and pans clean as she gazed out across the terrace at her family. Stefano bent over to help his father mend an old torn net, and Marco chased frogs across the patio. She stood there even after the last dish was washed and dried, watching as the sky faded from gray to black, the low, dense clouds wafting across the sky like a heavy blanket, illuminated by the moon above.

She stayed like that, watching them, as the last glimmer of daylight disappeared beyond the outline of the tiny island on the horizon. The moon, high above the clouds, cast everything below her into ghostly silver silhouettes as Princess Alice's lace curtains lifted and danced in the evening air.

Ten

Corfu
October 1946

Katerina tucked herself into the corner, where the mattress met the wall, just below the icons of Jesus, Saint Spyridon, and the blessed Virgin Mary. Knowing they were above her, watching over her, made her feel a little bit better. But not quite enough. She willed herself smaller. Chin to her knees and arms wrapped around her legs, she hunched her sharp shoulders forward and as low as they would go. If she made herself small, she reasoned, any witch or demon might overlook her. She had been like that for at least two hours, since the moment she woke and realized he was gone. The room was dark, too dark to see anything at all. But she knew from the silence that he wasn't in his bed. While Mama complained about his loud nocturnal breathing and deep snoring, Katerina was comforted by the sounds. They meant he was still there.

She had been tempted to climb into bed with her mother, to feel the safety and security that came with pressing her body against the curve of her mother's back. But she thought about how tired Mama seemed lately, the red tinge of her eyes, the gray pallor of her skin. Her mind raced to the scene just yesterday, when she came home from school to find Mama on her knees in the garden. At first Katerina thought she was digging up potatoes, but then she noticed how her mother's body trembled as her tears one by one watered the dry earth.

As much as she needed the reassurance of her mother beside her, Katerina chose instead to let her sleep. She was, after all, her mother's daughter, bred to put the needs of others before her own.

But then she heard it. It began as a low, slow hiss of a stray cat in the yard. The sound was enough to startle Katerina, who pulled her knees even closer to her chest, burying her face in her nightshirt. The hissing then stopped, evolving instead into a guttural yet high-pitched yowl that to Katerina sounded no longer like a cat but like someone, or something, was right outside the door, hunting their latest prey, which she feared must surely be her.

Her mind raced. It had been nearly a month since she'd overheard the men at the port, and she could not get the horrific images out of her head. Eleni Papadaki *"hacked to death with an ax, her skin ripped from her body."* Katerina closed her eyes again, but all she could picture was an image of Eleni Papadaki's skinless body clad in a fur coat with red lipstick coming for her. She had been brave long enough. Katerina sprang from her mattress and dove into the bed beside Mama, the old springs heralding her arrival. Katerina clung to her, pressing her body against her mother's back, and buried her face in Mama's hair.

"Darling, what is it?" Mama woke with a start. "What's wrong? What happened?" She sat up in bed, running her hands over Katerina's body. "Are you hurt?"

"I tried not to wake you," Katerina cried. "I tried so hard. But I heard something outside. I thought it was the cats, but, Mama, I don't think it was." She struggled to catch her breath between sobs. "I don't think it was a cat at all. And it was so dark, Mama. I don't know what was out there, but I think it was trying to come in here."

"It's all right, my sweet. There is nothing for you to be afraid of. Nothing at all," Mama said. She hugged Katerina closer to her chest as her eyes fell on Baba's empty spot in the bed beside her. A knot formed between her brows.

"But, Mama, I heard it. You've never heard such a horrible noise. It was so scary." Katerina took her mother's face in her tiny hands and looked deep into her eyes. "You must believe me."

"Oh, I do believe you," Mama whispered as she pulled Katerina closer and wrapped her arms around the trembling child, wiping the wetness from Katerina's cheek with her fingertips. "I do believe you were scared. But I want you to know that even when you feel scared, even when you hear strange noises, you have nothing to fear in the dark, my love. Remember, the goddess Nyx is always with you, watching over you in the night."

"Tell me again, Mama. Tell me the story of Nyx. You say she is always with me, but I don't remember meeting her."

"Oh, my darling, you have met her many, many times." Mama rocked Katerina back and forth in her arms, just as her own mother had done so many years before. She leaned in and kissed Katerina's head. And then she spoke again. "Night after night, since the day you were born, Mother Nyx has kissed your pink cheek and covered your sleeping body in her heavenly veil. Remember I told you that Nyx is the goddess of the night. She lives with her husband, the god of darkness, in a palace beyond the gates of Tartarus. Well, a long, long time ago, my sweet, when there was nothing in this world but chaos, Nyx rose out of the turmoil to guard the universe in the dark hours when her daughter Hemera—the day—was resting. Nyx wears a long, dark robe and has black hair that flows behind her for miles and miles like a churning river current. Everything about her is dark. Her dress, her hair, and even her skin is the faintest black, like the sky just before the dawn. Fastened to her hair is a long black veil, which trails behind her and casts the earth in darkness as Nyx flies across the sky each evening until Hemera is well rested and ready to shine her light on the world again. Now, Nyx is not just goddess of the night. Remember, I told you she has many, many children. Nyx is also mother to Hypnos, sleep, and to death and also to nightmares."

Katerina freed herself from her mother's embrace. She huffed, a whimper escaping from her lips. "Come now, Mama. How do you expect me to feel better knowing Nyx is watching me? I think she sounds scarier than the noises outside."

"Yes." Mama laughed. "Yes, you are right; that is what most people would think." She enfolded Katerina into her embrace once again. "But let us not be like most people, Katerina. I want you to always be brave, brave enough to do your own thinking, find your own reason, even when others around you claim to be so smart and clever. Because there, hidden sometimes among the darkest shadows, so easily overlooked by others, is where truth and beauty hide."

Mama went on. "Now let's look at Mother Nyx. Yes, some of her children may frighten you, but while Nyx is the mother of nightmares and death, she is also the mother of dreams and sleep. Just think for a moment of how beautiful and magical dreams and sleep are." She stroked Katerina's hair with her fingertips, calming Katerina with her soft touch.

"Think of how it feels to fall fast asleep in your bed after a long day of doing your chores in the sun, the sweet release as Hypnos comes to carry you away. Now think of all the enchanted places you can visit and all of the wonderful things you can experience only in your dreams. Think of the parties with beautiful silk dresses from Paris and frosted cakes kilometers high and porcelain dolls with hair the color of honey. These are Mother Nyx's gifts to you. She knows that I am a poor woman, and as much as I would like to, I cannot give these things to you myself, Katerina. But Nyx wants you to have them. She instructs her children to visit you and give you this precious escape. Each night Mother Nyx casts her dark veil on the earth so you can float off to sleep and live a life in your dreams that I dare not even dream of myself. So you see, my love, yes, sometimes there can be frightening things in the night, but there is also great beauty and kindness. Never forget that, Katerina. Always remember to look deeper than the darkness. You'll be surprised sometimes what you'll find hiding there beyond the black, just waiting to be discovered."

Katerina lay quietly beside her mother. She closed her eyes and thought of all the wonderful things she had experienced and places she had escaped to in her dreams. In her sleep she had feasted on chocolates and an entire table piled high with treats. She had run carefree and effortlessly across the island, through fields of beautiful wildflowers, and up and down the mountains. She swam across the sea with dolphins, soared through the sky with birds, and rose high into the clouds on her magical swing. In her dreams she was never hungry. In her dreams she had new shoes and dresses that fit her and she was never too hot or too cold. In her dreams she was happy. In her dreams Marco was happy too.

Katerina hugged her mother tighter. She opened her mouth to speak but heard Baba's footsteps approach, the crush of gravel beneath his feet growing louder by the moment. She glanced at her mother, who smiled slightly and nodded her permission to go to him.

Katerina sprang out of the doorway and into his arms.

∞

"Baba. Where have you been?" Katerina scolded as she clung to Laki.

"Katerina, quiet. You'll wake the entire island." He closed his eyes and buried his face in her neck, inhaling her scent.

"Baba. Where have you been? Why did you leave me?" He put her down as she spoke. Katerina stood facing Laki with hands on her hips and a pout on her lips. Her silken hair was loose to her waist and her toes peeked out from under the yellowed and frayed nightshirt.

"Shh, Katerina, please . . ." He took her hand and led her toward the garden wall. "Come now, quiet down, or you'll be the one to deal with Thea Voula when she wakes up. She's cranky on a good day, screaming at her poor husband day and night. Imagine the horror she'll be with no sleep." Laki rubbed his hands on his head until his hair stood straight up, then crossed his eyes and snarled his teeth while stretching his shirt out straight at the chest, mimicking but not quite matching the size of Thea Voula's humongous bosom.

Katerina stared at him and brought her hand to her mouth to smother her laughter. Her blue eyes shined bright and wide. In a family of dark almond eyes, she was the only one to inherit the robin's-egg blue eyes of her great-grandmother. Everyone agreed how fitting a blessing this was since Katerina had also inherited her name.

Placing her hand in his, Laki led her farther along the courtyard, away from the house and even farther from Thea Voula's open windows. Voula lived in an old house built into the hill, just above theirs. Not only did her terrace provide an unobstructed view of their courtyard in the daylight hours, but the pitch of the slope offered perfect acoustics that would have made even the ancient playwrights proud. Even when the fierce maestro winds blew in, Thea Voula slept with her windows wide open. She insisted the sea air was medicinal for her gout, but everyone knew better. They knew it was so she wouldn't miss a moment of the dramas and comedies playing out in her very own courtyard amphitheater below.

Only when they reached the wall overlooking the olive grove did Laki nod his head, signaling it was safe for Katerina to speak.

"Baba, where did you go? Why did you leave me? You know how afraid of the dark I am. I heard a noise. It was loud and creepy, and I swear to you it was a witch or a ghost coming for me. I know it was, Baba. I heard her calling my name." With her eyes opened wider, Katerina nodded again and again as if to convince him she spoke the truth. "I waited for you to save me. Where have you been?"

Katerina stepped closer to Laki and wrapped her arms around his legs. She trembled as she pressed her body against him.

"Please don't leave me alone again in the dark. Mama tells me Nyx is watching over me." She leaned in closer and whispered now. "But Nyx scares me too."

Laki looked down at Katerina and threaded his fingers through the silk of her hair. She trembled still, even as she stood in his protective arms, even as the first rooster crowed, signaling the frightful night would be over at last.

"Hush, Katerina. Your mother is right; there is nothing for you to be afraid of," Laki whispered, wishing he could find truth in those very words himself.

He rubbed his hand around and around on the nape of her neck, and then up and down the length of her back, just as he would when she was a baby and her sleepless, colicky screams could be heard across the island all through the night. Like a blind man reading Braille, he thought of how each bone that jutted out beneath his fingers and under the worn fabric of her nightshirt told a story. It was the story of a thin child, of a desperate man with a family to provide for, and also of a young girl who feared fairy-tale witches more than the real-life dangers that existed around them, even in the brightest moments of the day.

Pulling Katerina closer, Laki thought of the horrible stories from all across the country that he had heard from the men at the port. Families on either side of the political spectrum torn apart by ideology. And now even here on Corfu, he had begun to see with his own eyes brother pitted against brother, cousin against cousin, and with deadly and devastating results. It was too much to process, too much to comprehend. He turned to look upon the face of his sweet girl. He would do anything in his power to protect her. He patted the space beside him and motioned for Katerina to sit next to him on the low wall overlooking the grove.

"Katerina, look."

He pointed across the olive grove, into the distance and toward the horizon. There, where the sky met the sea, the first glimmer of dawn's orange light peeked through the black.

"See, my darling, just as your mother told you, Nyx is lifting her veil and gathering it again so that the day can begin. Right now, look across to the horizon and you can see Hemera passing her mother. No matter how tired she is, Nyx makes her nightly journey for the good of her daughter, just as I sometimes make my nightly journeys for you. So remember your mother's words, Katerina. Even when you wake up to find I've slipped away for my own evening chores, even when you are afraid and think you are alone, Mother Nyx will always be here, watching over you, protecting you in the dark."

∽

Katerina burrowed deeper into her father's lap. She watched as the sky turned from black to orange and red, then to gold before her eyes. Shifting her body around, she rubbed the scruff of her father's beard with her hands. Placing a kiss on his lips, she pulled herself back to get a better look at his face.

In that very moment a golden light washed over them, baptizing them in the magical blush of dawn. Katerina marveled at the metamorphosis taking place before her eyes. In the purifying light of sunrise, Baba no longer looked like a broken and tired man. Gone were the red in his eyes and the cavernous dark circles beneath them. Gone were the sallow tone of his skin and the angular, hollow cheeks. In that moment when Nyx and Hemera met at the cusp of day and night, Katerina experienced the magic that can exist only in the very moment when a new day dawns. In the enchanted glow of daybreak, Baba looked healthy and untroubled, like Odysseus throwing off his beggar's robes and revealing his true self.

Katerina smiled. She wrapped her arms around her father and squeezed with all her might. Mama and Baba were right; the goddess's magic was indeed magnificent.

Eleven

Corfu

October 1946

"Why does coffee always taste better when you make it?" Clotho smiled at Yianna as she lifted the cup to her lips.

"Don't you know everything tastes better when someone else makes it for you?" Yianna pulled her chair closer to Clotho.

"I brought you something." Clotho reached into her bag. "I saw this at the market in Sidari when I brought my honey to the market. I thought of you right away."

Yianna wiped her hands on her apron and leaned in. It was a magazine. Her eyes shot open wider as she clapped and brought her hands to her mouth. A small sigh escaped from between her fingers, and then she was silent for a few moments as she fixed her gaze on the magazine's cover image. She blinked a few times, looking from the magazine to the face of her friend. "Oh, Clotho. Oh, Clotho," she repeated over and over again.

Clotho handed Yianna the magazine. On the cover was a photo of King George dressed in his finest military attire, waving from the balcony of the royal palace in Athens. It was a photo from just weeks before, when the king at last returned from exile, restoring the monarchy to Greece.

Yianna traced her fingers along the king's face. "Oh, isn't he handsome?" she said.

Clotho nodded in silent agreement.

Yianna then opened the magazine and flipped through its pages, poring over each and every photo, taking in each exquisite detail. There was the king waving from his car, the streets of Athens packed with citizens waving Greek flags and welcoming the king home. Beside him sat a couple, a handsome young man also dressed in military attire and a delicate young woman in a white suit, her curly hair peeking out from beneath her dark hat. The young woman smiled broadly, her light eyes twinkling as she waved to the crowd. Yianna lingered over the photo, tracing her finger along the perfection of the woman's suit and hat.

"That's Frederica and Paul. It says here that Princess Frederica and Prince Paul accompanied the king as he returned to Athens. The streets were lined with thousands cheering and welcoming the king and the monarchy back to Greece." Clotho leaned closer as she spoke. "Archbishop Damaskinos welcomed the royal family as they arrived to the cathedral, performing the liturgy and blessing the king upon his return.

"And here," Clotho said as she turned the page and pointed to the small black type beneath a portrait of the king in his military garb. "It says here that the king once said the most important tool for a king of Greece is his suitcase." She looked up at Yianna, smiling. "Let's hope he can finally put that suitcase away and bring back stability and hope to the country."

Yianna looked up from the page to Clotho, her brows furrowed, knowing full well that Clotho never learned how to read.

Clotho laughed. "The newspaper stand owner was kind enough to read though the article with me. I gave him an extra jar of honey."

Yianna's gaze went back to the magazine.

"Here," Clotho said, pointing to another picture. "It says that thousands more lined the street leading from the cathedral to the palace, cheering and clapping as George passed. The king placed a wreath at the tomb of the unknown soldier before entering the palace, where he stood beside Prince Paul and Princess Frederica and waved to the adoring crowd below. God bless the king." She put her three fingers together, making the sign of the cross three times as she said the words.

"It also says that there were police out in full force. That there was worry of anti-monarchist protests but thankfully there were none. They had the good sense to stay away."

"Do you think this will help? Do you think having the king back will quiet the Communists once and for all?" Yianna asked.

"I don't know," Clotho replied. "I wish we could be assured of peace, stability, and civility. All we can do is pray that is the case. But I hope so. Look at them," she said. "Refined, elegant. That's what we should be. What Greece can be. Not those barbarians hiding in the mountains, torturing and tormenting those poor villages. I don't know what will happen from here. But I pray the king can help restore peace."

"But I thought you could see into the future. Isn't that what everyone whispers about?" Yianna laughed. "Aren't you the daughter of a witch, the famous Marlena who disappeared on a boat bound for Africa never to be seen again?" Yianna pulled a dish towel from her apron, teasing Clotho as she slapped the towel at her.

"Yes. That's right." Clotho laughed at her friend. She then paused and looked deep into her coffee cup before taking one final sip.

"It's better that way, isn't it?" Clotho looked at Yianna and then turned her face out toward the sea. "To allow their imaginations to run wild. It's easier sometimes to let them believe the madness and the lies."

Yianna nodded in silent agreement. She leaned in and placed her hands on top of Clotho's. The women stayed like that a moment, the silence between them more meaningful than a million words combined. It was the silence of sisterhood, of keeping each other's secrets no matter the cost.

"Come on," Yianna said as she removed her hands from Clotho's. She lifted her cup and nodded for Clotho to do the same. "Read my cup like we used to, all those secret afternoons stolen away on your terrace when we were girls."

Clotho nodded.

They each turned their cups three times and placed them upside down on the saucer.

"There's something else in the article as well." Clotho flipped through the pages again, coming to the photo of King George walking into the cathedral. "It's only a small mention. But it says here that Prince Andrew's widow, Princess Alice, was also at the cathedral to greet the king and welcome him back to Greece."

Yianna placed both hands back on her cup to stop them from shaking. It did no good. The cup now trembled under her touch. Her mouth opened slightly. A small gasp escaped. She stood and walked to the edge of the patio. She stayed there for a moment, quietly collecting her thoughts. "So she's back in Greece, then. In Athens."

"Yes."

"Does it say how long she's been there? Or how long she'll stay? If she'll stay?"

"No. It only mentions that she was there."

"I see."

Yianna stood a moment longer, taking in the news of Alice's return to Greece. It was what she had dreamed of for so many years. What her mother had prayed for until her last breath. But it was not meant to be like this. How was it possible that Alice had returned to Greece, to Athens, and yet had not come back to learn what had become of Vasiliki? How had she not sought out the family she vowed to always help and protect? Had she forgotten about the promise she made to her friend in those frantic final moments at Mon Repos? The thoughts swirled in Yianna's mind like a whirlpool, spiraling deeper and deeper, swallowing her whole. *This isn't how it is supposed to be.*

Yianna walked back to her chair. She turned and forced a smile, although she was certain Clotho could see right through the facade. Clotho motioned for Yianna to sit down.

"Your boys are your jewels. This home, so filled with love, is your palace. Your family makes you a rich woman, Yianna, rich and blessed in so many ways. Don't ever lose sight of that. People wander the world in search of what you have right here. People live their entire lives praying for even a small taste of what you have in this home."

Perhaps those words were confirmation that Clotho had indeed been born with the gift of ethereal sight.

Yianna sat and reached for her cup, eager to change the subject. She turned it over. "Well, let's see what the cup says about it."

Just then, as Yianna lifted her cup to gaze inside to see what her future held, a deafening noise reverberated from the east. An explosion, the *boom* violent and loud and yet muffled, as if it had happened underwater. The sound of metal crushing and water bursting from the sea and screams erupting all around mingled in the air.

Yianna's cup dropped from her hand as she and Clotho ran to the end of the terrace to see what might have been the cause. The two women looked out, scanning the sea, following the billowing smoke that filled the air. There, to the east, in the narrow channel between Corfu and Albania, was a naval ship engulfed in smoke and flames. The entire front portion of the ship had been blown off, a twisted minefield of metal, smoke, and fire. From their perch on the cliff, amid the smoke and sea spray, Yianna could make out the British flag flapping frenetically in the wind. Just farther down the channel, to the south, was another warship, also bearing a British flag, racing toward the damaged ship. The air was thick with black smoke, obscuring the view of the bay of Sarandë in Albania.

Clotho and Yianna stood on the terrace, shielding their eyes from the sun, straining to see more of the accident even as the smoke blocked their view.

All around them, they could hear the shouts and screams of the villagers who also stopped to gaze at the disaster unfolding below. It seemed as if the entire village had come out to watch from their homes, many of them racing down to the port to try to learn more.

"Oh my God. Those poor men. They could not have survived that. Thank God Aleko stopped fishing in the channel years ago. He knew a fisherman whose boat was fired on from Albania after drifting too close to her waters. He said he would never take that risk. Thank you, Saint Spyridon, for watching over him." Yianna made the sign of the cross three times. Clotho did as well.

They watched and waited. Over an hour later the second ship reached the damaged boat. They watched the frenetic activity as the sailors tended to their wounded and dying and the crippled ship began to be towed away from the carnage.

And then it happened again. A second explosion, as devastating as the first, reverberated through the channel and across the sea up into the village. The air was once again thick with smoke and screams. Yianna and Clotho clutched one another and watched in horror as the smoke and mist cleared to reveal the second ship engulfed in flames and smoke.

"Come on, let's get to the port," Clotho insisted. "We have to go. Come."

The women held hands as they raced to the port, stepping over the coffee cup Yianna had dropped when the quiet of their afternoon visit was rocked by the first explosion. The cup had landed intact on its side, the image of Yianna's future and fortune still left unread. There, amid the grounds and mud and muck, was an image clear as day. A large bird, black, wings outstretched, hovering over a house. Had Yianna or Clotho taken the time to glance inside the cup, they would have known at once what it meant. Marlena had taught them well.

Twelve

Corfu

October 1946

"Are you sure?" Katerina looked around again, making certain no one could hear.

"Yes. Come on," Marco insisted, grabbing her arm and pulling her along. "You said you want to."

"Of course I want to. I'm just afraid, I guess."

"There's nothing to be afraid of. I promise." He walked faster now and she was having trouble keeping up.

"Marco, where are you taking me?"

"Well, we can't very well go to the beach now, can we? Let's go to the cove. No one ever goes there. It'll be our secret."

"Will it hurt?" she asked.

"Of course not, silly." He laughed as he dropped her arm. "Come on." He ran ahead, motioning for her to follow. She ran as fast as she could behind him, anxious and exhilarated all at the same time.

Only the very young or the very determined would dare make the trip down the slope to the secret spot located on the farthest side of the highest hill on the island. It was a small, rocky inlet lined with majestic cypress trees with just a narrow strip of sand that disappeared even before the high tide fully set in. Their time would be limited, but at least they would be hidden from prying eyes.

But still, Katerina and Marco knew they could take no chances. They walked up and down the shore looking in every hidden crevice and behind every rock, to be certain there would be no witnesses.

Convinced they were alone, Marco ran back to where she was waiting and began to peel off his shirt and pants until he was standing before her in only his undershorts.

"Oh, come on. Go ahead. Don't be shy. I won't look," he said, turning his head away.

She nodded, finding her courage, and unbuttoned her plain brown dress. She removed it and placed it carefully on a rock. She stood on the shoreline in the cream-colored slip she had inherited from Calliope just last month.

Gathering all of her courage, she walked toward him.

"Are you ready?" he asked.

"Yes. I'm ready," she confirmed, taking his hand.

Months ago Katerina had mentioned to Marco how angry it made her that even now, even as the girls of the village were allowed to sit beside the boys in the classrooms and learn to read and write, girls were still not allowed to bathe in the sea or learn how to swim. It never made any sense to her. Even a simple dip among friends was viewed as immodest and scandalous. Katerina was enraged each time she walked past the port to see the boys racing into the water, laughing and jumping from the pilings at the dock. Why were the boys allowed the freedom of cooling off in only their undershorts while the girls were forced to swelter with only a paper fan and the shade of the olive trees for relief?

Had anyone spotted them and reported back that the children had been seen bathing in their undergarments, it would have been the switch for them both for sure. Katerina's parents rarely, if ever, punished her in this way. But frequent beatings, with a switch or a belt or a shoe or a wooden spoon, whatever happened to be handy, were standard practice for all of the other children of the village. Katerina understood the calculated risk she was taking with each step she took deeper into the water. Her parents would not tolerate the gossip and shame that this little excursion would bring upon the family. And yet the drive to know what it felt like to be weightless in the water, to swim out in the cool sea, to live in the day what she had until now experienced only in her dreams . . . it was a risk she was willing to take.

Together they walked into the water, Katerina hesitating once the water reached her thighs. Marco encouraged her to go deeper still. "Just to your waist. That's all," he assured her.

"Okay. I'm going to hold you and you lie back. You're going to float on your back and I'm going to hold you up," he said. "You trust me, don't you?"

"Of course I do. I trust you more than anyone in the whole world," she said, picturing in her mind Baba's story of the rose and the soil. It seemed to her a silly question. He was her best friend, after all.

She nodded her head and summoned up all of her courage. And just as she was about to lean back into his waiting arms, they heard it.

The explosion was deafening, reverberating across the water and the cliffs. She shot straight back up and they looked at each other. "What was that?"

"I don't know," Marco replied. "I don't know." They looked out across the sea, but the view to the northeast, where it seemed the noise had come from, was obstructed by the cliffs.

"Come on. We have to go back," Marco insisted. He held Katerina's hand as they hurried back to the shoreline and dressed, not even bothering to dry themselves before scurrying back into their clothes.

They ran the entire way, all the way up the rocky terrain of the hill and back down the mountainside along the dirt paths and back to the village.

Katerina found her father in the crowd and ran into his arms while Marco spotted his mother standing with Clotho among the dozen or so villagers who were hovering over the radio.

"Just after three o'clock this afternoon, disaster struck the British destroyer HMS *Saumarez* as it was passing in the waters between Corfu and Albania off the bay of Sarandë. Early indications appear as if the ship hit a mine, receiving critical damage with reports of dozens of crewmen killed or missing. Just over an hour later, disaster came again when a second British ship, the destroyer HMS *Volage*, was also hit by a devastating explosion. Rescue and recovery efforts are under way. We will keep you posted on the latest of what may play out to be an international incident with deadly and devastating consequences."

They stayed like that for hours, lingering in town, watching the wounded warships from the shore as the smoke turned the sky above from blue to black, listening to the radio, hoping for more updates or information. Slowly, as the afternoon gave way to evening, the fishermen, who had begun their day casting nets but ended it by responding to the British calls for help, began one by one to bring their boats into port.

∞

As the hours passed, Yianna continued scanning the port for any sign of Aleko's boat. She walked around the square, asking the other fishermen if they had seen her husband and son.

"Yes, I saw them earlier today on the western coast, near Sidari," an elderly fisherman reported. "Don't worry. They were on the other side of the island, nowhere near the explosion."

But Yianna's fear began to grow as the light started to fade and still there was so sign of Stefano and Aleko.

"Dimitri." She ran toward another fisherman. "Dimitri, have you seen

Aleko and Stefano?" she asked, getting more and more frantic by the moment.

"I saw them hours ago. We passed each other just after the first explosion. Aleko told me they were going to get a closer look. Stefano wanted to see the damaged warship up close."

"Up close?"

"Yes. You mean they're not back yet?" Dimitri's face fell, as did her heart.

Yianna sank to her knees in the dirt.

Thirteen

Corfu

October 1946

They were everywhere.

There were dozens of them, hundreds, even. Bodies littering the beach as far as Laki could see. It had been a particularly high tide, the current stronger and more violent than normal. And this was not normal. Not at all.

He stepped carefully, creeping through the labyrinth of arms, legs, and torsos, surrounded by grossly misshapen bodies tossed onto the sand by the violent current, contorted into unnatural shapes. He worked methodically and efficiently. Emotionless. He had a job to do. Nothing more.

He made his way down the beach. Hands dipping in and out of pockets, tugging and turning bodies, one after the other. He no longer bothered to look at their faces. What was the point?

The body was facedown in the sand, its pockets wedged under him. Laki pulled the corpse toward him, onto its back, and reached his hand in to search the corpse's pocket.

As he did, the dead man's cold hand sprang up and grabbed Laki's forearm. "Give me back my ring. You must give me back my ring."

Laki's eyes opened to the darkness. He sat up in bed, running his fingers through his hair, trying to regulate his breathing, trying to convince himself that the dream meant nothing. Still sitting up in bed, using his right hand, he put his thumb, index finger, and middle finger together and made the sign of the cross three times.

They had stayed at the port for hours, waiting with Yianna, scanning the sea, hopeful Aleko and Stefano would make it back and to find it was all just a misunderstanding, a father-and-son adventure gone on too long. But as night set in, it became clear to everyone that Aleko and Stefano would not be coming home.

It shamed him to admit it even to himself, but he had thought about going to the cove, knowing there would be more bodies washed onshore with pound notes in their pockets and gold on their fingers. But Laki could not bear the thought. What if the tide brought Aleko and Stefano to the shore as well? *Let someone else find them*, he thought. He could not be the one.

He stood and walked over to where Katerina slept, curled up in the corner of her cot. Kneeling, he kissed her cheek and then climbed back in bed beside Maria.

Staring up at the ceiling, he put his hand in his pocket and held the dead soldier's ring between his fingers.

Part Two

Fourteen

Mon Repos, Corfu
October 1922

They knelt side by side in the church where they had come countless times to pray. Above them the ceiling dripped with dozens of silver lanterns dangling down as if raining silver teardrops from the heavens. The walls were all adorned with rich amber- and gold-painted icons depicting various saints, including the one they had come to pray beside. Musky incense and the haze of candles lit by the faithful perfumed the air. The scent was familiar and comforting to them.

They knelt in the tiny room beside the silver casket that held the mummified remains of Saint Spyridon, the miracle worker of Corfu. With bent, covered heads, the women each made the sign of the cross three times before placing their hands on the casket and kissing the glass, where beneath, the sunken gray face and red velvet–adorned corpse of the saint was visible.

It was there, on that unusually warm October morning in 1922, that Princess Alice of Greece and her maid, Vasiliki, prayed for a miracle.

It felt like months, but it was merely two days ago that Andrew had been summoned to Athens for a military tribunal holding him accountable for the disastrous outcome of the Greco-Turkish War just weeks before. It was a staggering defeat for Greece, with more than fifteen thousand Greeks taken as prisoners of war and a hundred thousand more killed when the ancient city of Smyrna was set aflame, reduced to ash.

Alice was well aware of what was at stake. She had learned the fate of other officers found guilty: sentenced to the firing squad along with their entire families for their part in the catastrophic defeat.

On that morning, two days after Andrew was summoned to Athens, Alice and Vasiliki knelt in prayer beside Saint Spyridon and then returned to Mon Repos to await news of their fate.

Alice paced the floors for hours. From room to room she wandered, up and down the curved staircase, back and forth under the octagon ceiling dome that flooded the second floor with sunlight. She stopped pacing only to gaze out the massive floor-to-ceiling windows at the azure Ionian beyond.

"Can I get you anything, ma'am?" Vasiliki asked, always making sure to stand directly in front of the princess, allowing Alice to easily read Vasiliki's lips. Alice's deafness had been a carefully guarded secret among the royal household. As a child, the princess had learned to compensate by reading lips so well that only a few within the family's inner circle knew of her impairment.

As the hours passed and the tension mounted, Vasiliki thought it best to get the young children out of the house, to leave Alice to her thoughts as the older girls finished their lessons for the day. Philip and Yianna were quite a sight as they walked down the staircase, holding the banister to steady themselves and then running through the grand entrance hall and out the door, past the imposing columns of the palace's entrance. The children walked along the wide gravel path through the thick of the forest, beyond the expansive gardens and olive grove, and down the ancient stone steps leading to the sea as Vasiliki followed closely behind.

When they reached the sandy beach known as the swimming spot of kings, the children ran and chased each other along the shoreline. Their giggles and squeals filled the air as the gentle current lapped at their feet. Together they skipped and threw stones into the water as Vasiliki sat on the sand watching them, envious of their innocence.

Vasiliki then took their hands and led the children out along the narrow pier extending thirty meters from the shoreline out into the sea. Philip, forever mischievous and adventurous, tried breaking free from Vasiliki's grip to run the length of the pier himself. Holding tight, she knelt down before him and whispered, "No," before placing a kiss on the tip of his nose. Philip giggled, rubbing his nose, his blond hair lifting in the breeze as his blue eyes sparkled in the brilliant sunshine. Yianna then leaned in and did the same, planting a kiss on her playmate's nose before taking his hand in hers again.

Vasiliki looked to the sky and noticed the sun had tucked behind the craggy brush-covered hills that jutted out into the sea to the south. It was time to head home. But before going back, there was one last thing Vasiliki knew she needed to do. Just beyond the pier, seemingly carved into the hillside as the cypresses, olive trees, and brush hovered protectively above, was the freshwater spring known as Kardaki.

"Here. Come wash your hands," she instructed the children as the cool water splashed on them, rinsing away the dirt and the sand. Cupping her hands, Vasiliki pooled the water in her palms before offering each of the children a sip. When Philip and Yianna had their fill, together they walked back up the stone steps, through the dense of the forest and gardens and olive tree grove toward home.

Vasiliki made the sign of the cross as they passed the old chapel. Regardless of the outcome of the tribunal and what awaited her back at the house, she knew she had done all in her power to keep young Philip safe. She believed in the power of prayer. She believed that as protector and patron saint of Corfu, Saint Spyridon would watch over Philip as he did each child who was born to the lush green island. And Vasiliki knew that when the children sipped from the cool waters of Kardaki, the water had refreshed Yianna and Philip but also bonded them forever to this place and to each other. Vasiliki knew the legend of the fountain that dated back generations, to the time when the Venetians ruled Corfu. She remembered the stories her mother would share with her in the evening as the dusk settled across the island, before her mother and her stories were lost to the madness that consumed her whole. Vasiliki remembered nestling in her mother's lap as the supper fire's orange embers cooled to gray while the cricket and cicada songs filled the air and her mother spoke of the legends and myths and mysteries that made Corfu as magical as it is beautiful.

Vasiliki recalled each of those stories vividly, especially the legend of Kardaki. The spring was guarded by the figure of a lion carved in the 1500s whose raised paw protected the spout, and it was said that that anyone who drank from Kardaki was destined to return home to Corfu one day, forever bound to the lush sickle-shaped island in the Ionian Sea.

As they walked home, Vasiliki picked a cluster of wildflowers and roses from the plants that lined the pathway leading from the beach to the palace. She stopped a moment when she reached the top of the hill and looked down once more at the swimming spot of kings. Delicate yellow wildflowers dotted the landscape and swayed in the breeze as if they might leap from the cliff and into the sea. She watched as Philip chased Yianna through the field, darting between the blossoms, and wondered if this sweet child might one day grow up to be a king himself. *Imagine that*, she thought, fully understanding that Philip was quite far down the line of succession now that Andrew's brother, King Constantine, abdicated and his son, King George II, now sat on the throne.

She was lost in her thoughts as they approached the circular drive of the house and stopped a moment on the stone patio that overlooked the sea behind Mon Repos. There in the distance she spotted a few small fishing boats, blue-hulled and bobbing on the water. She scanned the sea as far as she could, across to the mainland and up toward the north, but there was no sign of Andrew's ship. She sighed deeply, taking the children's hands in hers once again.

"Come," she said, taking turns lifting their tiny hands to her mouth and kissing their fingers. "Let's go inside." She lingered a moment longer, gazing up at the majesty of Mon Repos, the curved portico, grand terraces, and intricate iron railings at once so strong and delicately elaborate. Inside, Vasiliki was met with a frenzy of activity. She knew the outcome even before she laid eyes on Alice.

It was done. Princess Alice had received word that Andrew had been arrested, and rumors swirled that a Greek military guard was en route to Mon Repos with orders to execute the family. At once, a British ship had been summoned to Corfu to evacuate Alice and the children from Greek soil and deliver them to safety.

Away from Greece. Away from Corfu. Away from Mon Repos. Away from Vasiliki and Yianna.

In those frantic, final hours, Alice hastily packed up her belongings while her girls ran up and down the stairs, gathering and tossing the family's documents and correspondence into the blazing fire of the sitting room. Vasiliki prepared the young prince's belongings and fashioned a bed from an orange crate for Philip to sleep in on the journey. She raided the linen closet, lining the crate with blankets and towels so the young prince would have a comfortable place to rest his head.

"Here, ma'am," she said to Princess Alice with tears in her eyes as she slipped an icon of Saint Spyridon under the makeshift bed. Philip smiled up at her, sucking his thumb and twirling his blond ringlets around and around with his finger. Vasiliki, who loved Philip as her own, leaned in and kissed him.

She then turned to Princess Alice. "Your child is Corfiot," she said. "Never forget that. Saint Spyridon will always protect him."

The two women embraced. As she pulled away, Princess Alice stared deep into her eyes. Vasiliki had entered Mon Repos as a servant but would leave a trusted friend to a princess.

And then Princess Alice spoke. "I will never forget your kindness and how you loved my family, Vasiliki. I will return to Greece one day. This is my home. You have helped make it my home. And your family will always find a home with mine."

Vasiliki cried as she watched Princess Alice and the children drive away. Their car sped down the long bougainvillea-lined drive, along Garitsa bay, at last arriving at the port. They then boarded the British ship *Calypso* and sailed away from Vasiliki and Yianna and their beloved green island and into the night.

That evening, sleep escaped both Alice and Vasiliki. Each spent hours down on their knees, praying in the darkness, mourning what they shared and what was lost. At the brink of dawn, each of the women stared out across the horizon as the day's first light broke through the black.

As the sun began to rise, Vasiliki replayed the words in her mind.

"I will return to Greece one day. This is my home. You have helped make it my home. And your family will always find a home with mine."

It was those very words, spoken from a royal princess to her young Corfiot maid, that would haunt both women for the rest of their lives.

Fifteen

Tinos
August 1930

It's amazing sometimes the things that blister in our memory. The moments, fleeting, seemingly insignificant at the time, that sear into the fabric of our being, shaping us from who we once were to who we can't help but be.

Sometimes it's not until years later, as the gray sets in and you see yourself in your children or maybe your children's children, that you look back on your life, reevaluating, recalling a childhood memory, and realizing how you were forever changed in that moment.

But for some, the gift of hindsight is an unnecessary one. Because there are those who even as children feel the shift the moment it happens, aware as they are robbed of who they might have been.

It was like that for Maria, the year she turned twelve and everything that was once so beautiful and bright faded to dust before her eyes.

August 15. She knew what day it was even before she opened her eyes. Panagia's Day. She didn't know what was more exciting to her, the thought of putting on the new dress Mama had sewn for her or the idea of finally eating meat after her two-week fast. Mama said that some of the other parents did not make their children fast from meat and dairy for the entire forty days leading to Panagia's celebration, but Maria didn't mind. She wanted to be faithful and abstain, just like her mother. While she sometimes craved the taste of meat, she quite liked planning meals with Mama, coming up with creative ways to make fish and vegetables as delicious as a souvlaki from the taverna.

But that wasn't the only reason she fasted. Maria secretly hoped that fasting might set her apart from the other children. She hoped that Panagia might make special note of her devotion, sacrifice, and prayers. After all, thousands and thousands of people came to Tinos to celebrate Panagia's feast day each year. Those were lots of prayers for the Virgin Mother to sort through. Maria knew she needed all the help she could get to stand out from the others and make sure that her prayers were heard.

It was oppressively hot that morning, and Maria had woken to find the mattress drenched in her sweat. She opened her eyes to see her mother standing over her, smiling and waving a plastic fan back and forth above her in an effort to cool her as she slept. The windows and door were thrown open in hopeful anticipation, but there would be no relief that day. Even the sea breeze could not summon the energy to permeate the heavy August air.

"Good morning, my love." Her mother smiled down at her serenely even as she continued waving the fan furiously.

They dressed quickly, Maria in the new blue dress with white buttons shaped like little flowers that Mama had repurposed from an old dress of hers. Mama wore her simple brown skirt that fell to her ankles and a white blouse tucked in neatly under her waistband. Her hair was plaited in a long braid that she wrapped around her head, secured at the nape with pins, and covered in a white kerchief. They raced out the door in record time, not stopping for breakfast as they continued their fast in preparation to receive Holy Communion.

"Are you all right, Mama?" Maria asked as Mama stopped to catch her breath on the sea wall as they approached the church. They were thankful for the slight hint of breeze along the waterfront.

"Of course. I'm fine," she insisted, coughing into her handkerchief. "It's just the heat."

Inside the church they stood with the faithful, bowing their heads and crossing themselves as the musky incense and ancient chants wafted through the cavernous room. Despite the discomfort of the heat, the haze and ancient chants were soothing.

Maria stepped up to the altar when it was her turn to receive Communion. She tilted her face toward the priest, lifting her chin and opening her mouth as he dipped the golden spoon into the silver chalice, placing the wine and bread, the blood and body of Christ, into her mouth. She closed her eyes as the priest recited the familiar words: "The servant of God, Maria, receives the body and blood of Christ for the forgiveness of sins and eternal life."

As they walked home after services that afternoon, they happened upon Mama's old friend Stella. Because Stella had no husband or children of her own, Mama always made an effort to welcome her into their home and didn't hesitate that day in inviting her back for their holiday meal. Baba had slaughtered a baby lamb for the occasion that Mama had slathered in olive oil, salt, and fresh oregano and rosemary before impaling the lamb on the spit, where it had been roasting slowly for hours, since even before the sun came up.

Everyone spent a joyous afternoon and evening feasting on roasted lamb and sipping sweet homemade wine. Baba, having had more than his share of both, danced a joyous *zeibekiko*, spinning round and round, slapping at his foot and leaping into the air as Mama smiled brightly, tossing rose petals at him and clapping from the sidelines.

It was to be the last joyous memory Maria had of her childhood.

The embers beneath the lamb carcass mimicked the sky, first blazing red and gold and then slowly fading to cool gray. And like the embers, the oppressive heat of the day gradually dulled and gave way to the cool night air. But even so, Mama's cough lingered.

The cough persisted, and after several weeks, as summer gave way to fall, Mama could no longer blame her condition on the weather. At Stella's insistence, she visited the doctor, who confirmed her worst fears. The bloody cough that had begun as a nuisance was more than just an infection. Mama had merely months to live and would be gone before winter's end.

Maria cried as Mama held her close and shared with her the news. They sat together on the patio, watching the sun disappear beyond the hills of Siros in the distance. Maria clung to her mother as the tears streamed down her face. "But who will protect me when you're gone? Who will watch over me and make sure I'm safe when I'm sleeping?"

"Goddess Nyx will always watch over you, my sweet," she said. "Even when I am not here, you will always have the magic of a mother's love hovering above you. I want you to think of me each time you watch the sunset and each time you wake to see the sunrise. Let that always be a reminder of the lengths and depths that I will go for you, to the ends of the earth and back again. Nyx and I will always be watching over you. I'll be right there beside Nyx, joining her in her golden chariot, whispering to her son, Hypnos, to bring you pleasant dreams and beckoning Hemera to forever shine her light on you."

They stayed like that, holding each other in the dark, until Maria was nearly asleep. Mama then led Maria to her bed, where she tucked her in and knelt beside her, fanning her until she drifted off to dreamland.

In the months that followed, Maria savored and cherished each moment spent with her mother. And there, beside them every day, was Mama's friend Stella. Each morning and each night, as Mama led Maria in prayer, they added Stella's name to the list of the people they asked Panagia to protect and provide for. Because truly, Mama insisted, the blessed Virgin Mother herself must have sent Stella to their side. She praised God and thanked Panagia again and again, convinced Stella must have been the miracle she had prayed for.

When Mama became too frail to get out of bed, Stella would stay all day and late into the evening, and sometimes all night, bathing Mama and feeding her broth when she was too weak to lift the spoon herself. And when Mama was nearing the end, when she was too weak to lift even her head, Stella gently helped Mama from her marital bed, whispering soothing words of comfort, and placed her in the bed with Maria so she could sleep beside her daughter.

That very night, in the home where she had learned of the power and beauty of a mother's love, Maria learned the devastation and pain of a friend's betrayal. Maria held Mama as she cried, the bed soaked through with their tears, listening to Baba's grunts and the moans emanating from the marital bed as they watched Stella's silhouette rise and fall above him in the darkness.

In that moment, as she wiped the tears from her dying mother's cheek, Maria made a promise. She swore that if Panagia were ever to bless her with children one day, she would do her best to love them as fiercely and completely as her own mother had loved her. And she made another promise as well: she vowed that she would never make the same fatal mistake as her mother. Maria would never put her faith and trust in another woman. If and when the day came that she needed to share her secrets or speak her innermost thoughts and feelings out loud, she would do so only on her knees at daybreak, when no one but Mother Nyx was awake to hear them.

Sixteen

Corfu
1930

Yianna had been so excited when her father gave her a few drachmas and told her she could walk to the *periptero* herself to buy a sweet treat. The periptero, a tiny newsstand kiosk, was the very fabric of Greek life and dotted just about every town square all across Greece, from the grand avenues of Athens to the tiny cobblestone squares of provincial villages. The periptero near Yianna's house was owned by a kindly old woman named Nitsa who had grown up alongside Yianna's grandmother. Nitsa was one of the few in the village to warmly welcome Yianna and her mother back from Mon Repos while the other villagers called them names like "Princess Dirt Floor" and whispered, "Thinks she's too good for us now," whenever they crossed paths. The old woman always made a fuss over Yianna, fawning over her and telling her how beautiful she was, just like her grandmother when she was young. Yianna loved hearing stories of her grandmother in happier times, as a young girl and young wife and mother, before the madness that fractured her family.

"She was the kindest soul you could ever meet. I loved her like a sister," Nitsa would say. "And she loved your grandfather from the moment she laid eyes on him. She adored him with all her heart, just as she loved your mother with every fiber of her being. Don't listen to those who tell you your grandmother was mad and that she tossed your mother out on the street. It's not true. It can't be true. Your grandfather broke her heart. How could she be the same after that?" The old woman would say this again and again before handing Yianna her change and always an extra sweet treat. "And don't let anyone tell you she didn't love your mama. I don't believe it. She had her reasons. Don't listen to those gossips, sweet girl. Only your grandmother and God know the truth." The old woman would set Yianna off with a toothless smile and a kumquat wrapped in a tissue.

Yianna walked toward home again, replaying the old woman's words in her mind. Her own mother never discussed it, but Yianna knew the stories of how Princess Alice saved her mother by offering her a job when she was destitute, going door-to-door looking for work when she was just thirteen years old. Her grandmother's descent to madness was the stuff of old village legend, the source of much gossip and speculation both then and now. Their family's tragedy was a favorite topic for village busybodies who would rather dissect and discuss the failings and affairs of their neighbors beside the evening fire than examine the state of their own homes in the light of day.

By all accounts, Yianna's grandmother, Nikoletta, had been a kind and loving woman who doted on her only daughter, Vasiliki. But then everything changed when her husband left for America and never came back. The once devoted and loving wife and mother became increasingly desperate and erratic as whispers of her husband's abandonment, and his new, light-haired American family, grew louder. Some said Nikoletta threw Vasiliki out because she could no longer afford to feed her; others said her heart was so badly broken by her husband's betrayal that she simply lost the ability to love.

As much as Vasiliki loved to sit and tell her daughter stories of years gone by, of life in the palace of Mon Repos, she had never once spoken about what happened with her own mother and how she had so painfully and publicly been betrayed.

Yianna made up her mind as she walked home. *I'll do it*, she thought as she sucked on the kumquat, savoring the sweet and sticky treat. *I'm going to ask her what happened. I'm older now. She has to tell me.* She then bit into the orange flesh of the fruit, savoring the sugary brine mixed with the tart citrus. She walked with purpose as she headed home. At last she would have answers. She took one last nibble of the kumquat, saving the rest for later.

"Demon's daughter! Demon's daughter! Demon's daughter!" The chorus grew louder with each step as Yianna approached the square between the schoolyard and the church.

She licked the last of the sugar from her fingers as she rounded the corner, went past the church, and headed toward the cemetery. The voices grew louder still. She was not surprised at all once she spotted the girls and then confirmed the target of their taunts.

"Look at the demon's daughter. Why are you walking? Why don't you just fly away like your mother?" the girls yelled.

Yianna stayed behind, not wanting to draw attention to herself as she, too, was often the subject of their teasing and taunts. But then one of the girls picked up a rock and Yianna could stay silent no more.

"Leave her alone!" she yelled as she ran to Clotho's side, attempting to shield her. The two girls had always been friendly, but Clotho, like Yianna, tended to keep to herself. This was the first time their relationship went beyond superficial banter. It would not be the last. "Leave her alone!" Yianna screamed again.

But the girls would not. The rocks and names kept coming. "Witch. Sorceress. Demon's daughter." They blamed Clotho for the drought that threatened their parents' crops and screamed at her to go back to Africa to join her mother.

"Demon's daughter. Devil child. So ugly and evil that even your witch mother abandoned you."

While she was not the intended target, it was as if Yianna could feel Clotho's pain. The words hit their mark with exact precision, wounding perhaps even deeper than the stones. Yianna stood her ground, flailing her arms in an attempt to make them stop. She watched as Clotho cowered, kneeling in the dirt and covering her head to protect herself against the barrage. And then Yianna watched as it seemed something overtook Clotho before her very eyes.

Clotho took a deep breath and whispered a few words, inaudible even to Yianna. The girls all stopped their insults for a moment, quieting down in an attempt to hear what Clotho had to say. She stood tall and raised up her arms, fists pointed toward the sky. Again she whispered something that sounded to Yianna like gibberish, a mishmash of sounds that made no sense at all. Clotho then began to slowly lower her arms until they were pointed at the girls. She opened her fists and stretched her fingertips out, pointing toward the girls as she began to laugh uncontrollably, her head rolling back, her entire body convulsing and shaking. It was a wild laughter, unbridled and unnerving.

Terrified, the girls looked at one another and then to Yianna. Yianna stood silently beside Clotho as she continued to laugh. Scared now, the girls dropped their stones and ran away, yelling, "She cast a spell on us! Oh my God. The witch's daughter cast a spell on us!" She heard the girls crying as they ran home, each frantically making the sign of the cross as if to protect themselves from the supernatural damage already done.

When the girls were out of sight, Yianna turned to look at Clotho. Clotho turned toward Yianna, eyes wide open and unblinking. And then she winked as her lips unfurled into a broad smile.

Yianna exhaled long and deep. "Are you hurt?"

"No. I'm fine," Clotho insisted as she brushed the dirt and dust from her blouse and skirt. "I'll just be going home now." She wrung her apron in her hand. "Thank you for helping me."

Yianna grabbed her other hand and held tight. "Let me walk you. I think I would really like to have a friend."

"Yes. I would too," Clotho replied, still holding Yianna's hand. "I would like that very much."

"Good. It's decided then." Yianna smiled and dug her hand into her pocket and pulled out a crumpled tissue. "Here. Have the rest. I was just going to throw it away anyway," she said as she offered Clotho the rest of the kumquat.

That day, the day Yianna wiped the blood from Clotho's face with the hem of her dress and helped her hobble up the hill toward home, Yianna learned the secret that would bond the newly formed friendship into a forever friendship.

Yianna knew the story of Marlena, just like the rest of the villagers. There were some who said that after being revealed as a witch, Marlena walked away from the church and threw herself off the mountain and into the sea. Others insisted Marlena had returned to Africa, where she practiced her evil sorcery, abandoning her child and husband. While there were differing opinions on what happened to Marlena, everyone on the island was in complete agreement on one thing. After her true identity was revealed, Marlena was never seen or heard from again. The sorceress had simply disappeared.

Together, the girls hobbled up the steep hill, at last reaching the bamboo frond gate leading to Clotho's house. Clotho hesitated before entering and turned to Yianna.

"You are my friend, aren't you?"

"Of course I am." Yianna laughed, thinking what a silly question that was.

"Truly my friend?" Clotho asked again.

"Of course," Yianna replied, enveloping Clotho in a hug.

"Okay, I trust you." Clotho pushed open the gate.

The girls stepped through the door, revealing a patio unlike anything

Yianna had ever seen. It was overflowing with plants and flowers and veg-etables and fruit trees.

Surely this was what the garden of Eden must have been like. They walked down the stairs amid the plants and flowers and trees. There were bountiful rosebushes in every color with blossoms as large as a grown man's hand. Wisteria draped across the entire length of the patio, making it appear as if the sky itself was crafted from lavender blossoms. All around them bees buzzed and hummed, but never once did Yianna feel afraid; their soft serenade was more like a comforting lullaby than a menace. Lemons, which looked more like grapefruits, dripped from tall elegant trees and tomatoes red as blood and large as dinner plates covered the vines that climbed and twisted across the patio.

And there, at the far end of this enchanted garden, a woman stood tall, whispering to a sunburst-orange hibiscus as one might whisper to a lover. Yianna gasped when her eyes came to rest on her.

The woman turned, a wide hat pulled low on her forehead, casting a shadow across her cheeks. Her face erupted in a broad smile when she spotted Clotho. She reached out her arm, waving her fingertips, beckoning her to come closer. And then she spotted Yianna and stopped. She lifted both hands to adjust her hat, pulling it back to get a closer look. Her eyes narrowed as she stared at Yianna, silent and motionless. Yianna could not be sure, but in that very moment she thought she saw a cloud pass over the beautiful woman's face. It was not anger. Yianna ruled that out at once. No, to Yianna it appeared that the woman's face was shrouded in sadness, a deep, soul-piercing sadness. It was the same black look she had seen in her own mother's eyes.

Clotho said nothing. She simply reached behind her, grabbed Yianna's hand, and pulled her forward. Yianna felt frozen, yet somehow her feet found their way. She stood there, beside Clotho, silent and confused and slightly scared. And then Clotho spoke. "This is my friend, Yianna."

When she heard these words, the woman's face erupted in a wide, bright smile. Her fingers fluttered to her face, and she dabbed at the wetness in her eyes with her long, tapered fingers.

She walked toward the girls, knelt before them, and spoke. "Hello, Yianna, friend of Clotho's. It is so very nice to meet you." She leaned in and kissed Yianna on each cheek.

"Welcome to our home. I'm Clotho's mother, Marlena."

Seventeen

Corfu
1935

It had been five years since the day Yianna first helped Clotho hobble up the hill to home. Five years since she had first laid eyes on Marlena tending her garden. It was the first of countless afternoons the three would spend together. It was always just the three of them, always when Clotho's father was away from home. He never knew of the friendships and bonds that were formed and the secrets shared on that patio. No one ever did.

At first Marlena and the girls met only monthly, when Clotho's father left to sell his honey in the markets of Corfu and the neighboring islands of Paxos and Antipaxos. But then his trips became more frequent, allowing the girls to enjoy weekly visits under the shade of the arbor. And after a while, when Clotho and Yianna were approaching their fifteenth birthday, Marlena invited Yianna to visit as often and as long as she would like, after Clotho's father left one morning and never returned.

The afternoons were filled with treats like honeyed walnuts, candied kumquats, and baskets of plump figs and blackberries. But the sweetest treats by far were always Marlena's marvelous stories and lessons. As the years went on, she taught the girls how to speak to the flowers and plants to coax them to grow and thrive, even when the skies refused to open up and others across the village complained nothing would grow through the drought.

As they grew from children to adolescents, Marlena taught them the art of coffee cup reading, demonstrating and explaining how to sip and twirl one's cup to coax the grounds into revealing their stories and omens. It was in the coffee grounds that they at last learned the truth behind Clotho's father's disappearance. The image appeared in Clotho's cup, etched into the black mud clear as day. It was the image of a man, standing between two homes, facing one with his arms outstretched, his back turned toward the other.

"What does it mean?" Clotho asked.

"Your father has a new family. He won't be coming here again," Marlena explained, the relief lifting from her like early morning mist once the sun appears.

As the girls grew into young women, Marlena began to help them decipher their dreams. Night after night, Yianna dreamed of a woman alone and crying, who could not find her way home. Marlena explained that this woman was symbolic of Yianna herself, that she felt lost between her past and her future and was afraid of never quite finding her place.

And then one day, when the girls were nearly seventeen years old, Marlena shared with them one final gift. She had read the omen in her own cup and knew that her time on this earth was limited. She had a gift, she said, a final gift that she placed in Clotho's hands so the girls could continue the conversation even long after she was gone.

It was a book of dreams.

The pages of the dream book were filled with drawings—ethereal, evocative images showing people doing things they can only do when the mind is alive but the body is resting. On one side of the page there were drawings of people flying between the clouds with the gulls, swimming in the depths of the sea alongside dolphins, walking on water just as Jesus had, and speaking with loved ones who had long passed on. Then on the other side were drawings of what those dreams represented, of money found and money lost, of a new child's arrival and the damage of a heart broken. It was a work of art, meticulously and painstakingly crafted, a gift from a mother to her daughter and the one cherished friend shared between them.

That same day Marlena finally spoke the words she had been thinking about for so long. "It's time you learned what happened. The truth," she said as she closed her eyes and inhaled deeply as if at once summoning her memories and her courage. Exhaling slowly, she opened her eyes and waved her hands in the air toward the girls, summoning them to sit beside her.

Once they were seated, she took each of their hands in hers. Leaning in toward Clotho, she began to speak. Her voice was soft yet steady. "On the day that my life and your life, Clotho, were changed forever, yes, I was indeed guilty of something." She looked from the girls out across the horizon, breathing deeply, inhaling the scent of her garden, which seemed to infuse her with the courage to continue. She sat taller in her seat, shoulders back, and continued with her story.

"Yes. I was guilty. But not of what they accused me of. Not of being a sorceress. There were many times throughout the years when I wished it were true. It would have made things easier." She laughed. It was a quiet, layered laugh.

"Niko whispered promises to me in the dark. And I believed him. He knew my marriage to Clotho's father was an unhappy one. He made me believe that he was different, that he loved me and would save me." She glanced at Clotho under the frame of her eyelashes. "That he would save us both. He said we would sail away together with you, Clotho, and begin a new life in Italy. We would be a family. It was to be a fresh start filled with love and happiness and no more pain. And I believed him." She closed her eyes again and once more inhaled the scent of her roses, gardenias, and rosemary.

"We were supposed to sail away that night, Sunday night. I walked into church that morning so filled with hope, and thanked God again and again for granting me the miracle of a fresh start. But it was all a lie. Niko's wife found my hair comb in his boat. He made up the story about his boat and my being a witch in order to save himself. He saved himself, and he ruined me in the process. I confessed everything to Clotho's father after he beat me again that afternoon. The first punch broke my nose. The second split my lip, spilling blood down my blouse and into the earth as I staggered out into the garden looking for a corner to hide in. I don't remember the third. I only remember waking up here, in the garden beneath the rosebushes, covered in cuts and blood from where the thorns tore at my skin. I remember staggering out of the gate and to the edge of the mountain. Standing there, staring out across the horizon as I considered throwing myself in the sea." She turned to face the girls. Her eyes narrowed as her brow furrowed into a knot. She smiled then, the knot unfurling as the edges of her lips lifted upward, revealing a bright yet tentative smile.

"There were times through the years I thought perhaps it would have been better that way, to have thrown myself into the sea as so many believed I had." Her smile widened as she reached her arm out, placing her fingers beneath Clotho's chin, lifting her face as she gazed at her. "But I couldn't leave my daughter. I couldn't leave my child. I got down on my knees and prayed that night. I knelt there as the sun set beyond the horizon, across the sea where I thought I would be sailing away from my hell. I stayed there and prayed until the sun came up again the next day. And somehow, in those desperate hours of the night, I found the strength to stay, to be a mother to my child. I made a decision to remain here, hidden away in this house with a man who hurt me, a man who never loved me, so I could watch over Clotho and make sure that she was loved and protected and that no one would ever hurt her. The one thing I asked of him was that he never touch our child. And he never did. He honored my wish. Your father never touched you in anger. And for that, I am grateful." She smiled at Clotho, tracing her finger along Clotho's long black hair.

"So I have been here, in this house, since that day, confined to a life in the shadows, watching over my girl and infusing as much color and light and life into our little world here on our patio as I can. I don't have the power to erase the black. I don't have the powers and the dark magic that the villagers whisper is mine. But I am powerful nonetheless. I have learned this over time, through the years. I am powerful," she said as she sat taller now, as if the words infused her with the very strength of their claim. "I can add light and love and color. I can pierce the darkness with these things. This is my power, and it is infinite." Marlena reached out her arms and squeezed the girls' hands. "I am powerful because I can love."

"But what about the flower?" It was Yianna who asked. "They said it was from Africa. How could that be?"

Marlena walked to the other side of the patio and plucked a beautiful flower so deep purple in color that it was almost black, so fragrant that Yianna thought her own mother on the other side of the mountain might be able to smell its sweet scent. Marlena tucked the flower behind Yianna's ear.

"This flower has been watered by the tears of my family, by my grandmother and my mother and now by me. For years now, the women of my family have put all of our worries and love into our gardens, and this beautiful flower, created from generations of clippings and crossbreeding and pollination, and our joy and our pain, is the result. It does not grow in Africa, dearest Yianna. It only grows here, in my garden. That's why no one had seen it before. That's why they believed him."

Marlena passed away just weeks after she shared her story with the girls. It happened exactly as the omen in her cup revealed it would. She slipped away from this world peacefully and quietly on a beautiful summer afternoon as she was tending her garden. And it was there that Clotho buried her mother, beneath her beloved roses and gardenias and the magical purple flower that had cemented Marlena's fate.

Eighteen

Germany
April 1937

Alice sat on a low stool near the fire. It was April, and despite the brilliant sunshine and cloudless sky above, there was still a damp chill in the air that she felt straight through to the marrow of her bones. She wiped her hands on a dish towel and buttoned up her cardigan before inching closer to the fire and going back to her task. She had been at it for two hours now and there was still more work to be done.

She reached over to the bushel of potatoes beside her on the floor and picked up another. With meticulous care, she first used the point of her knife to dig and cut out any eyes before skimming the surface of the potato with her blade. She lifted the potato to the light, a pure white specimen with no trace of the russet's peel. Perfect. Alice took great pride in her work.

"What time is it, Julia?" Alice asked.

"It's nearly nine. Shouldn't you be going? I can manage from here," Julia said as she walked over to Alice, placing about a half dozen of the newly peeled potatoes in her apron. She walked back over to the stove, where she dropped the potatoes in a large pot of boiling water. This was the first step in making *Kartoffelkloesse*, the potato dumplings that Julia, and the boardinghouse, was famous for.

Alice had been living in the house for a little less than a year now. She mostly kept to herself in the small room she rented, except for the time she spent with Julia, the young kitchen maid and Alice's newest, and only, friend.

When Alice first arrived, the owner of the house had warned the staff and tenants that their boarder asked to kindly be left alone. She cast a mysterious figure, dressed rather simply in conservative skirts and sweaters and always in muted tones. Yet the rich silks of her blouses, finely knit cashmeres, and thick wools of her wardrobe belied the rumors that she was a schoolteacher who was retired of her position for publicly speaking out against Hitler. Alice was well aware of the whispers and innuendos, finding the aura of mystery about her preferable to invasive questions about her life and past.

When she first arrived, Alice had stayed in her room, choosing not to join the other guests at the communal dining table, opting instead to have her meals delivered three times a day to her door. And then one morning she opened the door as Julia was delivering her breakfast. Typically, Julia was relegated to making the meals and not serving them. But with the boardinghouse at full capacity, all of the staff found themselves taking care of things that were not typically in their job description.

"Good morning," Alice said, still clad in her robe. Her bare feet peeked out from beneath the silk hem. She exhaled a long, thin stream of cigarette smoke that wafted into the drafty hallway.

"Good morning, ma'am," Julia said. The china rattled with her nerves. She clutched the tray tighter and cast her eyes downward. "Would you like me to bring your tray inside?" she asked, biting on her lower lip. Julia did her best to fix her gaze on the tray. A delicate rose teacup filled with strong black coffee, a plate of black bread with home-churned butter and blackberry marmalade, and a soft-boiled egg perched in a white porcelain egg had all been carefully placed atop a delicate lace doily.

"I can take it, thank you," Alice said, taking the tray from Julia's hands.

"Very well, ma'am," the kitchen maid responded before turning on her heel to leave.

"Just a moment, please," Alice said. "The doily, it's lovely. Did you make it yourself?"

"No, ma'am," Julia responded, still not meeting Alice's gaze. "I wouldn't know how. I never learned."

"It has brightened my morning," Alice said as she placed the tray on the desk by the window overlooking the gardens. She lifted the coffee to her lips and took a sip of the hot, bitter liquid. She then turned to face Julia, who was still standing in the doorway.

"I'd be happy to teach you, if you like?"

Julia slowly looked up. "Teach me, ma'am?"

"Yes. To crochet," Alice said as she smeared a thick layer of butter on the bread and took a hearty bite. "I studied at the Royal Hellenic School of Needlework and Laces in Athens. They're known worldwide for embroidery, but I always preferred to crochet. I can teach you all sorts of patterns and techniques. That is, if I can remember them all." She laughed, a deep, robust laugh that startled them both.

Julia stuttered slightly, "Th-thank you. That . . . that would be nice." She nodded and began to take her leave. But Alice was not done with her just yet.

"Wait," she said as she layered the jam on top of the bread and butter, shaking her head from side to side in delight as she tasted the creamy sweetness of her simple breakfast. "Do you play canasta?"

From that moment on, while still remaining aloof with the other guests and staff, Alice invited Julia into her room each afternoon. It always began the same way, with a lesson in crocheting, Alice patiently guiding Julia's fingers, showing her how to maneuver her needle to dip in and out of the yarn to form perfect stitches and eventually circles and rosettes. When the yarn and needle were put away, the cards came out for a round or two, or five, of canasta, depending on Alice's mood that day and also who was winning.

What began as friendly lessons and card games, a way to pass the hours as they were tucked away in Alice's tidy back bedroom, over weeks and months evolved into long conversations about art and history and life. Julia shared with Alice how her journalist father had been thrown in prison for printing unflattering articles about Hitler. With her mother home, caring for her younger sister who was born with a muscular disability and confined to a wheelchair, it fell to Julia to find work to support them.

"And how did you come to stay here, with us?" Julia asked one afternoon after Alice won three straight rounds of cards. She had learned early on about Alice's hearing impairment and made sure to always lift her head, looking at Alice as she spoke, making it easier for Alice to read her lips.

Alice shuffled the deck and dealt the cards one by one as she shared her story.

"I lived in a palace on the island of Corfu with my husband and children. One night we fled for our lives, away from our home and away from Greece. I have been adrift since that night."

Julia fanned out the cards in her hands, all eleven of them, clearly trying to hide her shocked expression behind her cards as Alice spoke.

In a tone devoid of emotion, Alice explained that while she was living in exile in Paris, doctors diagnosed her with schizophrenia and she spent years locked away in a Swiss hospital for treatment. "One morning I told the doctors that the Virgin Mother came to me. I explained how she visited me in my room. She sat down on my bed and we had a lovely chat. She assured me that she would watch over my children while I was away from them. And then the Virgin Mother took me into her embrace and said to me the words I will never forget. She said, 'I know you are tired. So very tired, Alice. I will watch over you so you can finally rest. I will be beside you. And you will finally know what peace is.' I told my doctors of my vision, assuming they would see her visit as a great blessing, just as I had. Instead, they prescribed electroshock therapy to cure me of my psychosis. Another blamed it on my hormones and ordered my ovaries examined."

"And what about your husband?" Julia asked, lowering her cards below her chin and plucking a card from the pile. She searched her hand for a match and then glanced up at Alice.

Alice's eyes narrowed with intensity as she shuffled the cards and began to deal them one by one. "Last I heard he was living in Monte Carlo with his mistress." She looked away from the cards, pursing her lips as she squinted her eyes. "Or was it Nice?"

"And your children? What of your children?"

"My daughters are all married. And I have a son. His name is Philip. He is in school, although I'm not sure where."

Julia raised her cards to her nose. She peered over the top of her hand, her forehead knotted in confusion.

Alice's face erupted in a broad smile as she laid her cards on the table to win her fourth hand of the morning.

After that day, Alice began to emerge from her room little by little. And while she had no interest in the other guests, she could often be found in the company of Julia as the young kitchen maid prepared meals in the boardinghouse's cavernous kitchen.

One afternoon Julia was unfocused, unable to remember even the simplest stitch during her lesson. Alice placed her hands on Julia's, attempting to guide them. "You're shaking." She took the needle and yarn from Julia's hands and placed them beside her. "What is it?"

Julia's lips trembled as she looked up at Alice. "I overheard them downstairs as I was serving breakfast. The conversation around the table." Julia's eyes darted around the room even as they misted over with wetness. "They said the Jews are having their businesses taken from them. Even their homes are being taken away."

Alice brought her hands to her lips. She had heard whispers and rumors that the Reich was becoming more aggressive in their tactics, but this was unexpected. "Is your family Jewish?"

Julia shook her head no. She began to cry now. "They also said that the terminally ill and crippled are being taken away to Württemberg, where they are being euthanized. My sister. What will happen to my sister?" She collapsed in a heap of tears.

Within seconds, Alice sprang into action. She walked over to her closet, empty save for a handful of skirts, blouses, sweaters, a coat, and one suitcase. She opened the suitcase, rummaged through a few bags, and then returned to Julia. "I want you to take this," she said, handing the young girl a handkerchief.

Julia opened it to find a ring, a simple yet stunning sapphire ring as large as her knuckle.

"Give this to your mother and tell her to take your sister and leave Germany." Alice then lit a cigarette, tilting her head back as she savored the first drag. "Now, shall we play another round?"

∞

When she finished peeling the last of the potatoes that bright and cool April morning, Alice brought them over to Julia at the stove. Alice watched as Julia mashed the cooked potatoes with a fork and shaped them into a ball, inserting a cubed piece of sourdough bread into the center. She then dropped them again into the boiling water, careful not to overcrowd the pot, to help prevent them from sticking together. Alice reached out her hand and snatched one from the plate.

"You'll ruin your appetite," Julia chided. "Shouldn't you be getting ready to go? What time are you meeting them?"

"At three. At the Hotel Dresden. I'm told they have a lovely patio overlooking the Rheine."

"Please." Julia swatted at her with her dish towel. "You can't be late. Please, go."

Alice went upstairs to her room to get ready. She took one last look in the mirror, pinning her hair in a low bun at her nape, her thick curls forming the natural wave all the fashionable ladies of the time spent hours creating. She slipped her stockinged feet into low-heeled brown shoes, tying the laces into a secure double knot. Her suit was a brown wool, her straight skirt falling to mid-calf; her jacket, unadorned and buttoned to the neck.

She refused the offer of a taxi, preferring instead to walk from the train station to the hotel. Alice looked at her watch. Three p.m. She was right on time . . .

They were seated at a round table in the corner of the sunlit terrace overlooking the river when she arrived. Alice spotted them instantly and smiled as she walked toward them.

"Hello, Mother." Cecilie was the first to greet her, extending her arms out and kissing Alice lightly on each cheek. Her dark hair fell into sculpted waves at her chin, her dark doe eyes rimmed with black kohl, her lips stained crimson. She wore a burgundy blouse tucked into wide-legged herringbone trousers. Beside her was her husband, Georg.

"Hello, dear. You are looking well, if not a bit pale."

"I'm pregnant, Mother."

"Oh. How lovely. Congratulations," Alice said. "This is . . ."

"Four, Mother. This will be our fourth child," she said, taking Georg's hand.

"Yes. Your fourth child, of course," Alice said. She then turned her attention to Philip.

"Hello, Mother," he said, extending his arm to shake her hand.

"My, look at you. So tall and handsome you are. You've grown so much."

"I'm fifteen now, Mother. I haven't seen you since I was ten."

"Yes. That's right." She took her seat and motioned for everyone else to do the same. "Shall we have some tea?"

The next morning Julia brought her tray to Alice's door.

"How was it?" she asked. "How were the children?"

"It was pleasant. Cecilie has taken such good care of Philip. I'm afraid the poor boy has been tossed around since I've been away. More than her sisters, Cecilie has done her best to step in and help him as much as she can. Apparently my husband makes a show of it, promising to come and spend the holidays with Philip, or to bring him back to the South of France with him. Cecilie has come to call them empty promise telegraphs. Andrew never does as he promises, and Philip is left disappointed by his father time after time. And I'm going to be a grandmother again. Cecilie is expecting."

"Do you think you'll see more of them? Are you ready to go back to your family?"

"I think so. I think I would like to. I think that when the baby comes I might go and stay with Cecilie. A new baby is always an opportunity for a fresh start. Perhaps this is ours? Besides, Philip does seem a bit lost. His sisters are busy with their own children, and with his father proving so unreliable, it would be nice to spend more time with the boy."

∞

April soon gave way to May, and the summer passed quickly. Then, as the soft oranges and rusts of fall gave way to the harsh gray and white of winter, Alice began making preparations to leave the boardinghouse and visit with Cecilie.

"Philip will be there from school as well," Alice reported to Julia. "His father wrote, telling him they would spend Christmas in Cannes together. But Philip has had enough of his father's empty promises."

Instead of purchasing gifts for the family, Alice worked with Julia to perfect her Kartoffelkloesse recipe as well as several other local specialties like blackberry jam and sweet home-churned butter with cinnamon. "They have everything that money can buy, and even things money should not buy. The excess is offensive to me, quite honestly. Instead, I'm going to prepare Christmas breakfast for the entire family," Alice announced. "This will be a Christmas we will all remember forever. The start of a new chapter in our lives."

∞

When the telegram came that mid-November morning, Julia volunteered to bring it to Alice with her breakfast tray. Clad in her robe, Alice opened the door, a broad smile on her face when she saw Julia. The smile dissolved when she glanced down to see the telegram addressed to her on the lace doily. Alice opened the telegraph and lifted it to her face to read.

November 17, 1937

Alice,

I regret to inform you that Cecilie, Georg, and her two young sons, Ludwig and Alexander, were killed yesterday when their plane crashed in thick fog en route to Cousin Lu's wedding in London. The body of Cecilie's newborn was found in the wreckage. It is believed she gave birth on board and the pilot attempted an emergency landing.

I will telegraph again with news of the funeral.

Andrew

Without words or outward emotion, she placed it back down on the tray, turned, and closed the door behind her.

It was the first time Alice had heard from her husband in ten years.

Part Three

Nineteen

Corfu
December 1946

Katerina sat beside her father crocheting as the adults engaged in lively and loud conversation. Just yesterday, Clotho had taught her a new rosette pattern and Katerina focused intently on her fingers and thread, carefully dipping her needle in and out and around to form perfect little flowers. It was unseasonably cool for an early December evening, and Katerina leaned into the cooking fire every so often to warm her hands. Calliope was there as well, seated beside her mother, glaring at Katerina.

Despite the raised voices, Katerina did her best to focus on her pattern and tune out the conversation. That was until Thea Sofia turned her hawkish focus from the latest village gossip to the tragedy of Marco's family.

"Sofia, you can't be serious." Laki exhaled. "This is ridiculous. Haven't things been difficult enough without your tall tales? Hasn't that poor woman lost enough already without you condemning the rest of her life as well?"

"I'm telling you, there is something about that family. If I was her, I would bring the priest up to that hovel of a home and have him exorcise the demons from that place." Sofia leaned in and whispered, "Before she loses the younger one too."

"That's enough," Laki insisted.

"It's true," Sofia replied. "Since we were children, since before that even, everyone whispered and warned about the dark magic surrounding Clotho's home. But I don't think it's Clotho's magic we should fear. It's Yianna's home that seems to be cursed. Look at how tragedy stalks that family."

"Sofia, please. Think of what she's been through. She lost her child. She lost her husband. It's enough to drive anyone to madness," Mama said as she refilled the glasses with homemade wine.

"It runs in the bloodline, you know," Sofia added. "There's no escaping the madness in Yianna's family. And now look at her. That poor boy will starve to death because his mother has lost her mind."

They sat on the patio sipping the wine that Baba had fermented from the summer's last grapes. It was Sunday, and it seemed as if the entire village had come out to church earlier in the day to pray for the souls of Aleko and Stefano. Traditionally the entire village would have gathered together after the funeral to provide comfort and food for the family. But there had been no funeral for Aleko and Stefano. Two months had passed since the explosion, and their bodies had never been found. Greek Orthodox church law dictated that no funeral could take place without the bodies present.

The mayor felt it was his duty to step in and try to help Yianna in some way, making the trip up the mountain several times, attempting to convince her to allow him to petition the church for a funeral on her behalf. But in the end, Yianna wanted no part of it. No funeral. No memorial. Nothing. Funerals were finite. She still held out hope that someday, in some way, the sea might take pity on her and return her husband and son.

After the accident, Yianna had retreated to her house, alone. As the villagers came by to pay their respects and offer condolences, she sometimes whispered thank you but often said nothing at all, meeting their eyes with a vacant look before turning again to stare out across the channel between Corfu and Albania. Even Clotho was not able to comfort her or reach her. Clotho's figs and honey went untouched, her questions unanswered, her hugs unreturned.

The radio now referred to the explosions as "The Corfu Channel Incident" and they had learned so much, and yet so little. It was indeed Albanian mines that caused the blasts that killed forty-four British sailors that day and badly damaged the two naval ships. The international community was in an uproar with threats of war and sabotage lobbed back and forth between the British and the Albanians. But no news report ever mentioned the Greek fisherman and his son who were also among the lost that day. To the rest of the world, it was as if they had never existed.

For days Yianna had stood staring out across the sea, holding Stefano's leather bag to her chest and praying for a miracle. She thought it possible the old fisherman was wrong, that they had not sailed closer to the damaged ship. "Perhaps they sailed off to discover the land of the Phaeacians. For sure they must have sailed off and away on an adventure to Ithaka," she said to anyone who would listen. "You know Aleko never could refuse Stefano's requests."

Marco told Katerina that night after night he listened as his mother cried, pleading with God to turn back the hands of time, to compel Aleko to do the one thing he never could do, to say no to his son.

Katerina put down her needle and yarn and leaned into Baba as Sofia droned on.

"Well, I couldn't believe my eyes and ears. It was simply not to be believed," Sofia said. "I made the trip all the way up that mountain. I mean, I was kind enough and went out of my way to bring her food, which, trust me, I could have used to feed my own children. She could barely afford to feed her family before all of this happened. Could you imagine now? I placed a platter of fresh fried mullet on her table, and do you know what she said to me? She actually said, 'Take it back. Take it out of my house and out of my sight.' So of course I asked her why, what was wrong with my dish. Everyone knows I'm the best cook in the village. And do you know what she said?" Sofia paused and looked around at everyone, raising her eyebrow and shaking her head.

No one spoke.

"'The fish ate my son.' That's exactly what she said. 'The fish ate my son. I will never eat fish again.'" Sofia waved her arms in the air toward the heavens. "Can you imagine such a thing?"

Everyone was silent for a moment, allowing the magnitude of Sofia's words to sink in.

Sofia began again. "She's gone mad like her grandmother did. It's only a matter of time before she starves that poor boy or tosses him out into the street like her own demented grandmother did to her mother. At least her mother had the good fortune to end up in a palace for a while. Marco will end up on the streets, I fear, another filthy urchin begging for scraps in the gutter." She shook her head and scratched her inner thigh as she huffed.

Katerina felt her cheeks flush hot and pink, despite the cool temperature. She wiggled in her seat, tempted to jump up and make Thea Sofia take back her hateful words. Just then she felt Baba's arm around her, pulling her closer to him. She looked up at him, the sadness in his eyes matching her own. Mama stood up from her perch near the outdoor kitchen, clearing the glasses and dishes with a clang.

Katerina wanted nothing more than to run to Marco and check on him in that very moment. She felt a need to make sure he had eaten dinner and to see with her own eyes that his mother did in fact care, that she had not abandoned him in her grief, that he would not end up destitute and alone on the streets. But she did not. The hour was getting late and the light was getting dimmer, but she vowed to go visit Marco first thing in the morning.

Katerina dug her nails into the ball of string when she noticed Calliope glaring at her. Her cousin was up to something. It was hard to make out Calliope's features in the low light, but then she smiled, her pink lips gliding over her bright white teeth like a snake across the floor; just as dangerous, if not more so.

"Aunt Maria, the fire is running low. Let me help you get more kindling," Calliope said, "so you don't have to burden yourself anymore." Calliope never took her gaze from Katerina as she spoke.

"Thank you, Calliope," Mama replied.

"Come on, Katerina. Come with me. We'll go together and gather twice as much."

As soon as the words were out of her mouth, Katerina and Mama exchanged knowing glances. Katerina's fingers wrapped tighter around her crochet needle. "You don't need me to come with you. You can do it."

"What, are you scared?" Calliope taunted. "Come on." She walked over to where Katerina sat and grabbed her arm, glaring. "Come on, cousin."

"I think we're fine for the evening. There's enough to last me till morning." Mama spoke in a calm and deliberate tone.

"Maria, don't be ridiculous," Sofia chimed in, pointing to the few scraps of wood left on the pile. "Katerina, go with your cousin. Make yourselves useful. How do you ever expect us to marry you off if word gets out that you're lazy? You'll end up old spinsters like that sorry Clotho. Go on now, make yourselves useful."

"But, Mama, you know I can't go out in the dark." Katerina stared deep into her mother's eyes, pleading for help.

"Yes, you can. And you will. Don't be stupid. Go." Sofia raised her hand and threatened to swat Katerina if she didn't move.

Given the choice, she would have taken a swatting from Sofia. But Katerina knew there was no choice to be made. She had to go or Calliope would brand her a baby and a coward and torture her for days on end. Swallowing hard, she willed the bile and the fear away, but it did no good. Plump, hot tears spilled down her face. But she had no choice. As with everything else in Katerina's life, this decision was not hers to make. She removed the thread from the crochet needle, and wrapping her fingers tightly around the metal, she tucked it into the pocket of her apron.

Katerina had no idea if crochet needles were appropriate weapons to use against witches and demons, but right now it was the only hope she had.

She walked with Calliope into the woods where the kindling would be dry and plentiful. Silently, she began to work. The quicker she accomplished her task, the quicker she could go back. She heard a rustling sound and turned around. Calliope was no longer behind her but had run away from her, sprinting out of the forest. "Careful, don't let the witches get you." She laughed as she ran, the sound of leaves and twigs crunching mixing with her laughter.

In the distance, a dog barked, startling Katerina. She jumped, instinctively covering her head, the kindling falling from the folds of her apron and to the ground below. The fear and frustration were too much. Katerina began to cry. She brought her hands to her mouth to quiet the sobs. But it was no use. No amount of muffling could silence her.

"Katerina." The voice came from the shadows.

She had expected this. But nothing can prepare you for the actual moment a demon speaks your name.

She fell to the ground wailing and shaking, head to her knees, knowing this was the end.

"Katerina," the voice said again. "What's wrong with you? Why are you screaming?"

She lifted her head and squinted into the dark, straining to catch her breath.

"Get up, dummy."

"Marco?" she whispered, still afraid to speak out loud. Arms covering her head, she lifted her face slightly to look up.

"Yes, it's me. What are you doing? Why are you down there rolled up in a ball?"

"Marco, you scared me nearly to death. I mean it. I almost died, right here on the ground. What's wrong with you?"

"What's wrong with me? I'm not the one lying on the ground like a pile of donkey poop."

He walked toward her. In the moonlight she could see that he wore no shoes. His pants, which were ill fitting just weeks ago, now were crusted with dirt and seemed to be falling off of him. With no belt, Marco had done his best to keep them from falling around his ankles by tying a fishing rope around his waist. She had not seen him in days, and his changed appearance startled her. But Katerina did her best to muster a smile for her friend.

Brushing the leaves from her skirt and hair, Katerina finally stood and faced him. "What are you doing out here in the dark all alone? Aren't you scared?"

"No. Why would I be scared, you silly girl? There's nothing to be afraid of. I was hungry and I came out here to eat."

"Eat? What are you eating? There's no food out here." She looked across the forest, nothing but trees and twigs all around.

"Sure there is," he said as he opened his mouth into a wide circle and inhaled deeply. He rubbed his hands around and around on his belly. Even in the dim, gray light of the moon, she could still see the black dirt caked under his fingernails. "See?" He smiled at her and took another deep breath. "You smell that food cooking over there at the mayor's house? It smells like roasted chicken." His eyes widened. "It smells so delicious." He took in another deep breath, his chest expanding up and out. "I'm eating the smells. They're filling my belly, and I'm not even hungry anymore."

Katerina looked at Marco and smiled.

"Here," he said, inhaling again. "You have some."

She breathed in and rubbed her belly with both hands, just as he had. "Yes, you're right. It smells wonderful. I think I'm full now too." She shook her head up and down, eyes wide in agreement.

They walked along in the dark as she collected more kindling. He promised to keep her safe from the evil spirits who roamed the island paths at night searching for children to steal. She promised to save him a small piece of fish from her dinner the following night.

As they turned and headed once again toward home, Katerina silently thanked God for answering her prayers and bringing Marco to her side. She was grateful for the company of her friend, but also for the sounds of waves crashing in the distance and of twigs snapping beneath her feet, masking the sound of her still empty and rumbling belly.

Twenty

Corfu

July 1947

The silk ribbon adorning Katerina's hair tickled her nose as she skipped through the gate and bounded up the stairs and through the doorway. Her dress was made of white silk and filled up like a balloon as she twirled and spun and then skipped again through the massive double doors and into the house. The room was bright and sunlit with a ceiling so high she wondered how anyone could reach it to sweep spiderwebs from the rafters. She spotted a table set against a window overlooking the garden and ran to it. The table, as long as her eye could see, was piled high with every sweet treat she could imagine—honey-soaked baklava; flaky, custard-filled bougatsa; bowls overflowing with berries; and even piles of chocolate and ice cream in every color and flavor that somehow managed not to melt, despite the heat. She leaned in to inhale the magical aromas and reached her arm out to select her first taste. As she brought her finger to her mouth, she stopped. "Marco would love this. Marco should be here with me," she said out loud. She turned and ran out the door, back through the gate, and up the mountain to get Marco and bring him to this magical house so they could enjoy these special treats together.

"Katerina."

Mama's voice pierced the silence.

She willed Mama away. For just a little while longer. She was so close to him. She could see Marco's house in the distance. She just needed a little more time to bring him back so he could taste just a few of the sweets. She wanted to do this for him. She needed to do this for him.

"Katerina," Mama said again, shaking Katerina's shoulder, transporting her in an instant from the mountainside to her little mat beneath the icons.

"Thank you, Hypnos, for the treats. It was a beautiful dream," she whispered before she opened her eyes to face Mama and the day.

"Katerina, hurry, get dressed or we'll be late. You know everyone will show up today; even the ones who never come to church will be there. Bright and early, washed and pressed, standing so piously in front," Mama said, walking back over to the outdoor fire where she was frying a pile of smelts that she would serve for supper after church.

"Hypocrites," Mama added as she lifted the last batch of fish from the smoking pan of olive oil with her spoon.

There was a time when Mama would coat the tiny fish in flour and salt before immersing them in the pan of boiling oil and then dousing the steaming plate with a spray of lemon juice. Despite Mama's warnings, Katerina never could bring herself to wait for the crispy treats to cool. Three and four at a time, she would pop them into her mouth, the sizzling briny skins burning her as she chewed, popping and crunching, unleashing their heavenly flavor in her mouth. With no flour or salt in the pantry for months now, the smelts, while still better than a bowl of bland fish-bone soup, were not nearly as crunchy or good.

"Come, my love," Mama said. "It's time for church. Today is the memorial service. Come now."

Katerina wiped the sleep from her eyes and rolled herself out of bed.

Today was Sunday, but not just any Sunday. Today was the forty-day memorial service for the mayor's mother, Thea Olga.

Everyone knew the church would be packed today for the memorial service. It was not that Thea Olga was particularly popular; her ill temper was as legendary as her aim. But even those who had not bothered to show up for her funeral would be there today, as it was tradition that the family provide and serve *koliva* following the service. Made with wheat berries, sugar, raisins, pomegranate seeds, and nuts and shaped into a dome, symbolizing Christ's tomb, the koliva was placed onto the altar with a lit candle in the center. At the end of the liturgy, the priest would say a prayer over the platter, extinguish the candle, and then crack open the mixture, symbolizing Christ's resurrection. At the end of the service the sweet treat was distributed to the entire congregation.

With Greece now fully plunged into a civil war, famine and deprivation were widespread across the entire country. All across Greece food rations were slim, and often nonexistent. But despite the rationing of food and increasing threat as the partisans and their campaign of terror inched south, everyone in the village knew that the mayor and his wife, Lina, were far too proud to scrimp. Even in times of war.

They made an odd couple, the slight and slim spectacled mayor with his tall, thick wife. Like most marriages in the village, theirs had been arranged, an agreement made by their fathers when the bride and groom were still children. And while the mayor made no secret of his political aspirations, aggressively campaigning for office once he turned twenty, everyone in town knew it was his wife's substantial dowry that financed his ambitions and fancy suits.

Katerina splashed water on her face and rinsed her mouth. She quickly dressed, putting on the brown woolen dress that Calliope had grown out of last year. Katerina scanned the house for her parents but didn't see them. She ran outside and looked across the patio. Checking once more to make sure no one was watching, she ran to the stove and snatched a handful of smelts from the pile Mama had been frying earlier. Katerina wrapped them in a yellowed piece of newspaper, tucking the package into her pocket just as Baba emerged from the outhouse.

"Come on! Let's go," he shouted as he knelt down and patted his chest with his free hand.

Katerina sprang forward and into his arms. He lifted her up and carried her to the gate as Mama emerged from the garden. Together, they walked down the whitewashed steps, past the wall of red roses dotted with dozens of plump bumblebees that darted about and filled the air with a chorus of soft hums.

$$\sim$$

As expected, it seemed the entire village was packed into the church that morning.

Friends and neighbors stood together during the liturgy. Old men in ill-fitting, moth-eaten jackets, elderly women shrouded in widow's black, and young mothers in their Sunday dresses whose hands were raw from scrubbing their children clean. Freshly washed children stood with their families, doing their best not to fidget and counting the minutes until the service was over.

While the other boys' intermittent cries of "Ow!" echoed through the church, results of their mothers' pinched reminders to be still, Marco stood barefoot, feet clean, quiet and motionless at his mother's side. Yianna appeared now a shrunken, hollow figure, thin and pale, her shoulders stooped forward as if she didn't have the strength to hold them up. Since the day of the explosion, she had been shrouded in the shapeless black uniform of perpetual mourning. Her black headscarf was pulled low on her forehead, almost obstructing her eyes, which were sunken and red.

Katerina looked over at Marco from where she stood on the far side of the church, between her parents. She fingered the newspaper-wrapped fish in her pocket and watched as he stepped up to receive Communion, opening wide so Father could spoon the body and blood of Christ in his mouth. Head bowed, he returned to stand by his mother, who stayed rooted in her spot, having refused to receive Communion since her son and husband were lost. She looked down on him, her eyes blinking as the corners of her mouth pulled slightly upward.

Marco took her hand in his.

Several of the men stood with their families, heads bowed, hands clasped, while others congregated by the door, darting in and out of the church for a cigarette, hoping their wives, and Father Emanuel, wouldn't notice.

After service, as they exited the church single file, the priest's wife placed a spoonful of the koliva into the palm of all the congregants while Lina stood behind her. Eagle-eyed and short-tempered, just as her mother, Olga, had been, Lina seemed to have the uncanny ability of measuring each spoonful down to the gram. Each time she thought the portions too generous, she would huff and grunt and her sausage-shaped finger would fly up and *tap, tap, tap* the priest's wife's shoulder.

Despite Lina's miserly portions, a hint of sweetness was enough to put a smile on everyone's face that morning. Even after the last trace was licked from their palms, the villagers lingered in the churchyard, catching up on the latest news and gossip. The men clustered together in the shade of the church bell, many fingering worry beads, sharing news of the royal family in Athens and the war against the Communists. Katerina exited the church, listening to the conversations all around her as she searched for Marco.

"There is no way King George could have just died, suddenly, like that. He must have been poisoned," Mr. Andonis insisted.

"What are you saying?" the mayor asked.

"It can't be coincidence. Coincidences don't happen in time of crisis and war. Come on, men. Think about it. Are you willing to believe that King George suddenly dropped dead not even a year after returning from exile?"

"When I first heard I thought it was a joke. The man died on April 1, to make the whole thing even crazier." A tentative laugh escaped the mayor's lips.

"I'm saying I fear there's so much talk of the partisans along the northern borders. What if they are already in Athens?" Mr. Andonis asked. "What if we are so concerned about the threat from the mountains and the north that we are not paying attention to what might be happening within the walls of the palace itself?"

"Do you really think he was killed?" Baba lowered his voice as he looked around to the women and children gathered among them. "If there's no protection for a king in Athens within the palace walls, then what's to become of us?"

"It's very much a possibility." Mr. Andonis inched closer as he lowered his voice too. "And you can forget the idea that the violence is confined to the northern villages. Just look across the water to see how close the danger is. We used to think the sea was enough to protect us from Albania, but not anymore. Just yesterday I was in Corfu Town and I saw my friend Dimitri, the police officer. We went for a coffee and he hung his head in his hands, telling me what he witnessed on Lazaretto."

"The leper colony island?" the mayor asked.

Mr. Andonis nodded. "Yes. The small island just a kilometer from Corfu Town, where we stroll and sit and have our coffees, ignorantly thinking we are safe here at home on our civilized island. The same island used by the Germans to execute Greek resistance fighters during the war is again being used as a death camp. Hundreds of Communist prisoners are being held there as we speak, captured here on Corfu and on the mainland. Dozens executed daily, lined up and shot, against the same wall where the Nazis executed our people. We called that an international outrage, and now we sit here silently as we execute our own." Mr. Andonis looked around at the men. He took a deep breath. "Yes, I do think it's possible that the death of the king was not an accident. Unfortunately, I fear anything is possible in this climate."

"I agree. I hate to admit it. We need stability," the mayor said as he wound worry beads around his fingers. "If King Paul can stay the course, then we'll drive out the Communists. But we have to have a united front against them. Let's just pray he can stay safe. And alive."

"Well, I challenge anyone to get close enough to Paul with Frederica beside him. Good luck to them." An old fisherman laughed. "Forget the royal guard. She won't leave his side. Even on tours of destroyed villages, she's right there beside him. When they drove up to console the villagers in Epirus, the roads were so badly damaged that the king and queen had to get out of the car and walk part of the way, and then ride a donkey into the towns. No one believed that it was actually the queen walking into the village in mud-caked boots. But she did. And she brought her ladies' council as well. Imagine," he said with a snort as he fingered his worry beads. "The villagers actually didn't believe it was her and asked to see her crown."

"It's no laughing matter," Mr. Andonis said. "Apparently Frederica and her ladies all carry poison in their purses. They would rather kill themselves than fall into Communist hands."

"Is that what we need to do as well? Carry poison to save ourselves and our families from their barbaric brutality?" Baba looked around to each of the men. None of the men responded; they just continued smoking their cigarettes, dangling worry beads from their fingers.

※

"Marco," Katerina called out as she approached the throng of boys huddled together and laughing in a cluster.

She elbowed and pushed her way through the pack. In the center, with

one arm hoisted in the air in triumph and the other clutching a homemade
bow and arrow, stood Stamati, the mayor's son. Katerina pushed in closer
still but then stopped, clutching her stomach and turning around when she
noticed the blood-steeped earth at his feet and the pile of dismembered
frogs and salamanders, many with Stamati's crudely homemade arrows
sticking out from their severed limbs.

"Take that!" Stamati yelled as he aimed and fired another arrow into
the back of a frog that struggled to escape.

"What's wrong with him?" Katerina asked as she pulled at Marco and
led him to the other side of the church, away from the villagers who hovered
around the mayor and his wife pretending to lament the loss of Olga, but
secretly waiting to see if seconds of the koliva would be offered.

"He's just showing off," Marco replied, looking behind to make sure
no one had followed them.

"As usual. Here." Katerina pulled the crumpled piece of newspaper
from her apron pocket and held it out toward Marco. "Go ahead." She
motioned for him to take the package. "Go on, she can't see you."

Marco took the package and opened it slowly. His face lit up as he
looked down at the pile of tiny fried fish. "Are you sure?"

"Yes. Eat it."

Lifting the newspaper to his face, Marco took a deep breath, as if
filling his belly with the mere scent alone. He closed his eyes and inhaled
again before shoving the entire pile of fish into his mouth. When he was
done, he lifted the newspaper to his mouth and licked the paper clean.
"That tasted so much better than it smelled."

Marco and Katerina began to walk toward the front of the church.
Marco stopped when they reached the well. Katerina understood at once.

Hand over hand, Marco lowered the bucket down the well and then
pulled up a full pail of water. Katerina took hold of the bucket and tipped
it over, allowing the water to fall into his open hands. Marco washed his
hands thoroughly and splashed the water on his face, rubbing the water on
his mouth again and again, making sure his mother wouldn't smell or taste

fish when she bent to kiss him good night, if she remembered to kiss him good night.

∝

Back in the churchyard, the women had finished cleaning the cemetery, pulling the weeds, and tidying the graves of their loved ones, as they did each week. They had now gathered around, chatting on the far side of the olive tree next to the cemetery wall.

With no grave to pull weeds from and no headstone to scrub, Yianna sat on the stone wall staring blankly into space. She held her dead son's schoolbag firmly in her hands. Since the day he disappeared, Yianna carried it with her everywhere. The brown leather faded and worn, the color and consistency of butter in spots from incessantly caressing the leather as she once had Stefano's face.

Yianna wanted nothing more than to return home, where she could close her eyes and see his face. She could conjure him at will, as if he were standing before her, telling her what he had learned in school that day or about an adventure he could not wait to set out on. He would come to her and speak to her and she could caress his cheek. Alone in her memories, Stefano was still with her, in the world between dream and reality, between the living and the dead.

Yianna mourned her husband, and there was no question she ached for him, the sadness often overwhelming. But the loss of a child and longing for a husband were not the same. Losing a child was different, unfinished and raw, overshadowing everything else. She wanted to join him and at times he called to her from the sea, beckoning her to come. And several times she nearly did, standing ever so close to the edge of the cliff, just a breath away from being reunited with him. It was always in that moment of weakness, as if he somehow knew, that Marco would come to her, place his hand on her shoulder, or take her hand in his. And he would bring her back to this world, if only for a moment.

She closed her eyes against the jumble of voices all around her and tried to conjure up her son's face. But he would not come to her here. She stood to go home, so she could be with him, but then she remembered Marco. How he had smiled when he spotted Katerina, how he asked her to stay this time, to visit. *"Please, Mama. Can we stay today, just for a little bit? Katerina's my friend. And look, the other mamas are here today also. Maybe you can find a friend too."* She didn't have the heart to say no. She didn't have the strength to explain that these women were not her friends. She just looked down at Marco, attempting to blink away the tears and appear happy for him, giving him the chance to stay just a bit longer. It was a monumental effort, the half smile of a woman who refused to allow herself any joy, who struggled in her faith and felt betrayed by God. And yet Yianna prayed incessantly that God might protect her only surviving son. It was this way for Yianna, and seemingly had been her entire life. She was a woman caught between two worlds, dangling precariously between tragic reality and what might have been.

Yianna cringed as she saw Sofia exit the cemetery and walk over with purpose, sitting too close to Yianna on the wall. Thea Voula, with her bad knee and cataracts, hobbled along as well, as the other village women took their places. Sofia held center court among them with her legs spread open and her bamboo walking stick held firmly in both hands.

"Did you hear the news? They are to be married. The radio reported it yesterday. Can you imagine?" Sofia flailed her arms with excitement. "Yianna, it's something to celebrate. In this dark time, at last something to celebrate. He's getting married."

Yianna turned to Sofia, unsure of what she meant or who Sofia was speaking of.

"It was announced by the palace, by King Paul himself. Prince Philip is engaged to Princess Elizabeth of England. Imagine that, a child of Corfu marrying into the British royal family. And to think, you knew him once." Sofia snorted and laughed.

"I really must be going home," was all Yianna managed to say.

"Come on. Stay for just a little longer. It will be good for you to be out of the house. It'll be good for Marco to see you here with your friends. We are here for you, Yianna. We are your friends." Sofia placed her hand on Yianna's arm. Yianna flinched, recoiling at her touch.

"Do you think Queen Frederica and King Paul will go to the wedding?" Thea Voula asked as she adjusted her brassiere.

"I imagine they will. Although the radio report said that Philip renounced his right to the Greek throne, and our religion too," Sofia added.

"So he is no longer Greek?" Voula asked.

"He was born here. He will always be Greek. No one can take that from him. But I imagine he had to give up our church so he could be part of hers. They are to be married in her church, after all. I mean, we could never have a royal wedding in Saint Spyridon, could we?" She laughed. "Where would they fit everyone?"

The women dissolved into laughter as Yianna sat in silence, clutching Stefano's bag to her chest.

"What do you think, Yianna? Do you think you'll get an invitation?" Sofia laughed again.

Yianna did not respond to Sofia, did not show any emotion at all.

And then it happened. She could fight it no longer. The swirling whirlpool of loss enveloped her whole.

"My boy is gone." At first it escaped her lips as a whisper.

The women leaned in closer, unsure of what she said.

"My boy is gone." Her voice grew louder with each word.

All eyes were on Yianna.

"Where is my son?" She was frantic now. "I don't know where he is."

Yianna turned to face the women, addressing them directly, her arms raised to the heavens as if asking for help, or perhaps blaming the heavens. It was one and the same.

"Every night he calls to me. He calls *for* me. Every night I hear my Stefano, pleading for me. 'Mama, where are you? I'm cold and scared. Please, Mama,' he begs. 'Please come and warm me.' And I can't. Do you know what it is to hear him crying for me, begging for me to go to him and save him, like I did so many times before when he was frightened in the dark? But I can't save him this time. I can't save him and I can't comfort him and I can't help him rest because I don't know where he is." She was sobbing now. "I can't save him." Her voice got louder, panic rising with each word. "I don't know where he is. Where is my son? Where is my son?"

∾

Katerina and Marco heard Yianna's cries as they were leaving the well. They locked eyes and ran together as fast as their legs could carry them. Once they reached Yianna, Katerina hung back, wanting to help but knowing it was not her place.

"Mama, I'm right here. It's all right now," Marco whispered to his mother as he stroked her hair and cradled her in his arms as she had once cradled him, before his father and brother were lost, taking the mother he had once known to the bottom of the sea with them.

Not one person stepped in to help her. Not one person moved to console her or to dry her tears. They had tried before, and she always shooed them away, not interested in their pity or their help. This was not the first time the entire village witnessed Yianna's breakdown. By now everyone was well aware of the fragility of her pain, a Pandora's box of grief unsealed before an audience.

Even Clotho could do nothing for her when Yianna was in such a state. No amount of coaxing or reasoning could help. Her sorrow was just another cold fact of their lives. Unchangeable. Something to acknowledge, then step over, like a wounded bird in the road.

Yianna softened when she looked into Marco's face, her eyes regaining their focus, and at last she quieted down. She caressed Marco's cheek as he tried helping her to her feet, but she remained there, a crumpled, shapeless black heap on the ground. Then someone else stepped forward to help Yianna, to offer the support she refused again and again. With giant, purposeful strides, Baba walked over to where Yianna now sat on the ground as Marco continued to try coaxing her to stand. Baba nodded to Marco and put his arm around Yianna, lifting her gently to her feet and whispering something in her ear. She looked into his eyes and smiled, gratitude showing on her face and even through her tears. She mouthed the words, "Thank you, I knew you would come."

Everyone watched as Yianna leaned into Baba, resting her head on his shoulder as they walked together down the road, disappearing behind the olive grove as they began the journey back to Yianna's house.

Katerina knew that Mama would still be inside the church, preferring to pray privately rather than join the other women as they chatted and gossiped. She waited and watched as her mother emerged from inside. "Come, Mama, let's go home. It's time to go," she said as she led Mama away.

"Where is your father?" Mama asked.

Katerina could feel the eyes of the women on them as she escorted her mother home.

Twenty-One

Corfu

April 1948

Katerina and Marco slipped away and walked together toward the farthest end of the island where the path was rocky and overgrown. Katerina did her best to keep up, but every now and then she stumbled over a tree branch or a rock. She stopped for a moment and looked down at her leg, at the pale scratch down her calf where a thorn had caught her. It stung and at once turned from white to red. She thought about turning back, but then he looked at her and smiled, waving her along with his hand.

"I'm nervous." She stopped, looking behind her as if to turn back. "We shouldn't be doing this."

"Oh, come on. You said you wanted to." He took her hand and smiled, the sight at once melting her resolve as well as her fears. She had made a promise and she didn't want to disappoint him. After all, he was her best friend.

They had talked about this for weeks, planning when and how they would escape unnoticed for a few hours. They had tried once before, but then they heard the explosion that changed everything.

She couldn't believe that finally the day had come when he was really going to teach her how to swim.

"There's a tiny inlet, just over the next hill. It's a tricky climb to the other side of the mountain, but if we're careful we'll be fine. No one ever goes there. You'll be swimming in no time." Marco smiled at her as he untied and reknotted the rope at his waist.

She tugged at her slip, which had bunched up between her legs, making the walk in this uncleared part of the woods even more uncomfortable. Despite her uncertainty and nerves, she knew it would be worth it. She couldn't wait to feel free, to know what it was to glide through the sea, to dive under the surface of the water and float freely where no one could see her, where being the smallest didn't matter.

"Do you dream, Marco?"

"Yes. Sometimes."

"What do you dream about?"

"I dream my brother and father are still here. That my mother is still here."

Katerina stopped and faced him. "But she is here."

"No, she isn't. She went with them, Katerina. I know she didn't mean to. But she did."

They walked in silence for a few minutes after that.

"What about you?" Marco asked. "What do you dream about?"

"I dream of having a nice house, like the mayor's, where there is plenty of food to eat and Mama and Baba don't have to worry about anything but what pretty dress Mama will wear and which delicious food we should have for dinner."

"I like that dream," he said.

"And I have another dream sometimes too. There's a lady in white who comes to me. She seems very nice and she's always smiling. Clotho tells me she is watching over me. But I don't know who she is."

"That sounds like a nice dream."

"It is. But it makes me sad also."

"Why?"

"Because I can't remember the last time I saw Mama smile."

They walked in silence for the rest of the way, the silence of best friends whose most meaningful conversations needed no words.

"There, it's just behind that abandoned house." Marco pointed to the tiny stone and mud home they could just make out through the dense brush and tangle of olive tree branches and leaves at the other end of the clearing. It was no more than a pile of rocks and the skeletal remains of a wall and window that had once been home to a fisherman several generations ago.

"Come on, let's go." He grabbed her hand, ready to sprint to the cove, but then stopped when he heard a noise. It seemed to come from just behind the fisherman's house. "Did you hear that?"

"Hear what?"

"It sounded like a scream." Still holding her hand, he crouched down into the high grass, motioning for Katerina to do the same. "There, there it is again."

The sound was louder this time.

"What was that?" Katerina trembled and grabbed his arm, thinking immediately of the stories Calliope had told her, of the demons who walked these uncharted paths and for whom a decrepit house would be the perfect place to hide and devour stolen children.

They heard the noise again and both Katerina and Marco turned toward it. Squinting through the brush and the cracks and crevices of the wall, they could barely make out the outline of two bodies on the ground, a tangle of limbs in the grass.

"What are they doing?" Katerina asked, straining her neck to see.

Marco didn't answer. He placed his finger on his lips and motioned for her to be quiet.

"Wrestling." Katerina turned to Marco wide-eyed, silently mouthing the word. "They're wrestling."

The children crouched lower now and watched again for a few moments longer. Marco and Katerina could just make out the figures through the brush-covered hole where there once was a window. The person on top pinned the other to the ground. And then suddenly the bodies flipped, shifting positions. One of the figures stood then, putting on a shirt, and walked to the other side of the stone wall.

"It's Mr. Andonis," Katerina whispered. "Look, Marco, it's him."

"Shh." He pressed his finger to his lips again. "Katerina, be quiet. Please. Don't let them hear you."

"Do you think he'll tell that we were here if he sees us?" Katerina was overcome with fear that their secret mission would be found out. "We can't let him see us, Marco. We'll both be in so much trouble. We should go."

"But what about your swimming lesson?" Marco asked.

"Not now. Not today. My parents will be so mad at me. Marco, we have to go."

∞

Marco didn't quite understand what he had seen, but he knew that Katerina was right; they needed to leave this place, quietly and quickly. But a single thought swirled in his head and unsettled his empty stomach. Mr. Andonis had taken great pains to steal away here, to this desolate place, hidden away from the eyes and ears of the other villagers. But why would he come all this way to wrestle behind the dilapidated house? It made no sense.

It seemed Mr. Andonis also had something to hide. Marco grabbed Katerina's hand as he led her away from the crumbling house as fast as their legs could carry them.

Twenty-Two

Corfu
May 1948

Maria walked in the woods, but she wasn't the least bit afraid. She felt oddly at ease here, serene, although she was alone on this unfamiliar path. The moon was high and directly above, pale gray light filtering down between the trees, helping her find her way.

She could see the opening in the distance. She knew the clearing was there, just past those trees. She knew that was where she needed to be, where *she* would be.

She had waited so long to see her, and she had missed her so. But now the waiting was over. And they would be reunited once again, the way it was meant to be.

With each step closer to the clearing, her legs became heavier, weighted down as if she were walking through waist-high sand. But nothing would stop her from seeing her again. She continued on.

Just a little farther down the path. Just a few more steps, another moment or two, and she would be in the only place she had ever truly belonged: her mother's arms.

The trees gave way to a large clearing in the center of the forest. The light was brighter here. And then she saw her. "Mama," she cried. "Mama. Mama."

Mama lifted her head and smiled when she spotted Maria coming toward her. Her eyes welled, and when she blinked, tears rolled down her face. But then her facial expression changed. They were not tears of joy.

"Mama. Mama," Maria called again as she began to run.

"No. Stay back," her mother warned. "Stay away." She lifted her arms and waved them wildly. "Go back. Go back."

Maria spotted the blood as soon as her mother lifted her hands. And then she saw them moving in, and in an instant they had surrounded her. There were dozens of them, large wild dogs surrounding her mother, snarling at her and growling fiercely.

"Run, Mama! Run!" she shouted. But Mama remained still.

Maria stood, planted in that very spot. She watched as the wild dogs attacked, ripping apart her mother, tearing her flesh, shredding her into nothing before her very eyes.

Maria woke from her nightmare, gasping for breath, the sheets soaked with perspiration. She glanced across the room and spotted Katerina asleep on her mat, her profile illuminated in the moonlight. Maria hugged her arms around herself and turned to her side. He was gone, again.

Closing her eyes once more, Maria replayed the dream in her mind.

Maybe I'll ask Clotho what it means. But then she thought better of it, realizing she had known the meaning of her nightmare all along.

Twenty-Three

Corfu

June 1948

"Do you renounce Satan?" Father Emanuel asked. Clad in his black robes and with his long hair cinched in a low bun at his nape and facing west, where the sun sets and where ancients believed the gates of Hades were located, the bearded priest stood at the entrance of the church holding his liturgical book.

"I do renounce Satan."

"Do you renounce Satan?"

"I do renounce him."

Father Emanuel asked three times in all. And three times the godparents answered the same way.

Thea Voula and her husband beamed with pride, watching as baby Thalia, their first grandchild, was christened and welcomed into Christ's kingdom.

Father Emanuel then turned to face east, where the sun rises, so the godmother could accept the light of Christ into Thalia's life.

Katerina stood in the church and did her best to ignore Calliope, who fidgeted beside her. The cousins both wore their hair tied off their faces, held in place by a yellow ribbon that Laki had cut in half with his fishing knife that morning so each of them would have something pretty to wear to the baptism.

Sucking on her fist and cradled against her godmother's chest, Thalia slept peacefully throughout the entire service, until Father Emanuel hoisted her naked body into the air and plunged her feetfirst into the baptismal font.

"The servant of God, Thalia, is baptized in the name of the Father and Son and Holy Spirit." His words were barely audible over the screams of the infant.

Unlike some of the other stern and humorless priests who had come and gone from their tiny congregation, Father Emanuel was a gentle soul who had actually taken the time to build a fire and warm the water before pouring it into the font. But despite the warm temperature of the water and the kindly priest's gentle touch, baby Thalia continued to scream.

After the service, everyone filed back to Thea Voula's house for the traditional baptismal luncheon. In happier, more prosperous times, there would have been a whole lamb or perhaps even a pig roasting on a spit for everyone to feast on. But this meal was like others had been for as long as anyone could remember now that war, loss, and hunger were infused into the fabric of everyday life. Today the baptismal feast consisted of roasted fish, lobster, sea urchin, and vegetables cobbled together by the nets and gardens of friends and family.

Traditionally the men and women would have retreated to opposite sides of the house to share their latest news. The men would argue over politics while the women caught up on the latest family news and village gossip. But not today. Today, men and women huddled together as there was much important news to discuss. The women fanned themselves with plastic fans purchased at the periptero as they sipped chamomile tea harvested from the hillside and fresh lemonade from lemons plucked from their gardens and sweetened with local honey. The men smoked home-rolled cigarettes as the periptero had run out of boxed cigarettes weeks ago.

The men fingered their worry beads furiously while the women leaned in and clasped their hands in prayer as they comforted Toula, a young mother from Erikousa. Toula cried as she shared her story, explaining that her mother's village in Epirus had been overtaken by Communists. Toula twisted and knotted the hem of her skirt as she told how her elderly parents were forced to escape on foot ahead of the brutal pillaging of the village. Her parents had joined the thousands fleeing the northern border and flooding into cities like Ioannina and Athens to escape the Communist brutality, only to find themselves facing famine and horrible conditions among the refugees.

Irene, baby Thalia's godmother, explained that she had just returned from visiting her sister in Athens and was shocked to find the store shelves empty and the streets flooded with refugees as Athenians waited hours in line for a small bowl of soup from local soup kitchens.

"It's going on here as well." Mr. Andonis fidgeted with his worry beads. "I was in Corfu Town last week to stock up on supplies. I could not believe the change since just last month." He shook his head. "The color of our beautiful town, the way the Ionian sunlight falls on the reds and rusts of the homes and the church bell towers, bathing the entire city in its ethereal light. It's one of the reasons I fell in love with this island. It's as if the very color has been dimmed, the fabric of our lives threadbare and worn. Even the Germans could not manage this. But now . . ." His voice trailed off. "I don't know that any of us are safe."

Laki leaned in. "What happened? What changed?"

"There was a group of children, no more than five to seven years old. They were in a truck and stopped along the road to get some water near where I was waiting for the bus. They were filthy. Most wore no shoes. Their heads were shaved and they were emaciated. They looked like skeletons. It broke my heart."

"But whose children?" the mayor asked. "And where were they going?"

"I asked the same thing and was shocked at the answer. They were being taken to Queen Frederica's *paidopoleis*. Here, in Benitses. Children with nowhere to go, no family of their own, whose parents had been murdered or had simply disappeared. Children who were sent away by their own mothers and fathers, parents with no way to feed their sons and daughters, knowing their only hope of survival was to bring them into the queen's care. This is the state we find ourselves in. I know Frederica started her children's villages to save the children of war along the mainland. But now there are desperate families here too." He shook his head and closed his eyes. "I'm sorry. Maybe I was naive, but I never imagined the need to be so great here. There has always been poverty and suffering, I know. But this is more." Mr. Andonis took a deep breath and let his head hang.

He stirred something in everyone listening that day. They were tired. And they were hungry. And there was reason to be concerned, even scared, as the water surrounding the island seemed no longer enough to save them from the Communist threat across the channel.

"God bless those children." Sofia made the sign of the cross three times. "And God bless Queen Frederica. Singlehandedly she and her friends are doing what all of those self-important men in suits have promised to do."

"She made a promise to us and she is keeping it. My mother's people are from Agia Triada, and the village was devastated. The partisans swept through and burned the entire village to the ground. Dozens of children were left orphaned. Those poor children now have a home and food to eat because of the queen herself," the mayor's wife, Lina, said.

"While men kill each other, it is a woman who is saving the children of Greece." Laki shook his head as he spoke.

"What does it matter who is saving them, as long as they are being saved?" Sofia added.

"They say he's a puppet. That she's the one in charge," the mayor said as he twirled his worry beads around and around on his fingers.

"That's ridiculous." Lina brushed off her husband's argument as if it were absurd. The mayor bristled at her boldness but said nothing in return.

"So the queen saves the children, but who will save us?" Laki ran his fingers through his hair as he paced the patio, looking down from Voula's house to his own home below. The cracked pavement and crumbling walls were clearly visible from this vantage point.

"She said it in her radio address. Don't you remember?" Mr. Andonis replied. "She said it on Christmas Day, wearing a black dress of mourning on Christ's birthday. She said she was in mourning for the state of our country and that she would now be the mother of Greece, a mother to all the children left motherless by this damn war."

"And she has kept her word. She was serious about doing everything in her power to help." Sofia nodded her head up and down as she spoke.

"Serious enough to leave the king in Athens as he recovers from typhoid," Voula said as she adjusted herself in her chair. She leaned in as she spoke. "She wouldn't listen to the soldiers. She refused to stay home when they told her it was too dangerous to visit Konitsa. She went anyway. My cousin Lambro saw her with her very own eyes," Voula boasted. "She was standing as close to her as I am to you." She tapped at Mr. Andonis's leg with her walking stick for emphasis. "She could smell her perfume and see each curl of her hair and the blue of her eyes. Lambro said she stepped out of a car and onto the road looking like an everyday woman in a simple coat, not a member of European royalty. She went not as a queen but as a Greek, as a mother. The road to Konitsa was littered with bodies and craters, remains of the brutal fighting. Why, some parts of the road are still nearly impassable. Frederica was the first to cross the bombed bridge once it was fixed, you know. But despite all this, despite the danger, Frederica insisted she go see the villagers herself."

Voula stopped her story for a moment, raising her eyebrows and looking around the room, savoring every moment of having all eyes on her, a captive audience spellbound by her story. She then closed her eyes and bowed her head and made the sign of the cross three times, each movement of her hands slow and articulated. The others followed suit. She continued, "The queen cried when she saw the children. Oh, how she cried, the tears only a mother can cry. Only a mother can understand our pain."

"Yes, yes," the women agreed, nodding their heads in unison, repeating Voula's words. "Only a mother can understand our pain."

"Frederica held them in her arms. She didn't care they were dirty, covered in filth and lice. She caressed them and showed them love. The entire village destroyed. Parents, dead." Voula stomped her walking stick into the ground for emphasis. "Those poor children had slept on the cold schoolhouse floor for weeks, existing on nothing but dried figs. With no family left to care for them, they were alone, until the queen risked her life for theirs."

"They almost killed her own child, and by the grace of God he was saved," Mr. Andonis continued. Voula narrowed her eyes and pursed her lips, visibly annoyed by the schoolteacher's interruption. "It happened when they were in exile in Egypt. Prince Constantine was only a toddler, and terribly sick. He was intentionally misdiagnosed by a doctor with ties to the Communists. Thankfully she knew enough to summon another doctor who accurately diagnosed the child. His appendix would have burst. This man, this monster, sat by and watched, allowing a child to suffer, watching as Constantine hovered near death, all to further his own sick political agenda. From that day on, Frederica insisted she would devote her last breath to helping mothers care for the children of Greece. She said no mother should endure what she endured.

"Did you hear that, Costa?" Mr. Andonis said to Voula's husband. "You, who went on and on about how a blue-eyed, blonde-haired German can't possibly understand what the people of Greece need. Don't you ever forget that it is your so-called German born princess who is actually saving our children while your full-blooded Greeks are destroying them."

Costa said nothing in response.

"Well, thank God for that. It's getting worse in the north," the mayor added. "The Communists are taking children away by the truckload, telling families the only chance they have of saving their children from the war is to send them away. These poor families have no choice. Can you imagine?" The mayor wiped his glasses with the corner of his suit jacket.

No one responded to the mayor's question. For the first time that anyone could remember, not one of them pretended to have the answer.

∾

On the other side of the room, Maria busied herself by cleaning up and washing the dishes and glasses from the luncheon. While Laki and Katerina relished the company and conversation of social gatherings like these, Maria always managed to steal away and busy herself in the quiet isolation of kitchen work and cleanup. At first Voula had declined Maria's offer of help. Maria insisted and persisted, saying it was the least she could do to help welcome Voula's grandchild into Christ's kingdom. Voula finally stopped her feigned protests and allowed Maria full run of the housekeeping.

Maria spotted Yianna on the other side of the patio, sitting off by herself.

"Yianna, is there anything else I can get you?" Maria asked as Yianna nibbled on a piece of bread with olives.

"No, Maria, thank you." With pin-thin arms she waved her away.

"Have some potatoes. Here, just a small one," Maria tried again, piercing a potato with a fork and offering it to Yianna, knowing full well that the potatoes had been baked in the same pan as the fish.

"No, thank you. This was perfect," Yianna insisted. She turned her head in the direction of where Voula was still holding court with yet another story about Queen Frederica. "God bless our queen."

"God bless her indeed," Maria agreed. "Do you really think a woman can be the salvation of Greece? That a woman can be the one to right so many wrongs?"

Yianna wrung her hands, twisting her fingers. "No. A woman can't." She looked up and into the eyes of Maria and exhaled. "But a mother can." And with that she stood and walked over to where Clotho was holding baby Thalia in her arms. Maria returned to the sink to finish the last of the dishes.

∾

Silently, Clotho handed the precious bundle to Yianna.

Yianna said nothing as she cradled the sleeping baby in her arms, inhaling her baby scent. Her face went blank and she closed her eyes, chin tucked to her chest. Clotho reached her hand out, touching her shoulder.

"You are lucky, you know, Clotho," Yianna said, her voice cracking.

Clotho chuckled and shook her head. "Yes. I'm very lucky. Anyone can see that." She laughed a nervous laugh.

"You are. Trust me," Yianna said. "Everyone says children are the greatest gift. How blessed we are when we have them, Clotho. How God smiles down on us when we become mothers. The greatest gift from above. The reason we are put on this earth."

"Yes," Clotho replied. "Children are a blessing, Yianna. You are blessed. Marco is a good boy. I saw him laughing earlier with Katerina. It's nice to see him smile. He deserves joy. And so do you. You still have a son here, with you. It is all right to feel joy, if not for yourself, for him. For Marco."

"No, Clotho. There is no joy for me. Because I know the day a woman becomes a mother is the day she learns what pain is. I'm not talking about labor pains. Those come and go and a woman always forgets. The pain I'm talking about lasts a lifetime. It's when you realize that you will live in fear every moment for the rest of your life. Because despite what everyone tells you, that is what it is to be a mother."

"Yianna, come now. The day a child is born is a joyous day, a blessing."

"Listen to me, Clotho. I'm telling you the truth. I'm the only one who will. I know as well as you do how they all stare and whisper, not just about me but about you too. 'Poor childless Clotho. What is a woman without children? Incomplete. Is she even a woman?' But I want you to know something." She lifted her chin and took a deep breath as she cradled the baby to her chest. "You are better for not having children, Clotho. I wish I was like you. I wish I never had children."

"Yianna, I know your heart is broken. I know you're hurt, and I am so sorry. I wish I could take your pain. But don't wish your family away like that. Your family was a blessing, the greatest blessing."

"No, Clotho. I wish I never had a family. Because then I would have no one to lose."

Clotho opened her mouth to speak, but remained silent.

Yianna stared out blankly across the green of the island. "God took my son, Clotho, but even before that day, I lived in hell. Each time I held that perfect baby boy in my arms, each time I kissed his soft pink skin and looked into those beautiful eyes, each time he said, 'Mama, I love you,' my heart was so filled with love, I thought I would burst from it. But that love, the joy he gave me, came at a steep price." She bit her lip. "It destroyed me."

She closed her eyes and her face became ashen as the tears spilled down her cheeks and onto the sleeping baby. "I loved him too much." Yianna stood for a moment and then handed the baby back to Clotho. She hugged her arms around her body, closing her eyes and squeezing tighter, as she once might have hugged her son to her chest. Nothing but emptiness now in the space he once filled.

"And I can tell you, Clotho, the pain is greater than the joy. It is deeper, deafening. They all know it's true." She motioned over to where the women sat by the wall. "Those same women who tell me how very sorry they are, who tell me they pray for me . . ." Yianna's voice drifted off, almost a whisper now. Her lips quivered as she sucked in the salty sea air, allowing it to fill her lungs before she exhaled and spoke again. "Those same women who tell me how very sorry they are, privately they thank God for what happened to me."

"Yianna, no one here has meant you any harm. Not to you, and certainly not to your children."

"Oh, but they do." Yianna's eyes grew wide, wild as she looked out toward the horizon, and then she focused again on Clotho, narrowing her eyes now into a steely fixed gaze. "They thank God for taking my son—because in taking mine, God spared theirs. I'm not crazy, Clotho. You know that as well as I do. They want to believe I'm crazy because they think it makes them look more sane. My pain is a gift for them. My pain means they were spared."

Yianna then walked to the gate. Her hand trembled as she pulled the latch. She held the gate open and turned back toward everyone gathered on the patio. She scanned each and every face as tears ran down her cheeks. She opened her mouth but then closed it again, a soft moan escaping her lips. Still clutching her dead son's leather bag close to her heart, Yianna walked away from the christening party and toward home.

Twenty-Four

Corfu

October 1948

Marco considered himself lucky. The tide was exceptionally low that day, allowing him to walk farther along the cove jetty than normal. Out here, just beyond the tide pool where the current churned treacherously, thumb-size barnacles clung to the rocks untouched and unharvested, even as the villagers fished and foraged for ways to feed their families. The blade of the knife he had found in his father's old fishing bucket was quite dull, just sharp enough to pry stubborn mollusks from their grip. He sucked the briny flesh from the shells, savoring the salty treats as they slipped down his throat. As he tossed the shells into the sea, Marco looked out across the water and spotted a cluster of black spiky sea urchin just a bit farther past the breakwater. He inched along the jetty, each step measured and mindful. Had the other boys spotted him out there, arms out for balance, shuffling along slowly as an old woman might, they no doubt would have mocked him. There was no question that Marco was more careful, taking far fewer chances than other boys his age. Unlike those children,

154

yet unmarked by tragedy, Marco understood full well the destruction left behind when a young life was lost. He could never do that to his mother, even as he questioned if she would truly grieve for him as she did his brother.

Time and again, Marco wondered if his mother was angry with God not just for taking her child but for taking the wrong child. Stefano was the smart one, the obedient one, and, Marco had always thought, the favorite. Marco knew that his brother was all of those things. But perhaps even more importantly, Stefano was also his mother's hope for the future. His mother's hopes and dreams and any potential of a different life were pinned to the back of her beloved elder child, and then lost at sea with him as well. The young boy who dreamed of becoming a teacher one day, who sat by the fire reading to his mother and then whispered with her deep into the night, retracing Odysseus's route and debating with her which was more terrifying, the one-eyed man-eating Cyclops or the Sirens who seduced their prey and then devoured them in insidious ways. Night after night Marco had wished they would just shut up already. It was bad enough that he had to listen to Mr. Andonis drone on and on about the ancient myths and their lessons during the day, but to hear Stefano and Mama chatter as he tried to sleep was torturous.

What he wouldn't do to be kept awake by those whispers again in the night.

Marco still struggled with his studies and could barely read and write, despite the best efforts of Katerina to get him to focus. But he had become adept at deciphering and predicting the weather. Like generations of fishermen whose lives and livelihood ebbed and flowed with the winds and currents, Marco had taught himself to understand what each subtle shift in the waters and winds meant. He was not a fisherman, nor would he ever be. But for Marco, understanding the winds and sea was survival nonetheless.

As tempting as the thought of sea urchin was, as their soft and salty flesh would surely keep the hunger pangs at bay, Marco thought better of it. He tucked his knife into the waistband of his pants and headed back toward shore. All around him, even before his feet reached the sand, the winds began to rattle and shake the cypress and olive trees that lined the cove as the tide rushed more urgently toward the beach.

He had planned on meeting Katerina at Clotho's and hated missing out on the treats she would no doubt have ready for him, but even the promise of figs and blackberry jam could not keep him from his task. As the wind and waves picked up, he knew his place was home.

With each storm since that terrible day, each time the maestro blew in from Italy to the east, across the Adriatic Sea and to their village, Mama immediately took her place. Marco raced home from the beach up the mountain path knowing exactly where he would find her. Knowing it was time to take his place as well.

As he burst through the gate, he saw she was already there, clutching Stefano's bag to her chest, fingers stroking the weathered leather. Mama stood out there on the terrace, just beyond her garden, just as she had the day her son and husband set off to cast their nets before they were lost to her forever.

Unnoticed by his mother, who never took her gaze from the sea below, Marco walked into the house. He scanned the fireplace, not surprised when he didn't find any supper waiting for him. He reached his hand out over the pile of ashes in the center of the hearth. As cold as they had been when he left the house this morning and days even before that.

He walked to the farthest corner of the house and dragged his thin mat across the floor. Placing it in the doorway, he sat down. He pulled his father's old sweater on and then wrapped a tattered woolen blanket around his bony frame, resigning himself to another night of keeping watch over her. At least here, with the mat in the doorway, if sleep overtook him, he would hear her if she called to him.

"You can count on me, Mama. I'll be right here for you," he said as he wrapped the blanket tighter around his shoulders.

As the sky turned from bright blue to navy to gray, Marco knew that time was running short. Soon darkness would descend, and she would no longer be able to watch the water rise and fall, straining her eyes with each crest and swell, praying her boy might somehow, by a miracle, appear.

Marco stayed like that too, watching her, unable to tear himself away in case his mother needed him or called his name. But she never did.

"Save my son," Mama cried. "Dear God, please. Help me find the strength to save my boy." She collapsed to the ground as the words escaped her lips. Her sobs filled the air, primal and pitiful, as she raised her arms, first up toward the darkening sky and then down toward the sea below.

Marco watched from the doorway as his mother fell to her knees. He rubbed his belly, still empty, and inhaled deeply, hoping what was left of the breeze might carry the aroma of a meal to him. But there was no scent on the breeze, just as there was no mention of his own name on his mother's lips.

Twenty-Five

Corfu

October 1948

"Do you think you will ever have children of your own?" Katerina asked.

"These are my children." Clotho smiled as she plucked a giant white gardenia from the waxy tree and tucked it behind Katerina's ear. "Remember, you must treat them like they are your family. You must talk to them, nurture them, and they will reward you."

Clotho turned to the fig tree, inspecting each specimen, choosing only the fruit that was a deep black-hued purple and perfectly ripe. She piled the last of the figs into a basket and handed it to Katerina. "You know I would love for you to stay, but it's nearing supper, Katerina. Don't you think you should be heading home? Your parents will worry."

"I'll just wait a little bit longer." Katerina's voice was heavy with disappointment. "Marco said he would come today."

Katerina placed the basket down on the table just as the wind kicked up, rattling the arbor above. Katerina lifted her gaze and watched as the leaves and plants performed their frenzied dance on the breeze. "There's a maestro coming."

Clotho nodded. A tight smile crossed her lips.

"He won't come today, will he?" Katerina asked, although she already knew the answer. "He'll stay with her. I know he will."

"He'll stay with her." Clotho reached her hand out and placed it on Katerina's.

"It's not fair, Clotho. Can't you do something? Can't you talk to her? She's your friend. I'm so sorry and I know how sad she is. But Marco is sad too. He misses his father and Stefano. And he misses his mother too. He needs her. I know he does."

Clotho sighed. "I know. We all do, my sweet girl. But Yianna's grief is not for us to debate or judge how long or deep. Some things are beyond words, beyond understanding, beyond even the best intentions of the dearest friends. Grief is a wound that never heals, Katerina. Yianna will live with this deep, gaping wound for the rest of her life. I pray she finds a way to live with her pain." Clotho was silent for a moment, shifting her gaze from Katerina off to the horizon. "Because there is no other choice."

Clotho reached over to tuck a tendril of hair behind Katerina's ear. "Her soul is tired, Katerina. An exhaustion you and I could never understand no matter how hard we tried. We can only hope she finds the strength to come back to this life, for herself and for Marco. And until then, you and I will do our best to look after him, won't we? Marco is not alone. He has you and me, and that's more than some people will ever have in life." Clotho stood and looked out across the horizon again where low, gray clouds were drifting across the sea and toward the village.

"We'll look after him, Clotho. Even if she doesn't find her way back." Katerina bit her lower lip and looked up at Clotho, her blue eyes brimming with tears.

"We will." Clotho smiled, tapping Katerina's nose with her finger.

She then walked to the outdoor stove where a pan of potato pita was cooling. Clotho had made the pita earlier that morning, hand rolling the dough and filling the pie with boiled potatoes, fresh dill, milk, and what little feta cheese was left in her pantry. She had drizzled the dish with fragrant green olive oil and roasted it over the open fire all morning until the creamy mixture bubbled and browned and the dough turned crisp, dark brown, and flaky. She grabbed the large butcher's knife and cut the pie in three pieces, wrapping two of the pieces in dish towels and placing them in the basket beside the figs.

"One package is for your mother and the other is for Marco and Yianna." She narrowed her eyes and wagged her finger at Katerina. "So don't bother stealing food for him like you do the fish from your mother's stove," Clotho chided, her pursed lips slowly unraveling into a wide smile. "Give it to him at school tomorrow and be sure to tell him that it's potato pita so Yianna knows it's not fish and, God willing, she'll eat some as well."

Katerina exhaled in relief. "How did you know about the fish? Please don't tell my mother. I was only trying to help Marco. It's not really stealing, is it?"

"I won't tell. I know you are only looking after your friend. Your secret is safe with me. Now go. You mother will be worried about you." With a wave of her hand, Clotho shooed her away.

Katerina hugged Clotho one last time. She picked up her basket and without another word began the long walk home.

Walking more gingerly than usual, with deliberate, measured steps, Katerina made her way down the trickiest part of the hillside. Normally she would race down the rocky terrain as fast as her spindly legs could carry her, without a care of tripping or falling. Skinned knees and scraped elbows were of no concern to her. They were as much a part of who she was as her tanned sinewy limbs and clear blue eyes. But Katerina was cautious this time, holding tight to the basket, placing one hand on top of the dishcloth that covered the pita Clotho had wrapped for Marco. She took every precaution to make sure her precious cargo would reach Mama, and especially Marco, intact.

Once she reached the bottom of the hill, where the precarious terrain

gave way to more level earth and a well-traveled dirt path, Katerina quick-
ened her pace. As she walked briskly toward home, she looked out across
the sea. The maestro winds that had just a short while ago announced
themselves by gently kissing the back of her neck had grown emboldened.
Blustery and unabashed, the squalls whipped the surf into a seemingly
endless vision of angry whitecaps and swirling currents.

Katerina walked even faster now, wishing she had not stayed so long
at Clotho's, wishing she could reach Marco right this moment, present
him with Clotho's delicious pita, and fill his belly while easing his mind.
Katerina knew, as did everyone in the village by now, that the maestros
brought more than just the whitecaps to the surface. As the current churned,
so did Yianna's mind.

Katerina at last reached home just as Mama was preparing to cook
dinner. She handed her mother Clotho's figs and pita and ran to build a fire
before being told to. She hoped that by some miracle Marco might come
down the mountain and visit her that night, while the pita was still fresh
and warm. But in reality, Katerina knew better; she knew he would not
leave his watch until the sea returned to her glassy stillness.

As the fire spit and crackled to life, she sat a moment. She watched as
the embers ignited, then floated up and away on the maestro breeze like
red-hued faeries dancing in the air. She then looked out to the horizon
where the last remnants of daylight disappeared and the ethereal blue-gray
glow of twilight gave way to the ashen dead of night.

Katerina felt the familiar nighttime uneasiness wash over her. She
heard a noise beyond the garden, the sound of heavy footsteps and twigs
breaking underfoot. Startled, she stood to go closer to the house where the
light from the fire kept the darkness at bay. Just as she turned to go, Baba
came bounding up the steps two by two. He ran right over to Katerina and
scooped her in his arms. She nestled there, burrowed into his neck like a
tiny kitten.

"You're trembling," he said. "Look at me. Remember what I told you
about the darkness?"

With her arms still draped around his neck, she looked up at him and nodded her head. "Yes."

"Tell me," he said. "Tell me so I know you understand. So I know you can repeat the words, even when the day comes that I won't be here to say them for you."

"Remember . . ." Katerina whispered, her voice soft as a kitten's purr.

"Louder," he insisted. "Louder so everyone across this village in every home and in every hovel can hear you. Say it like you believe it, like you know it to be true. So that Nyx herself can hear my daughter's voice, strong and steady, fearless as she is."

"Remember," Katerina repeated, her voice still trembling slightly, but louder than before. "There is magic to be found in the darkness. Fierce, beautiful magic. There is nothing to fear because Mother Nyx watches over us, hearing our prayers in the night."

Katerina held tight to Baba as darkness descended all around them.

Twenty-Six

Corfu

October 1948

She met him on the path to school, just as she hoped she would.

"Did you eat anything this morning?" Katerina asked Marco as she fingered the pita and figs that were still safely hidden in her pocket from the night before.

"No." His eyes turned downcast. "Mama was already gone when I woke."

"Well, here. I have this for you." Katerina handed Marco the pita and figs that she had guarded in her pocket overnight. "Clotho sent it."

He broke the pita in half, wrapping one portion in paper and placing it in his pocket to save for his mother. The other half was devoured in an instant, his eyes wide and bright, a smile at last crossing his face. Together the children walked to the schoolhouse.

"Did you study?" she asked. Now that Katerina and Marco were twelve years old, it was their turn to recite Cavafy's "Ithaka" poem before the class.

Katerina had been practicing for days now. Marco had promised her that this time he, too, would study and learn the assignment.

He looked at her, silently untying and tying the rope he used to keep his pants up.

"Marco. Come on. You promised me you would try. Mr. Andonis will be so disappointed you didn't even try."

"There was a maestro last night," he said.

Her cheeks flushed. *How could I forget?* "Let me help you," she said. "I'll say it first and then you can repeat it back. Even if you remember just a small part of it, I'm sure Mr. Andonis will be really pleased. Ready, listen . . .

> "'As you set out for Ithaka
> hope your voyage is a long one,
> full of adventure, full of discovery.
> Laistrygonians and Cyclops,
> angry Poseidon—don't be afraid of them.'"

"Now let's say it together. Okay, 'As you set out for Ithaka . . .'"

But Marco had already lost interest as they approached the entrance to town. They were joined by several of the children who ran and skipped and spoke in a jumble, making it hard, if not impossible, for Marco to focus. Katerina refused to give up on him, continuing to recite lines even as Marco ran ahead with the other children. She was so consumed with getting Marco to focus that she didn't notice Mr. Andonis running toward the children. He waved his arms frantically and yelled again and again.

"No! Go back!" he shouted. "Go home. School is canceled today. Turn around and go home right now!"

But the schoolteacher's urgent tone and words had the opposite effect on the children. Instead of going back, they inched forward, eager and anxious to see what had caused this unexpected reprieve from a day of lessons.

"Katerina, go." His eyes bored into hers, imploring her. "Please." But it was too late.

Katerina could see beyond the schoolteacher's flailing arms, above his head to the ancient olive tree beyond, where Sunday after Sunday, generation after generation, the villagers would gather under its canopy of shiny leaves, offering shade and shelter from the blazing sun. She could see the sturdy trunk, home base for carefree games of tag, and her branches, elongated and sturdy, perfect for climbing and swinging. As Katerina looked beyond Mr. Andonis, she saw a body there, swaying ever so slightly back and forth, suspended from a rope tied around a branch and knotted around the person's neck.

Katerina inched closer, as did all the children. Mr. Andonis stood powerless in the middle of the road as the children crept slowly past him, toward the lifeless body. Only Marco stood in place, paralyzed. The breeze caught the woman's hair, lifting the brunette veil, streaked with premature gray, which had until that moment hung loose to her waist, obscuring her face.

"No," Katerina cried when she saw her. "No! No!" she yelled as she reached her arm out for Marco, who was inching backward as the other children surged forward.

Marco stood there silently as the screams and cries erupted all around them. By now more of the villagers had heard the news, many running toward the square.

Marco stood motionless as his mother's lifeless body hung from the yia-yia tree.

Katerina followed the thick twine with her eyes, wound several times across the branch and tied around Yianna's neck. She noticed, too, the handmade stool, carved from olive wood and knotted with rough twine to hold the legs in place. The stool, overturned on its side, just out of reach and inches from Yianna's dangling feet. Katerina wondered if in her final moments Yianna realized she had made a mistake and tried to will it upright again.

How could she leave Marco alone? Katerina thought, unsure if she said the words out loud.

"Her soul is tired, Katerina. . . . We can only hope she finds the strength

to come back to this life, for herself and for Marco." Clotho's words echoed in Katerina's ears. *"You and I will do our best to look after him, won't we? Marco is not alone. He has you and me."*

"Marco," Katerina said, turning to him. "Marco." The tears streamed down her cheeks, and she was unable to say anything more. Marco said nothing. He just stood there, staring at the lifeless body of his mother.

Katerina stepped closer to him. She placed her arm on his shoulder. He inched closer to her, shoulder to shoulder now. She took his hand in hers. Katerina stood beside her best friend in the middle of the dirt road as they looked up at the body of his mother dangling from the yia-yia tree.

⚮

As the villagers stood around, some crying, some praying for Yianna's soul as they made the sign of the cross, others shook their heads in whispered confirmation that Yianna had been insane all along.

"It's bad enough what her grandmother did, throwing her only child to the streets. This is even worse. Now that poor child has no one."

"Well, there's Clotho. Do you think she will take him?"

"And what would that be like for the poor child? Imagine that!"

Katerina, Maria, and Marco all huddled together with Clotho, who had come down the mountain, sensing something was wrong. Clotho enveloped Marco in her arms the way Yianna used to, the way a mother should. Marco looked up at her. There were no tears. Just a blank stare. This broke everyone's heart for the second time that morning.

It was Mr. Andonis who found the note tucked in Yianna's apron pocket, as Laki cut the rope and laid her down on the ground at the base of the tree. Mr. Andonis's face turned ashen as he read it. Without saying a word, he handed the paper to Laki, whose hands shook as he read the paper as well.

"What does it say?" The mayor pushed through the crowd. "What is it?" he more demanded than asked.

Laki handed the note back to Mr. Andonis, nodding in agreement for him to read it aloud, then bent over, burying his head in his hands.

Mr. Andonis lifted the paper to his face, his hands and voice trembling as he began to read.

I did this. Alone. Do not look for justice or blame. There is no one to blame but me. I know the church will not bury me because I took my life. Throw my body from the cliff down to the sea below. I don't care. There is nothing left for me.

I did this not to escape my pain, as I know so many of you will think and say. I did this for Marco, so he can escape my pain. So he can have a better life, a life that was promised to him long ago.

My dying wish is for Marco to be taken to the queen's paidopoleis. There he will have the mother he deserves. Queen Frederica will give him everything I could not. There my beautiful boy will finally have a chance at life. I can only give him poverty and hopelessness. It is my dying wish that you, my neighbors and friends, bring Marco to Queen Frederica's care. She will love him and provide for him like I never could, like Princess Alice promised their family would.

Marco, you are a good boy and I love you very much. Before today death was your prison. But no more. Now it is your release.

Everyone in the crowd gasped. Laki sobbed uncontrollably beside Yianna's body. Maria stood still, holding Katerina's hand as she watched her husband crying beside the body of the woman the villagers whispered about, the woman whose home they swore he had often been spotted leaving at daybreak.

Several of the villagers watched the public expression of Laki's grief, whispering to one another as they held their hands to their mouths, attempting to shield their words from Maria. Their actions instead had the opposite effect, magnifying the nature of their assumptions, their accusations.

Clotho left the children with Maria and walked to where Yianna's body lay in the dirt in the shadow of the tree. She fell to her knees. Tears spilled from her eyes into the soil as she took Yianna's cold, stiff hand in her own, willing her friend back to life, wishing she could conjure up the magic to bring her not only back to life but back to a time before all was taken from her. For once in her life, Clotho wished the rumors were true. If only she truly were the daughter of a sorceress. If only she could summon the spirits at will, rewriting the rules of life and death and all that was in between. Instead, she knelt beside the cold body of her friend and cried.

Twenty-Seven

Corfu

October 1948

It was decided that the women would bring Mama's body into the school-house for preparation for burial. There would be no funeral for his mother, as the Greek Orthodox Church stated that anyone who committed suicide was not worthy of entry into Christ's kingdom, having committed a crime against the Holy Spirit. Likewise, she would not be buried inside the Christian cemetery, so the villagers instead agreed to lay her to rest in a simple grave outside the cemetery gate.

The villagers hastily buried Mama that very afternoon. Marco stood numb over his mother's grave, not knowing what to say or do. Clotho was beside him. Both remained silent as the dirt was tossed on the flimsy box that served as his mother's final resting place.

"Let's go," Marco said, turning to Clotho even before the last of the dirt was piled on the casket. "Please. Let's go."

"I'll come see you tomorrow." Katerina hugged him tight. At first his arms lay stiff at his sides. "I'll be there bright and early. You can't get rid of me, you know." With those words he threw his arms around Katerina. She hugged him back with all her might.

"Do you really think she's going to hell for what she did?" Marco asked Clotho as they started up the hill. "Like those ladies said. I heard them speaking with Father Emanuel. They said she'll go to hell for her sin. For taking her own life. Do you really think so?"

"Not at all," Clotho said. "Your mother was an angel on this earth, and she will forever be an angel in the heavens. She wanted so badly to help you, to take care of you and to protect you. But her grief and her sadness made it so very hard for her. She's free now, Marco. And she can watch over you and your brother, the way she was meant to. The way she always wanted to."

"Do you really think so, Clotho?"

"I know so, sweet boy."

✆

After the burial the men gathered over coffee and ouzo at the kafenio, discussing what was to come next. All except for Laki, who claimed he needed to get to his boat and pull in his nets. Not one person believed him. But not one person challenged him.

"But shouldn't he stay with Clotho? She doesn't have children of her own. She can care for him," Mr. Andonis argued. "They were friends. Yianna trusted her."

"I understand your point, but Yianna clearly stated in her note that she wanted the child brought to the paidopoleis. How can we deny her this final wish? They'll feed and educate him and, perhaps most importantly, protect him. That's what she wanted for her son. We can't change that," the mayor replied.

"Don't you think it would be better this way? To have him stay here?" Mr. Andonis pressed again. "That child has had so much loss. It's not right to take away the one familiar thing he has left. Life here in the village, with his friends and Clotho."

"No, I don't. I really don't. We don't know what the next few days will bring. Just last week there was a report of a prison break at Lazaretto, and yesterday partisans were spotted in the hills of Palaiokastritsa. The radio report said several smaller villages have emptied already, people abandoning their homes to stay with friends and family closer to the shore towns and Corfu Town. Even the monastery closed its doors as a precaution. They think some of the escapees may be hiding in the caves and water grottos. We don't know if they'll try to come up north," the mayor cautioned.

"Well, if they're trying to get into Albania, there's a good chance they'll try to head up this way. It's a much shorter journey here across the channel. They'd be found out in an instant if they tried to cross from port or closer to town," another fisherman said.

"And that's my point exactly," the mayor replied, running his fingers through his hair. "It won't be safe for any of us here if they come north. What happens next? Who will take responsibility for Marco then? We don't know how we'll protect our own children. You've heard the stories as well as I have. You know what they've done to villages all across the country. Children, women, entire families . . . gone. How can we in good conscience let him stay with Clotho when we don't know if he'll be safe here? There's no point in debating this. It was her dying wish, a mother's dying wish. You read the note and heard it exactly as I did. There's nothing for us to consider or debate. Yianna made the choice for us when she hung herself on that tree."

"I still think we should think about this," Mr. Andonis insisted once more. "Mr. Mayor, don't you think perhaps in her state of mind, Yianna was not rational in her thoughts? Don't you think that maybe in this case, she wasn't properly equipped to decide what was best for Marco?"

Just then, an elderly fisherman stood from the table where he had been furiously fingering his worry beads. He leaned toward Mr. Andonis as he spoke. "There is nothing to think about. All that matters is that Yianna is dead and we are all witnesses to her dying wish. Do you want the responsibility of having your own family stalked by Yianna's unsettled soul?

Because I don't. I want no part of it." He slammed his fist on the table and walked into the kafenio to get a glass of water.

All eyes were on the old man. No one spoke as they digested his cautionary words.

At last the mayor broke the silence. "I'll take him. Let him spend one last night here, with Clotho, and then I'll take him to the paidopoleis in Benitses in the morning and be back by lunch to monitor the situation. If there's partisan activity nearby, we'll leave together, as a village. It's safer that way."

The men looked at one another. One by one they nodded their heads in agreement.

"All right then," Mr. Andonis said. "It's decided. You are a good man, Mr. Mayor. And we are lucky to have you." He placed his arm on the mayor's back and toasted to him with his near empty glass of ouzo.

Twenty-Eight

Corfu

October 1948

Without a word to any of the other villagers, Katerina and Mama began to make their way toward home. It was now close to dinnertime, and Katerina had eaten nothing since that morning. But when they arrived home, Mama opened the door, walked inside, and slid silently beneath the sheets of her bed.

After a short while, Katerina went to her side. "Mama, are you all right?"

But there was no response from Mama; she just stared silently at the wall. "Are you all right, Mama?" Katerina repeated again. "Can I get you anything?"

"I'm fine," she replied at last, her voice no more than a whisper.

Tired and hungry, Katerina went back outside and hopped up on the garden wall, waiting. She was unsure of what she was waiting for—for Mama to rise from her bed, for Baba to come home, or for it to be morning so she could see Marco. She sat there in disbelief, trying to grasp the enormity of what had happened and what tomorrow would bring.

"Katerina." She heard his voice, thinking perhaps she must have dreamed him there. "Katerina." She heard it again. It was not a dream. She jumped from the wall and ran and threw her arms around Marco's neck. Clotho stood beside him, her hand on his shoulder.

"I'm leaving tonight," Marco said.

Katerina pulled away, looking from Marco's face to Clotho's. "Tonight?" She could barely manage a whisper.

"The mayor says it will be too dangerous to go in the morning." Marco's voice was flat, devoid of emotion.

"Dangerous, how?" Katerina asked, looking to Clotho for answers.

"The mayor came to the house," Clotho replied. "He mentioned partisan activity in the mountains and said it would be better to leave now." Clotho never removed her hand from Marco's shoulder. "The mayor will take Marco to the paidopoleis tonight."

Just then Baba arrived home. He looked even more ashen and shaken than earlier. He carried his fishing basket in one hand, the other hand stuffed deep into his pocket. "Where is your mother?" he asked Katerina.

"She's in bed. I think she's sick. She hasn't gotten up since we got home."

Baba said nothing. He took the basket of fish to the outdoor kitchen area and set to work, scaling and gutting the fish as he spoke. "I was down at the port and we just got word. The police in Corfu Town sent officers here. They caught a few of the escaped prisoners in the caves of Palaiokastritsa, but it's worse than we thought. The Communist navy sent boats from Zakynthos and Cephalonia to support the escaped partisans and bring them back to the mainland. The navy boats were captured, with none of the prisoners on board. The escaped partisans are still scattered across the island. Police think they're hiding in the mountains, here, in the north. Already there was a problem in Peritheia. A farmer was found murdered. They came on his land and asked for food and water. He refused them, saying they were a disgrace to the flag. And they killed him. The man was sixty years old. Some of the smaller villages are telling their residents to leave, to go down the mountains to the coast and to friends and family in Corfu Town until the threat passes." Baba finished cleaning the fish and put them one by one in a scalding hot frying pan placed on the outdoor fire.

"The mayor said the same thing." Clotho kept her hand on Marco's shoulder.

"When exactly?" Katerina asked Marco, biting her lip to keep from crying. "When are you going?"

"After the sun sets," Marco replied. "He said it will be safer for us in the dark, that he knows the back roads and he can get me to Queen Frederica, even in the dark."

Katerina looked out beyond the garden toward the sea where the pink-and-gold tinged sky confirmed that her time with Marco was running short. Never more had she wished Baba's words about the power and magic of the night were true.

"Then you have a few minutes to sit and eat with us," Baba said as he motioned to the table. "Here. Come. Let's send you off to the queen with a full belly, shall we?" He forced a smile as he passed the plate of fish around. Marco reached his hand to grab one, then suddenly stopped. He put his hand at his side again. "No, thank you."

Clotho got down on her knees before Marco. Taking both of his hands in hers, she smiled at him. "It's all right. You don't have to worry. And you don't have to hide. Not anymore." She lifted his hands to her lips and kissed them. She smiled broader and brought his hands to her face, placing his palms on her cheeks.

He looked into her eyes.

"I promise you. It's all right," she said once again. "She wants you to be happy, Marco. She wants you to be free."

Marco nodded. He reached his hand out and took a fish from the plate. And then he took another.

Just then, Mama emerged from the house. Although it was quite warm out, she had wrapped herself in a blanket.

Katerina walked to her mother's side. She reached up and took her hand.

"Marco is leaving tonight."

Mama nodded and wrapped the blanket tighter around herself. Marco walked over to her and hugged her around the waist. Mama stood motionless for a moment and then she hugged him back, leaning her cheek on his head. "I'm so sorry, Marco. I'm so, so sorry."

After a few moments, Mama pulled away from his hug. She took him by the shoulders and stared into his eyes. "Never forget how much your mother loved you, Marco. She loved you with all of her heart. She loved you more than anything. You may not understand this now, but I want you to always remember that she put you first. It's true. Every single thing she did was for you. Right up until the end. She fought for you. She fought as hard and as long as she could. You may not understand it now, but you will one day. I promise."

Clotho walked over to where Maria stood holding Marco. She placed her hand on his back. "We have to go." She spoke softly. Her words were deafening.

Marco turned to face Katerina, his face now tear-streaked.

Katerina was the first to speak. "It will be okay. You're going to be okay."

"How do you know for sure?" he asked.

"I know it in my heart," she said as she placed her fingertips on her heart. "Go, stay with Queen Frederica. She'll take good care of you. And then you can come home to me." Although her heart ached, she smiled broadly for him. "I wonder if it will be like the palace again. The one your mother lived in when she was a baby."

"Do you really think so?" he asked.

"Maybe. And maybe they'll remember your family and even give you your own throne." She giggled now, burying her face in her hands. They laughed together like they used to, before their innocence was lost, along with his entire family.

Clotho gently touched his shoulder. "It's time."

At once the tears sprang to each child's eyes.

"I'm going to miss you," Katerina said. "You're my very best friend in the world." She looked down at the floor. "My only friend."

"You're my best friend too," he said, pulling at his pants. "Actually, Katerina," he said as he looked down at the ground, kicking at the dirt with his bare feet. He tied and retied the rope and then looked up at her as he bit his lip. "You're not just my best friend. You're my family. The only family I have now." His tears began to fall faster now. One by one they slid down his cheek, streaming down his face. He tried to wipe them away with the back of his hand, which left a streak of dirt smeared across his cheek. "Will you promise me something, Katerina?"

"Of course. Anything." She held tighter to his arm.

"Promise me you'll always be my family. So I have a home and someone to come back to." He bit his lip harder now, but it did no good. There was no stopping the tears that he had kept bottled up for so long. Marco had been so brave for his mother, tamping down all of his own emotions so that she might feel something again other than loss and pain and numbness. So that she might feel something for him. But in the end, his bravery, stoicism, and sacrifice were not enough to bring her back to him. And now she was gone forever. "Promise me you'll be my family. Because otherwise I'll have nothing."

"Of course. I promise," Katerina said as she threw her arms around him again and held on this time as if she might not ever let go. "Of course." She clung to him, not caring about appearances or her mother's warnings about how proper, virtuous young ladies behaved. It didn't matter, not at all. Because she knew that this was where she belonged. Despite all they had experienced together—tragedies, adventures, silliness, and sadness—it was always the same. She felt safe with Marco beside her. And now, as she hugged him close, it was so very clear to Katerina; he would always be her best friend. He would always be her home. "And you promise me that no matter how nice your life with Queen Frederica is, you'll come back here, and to me."

All he could do was nod.

"You have to come back," she insisted, shaking his arms, needing to see his smile one last time. But Marco just stared down at the floor. She leaned in and whispered in his ear. "You promised me you would teach me to swim. You promised, right?" She smiled and squeezed his hand again. "You can't leave me here like this. I'll sink like a stone."

His face at last erupted in a smile. He hugged Katerina close. "I promise."

He wiped the wetness from his face again with the back of his hand and then reached out for Clotho. Hand in hand, they walked out the gate, away from Katerina and toward Marco's new life.

Katerina stood statue still and watched them go. The tears came heavier now. She wrapped herself around her mother's waist, pressing her face into her apron. The fabric smelled of smoky cooking fires whose stubborn remnants permeated the fabric. She inhaled deeply, the way Marco taught her when he insisted the mere scent of a meal cooking was enough to satiate his hunger. Nothing. She felt empty and depleted. Just as before.

Mama wrapped her arms around Katerina and together they watched Marco and Clotho walk away into the night.

After a few moments, Baba spoke. "Maria, we have so much to talk about. There's so much I need to say."

But Mama said nothing. She just turned and went back into the house, sliding once again silently between the sheets.

Katerina felt as if something heavy and unseen had attached itself to her, weighing her down. Slowly, she made her way over to the garden wall. She sat there, alone in her thoughts, attempting to process and understand all that had happened since this morning, all that had changed, all they had lost.

Dusk had settled in, and in the distance the sun, a deep rust-colored orb, sank low on the horizon. Just as the last glimmers of light reflected and danced across the sea, Katerina once again began to cry. It was deep and guttural, an aching cry, and it surprised her. She was unaware that she was capable of feeling such emotions, that these emotions even existed. This was not merely sadness. This was not merely pain. This was something more, something she could not explain or understand. It was as if something deep inside of her had been released, unleashed into the world before she was able to grasp what it meant or what it was. All she knew was that it existed. And because of this, Katerina understood that she was now forever changed.

She stayed there on the wall until the last glint of daylight was a memory. Over and over again she repeated the words her parents had recited through the years to comfort and calm her in the night. *"Never forget, you are never alone in the dark. There is nothing to fear because Mother Nyx is always above, watching you and protecting you in the dark."*

Katerina sank to her knees and began to pray.

"I know I'm not a mother, but please, Nyx," she whispered, "please protect Marco and bring him home to me. He doesn't have a mother to pray for him anymore."

Twenty-Nine

Corfu

October 1948

"Katerina. Wake up."

She opened her eyes, thinking she was dreaming. It was barely light out. Thea Voula's rooster had not even crowed his good morning yet.

"Wake up," Baba said again as he shook her.

Katerina opened her eyes and looked around. What she saw made no sense. Mama was stuffing linens and clothing and the keepsake box into a suitcase.

"What's going on?" She sat up and rubbed the sleep from her eyes. "What's happening?"

"It's the partisans," Baba answered. "They're here. They've been spotted near the beach. We don't know how many, but we can't take any chances. We need to leave. We'll be safer in the city. There's no way to protect ourselves here."

"Mama." Katerina looked at her mother.

"Katerina," she said, her voice barely a whisper. "Listen to your father. Please."

Katerina shot up from bed and dressed in an instant.

"Help your mother pack up whatever you can. Hurry, please. I'm running to the vegetable cellar and then we'll go. We'll leave with everyone from town. We'll all stay together until we can get to the coast and to one of the larger towns farther south, closer to Corfu Town."

Katerina did as she was told. She climbed up on the bed and grabbed the icons from the wall, along with the dried Palm Sunday crosses, and handed them to her mother.

∾

As Katerina and Maria packed up what they could from the house, Laki went down to the root cellar to see if there was any food they could bring with them. He scanned the shelves, a few onions and potatoes. He then turned to the shelves where Maria kept her gardening equipment. He could see a metal spade glinting in the darkness. Then he heard the heavy-footed crunch of gravel and twigs beyond the cellar, and as he reached his arm out to grab the spade, the cellar door burst open. Laki spun around, squinting, praying for his eyes to adjust. It was a man, tall and slim, silhouetted against the backlight.

"What do you want?" Laki demanded. "Leave us in peace." He kept his voice measured. He did not want to alarm or alert Katerina and Maria.

"This is my home. We have nothing of value here." He took two steps toward the man.

The man backed up, out of the cellar and into the morning light.

"Do I know you?" Laki asked. The man's hair was matted, his face covered in a graying beard and filth. Laki couldn't place him, but this man was uncomfortably familiar to him. "Do I know you?" he repeated.

The man looked at him, pulling at his beard and nodding his head.

"Laki. It's me. Panos. I was the schoolteacher here." The man stood his ground and didn't come any closer. "Before my political beliefs were found offensive and I was relieved of my position."

"Panos. What are you doing here?"

"You know exactly what I'm doing here, Laki. Let's not pretend." He laughed then, an unsettled laugh that unnerved Laki. "I just need something to eat."

Laki knew what happened to Greeks who were caught helping or feeding Communists. In the government's eyes there was no distinction between being a Communist and helping one.

"Just give me something to eat and some water and I'll leave. You have my word. There are more of us. I can't promise you that the others will extend the same courtesy."

Laki dug the bread and olives from his bag and handed them to Panos. "There's a jug of water beside the well. It's too heavy to carry. We'll leave it. You can have it. The water is fresh."

"Take your family and go," Panos said as he ripped into the bread with his teeth.

Just then, Katerina came bounding down the garden steps. Laki called out to her, "Katerina, stay where you are. I'm coming. Stay right there. It's time to leave."

Panos looked to Laki and put his fingers to his lips, motioning for him to go. Laki nodded, noticing the knife tucked in his waistband. He began running up the stairs, and as he neared the top, he shouted to Katerina and Mama. "Let's go! Come on!"

Laki made no mention of his encounter with Panos to the girls, or to anyone. They walked briskly along the road, meeting other families along the way. By the time they reached the center of town, meeting at the kafenio as the men had decided the night before, it seemed as if the entire town had emptied. The mayor was seated at a table, smoking cigarettes and speaking with the other men, who gazed out across the sea, debating whether they could safely evacuate the village by boat instead of walking.

"Absolutely not," the mayor insisted. "We can't fit everyone and we can't leave anyone behind."

"It's a moot point anyway. Look," Laki said, pointing to the east. "The clouds are moving in low and fast. It won't be safe to take the boats out; the winds are stirring up the whitecaps. We'll walk. We'll stay together and we'll walk."

Katerina came over to where the mayor was standing. Stamati stood beside him, carrying the homemade bow and arrow that he used to torture frogs and stray cats. Katerina tugged at the mayor's sleeve. "Mr. Mayor . . ."

"Katerina?" His eyes were bloodshot, his face, typically clean-shaven, covered in stubble.

"Was it a palace?" Katerina asked.

The mayor's eyebrows knotted in confusion.

"Was it a palace?" she asked again.

"I don't understand what you mean."

"You took Marco to Queen Frederica last night. Was it a palace? Was it a beautiful palace where he'll be loved and safe?"

Everyone, including the men who were planning the best way to evacuate, stopped to watch the exchange.

The mayor inhaled deeply and then exhaled again. A guttural noise escaped his lips as his chest heaved up and down in rapid succession. He stared at Katerina with his bloodshot eyes. A single tear escaped down his cheek. He moved quickly to wipe the remnants away.

"Did you see Queen Frederica? Did you tell her to take good care of him?" Katerina persisted.

But before the mayor could respond, shouts erupted from across the square. Three men were walking toward the villagers. One had a gun that he held out, pointing it at the crowd.

"What is this?" The mayor stood.

The men of the village all stood as well, facing the three strangers. At once everyone understood who they were, what they were. They wore filthy clothes that hung from their bodies, their faces and hands crusted with dirt.

The men of the village took a few steps forward as the women fell behind the men, grabbing and positioning the children behind them.

"What do you want?" Laki was the first to speak. "You have no business with us, with our families."

"You're no use to us," one of the men said. "Get on your way like you were planning to."

Then another of the men spoke. "We'll let you get on your way, but first give us your weapons. Hand them over or we'll shoot you all. The women and children too."

"We don't have any weapons." It was the mayor who spoke. "We don't have anything and we don't mean you any harm. Just let us leave."

The three men looked at one another, whispering among themselves. The tallest of the three pointed to a table at the edge of the café. "Place your valuables on the table. One at a time. Now."

Mr. Andonis spoke next. "Can't you see this is not a wealthy village? We don't have anything of value."

The man with the gun pointed it at Mr. Andonis. "I see wedding rings and crosses. They'll do no good on corpses. Take them off and put them on the table and then you can leave."

The mayor looked around to everyone assembled in the square and nodded for them to do as they were told. One by one, they stepped up to the table and put their wedding bands, crosses, and bracelets in a pile before stepping back to join the cluster of their friends and neighbors.

"Is that everything?" the man with the gun demanded.

"Yes," the mayor said. "That's all we have. There is nothing else."

"Leave." The man waved his gun. "Go."

"Please," the mayor said, motioning to everyone with his hands, a white streak on his ring finger where his wedding band had been. "Please, this way. Let's make our way toward the village entrance and down the mountain."

For the most part everyone was silent at first. But as the group began to walk past the partisans and away from the square, a few began to pray out loud, while others whispered to one another. Thea Voula's voice could be heard above the rest.

"Oh, dear God. Take me now. I can't take much more of this." Voula began to moan as she shuffled along. "It was Yianna. This is her." She leaned in to her husband, who ignored her. Finding no audience in her husband, she turned to another woman walking beside her and began to moan again, this time a bit louder. "This is Yianna's doing, I tell you. What she did was a sin against God and man. She opened the gates of hell and brought the evil spirits here to curse us."

Laki, Maria, and Katerina walked silently among the villagers, not reacting to Voula's tirade, pretending not to hear her.

"It's fitting that she'll rot in hell for her sin," Voula went on.

Laki could stand no more. "Enough," he said through clenched teeth. "For once in your life just stop with your acid tongue and lies."

"Fine for you to say," Voula snapped at him. "Lord knows it's your guilty conscience at work. This is your doing. All of it. All those nights you slithered into her bed. What promises did you make her at night that you broke in the light of day? It's blood on your hands, and now the rest of us are suffering because of it."

Hearing the commotion, the man with the gun walked toward them. "What's this about blood on your hands?" he asked Laki.

The mayor hurried to catch up with them. "It's nothing. Just a misunderstanding. Just a neighborly misunderstanding."

"A misunderstanding?" He waved his gun toward Voula, who leaned heavily on her walking stick.

"She's a silly gossip who doesn't know what she's saying," Laki responded.

"It's nothing," the mayor said again.

"That's for me to decide." The partisan reached his arm out, blocking Voula's path. "What do you mean he has blood on his hands?"

Voula looked around, perhaps unaware of the power given to her words, or perhaps embolden by it. "His mistress killed herself yesterday.

Hung herself from a tree, leaving her child an orphan and bringing Lord knows what evil spirits into our midst by damning herself to hell."

The man turned to Laki. "This woman killed herself because of you?" he asked, waving his gun.

Laki stood tall. "No. No. It's not true. Don't believe a word of it." He shook his head.

The man walked up to Laki, chest to chest now. "Why should I believe you over her? I think you're a liar."

"I am no such thing." Laki held his head high.

"I'm not so sure." The man waved the pistol at him again. "Come with me."

"There's no need for this," Laki said. "I haven't done anything wrong."

"Then you have nothing to worry about. I want to make sure you're not a liar. And then you can be on your way. But if you lied to me . . ." He laughed, a deep, disturbing laugh. "Well . . ."

Laki looked back at Katerina and Maria. "It's okay," he mouthed to them.

The man leaned in and patted Laki down. "Empty your pockets."

Laki looked up at him.

"Empty your pockets," the man repeated, louder now, waving his gun in the air.

Laki exhaled and closed his eyes. He placed his hands in his pockets, preparing to pull the fabric inside out. But before he did, Laki did one thing more.

"Katerina!" he shouted, loud enough for her to hear. "Katerina. Remember Orpheus. Promise me you'll always remember Orpheus. Have faith and look ahead. Always. I love you, my sweet girl, and I will always be behind you."

The man looked at Laki, confused for a moment by the distraction. But as Laki turned his pockets inside out, the dead soldier's ring fell to the ground.

"I knew you were a liar," he said, before shooting Laki in the head.

Part Four

Thirty

Buckingham Palace
November 1947

"There you are, my dear." Queen Frederica walked over to where Alice was standing, admiring the wedding cake. It was polite conversation more than anything. No one would have trouble spotting Alice among the wedding guests that day, as she was wearing a rather plain suit of gray velvet with a matching hat and simple pearls in a sea of silk and furs, tiaras, and jewels.

"It's a bit much, don't you think?" Alice asked, taking a deep drag of her cigarette, waving it toward the cake that was more than nine feet tall, covered in fresh fruit and embellished with the crowns and signets of the royal households that were now joined in marriage. "You've heard what they've taken to calling it, haven't you?" she asked, taking another deep drag.

"No." Frederica smiled. "I haven't heard."

"They're calling it the ten-thousand-mile cake, since the fruits and sugar and such had to be shipped from around the world to make it. Even as much of England still rations tiny portions of sugar and fruit."

"Well, that's the world we are living in, isn't it? Even Lilibet used ration coupons to purchase the satin for that beautiful dress. And her ring is stunning as well. You had it made, did you not?"

Alice pursed her lips together, her forehead wrinkling at the memory. "Yes. Philip requested the design. I simply offered him some of the family pieces. It's beautiful, but we had quite a shock when I went to Paris to retrieve the jewels from the vault and found Andrew had sold some of the stones years ago and had them replaced with paste."

Frederica's eyes widened.

"He is still managing ways to surprise us, even after his death." Alice fingered the triple strand of pearls adorning her neck. "And then of course Philip's sisters had a fit that their inheritance was to be used to secure Philip's marriage. Eventually Theodora and Sophie came to their senses, but Margarita was dramatic as ever, even threatening legal action. It was a mess, I tell you. But it's all sorted now," she said with a wave of her hand.

"The ceremony was beautiful," Frederica added, a not-so-subtle change of subject. "I was moved to see Philip still makes the sign of the cross in the Orthodox manner."

"Yes," Alice agreed, the expression on her face and in her eyes softening again.

"Of all of Paul's first cousins, I must admit I've always felt a special affinity for Philip. Maybe it's because we were both considered somewhat as outsiders. I have such fond memories of Philip and me and our Greek lessons." Frederica laughed. "When Paul and I were first married, I was afraid I would never master the language. Do you remember how Philip and I would try to speak together? How we would stumble and fall into a heap of frustrated laughter? It seemed impossible."

"Anything is possible with faith and dedication," Alice added as she lit another cigarette.

Frederica took Alice's arm and together they walked across the room, past the generations of royals and well-wishers and family. They stopped at a window overlooking the gardens.

"I've thought of you often these past months," Frederica said. "I've always admired your work with the Red Cross during the occupation, all those children you fed and sheltered. And when I learned of how you hid the Jewish family in your home from the Nazis, it inspired me even more. There is such need, Alice. We keep building more paidopoleis, and each time we do, it is not enough. I wonder if it will ever be enough."

"There is no greater gift than to help those in need," Alice responded. "I feel God has spoken to me, Frederica. Something happened to me while I was on Corfu. I left part of myself on that island. I can't explain it, and I'm not sure I understand it."

There was silence between them for a moment. A server walked past. Frederica placed her glass on his tray and then fixed her gaze on Alice again. "I'm sorry that the girls can't be with you here today," she said. "I know it must be difficult."

Alice pursed her lips. "Who would have imagined that all my girls would be banned from their own brother's wedding? Theodora and Sophie sulked and moaned for a few days. Eventually they got on with it. But Margarita . . ." Alice closed her eyes and shook her head. "Margarita vowed to confront Philip, but I wouldn't hear of it. I won't have them breathing a word of insolence to their brother or upsetting him in any way. It's neither the time nor the place. It's simply too soon to think that wives of German officers might be welcomed in England without raising eyebrows or causing an international incident. I hope with time, as the wounds of the war begin to heal, that they can come visit their brother and we can be a family again. But not now. Not today."

"Give it time. I remember when I first arrived in Greece from Germany. I was so in love and so excited about my new life. I wanted nothing more than for the people of my adopted home to love me as much as I instantly loved them." Frederica looked out the window, gazing across the expansive lawns of the palace, lost in her memory for a moment before her gaze fell again on Alice. "It was hurtful to read the headlines, the articles insisting that since my grandfather was the Kaiser, I could never be Greek."

Frederica's brow furrowed, recalling all the times she had worked tire-
lessly, traveling in horrid conditions, spending days away from her own
children to bring food and medicine to the poorest and most remote villages, only to have the left-wing newspapers plaster their pages with hateful
rhetoric. "Just give it a little time," Frederica repeated, her voice layered with
compassion. Although she knew that even now, even so many years and
good deeds later, the German blood in her veins was often still weaponized
as a political tool by anti-monarchists.

"I told my girls I will be their eyes and ears. I've been keeping a journal since I arrived. I promised I would write down every detail for them."
Alice's mouth unfurled at the corners, revealing a slight, tight smile even
as the crease in her forehead deepened. Like everything in Alice's life,
even this time of great joy and celebration was tempered by an underlying
sadness.

Frederica's eyes twinkled as a broad smile erupted on her face. "I will
take it for you. I'm going to visit my parents after the wedding and I will
hand-deliver your journal. I promise to sit down with the girls and tell them
every glorious detail. They'll feel like they were right here with us, sipping
champagne and feasting on that legendary cake."

"How is Paul?" Alice asked, switching topics.

"He is doing as well as he can"—Frederica paused—"under the circumstances. He so very much wanted to be here and celebrate. You know how
fond he has always been of Philip. But the situation at home is getting
more difficult by the day and he simply could not leave. What about you?
What will you do after the celebrations? Will you stay here?"

"Philip asked me to stay, but this is not my home, and it's not my place.
I'll go back to my flat in Athens. At least for now."

"Will you come visit us at Mon Repos? I know how much you loved
your time there. Maybe Philip will bring Lilibet? I will ask him to. Wouldn't
it be lovely for her to see where her husband was born?"

Alice fingered her pearls. "Yes. I would like that very much."

"We have a paidopoleis on Corfu now as well, not far from Mon Repos in Benitses," Frederica continued. "There is such need, it breaks my heart. Paul said it was the time he spent with you and your family at Mon Repos that made him fall in love with Corfu. He said those memories, those times were magical."

"Yes," Alice replied. "Corfu is a magical place, blessed and protected by Saint Spyridon himself."

"He told me once about a young woman who worked with you. She made such an impression on him. Paul must have been about twenty at the time. She was a maid, a sweet young girl with a daughter of her own. He told me how he loved watching Philip and this little girl run from room to room, hiding behind the curtains and squealing with laughter when they were found. On his last visit with you at Mon Repos, this young woman packed his bags. And when they were opened in Athens, among his clothing was an icon of Saint Spyridon that she had tucked away in his bag for him."

Alice tilted her head, her eyebrow arched as she ran her finger up and down along the smooth pearls.

"Paul carries that icon with him to this day," Frederica said, her eyes misting over. "With all we have seen and lived through, perhaps it is Saint Spyridon who has looked after us and kept us safe in these difficult times."

"Yes, my dear. My faith in the saint is strong and I think it is quite possible," Alice replied.

"Do you recall the woman's name? Perhaps when we go back we can thank her, tell her how much the icon has meant to us."

Alice looked at Frederica but remained silent.

"Do you know what became of her?" Frederica repeated.

"So much has happened since those years on Mon Repos. There has been joy, like today, and also much pain and damage, I fear. I know you know I was unwell for a time. I spent several years in a hospital in Switzerland. I'm afraid it was all too much for me and I needed to rest. I needed to rest my body and my mind and, most importantly, my soul."

"Yes. I understand. But you are well now."

"Thank God. I am very well now. But those years, and those doctors." Alice shook her head and stared out through the window, across the gardens. "I spent some time alone in Germany after, to settle back into daily life. And then Cecilie died . . ." Alice's voice trailed off. There was silence between the women for a few moments while she collected her thoughts. "I'm well now. But getting here took its toll." She looked now at Frederica, wondering if she understood. The confused look on Frederica's face showed she did not.

"Though I gained my health and life again, I lost a part of me along the way as well. I lost my memories, Frederica." Alice fumbled to take a cigarette from her pack, then struggled to light it. At last she managed it, taking a drawn-out drag and exhaling long and deep before she spoke again. "I don't remember much of our time on Corfu. Not all has been lost. I remember how happy we were. I remember that beautiful house, the verandas and the views, and that lush, beautiful garden. Oh, how I loved that garden and the flowers: roses, wisteria, gardenias, and lilies. It was glorious. And I remember feeling that at last our family was complete and that Saint Spyridon answered my prayers with the arrival of Philip. You can't imagine the shock I felt when they told me I had given birth to him on the dining room table. At first I thought it was a joke."

Alice looked across the room to where Philip was escorting Lilibet to the cake. "It was Dr. Freud who told me the memory loss was self-preservation, that the mind erases trauma to protect us. Did you know that?"

Frederica shook her head. "What about the night you fled, thinking your life was in danger? Do you remember that?"

"No. I have no memory of that night. None at all. I remember being on the *Calypso* as we sailed away from Corfu. I remember praying on my knees at daybreak as my boy slept beside me in a bed made from an orange crate."

"An orange crate?" Frederica laughed. "Oh my."

"Yes." Alice smiled. "I think losing my memories was perhaps God's way of protecting me."

"I understand," Frederica said, shaking her head and reaching out, placing her hand on Alice's elbow. "But for me, no matter how painful it is, and it has been so very painful, I don't want to forget. I want to remember it all. I want to remember every face of every child who cried in my arms. I want to remember every face of every mother who told me what it was to watch her children suffer, who told me what it was to have their children murdered before their eyes, for the mere fact that her husband supported the monarchy. All of it. As much as it pains me, as much as I will be haunted by them for the rest of my life, I don't want to forget a single moment. I can't forget them."

"I will pray for the Lord to protect and preserve your memory, Frederica. I know what it is to lose a child. After Cecilie died, I heard the whispers, what people said behind my back even as I buried my child and her children. *Mad*, they called me. They expected me to break down again, that Cecilie's death would kill what little life I had managed to resurrect for myself. But they were wrong. Cecilie's death reminded me that I needed to live, to be present in my children's lives, to be a mother to Philip. And to use my time on this earth wisely and in faith."

Alice motioned for Frederica to walk with her. "Come." Arm in arm, they strolled past kings and queens and princes and princesses and dukes and duchesses and royalty from nations across Europe and beyond. Alice and Frederica watched and beamed with pride as Philip, once known as the tiny prince of Corfu, pulled from his side the royal sword of Mountbatten. As Elizabeth stood beside him smiling, Philip raised the sword and sliced into the ten-thousand-mile wedding cake.

Thirty-One

Corfu

June 1950

It had been nine months since the Communist leaders took to the radio announcing they were ceasing hostility, effectively ending the war as thousands of partisans fled Greece, disappearing beyond the Albanian and Bulgarian borders. All along the north and even as far south as the central mountain region and Athens, life was forever changed for so many. Villages once teeming with life and laughter now sat empty and quiet. Some for a short time as families slowly made their way back home; some for forever as others realized there was nothing and no one left for them to return to.

And beyond the physical loss of lives and homes, the war had left a lingering toll on those lucky enough to survive. Even on Corfu, where the visible damage from the war was minimal and where cheers reverberated along the alleyways as the Communists were driven out. Still, wounds had been left simmering beneath the surface, changing the fabric of daily life for so many. Scattered across the island were families left forever fractured not only by the loss of life but by loved ones lost to opposing ideologies.

And nowhere was the lingering effect of the war more evident than in Benitses, where the doors of Frederica's paidopoleis remained open to continue caring for the littlest victims of the war and to help families left struggling.

Slowly over time, life once again began to resemble something close to normal in Corfu. The cafés along the Liston once again filled with islanders savoring their afternoon coffee as the music of the Corfu Philharmonic mixed with the squeals of children playing cricket in the expanse of Spianada Square overlooking Garitsa bay. Along the coast, hotels began to welcome visitors, and in Ipsos, the French businessman who had fallen in love with Corfu so many years before finally fulfilled his dream and broke ground on a grand luxury resort to be called Club Mediterranee. And beyond the Liston, as they had for generations before, the faithful knelt in prayer inside the incense-filled Saint Spyridon Church, praying for the saint's protection and guidance.

Katerina and Mama exited the church of Saint Spyridon and walked out into the street. It was their weekly tradition to attend services and then stop at Olympia, the café where mother and daughter had found work cleaning the kitchen and toilets at night.

The owner, Manoli, with his jet-black brows and mustache, always reserved a table for Katerina and Mama. It was difficult to find work after the war, with so many in need. But Manoli, who had lost his own brother at the hands of partisans, felt pity for the young widow when she showed up in her black veil and mourning dress explaining that she was desperate for work and could not return to the village where her husband had been murdered.

Although Mama urged Katerina to go back to school and finish her lessons, and despite the fact that Katerina dreamed of one day continuing her education, Katerina insisted on working beside her mother. With all they had suffered through, endured, and lost, Katerina hoped that in some small way she might help ease her mother's burden if she stayed and helped lighten her workload. At first they managed to eke out a living, working together through the night, returning home with the sunrise to sleep side by side in their tiny rented room in an alley behind the arched promenade. But then over time, Katerina began to see the changes in her mother, the exhaustion that no amount of sleep could erase, the lack of appetite that no favorite food could entice. Katerina watched helplessly as Mama withdrew further and further into herself.

"We'll go to Tinos together one day, Mama. Just as we planned." Katerina held Mama's face in her hands, staring into her eyes, searching for the mother who had once cared for her with such tenderness, missing her and longing for her. "I can't wait for you to show me your beautiful island. And we'll go pray together at Panagia's icon. We'll pray together and she'll watch over us."

Mama nodded her head slightly, the shadow of a smile crossing her lips. But Katerina had learned to recognize the signs, this facade of a smile, the emptiness behind her eyes. A vacancy that Katerina had come to fear.

"Come, let's look in the keepsake box together," Katerina announced one morning, longing to see the joy and the smile the trinkets from her life in Tinos would always bring to Mama.

Katerina placed the box on the bed and opened the lid. Together they gazed inside, smiling at the treasures held within. The emotion swelled within Katerina, like a flutter in her belly that worked its way up through her soul and deep into her heart. To see her mother smile filled her and sustained her. With the keepsake box opened before her, the corners of Mama's eyes crinkled with joy and her lips peeled back, exposing her gleaming teeth as her eyes widened. Mama brought her hands to her mouth, a tiny squeal escaping from beneath her fingers.

Katerina knew all too well that when you love someone, their pain becomes yours. It had been so very long, she had forgotten that when you love someone, their joy becomes yours as well.

"Oh, look." Mama held the wedding crowns up to the light that bled into the room from the one tiny window next to the door above the washbasin. "How pretty." She placed them on Katerina's head the way she used to back in the village, back before the gunshot rang out that morning, taking Katerina's father in an instant, and her mother bit by bit.

"Yes, Mama," Katerina agreed. "They are."

"Oh, look at the tiny flowers. They are so beautiful." Mama lifted them from Katerina's head, turning them this way and that to examine them once more before placing them back in the box. She then turned to Katerina. "Who is getting married?" she asked.

Katerina watched helplessly as her mother continued to slip away from her. The doctors called it dementia, but Katerina called it something else. It didn't matter to her in the least what the doctors diagnosed or discussed among themselves in hushed tones as they huddled together conferring on Mama's condition. Katerina knew without question what the truth was. She, like her mother before her, knew in her heart that sometimes Panagia shows mercy where otherwise there was none. When your heart has been broken beyond repair, sometimes it's simply easier to forget.

Each Sunday, mother and daughter sat together at Olympia, at a corner table under the arches where Katerina devoured an ice cream handcrafted for her by Manoli himself. Mama always nursed a coffee as they watched the elegant citizens of Corfu stroll by.

While she missed life in the village sometimes, this was one of the things Katerina loved most about their new life in Corfu. There was so much to see and do. It didn't matter that they had no money to spare beyond the simplest groceries and the rent on their tiny room. From concerts by the Corfu Philharmonic in the square, to cricket matches on the grass, to the litany processions of Saint Spyridon's mummified remains through the streets, every time Katerina walked out the door she felt there was something new to experience and discover.

But of all the glorious things she loved about life in the center of town, Katerina had come to love Easter in Corfu Town most of all. She loved how the entire city spilled out onto the *plateia* and across the park as the light of resurrection was passed from one candle to another until the entire square, thousands and thousands of people, were illuminated by candlelight as they all sang "Christ Is Risen" at the stroke of midnight. She loved how on Holy Saturday giant ceramic pots were tossed from the balconies surrounding the square as crowds chanted and cheered from below, all while dodging the shrapnel as the vases exploded on the street. It was Manoli who explained the tradition to Katerina.

"It comes from the Venetians. They would throw away old things from their balconies on New Year's Day, hoping God would bless them with better, newer replacements." He laughed. "We, of course, as Corfiots, had to make this our own. So we throw pots on the most important day of the year, the day Christ was resurrected."

"But why pots?" Katerina asked.

"What's the point of throwing my old pants out the window? Have you ever been excited to see dirty pants and underwear tossed to the street? Do they make a crashing noise? Do they threaten to decapitate those cheering below? No, this is Corfu; we need to make a show of it. To make some noise and be bigger and better, and add a little bit of danger. So, pots it is." He laughed as he handed her an ice cream.

It was always a special treat when every few months, Clotho would take the bus and meet Katerina and Mama for coffee after she finished selling her honey to the shopkeepers in the old town. In those moments, sitting with Clotho, Katerina came to understand how pleasure and pain were so intricately entwined. Nothing made her happier than to see her old friend and hear stories about how the other villagers had fared since the war. But seeing Clotho was also a reminder of the life she and Marco once shared, and then lost so suddenly and brutally.

"Maria, will you eat something?" Clotho asked.

"No, thank you," Mama replied. "I'm tired and need to go lie down. You stay here, Katerina. Enjoy Clotho's company."

"Are you sure, Mama?" Katerina replied. She wanted to stay here, outside with Clotho, taking in all the color and character of a Sunday afternoon on the square. The thought of returning to their tiny room made her stomach seize. But Katerina knew her place, and it was beside her mother.

"Stay." Mama leaned over and put her hand over Katerina's. "Stay."

"Thank you, Mama," Katerina said as she watched Mama shuffle home, away from her, away from the sidewalks and avenues teeming with life. Away from life.

"Clotho, will you ever move here?" Katerina asked, licking her arm where the ice cream dripped. "Will you come stay in town? Mr. Andonis is here now, teaching in the elementary school. Even the mayor's family left the village and is here. He says Pelekito is empty now, a shell of what it was."

"No." Clotho lifted her coffee to her lips and sipped the dark liquid. "No, Katerina. I'll die there on that mountainside."

"But aren't you afraid? And lonely?"

"No. I'm not afraid. Not in the least. And I'm certainly not lonely. Why, I have my mountain and plants and flowers to watch over me, just as I watch over them."

"Do you think that with the war over, Marco can come home now?"

"Oh, Katerina." Clotho leaned in across the table and reached for Katerina. She lingered there a moment, holding tight to Katerina's hand, cracked and leathery.

"Katerina, Yianna asked that he be taken to the paidopoleis. That's his home now. The good people of the paidopoleis will care for him and educate him, and when the time comes, when he turns sixteen, they'll help him find a job and he'll settle into his own life. Maybe he'll come back to the village then. It was his mother's dying wish, don't ever forget that. No matter how much you miss him, no matter how much I would have welcomed him into my home and taken care of him, none of that matters. It's what Yianna wanted." She leaned in closer now, taking both of Katerina's hands in her own. "Katerina, however much you want him home with us, it is against everything holy to stand in the way of Yianna's wishes for her son."

"And what about me?" Katerina asked. "Where do I belong?" It was a question that Katerina found herself asking lately. She felt so lost and so very alone. As much as she loved the bustle of the city, the constant stream of people, and the excitement of Corfu Town and all of the city's endless possibilities, Katerina had never been so surrounded by people and yet felt so very alone.

"Come, let's see what the cup says, shall we?" Clotho took a final sip and twirled the mud at the bottom of her cup three times. She then placed it upside down in the saucer, waiting for the mud to reveal her fate.

"I miss him," Katerina whispered, twirling her napkin, twisting it around and around before dropping it on the table before her, watching as it slowly unfurled. "Clotho, I miss him so much." Her head hung heavy, and she began to cry. It was as if all the tears, all the emotions she had not allowed herself to feel, not allowed herself to show, could be contained no longer. All this time she had tried her best to be strong for her mother, but her mother wasn't here. She had gone off to sleep in the middle of the day, to draw the curtains and lie in the darkness, a tomb for the living. And now Clotho was here with Katerina, a safe haven for her secrets, just the way it was when Marco was beside her.

Clotho lifted the cup. "Let's see what our fate is." She gazed into the mud that lined the inside of the cup. Clotho narrowed her eyes and looked again, nodding her head. "I see."

"What does it say?" Katerina asked.

"It says we are long overdue." Clotho grabbed her bags and straightened her father's old fisherman's cap. "Let's go." She motioned to Katerina to get up and together they walked down the esplanade as Garitsa bay glistened alongside them.

"Where are we going?"

"On an errand."

"Where?" Katerina asked again. But Clotho said nothing, even as they boarded the bus and she handed her drachmas to the driver. They sat and watched as the beauty of Corfu played out before them while they traveled south along the bay. Out the window the changing landscape of Corfu revealed itself to them, one beautiful vista at a time. The bus made its way down the freshly paved streets and crudely paved alleyways, past the ornate gates of Mon Repos, where Marco's grandmother had once worked, down the steep hills of Kanoni, and past the tiny, picturesque church of Vlacherna, which jutted out into the sea with Mouse Island just behind her. The bus continued south, past beaches and cafés and tiny villages, and at last Clotho stood to exit as they reached the village of Benitses.

"What are we doing here?" Katerina asked again.

"Come. You'll see soon enough."

It was a five-minute walk from the bus stop through the center of town. They stopped in front of a wrought iron gate, the sign above reading Saint Spyridon Paidopoleis of Corfu.

Katerina grabbed tight to Clotho's hand and squeezed with all her might. "Is this what I think it is?"

"Yes. It's Frederica's children's village. I thought we should come and see how Marco is. Don't you think?" She smiled at Katerina beneath her cap. "It's been too long."

"Yes." Tears sprang from her eyes and down her face. She breathed deeply in and out and could not believe they were really here. She thought she would have to wait until Marco was sixteen to see him. She never imagined she could see him before then. And here they were.

"Thank you, Clotho," she cried. "Thank you."

"I've only had one friend in my life I could trust, Katerina. One person I could put my faith in, and that was Marco's mother. I know what Marco means to you. I know how special your bond is. So let's go see him and let him know that he is loved and that we are here for him, always. Come," she said, smiling as she tipped back her cap.

They walked together through the gates and into the compound. They passed several tidy buildings and children dressed in simple, clean uniforms of white blouses and navy pants. The children all seemed clean and well fed. A small group of girls sat on the floor playing jackstones while the boys played tag in the yard.

At last they reached the office.

"Hello. We would like to see Marco Scarapolis, please."

The woman reached behind the desk and pulled out a large ledger and placed it on the desk. One by one she flipped through the pages, scanning them top to bottom as she traced along with her finger.

"We took the bus to come visit him," Clotho added as she squeezed Katerina's hand and smiled down at her. "Just to say hello and give him a hug. We don't want to disturb anyone and we don't have to stay long. We would just like to see him, please."

Katerina fidgeted and held tighter to Clotho's hand. She was shaking with anticipation and excitement and thought she might faint on the spot and ruin it all.

"What was that name again, please?" The woman smiled at them, cocking her head to the right.

"Marco Scarapolis," Clotho repeated. "He is thirteen years old and he was brought here in October of 1948."

The woman looked at them and smiled again, but it was a crooked smile, a confused smile. "I'm sorry, but there is no Marco Scarapolis here."

Thirty-Two

"Please, won't you come?" Katerina pleaded with Mama. "Please, Mama. It's the litany of Saint Spyridon. Manoli said he would save us a table. Please."

But Mama just rolled over to face the wall. "No, Katerina. You go ahead. I'm tired."

It pained Katerina to leave her mother in bed, in the dark, on one of the most meaningful days of the year. But Katerina knew that there was no changing Mama's mind. Some days were gray, the sadness permeating her, but she was able to function. And other days were black. And on those days, no matter how Katerina tried or what she said, there was no helping her mother; all she could do was bring her food and beg her to eat it. Besides, staying behind today was not an option. Today, Katerina was a girl on a mission.

Katerina felt the energy the moment she stepped out on the street. There was magic in the air on the day of the litany. It seemed as if everyone on the island came out to the plateia to watch as the priests carried Saint Spyridon's body, positioned upright in a glass and golden casket, through the streets, blessing the faithful as he passed. It was said that prayers made to the saint on the day of the litany were especially potent, and for that reason Katerina raced to Olympia to take her place along the saint's route.

Katerina had thought long and hard what she would ask for on this special day. In addition to health for Mama, she would ask the saint to look after Marco and help him find his way back home. Where had he gone and why? And most importantly, where was he now?

Even in this heat, thousands had come to the Liston at the crack of dawn to secure a seat, making sure they had a perfect view as Saint Spyridon was carried by. Villagers traveled by the busload from across the island while the faithful made pilgrimages from all across Greece to witness this mystical and legendary procession of the miracle worker of Corfu. Katerina was ever grateful to Manoli, who promised to save a seat for her, perhaps understanding that she needed something to look forward to. She approached the restaurant and gave Manoli a giant hug when she saw him.

"Your mama is not with you?" he asked, looking past Katerina.

"No. It's just me."

"Well, I have the best table saved for you. You should see these hypocrites. They wake before the sun to come pray beside the saint, and then they curse me and argue and yell when I tell them this table is reserved for someone special and they can't have it."

Manoli escorted her to a small table with a perfect view of the cobblestone streets, where the golden-robed and bearded priests would carry the body of the saint on their shoulders.

She heard the music, the slow, mournful drone of the philharmonic, heralding the arrival of the procession of the saint. *Dar dar, dar dum*—the musicians marched in time, dressed in their white fringed uniforms as their maestro led the way, his baton held high to keep time. Behind them, the priests walked slowly, about a dozen of them. Some held icons, arms raised high in the air; others waved incense at the faithful, who bowed their heads and made the sign of the cross. Among the cluster of priests, four had the honor of carrying the glass case holding the body of Saint Spyridon. Katerina, along with the thousands who now packed every niche of space on the plaza, knelt with bowed heads and made the sign of the cross and prayed as the saint's procession passed.

She took a last sip of her juice and stood to leave as the music faded and the procession made its way farther down the promenade. She spotted him in the crowd, across the plateia.

"Mr. Andonis," she shouted, waving her arms. "Mr. Andonis!"

"Katerina." His face erupted in a broad smile when he saw her. Weaving in and out of the crowd, Mr. Andonis made his way across the square, greeting his former student with a kiss on both cheeks.

"And next year, with the saint's blessings," they said to one another, the traditional greeting upon being blessed by the saint.

"Is your mother here?" Mr. Andonis asked.

"No."

He understood at once. "I'm sorry." He reached out his hand and touched her elbow.

"I was hoping I might see you. I heard you are teaching school here now. Do you like it here? Do you like your new job?" Katerina asked.

"Yes. I live not far from here, over in Kanoni, near Pontikonisi. I'm teaching in the elementary school. I have to tell you I miss our little village. I miss all of you. But it's a good job, and there was no reason for me to stay in the village when there are no children left to teach."

One is dead. One is missing. And I'm here, trapped between the world of the living and the dead.

"Are you near the mayor and his family? They moved to Kanoni too, didn't they?"

"Yes," Mr. Andonis said, nodding and smiling. "I live just down the street from them. It's convenient. I'm still tutoring Stamati . . . well, trying to, at least." He shot her a knowing look and the two burst into laughter. It was the first time in a long time Katerina laughed out loud in this way, remembering all the times the teacher tried in vain to hold Stamati's attention.

"I saw Clotho," Mr. Andonis said. "I went to the village. I wanted to see it myself. I hadn't been back since that horrible day." He glanced down at the floor, unable to look her in the eyes. "Two years later and everything has fallen into disarray. Only Clotho's house is unchanged. Maybe the old ladies were right all along. Maybe there's magic on that mountain after all."

"I think there is."

"She told me about your trip to the paidopoleis. I don't know what to say. I don't understand. I'm so sorry, Katerina. I'm so sorry. We all wanted to help him. To save him . . ."

"I know." It was Katerina's turn to look away.

"I keep thinking about Yianna. I never had the chance to spend much time with her, but she left an impression on me, as did her boys. I'll never forget how those boys would take care of one another. How they would stay and help each other when it was their turn to help me clean the classroom. That doesn't just happen. It takes a special mother to instill that in her children, especially boys."

Katerina was silent, his words confirming what she knew all along.

"There was one time I visited them at home. Stefano had asked to borrow a book and I brought it to him. Yianna made me a cup of coffee, and we sat outside on the terrace and she told me about her family. She told me where she was raised and where she hoped to return one day. It's a tragedy that day never came for Yianna, or her boys. Imagine if they had gone back to Mon Repos. Imagine if Princess Alice had kept her word, how different their lives would be."

Katerina said goodbye to Mr. Andonis with a promise to make time to continue reading her beloved classics and to find him when she was ready to continue her lessons, even privately. After hugging Manoli and thanking him, she began to walk south along the plateia back toward home. She replayed the conversation with Mr. Andonis in her mind. *Imagine if Princess Alice had kept her word, how different their lives would be.* It had been so long since Katerina thought about Marco's mother's story, of where she was born and who had promised to always care for her and her family.

"Imagine if they had gone back to Mon Repos."

Katerina picked up the pace now. She walked with purposeful strides and made it quickly to the street, where she turned and followed the foot-path with Garitsa bay to her right. She glanced up at the sun's position, creeping around the farthest end of the bay. If she walked quickly, she could make it there and back before dark. As she walked, the scent of peddlers selling roasted corn along the waterfront mixed with the heavenly scent of lamb roasting outside a neighborhood café. She breathed in deeply, the way Marco used to, but instead of being satiated by the scent, Katerina grew even more ravenous. But there was no time, and no money, to stop for something to eat.

She remembered the route from the bus drive with Clotho to the paido-poleis in Benitses. Eventually, if she continued along the bay, along the road hugging the water, she would reach her destination. After walking about forty-five minutes beside the sea, she followed the road inland.

She rounded the corner, away from the bay, and continued about a quarter mile uphill on Faekon Street. Just a little farther up the slope and there it was, the entrance to Mon Repos. There were two posts on either side of the driveway, with a solid metal gate, closed and locked. Farther up the hill she at last spotted a small area where there was a divide between the fence and the wall. She looked around to make certain no one was watching her, then she shimmied along and climbed up and over the space between the wall and the fence, landing on the other side. She crouched down, and through the trees she could see the grand driveway sloping uphill. She followed along, making sure to stay off the pavement, hidden by the dense cover of trees and flowers that grew in the forest surrounding the villa.

It was a crime to trespass on the grounds of the royal villa. But it was a risk she was willing to take. It was the conversation with Mr. Andonis that did it, his words jarring her memory and sparking her imagination.

What if Marco left the paidopoleis to come here, to the home his mother always dreamed of returning to? she wondered. *What if he told Queen Frederica of Alice's promise, and the queen fulfilled her family's obligation to Marco by bringing Marco home to Mon Repos?* She knew it was a risk. She knew it sounded crazy, but she could no longer sit by and wait and wonder and worry. She would never forgive herself if she didn't at least try to find him.

Every few moments she stopped to look around and whisper his name. "Marco, Marco." But she received no answer and saw no sign of him. She continued to search, and after about a quarter of a mile, the pavement and forest widened and cleared, revealing at last the most beautiful home Katerina had ever seen. She stood there for a moment, hand to the sky shielding the sun from her eyes, and gazed up at the beauty of Mon Repos. In the center of the circular driveway was a lush flower bed with a towering magnolia tree whose waxy leaves glistened in the afternoon sun and dripped with pristine white flowers. Beneath the tree, surrounding it, were a half dozen rosebushes whose red blooms perfumed the air, even from where she stood several meters away. The flowers were the same color as the red trim of the house and the red-painted bases of the massive gas lamps that flanked either side of the entrance. Beyond the house, the Ionian Sea glistened a bright, brilliant blue matched only by the sky above. Katerina had never seen anything more majestic and magnificent.

In that moment, crouched and camouflaged among the trees and plants on the grounds of Mon Repos, she finally understood the pain Yianna must have carried with her through her entire life. She pictured Yianna here, running along the paths and gardens as a child. What must it have been like to live here, surrounded by all this beauty? Yes, her mother was a servant, but this was her home. Marco had mentioned this to Katerina several times, saying his mother was always adamant about that. This was her home. To have lived here and to have lost it. To have lived here with the promise of returning one day, only to have that dream, along with so many others, ripped from her.

Katerina walked farther along the path, behind the house, careful to stay hidden in the brush. As she went deeper into the forest, she stopped and marveled at a massive, ancient olive tree, hulking and extraordinary. The tree was tremendous, her leaves and branches forming a canopy that only glimmers of light could penetrate, casting shards of daylight on the dirt below. The trunk was made of dozens of smaller, slim trunks, looking to Katerina as if it were not a tree at all but instead a circle of forest nymphs dancing together, arms stretching upward in an elegant dance. She wondered if Prince Philip had once chased Yianna around this very tree.

She continued through the forest for about ten minutes more, passing ancient ruins, a garden, and a small church along the way. Finally, the grounds sloped downward and she heard the soft rush of waves. As she grew closer to the beach, she heard the voices coming from below. She inched cautiously toward the cliff, peeking down, careful to be as still as possible and not give herself away.

She brought her hand to her mouth as she spotted them, an audible gasp escaping from her fingers despite her best effort to keep silent. The beach was crescent shaped, a lovely cove seemingly carved out from the lush green cliffs above. Extending out into the sea was a long, thin pier. Katerina watched as the children, three of them, climbed out of the water and walked out onto the pier. Waiting in the water below, arms outstretched, encouraging them to jump, was a man, their father.

She watched as the two eldest jumped, their laughter reverberating up over the cliffs and across the forest floor as they shouted, "Again, again!"

"Constantine. Let your sister have a turn," the father said as his son climbed back onto the pier, ready to jump again. "Come on, you can do this. You're a brave girl." The youngest stood on the pier with arms crossed, contemplating the water below. "Come on, Irene, jump. Sofía, hold her hand and jump with her."

Katerina nearly fainted as she heard the father speak to his children. This was not an ordinary family at the beach. Constantine, Sofía, Irene. These were the names of the children of the king and queen. This was the royal family. The father in the water was King Paul himself, the three children

Crown Prince Constantine and Princesses Sofía and Irene. The moment she realized who this family was, she heard a woman's voice, distinct and clear, in perfect but slightly accented Greek.

"Come on, children. Only a few more moments. It's almost time to go and get cleaned up for dinner." The woman sat on a large blanket on the sand wearing a large sunhat and dark glasses, but there was no mistaking the curls that peeked out from beneath her hat.

"Come on, Irene. One time before we go. You can do this." King Paul clapped his hands and waved to Irene to jump.

Irene took three giant steps forward, then leapt into the waiting arms of her father.

"Bravo, my girl. Bravo." Frederica stood, clapping and cheering her on from the shore. The children raced toward the sand and Frederica handed each of them a towel to dry off. King Paul was the last out of the water; when he reached Frederica, she handed him his towel and gave him a kiss as well.

Katerina was excited and terrified and nervous all at once. Her instinct told her to take this opportunity, to run up to the queen and ask her if she knew where Marco was. She straightened her spine, gathering her courage and preparing what she would say. *Curtsy.* She reminded herself to curtsy. She had taken just a few steps when she heard more voices coming from beyond the path. She ducked behind the tree and watched as two soldiers approached the family. Each of them had guns strapped to their waists. She looked again at the guns and up at the soldiers and pressed her body behind the tree, wishing the arms of the dancing nymphs could envelop her and hide her.

"Good afternoon, gentlemen." The king greeted the soldiers as the family collected their towels and clothing and began the walk back from the beach to the house, escorted by the soldiers.

"I'll be right behind you," Constantine said as he broke from the family and ran over to the fresh spring. The young prince steadied himself by holding on to the base of the spring and leaned in, drinking from the cool, clear water. He then cupped his hands and filled his palms with water, splashing his face and hair before running to catch up with his family.

Katerina was near tears. She so desperately wanted to run to the queen and wrap her arms around her legs and ask for her help, ask her if she'd seen Marco, ask for help in finding Marco. But Katerina also understood that breaking onto the grounds of Mon Repos was a crime. If the soldiers arrested her and threw her in jail, there would be no one left to care for Mama.

She watched as the family walked away from the beach, and from her. As they slipped from view, Katerina felt her hope slip away with them. When they were safely out of sight, Katerina scurried down to the beach to take a drink from the fountain. She was hot and thirsty, and she let the cold spring water run over her. She looked at the spring, noticing that the spout was shaped like a lion's paw. *Marco would love that,* she thought to herself.

Katerina climbed the steps back into the forest and began the walk home.

Thirty-Three

Theodora paced the floor. Back and forth. "Really, Mother. Just for to-morrow. Can't you make an exception for Elizabeth's coronation?"

Sophie and Margarita sat together on the green velvet sofa in the sitting room of the spacious second-floor Buckingham Palace apartment Alice had been invited to stay in. The grandeur of the rooms, adorned in life-size oil portraits, thick woven rugs, and plush fringed and sashed drapes, was a stark contrast to the rather austere and sparse lifestyle Alice had adopted back in Athens. The sisters glanced at their mother and then each other.

"Mother, think of everything we've been through. The celebrations Sophie, Margarita, and I missed. Philip's wedding. Losing Father and Cecilie. Having lost you for all those years. We finally have something to celebrate together, as a family."

"And celebrate we will." Alice sipped her tea and placed the cup back in its saucer.

214

"Mother." Theodora's exasperation echoed in the room. "The newspapers have already gone to town." She walked over to the desk where the morning's newspapers sat, still unread by Alice. She lifted the papers one by one and read the headlines. "'Philip's Mother, the Mysterious Greek Mystic.' 'Queen's Mother-in-Law: Secret Life Behind Convent Walls.'"

Alice smiled coyly, reaching for a pack of cigarettes. She was seated on a green velvet winged chair, dressed in the gray nun's habit and veil she had adopted as her uniform since returning to Greece after Philip's wedding. Inspired by Frederica's work with the paidopoleis, Alice decided she would further devote herself to helping her fellow Greeks. Without a second thought, she sold a topaz and diamond ring that Andrew had presented her when they were married and used the money to found an order of Greek Orthodox nuns called the Christian Sisterhood of Martha and Mary.

"Mother. It's not right. You'll stand out like an eyesore. Why, you're not even a real nun," Theodora huffed. "You've taken no vows. You and I both know you run your sisterhood more like a nursing program than a religious order. Please. Can't you for once?"

Alice stood from her chair. She ran her fingers down the length of her skirt, which fell to the floor. A large cross carved from olive wood dangled around her neck. Her hair was covered in a veil made from the same material as her dress; a thick white strap tucked under her chin kept the heavy material from slipping off her forehead. She walked over to the desk and picked up the newspapers. She glanced at the photos of herself on the front page and smiled. She would never admit it out loud, but Alice rather enjoyed her newfound notoriety as the eccentric mother-in-law of the queen.

"Oh, Theodora. I've long ago given up caring what people say or think. I know how they talk and joke about the nun who wears a habit yet smokes and drinks and plays canasta." She laughed, making smoke circles with her cigarette. "I know all about the gossip, and I also know the work that needs to be done. In my nun's habit, dressed this way, no one judges me. They don't care that my dress is not the latest fashion or my hair is not properly styled. Dressed like this, I can focus on my work, and I can help the people who need me most. That is all that matters."

"Yes, but, Mother. On the queen's Coronation Day?"

"Yes. On the queen's Coronation Day. And every day, as far as I'm concerned. You see those papers, those headlines, as a distraction. I see them as a way to bring attention to my work. And I want no further arguments or discussion about it." Alice directed her gaze at Theodora.

Before the girls could argue further, a knock at the door interrupted the discussion. Philip, tall and handsome, entered the apartment.

"Good morning, Mother." He kissed Alice on each cheek. "Good morning." Philip nodded in the direction of his sisters.

Theodora seized upon the opportunity to revisit the wardrobe discussion now that Philip had joined them. "Philip, would you please tell Mother that perhaps it would be best to wear more traditional attire for the coronation? At least for the church. Perhaps you can change when we come back for the luncheon?"

Alice took another bite of her apple.

Philip looked from his sister to his mother. "Mother? Is there a problem?"

"The only problem is that I seem to be an embarrassment to your sisters. Perhaps I should have stayed home, like Frederica."

"Mother, you know the protocol. Frederica couldn't come because she is a sitting queen. Of course we want you here. Lilibet especially wants you here. She wants you with us. As do I. And for all I care you can wear a sack tomorrow."

Alice folded her arms and glanced back at her daughters, a sly smile on her face. She brought her cross to her lips and kissed it gently, fingering the smooth wood. Alice silently and privately thanked God for the gift of her son. It had been a long and challenging road, with much difficulty and heartache along the way. After so many years apart, she was forever grateful for the man of dignity and honor her tiny prince had grown into, despite his unconventional upbringing. It was not lost on Alice how she had been absent in one way or another for most of Philip's childhood. And yet he was, without question, the most accepting and welcoming of Alice's children.

Alice cherished their time together here in England and dreamed of the day that Philip's commitments might allow him to return to Greece with her. She was proud of the work she had accomplished, the lives changed and helped through her sisterhood, and she looked forward to sharing it all with Philip. Most of all, she dreamed of the day she could return to Corfu with her son. But she had learned to be patient. That day would come. But for now, Philip's place was here, beside his queen.

Despite her daughters' concerns that she was an embarrassment to the queen, Alice understood the truth. In Elizabeth, Alice had found an unexpected ally and her son had finally found the stability he had craved as a child. And with Elizabeth's encouragement and blessing, Alice had been offered a second chance at being part of Philip's life. They were an unlikely pair, but grounded in their love of Philip and their desire to give him the family he never experienced as a child, the queen of England and the eccentric Greek nun had developed a fondness and affinity for one another that few, if any, could understand.

The following morning Alice and her girls were among the eight thousand guests packed into Westminster Abbey to witness the queen's coronation. As the queen's mother-in-law, Alice was seated behind the queen's family, including young Charles, who was the first child to ever attend his mother's coronation.

As the ceremony came to a close, Alice watched as the queen filed out of the church, followed by Philip and the royal family. She gave a little nod and a wink to Charles, who had behaved so well and sat so still throughout the three-hour service.

Head held high, her veil strapped to her chin and her gray habit trailing to the floor, Alice walked proudly and deliberately with each step as she led her daughters and their husbands down the aisle of Westminster Abbey and out to the cheering crowd outside.

Part Five

Thirty-Four

Bronx, New York

April 1960

"No," Katerina cried silently to herself. "No. Not again." She shut her eyes and buried her face deeper into the pillow, praying it would stop.

"Can't you hear her? She's crying." Stamati moaned as he swatted his hand toward her.

"Please. Stamati, can you go to her? Please. I'm so tired," she whispered. She had never imagined it was possible to feel this depleted, this utterly empty and numb. She had never imagined it was possible to want and love something with your entire being, to have your entire world fall into place when you heard your child's first cry in the delivery room. She also never imagined the exhaustion and gut-sinking feeling that came with hearing an inconsolable newborn's relentless crying in the night.

So much joy, so much pain. How was it that they could coexist?

It had been four months since she gave birth. Katerina had already suffered two miscarriages when she found herself pregnant again, this time with twins. She prayed on her knees incessantly for the safe delivery of her children and feared she would lose these babies as well.

Dawn was born pink and screaming.

Her twin, a baby boy, was born silent and still.

Dawn was indeed her miracle child.

"Please, Stamati," she said as her daughter continued to wail. "Just this once. Can you please go to her? I'm so tired."

"I have a job. This is your job. I don't ask you to get up and go to the restaurant for me," he said as he rolled over, away from her. His words stung, but she was not surprised by them. Nothing surprised her anymore. She had learned never to expect anything from him, and this way she was never disappointed. Stamati was not the one she would have chosen, but the choice had not been hers to make.

There had been no choices for Katerina, only obligation and duty. Hers was not a marriage of love, or even convenience. It was a marriage of circumstance. The first few years after Baba's murder had been so very difficult, but she and Mama had managed to survive. Dreams replaced by duty; laughter replaced by longing. Hours spent in the classroom with Mr. Andonis replaced by hours spent on her knees, scrubbing beside Mama.

Over the years, Mama slipped away. At first she refused to leave the room; then she refused to leave the bed. Eventually she stopped speaking and eating as well. Katerina lay awake at night next to her, wondering how she would manage to take care of her, how they would manage to survive.

From the moment they fled the village and arrived in Corfu Town, up until the very end, Mama vowed she would rather starve on the streets of Corfu Town than return to the place where she had been so publicly and brutally betrayed. It was the same for Katerina, who knew that only one thing could draw her back to Pelekito. Katerina had vowed that she would only return when Marco did.

It had been twelve years, and Katerina had kept her promise.

Marco had never returned. And neither had she.

Despite years of searching for him, of visiting the paidopoleis again, Katerina never found out what had happened to Marco, and so she lived with the painful reality that Marco had simply disappeared. There were so many times Katerina wished she could as well.

"Have faith and look ahead."

Baba's words echoed again in her ear the morning the mayor came to see her at Olympia, asking her to join him for coffee after her overnight shift. He said he knew of a place where they could provide for Mama, where she would be safe and have the medical care she needed and deserved. Katerina thanked him for the coffee and information and stood to go, knowing full well that she could never afford such a place. And then he reached up his hand, blocking her path.

"There's one more thing, Katerina," he said. "Stamati will be leaving for America in the next year. He's going to be a partner in a new restaurant in New York. We have everything in place for him. But he needs a wife to begin his new life. He needs a good girl we can trust to take care of him and provide a proper home for him and our grandchildren."

"Remember Orpheus."

No, unlike Orpheus, Katerina was never tempted to look back. But it was not because she was certain that faith and love followed silently in her shadow. It was because she was certain they did not.

On a crisp fall Sunday, just before her twentieth birthday, Katerina walked three times around the altar bound to her new husband by wedding crowns joined together by a ribbon. Like Mama before her, Katerina understood that hers was a marriage built not on a foundation of love but on necessity.

Katerina did her part that day playing the role of the gracious bride, smiling and receiving the well wishes of her guests. As Clotho folded Marlena's dream diary into Katerina's arms, Katerina smiled genuinely for the first time that day. The tattered and yellowed book meant more to her than all the gifts the mayor and his wife and their guests lavished upon the young couple.

At first Katerina was unsure if she could go through with it, leave Mama in a nursing home on Corfu and make the move to America. But then Mama found a way to make it easier on Katerina, just as she always had. As her departure date grew closer, with each visit to the nursing home, Katerina was met with no more than a blank stare. Mama no longer recognized or remembered Katerina. And just as she had so many times in Katerina's life, it was Clotho who helped her see the truth.

"She's releasing you," Clotho explained. "You're free to go now."

Mama slipped away one late summer morning weeks after Katerina welcomed Dawn into the world. And though she mourned the loss of her mother, Katerina also understood that now Mama was free as well.

While Stamati was often a difficult man with a penchant for gambling and a wandering eye, Katerina was grateful for the security her marriage provided. Each night when Stamati came home, Katerina quietly unclipped the stack of dollars he brought from the restaurant, slipping a few at a time into the box she kept hidden in her closet. Clotho was getting on in age, and Katerina knew the day would come when she would need to step in and care for Clotho the way Clotho had taken care of Katerina and Marco when their own mothers were unable to.

Katerina and Stamati lived in a tidy row house on Eastchester Road that she had fallen in love with the moment she laid eyes on it. It was the only thing she had ever asked of Stamati, to raise their family here. She remembered all the times she and Marco would stare up at the mayor's house back in the village and wonder what it would be like to live in such a place. As a child she was convinced that everything she wanted in life could be found within the walls of a magnificent home like the mayor's.

Marriage to Stamati meant Katerina could give Dawn everything she and Marco had dreamed of. She now had everything but Marco.

Katerina lay motionless in the bed, the blankets pulled up to her chin. It was quiet now. Dawn had settled down and Katerina was hopeful that she had fallen back asleep. But then the music from the neighbors next door blared through the wall. Loud Italian music. The floor and walls vibrated with their joy and dancing and laughter. There was so much joy on the other side of that wall.

And Dawn began to wail.

"Aren't you going to get her? For the love of God, make her stop crying," Stamati said, his face pressed into his pillow.

Katerina felt as if she were walking through honey, her limbs weighted down, almost unable to move them. But somehow she managed to lift herself from the bed and go to her daughter. She stumbled down the hall, caught between the world of asleep and awake. She wanted to cry for the exhaustion and the pain, but even the tears were too tired to come. Numb. She was numb. It was so very late and she was depleted. And still, the music and laughter from next door blared on. It was two a.m. *Where is the decency?* she thought. *They know I have a baby.*

She shuffled down the hall to Dawn's bedroom in her bare feet and nightgown, feeling her hand along the wall and flipping on the light. There she was, tiny and flailing in her crib, angry and red and wet with perspiration from crying. But the moment they locked eyes, Dawn's face erupted into a bright, toothless smile. Her eyes, still wet with tears, twinkled as her arms and legs kicked and punched the air. As Katerina approached her crib, the screams and wails gave way to giggles and coos.

Katerina bent over the crib and picked up her baby girl. The transformation was immediate. It didn't matter how tired she was. It didn't matter that she didn't love her husband, or even like him very much. It didn't matter that she was lonely or that her neighbors were terribly inconsiderate. Everything else fell away as Dawn snuggled against Katerina and nursed at her breast. This was what mattered. The only thing that mattered.

Thirty-Five

Bronx, New York
July 1960

"Shh. It's okay. It's okay." Katerina snuggled Dawn to her chest and walked back and forth from the kitchen to the living room and back again. It had been another challenging and sleepless night. The noise from next door had made it impossible for Katerina to fall asleep. She glanced out the window. It was still dark out. She had lost track of the time, but there was no longer any distinction between day and night, just as she could no longer distinguish between asleep and awake.

Dawn continued to fuss in her arms as Katerina gazed out the window. Daybreak. She watched as the day's first light penetrated the black.

She nuzzled Dawn closer, rocking her as she opened the door and went into the tiny garden that she had planted and tended with such care. Roses, tomatoes, figs, zucchini, and pots filled with fresh herbs covered every corner of the patio and tiny patch of grass. Above, the arbor dripped with sweet green grapes. In the daylight the arbor buzzed with the frenetic activity of bees, reminding Katerina of the symphony of her beautiful mountain village; all that was missing was the rhythmic crash of the surf in the distance. This tiny garden behind the house was her refuge. It would never be the same as her mother's lush garden overlooking the sea or Clotho's spectacular oasis perched on the edge of the mountain, but each time Katerina stepped outside and breathed in the scent of earthy tomatoes, sweet basil, and aromatic rosemary, something inside her stirred and ached.

"Look, my love. It's the day's first light. Isn't it beautiful? See," she whispered, pointing toward the sky. "It's daybreak, Dawn. Did you know that's why I named you? That's your name, sweet one. *Avgerini* in Greek, it means the dawn. Just like you, my light piercing through the black."

Katerina gazed up at the sky as the light changed from black to gray to bright morning blue. She often thought back to how frightened she was of the dark when she was a child. She remembered how her mother and father would console her in the night, assuring her that Nyx was watching over her as the goddess raced across the sky in her golden chariot. How she longed to be comforted by them one more time. How she longed to believe once more that the dark goddess was indeed watching over and protecting Dawn as she slept.

Katerina had so often wondered how life would have been different if her father had lived. Had her mother's heart not been broken in so many different ways. *Maybe they would be here with me.* But if her parents were with her, she would not be here, she would not be married to Stamati, and in the end, she would not have Dawn.

She rocked Dawn in her arms. The early morning light was soft, the light of new possibilities.

She walked in circles around the small patch of grass. No matter how she tried, no matter what she did, Dawn continued to cry. Katerina went to the steps that led to the second-floor balcony and sat down. She could no longer keep her own tears at bay. Dawn's unsettled screams and tears dissolved her resolve, her strength, and her spirit. As she sat there on the steps, Katerina also began to cry.

She did not notice the neighbor next door walk out into the yard and come toward her. She had seen the woman only a handful of times, but she heard her every single day. And every single night. This was the same woman who each morning went outside and grilled fresh peppers over an open fire. As the scent wafted into her home, Katerina had wondered so many times who on earth would eat so many peppers.

Her hair was wrapped in curlers with a pink chiffon scarf knotted on top to keep them in place. She took a hearty drag from a cigarette, un-filtered, which dangled from her lips, still stained with last night's red wine.

The woman said nothing as she looked down at Katerina, a crumpled heap of new mother seated on the stairs. This woman had been the source of so many sleepless nights, so much stress between Katerina and Stamati. She had begged him, pleaded with him, to ask the neighbors to keep the noise down, but he refused. "Just because you don't like to be around people and have a good time doesn't mean you can ruin it for others," he had said.

The woman tossed her cigarette to the ground and stomped it out with her slipper. She said nothing as she approached the fence. Silently, she reached her arms out over the divide, motioning for Katerina to give her the baby. Instinctively, Katerina pulled Dawn tighter to her chest, which made the baby scream even more. Katerina bit her lip to keep from crying even harder now.

"It's all right," the woman said. She spoke with a deep Italian accent. "My name is Violeta. I have five children. Maybe you've seen them running around here like animals." The woman blessed herself and shook her head, rolling her eyes and smiling. "I promise I won't keep her. I'll give her back. I can't fit any more children in my house."

Katerina held Dawn to her chest. She said nothing.

Violeta smiled at Katerina and leaned in closer. "I know how hard it is. And you don't have anyone with you. I don't see anyone go into your house. And I don't see anyone go out of your house except your husband. And you never leave. I never see you leave. Never, never, never," she said, waving her arms in the air as if her words were not dramatic enough. "I know you are alone. Here." She reached her arms out again. "Let me help you."

Reason told her not to do it, not to trust her child to this stranger, but Katerina was so very tired. She lifted her arms and Violeta took Dawn into hers. She smiled down on her and the baby's face softened and lit up. Violeta rocked back and forth and sung to her, the liveliest little melody in Italian. And then she reached down and loosened the swaddling, cooing and whispering and clucking as she did. And within moments, Dawn lay quiet and content.

"The swaddling is too tight. See?" Dawn raised her tiny hands into the air as she kicked her legs, enjoying her new freedom. "She wants to be free, this one." She smiled as she tickled Dawn's belly with the tips of her fingers. "These are things that our mothers help us understand and learn. The things we can't possibly know when we have our first babies."

Katerina said nothing.

"Your mother is not here."

She shook her head no. Her mother was not here.

Katerina looked at Dawn, so perfectly content in this stranger's arms. And at once she knew it in her bones: she was a failure, a failure at motherhood. She had lost three babies. Maybe God had made a mistake in allowing Dawn that first breath. Maybe she was meant to join her brother, her twin, and the two who came before. Maybe God had forgotten to take her too. And now Dawn was here, with a mother who failed her, who did not deserve to have a life trusted to her.

"We all make these mistakes. And then we learn. It's all right," Violeta said, as if she could read Katerina's mind. She leaned over the fence and handed a smiling Dawn back to Katerina. Violeta then walked over to the grill. Katerina watched as she slathered red and green peppers with olive oil and salt before placing them on the fire, cooking them until their skin was charred black.

"Mama," Violeta called out toward the house. "Mama. Come. I'm ready for you."

A woman emerged from inside, dressed in a pale floral housecoat, her silver hair tied in a bun at the nape of her neck. She shuffled along, using a cane that looked as if it had been hand carved from an ancient piece of olive wood.

"Here." Violeta smiled as she placed the charred peppers before the old woman. Dawn stayed quiet in Katerina's arms as she watched the old woman next door nimbly go to work, cleaning, cutting, and tossing the peppers into a bowl with olive oil, salt, and garlic.

"There," she said when she was done, wiping her hands on her apron, using her cane to point to the bowl of now marinating fragrant peppers. "Your father will be so pleased to see we have them ready for him. He's tired, Violeta," she said. "It's good that we let him sleep today."

"Yes, Mama," Violeta said. She waved goodbye to Katerina as she grabbed the bowl of peppers and helped her mother back down the stairs and into the house.

∽

It went on like that for weeks. Katerina would walk Dawn around the garden at daybreak, anticipating Violeta's arrival. At first, the conversation was minimal, Violeta extending her arms over the fence, asking to hold Dawn, offering advice for how to calm her and help her sleep.

Slowly, with each passing day, with each shared cup of coffee or piece of advice, something began to shift within Katerina. She looked forward to her mornings with Violeta, to their conversation, however minimal, as Katerina was still struggling to learn English.

It wasn't long before Violeta found an English tutor for Katerina who would come to the house a few days a week in the morning after Stamati left for work.

"Thank you." Katerina had been so moved by her kindness.

Violeta merely laughed and waved her cigarette in the air. "Really it's more for me than you. How will we ever manage to gossip about our neighbors if you don't learn to speak English?"

Perhaps as much or maybe even more than their friendly banter,

Katerina came to enjoy watching the frenzy of activity and often chaos that existed on the other side of the fence. There was always a child coming or going, interrupting Violeta: one who needed a shoe tied, or something to eat, or simply the reassurance of a mother's hug. Violeta lavished attention on every one of them, scooping them into her arms when they ran to her, smothering them in kisses. It was the same with her husband, a hulking man with a shock of black hair and a lush mustache to match. It made Katerina slightly uncomfortable, the way he swooped in sometimes, grabbing Violeta around the waist, pulling her to him, and kissing her hard. It didn't matter that Katerina was there, or the children or even Violeta's mother. No affection was off limits for the family next door.

Yes, it made Katerina uncomfortable, but even more so, it made her sad. Katerina had so much in life and she knew how fortunate she was. And yet there was a melancholy she could not shake, a loneliness that was her constant companion.

Katerina and Stamati coexisted. He left every morning for work and came home for bed, most nights anyway. He was rarely home for dinner and frequently met the men for a game of late-night poker. It was not how Katerina had envisioned marriage, but he left her in peace and she made sure his clothes were laundered, the house was clean, and there was always something to eat. As she watched Violeta and her husband, the easy laughter between them, the unbridled love, Katerina longed for something more. It was easy to see that Violeta and her husband not only had a passion between them, but also were each other's confidants and best friends. Watching them brought back the all-too-familiar pain and longing. She had once had a best friend as well.

One morning Violeta emerged from the house with a tray of coffee and biscotti. "Here, I thought you might like some." She handed a cup to Katerina as she took Dawn in her arms.

"Can I ask you a question?" Katerina said.

"Of course." Violeta smiled down at Dawn, who smiled back with a broad grin dotted with new teeth that gutted Violeta and Katerina.

"What do you do with all those peppers? Every day I see you out here roasting peppers. How can you possibly eat them all?"

Violeta looked at Katerina, furrowing her brows, and then she laughed. But there was something different about her laugh. It was not the easy laughter Katerina had come to expect from her neighbor. This was a measured laugh, and until this moment, Katerina had not witnessed anything that one might consider measured about Violeta. Everything about her was joyful, unfiltered, visceral, and raw.

"I roast them for my mother."

"But how can that tiny woman eat so many peppers?" Katerina was even more confused.

Violeta sat down on the steps and handed Dawn back to Katerina. She dug her hand inside the pocket of her housecoat and pulled out a cigarette and a match. "She doesn't eat them. They're for her memories."

"Her memories?"

"Yes. To remind her of life before."

"Before you came to New York?"

"Before the day that ruined us." She took a deep, long drag of her cigarette and then leaned back on her elbows, tilting her face toward the morning sun and exhaling a thin stream of smoke. She sat up again and turned to face Katerina through the fence.

"Our family's home was in the town of Civitella, nor far from the city of Arezzo, tucked away in the Tuscan hills. My father ran a grocery selling vegetables and salami and meats that he cured at home on our family's farm. He made the most delicious prosciutto. Creamy and never salty. I never knew his secret. I still don't. My father made everything himself, by hand, except for the roasted peppers. That was the one thing he asked my mother to make for him. Every morning she would go out to the garden and pick fresh peppers and grill them over a fire beneath an iron grate. I remember waking up to that scent every morning. My father never needed a clock or a watch. He said it was the scent of my mother's peppers that woke him up. Every day she prepared the peppers with olive oil and garlic and fresh herbs from the garden, and every day at nine thirty in the morning my father would load up his wagon and walk into town with the peppers and the prosciutto and the salami.

"It was June of 1944, and while the Germans were occupying Italy, for the most part they left us alone. My father would feed them when they came to the store. He always made certain to give them generous portions of prosciutto, and they told him they had never tasted anything like it back home in Germany.

"And then one night, a group of soldiers were drinking in the social club. Word got out that they were there. A group of young villagers entered the club and shot them right there, as they were drinking at the table. One soldier survived and managed to crawl back to his command." Violeta shook her head now, closing her eyes to the memory and what came next in her story.

"The next morning the town emptied. Everyone fled, afraid of what the Germans might do to us, to everyone, although we had no part of it. But then the priest received word from the German general that there would be no retaliation. Days passed, and slowly our friends and family and neighbors came back and life returned to normal. At least for a short while.

"It was Sunday morning, a few weeks later, and it seemed the entire town was at early morning mass as we celebrated the feast of Saints Peter and Paul. And that's when the Germans decided to come back." Violeta stood up now, shaking her head. She looked to the heavens and brought her hands together as if in prayer. Then she looked down at Katerina, seated on the steps, cradling a now sleeping Dawn in her arms.

"They began at dawn, burning the homes on the outskirts of the village, killing men, women, and children along the way. Some in their own beds, even the children. My father had gotten up early, the one day my mother's peppers did not wake him. He was in his cart, headed to the church with prosciutto he had cured especially for the feast. It made no difference to the Germans that he had fed them, that he had been good to them. They shot my father and my two brothers that morning. They went to mass, Katerina. They were murdered for going to mass. We should have been there as well, my mother and I; we went as a family every Sunday. But I was feeling unwell and my mother stayed home to take care of me.

"They killed more than two hundred people that day, shooting them five at a time, even throwing a grenade into the church where the priest had locked the doors, trying to save the parishioners." Violeta shook her head and shoved her hands deep into the pockets of her apron.

Katerina reached her arm out, grabbing hold of Violeta through the fence. "I'm so sorry," she whispered, not knowing what else to say, understanding in that moment that she was not alone in her life of loss. "My father was killed too. He was murdered . . ." Her voice trailed off.

Violeta and Katerina stayed like that, silent, holding on to one another.

Just then Violeta's door opened. Violeta's mother, her bun neatly pinned, housecoat freshly ironed and starched, shuffled out the door with her cane. The old woman made her way to Violeta and smiled as she spotted Katerina and Dawn.

"*Bellisima bambina,*" she said. "*Bellisima.*" The old woman then turned to Violeta. "Come, let's get the peppers ready. It's almost time for your father to get up."

Katerina watched as Violeta helped her mother with the peppers, placing them on the blazing hot grill until they blistered and blackened. Using dishcloths, the women rubbed the black away until all that was left was soft, fragrant flesh that they tossed with whole garlic and fresh oregano with translucent olive oil and salt. The old woman then leaned forward, inhaling the smoky, savory scent. "*Prego,*" she announced before shuffling back inside the house.

Violeta returned to her place on the stairs. She lit another cigarette, then picked a piece of tobacco from her tongue before exhaling a stream of smoke into the air.

"We found them piled onto one another, like trash tossed away. My mother and the others climbed into the pit to find their loved ones." She paused. "They carried each and every one of them out of that pile of death so they could bury their family members in dignity." She turned to Katerina, her eyes rimmed with tears.

"And that is why, Katerina. Why I have a house full of children and friends and noise and music and dancing and, yes, peppers." Violeta exhaled a puff of air from her lips. "So now you know why my house is the way it is, Katerina. I know it's chaos. I know it's too much sometimes, too loud, too crazy, too much of everything. I'm sorry if it disturbs you, but it's better this way."

Katerina said nothing as she rocked Dawn in her arms.

"Yes. It's better this way. Because there is no such thing as too much life. Even the yelling and the screaming, and even the fights and tears are better than the silence, Katerina. Anything is better than the silence."

Thirty-Six

Bronx, New York
September 1961

Katerina woke to the sound of raindrops on the tin roof that provided shade to the small patio adjacent to the garden. She rolled over in bed, praying the rain would stop. But it didn't. It rained all through the night and into the morning.

The rain spiraled her into a mood as gray as the sky. She felt the weight of the dampness, the heaviness of the clouds. She couldn't explain it. It had been months since she'd had such a feeling of melancholy. There had been such a difference since meeting Violeta. Their brief chats in the morning, over coffee, over the fence, had done so much to lift Katerina's spirits. With Violeta's advice, Katerina had actually gotten Dawn to sleep through the night. With Violeta's guidance, she was making great progress with her English lessons, practicing her new words and phrases over the fence each day. And then one afternoon as Dawn napped and Katerina sipped her coffee, Violeta ventured into uncharted territory.

"How often do you make love?" Violeta had asked without the slightest hint of embarrassment.

Katerina had excused herself in an instant, claiming she had forgotten something in the oven. Once inside, with the door shut behind her, she leaned against the door and laughed, turning as red as the tomatoes growing in her garden.

Katerina glanced out the kitchen window now as she prepared Dawn's breakfast. Again she saw nothing but gray in the clouds above. The radio report said it was a tropical storm with rain expected for days. There would be no coffee or visit with Violeta and her mother. There would be no witty conversation and laughter shared over the fence. There would be no one to help soothe and hold Dawn when Katerina needed reminding that she was not a failure as a mother. She lifted her chin and inhaled, taking in the scent of her kitchen. There was no comforting perfume of Violeta's peppers in the air. Katerina felt as empty as she had the day Marco promised he could satiate his hunger merely by inhaling the scent of a neighbor's dinner carried to him on the breeze.

She had never learned to swim, but she imagined this feeling was similar to having a wave crash down on you, pulling you under as the water filled your lungs, making it impossible to breathe. She felt it coming on, a force so slight and yet so powerful she often didn't notice it until it was there, moving her bit by bit until she'd lost her footing and gone under. That was how she felt that morning as the rain pelted against the tin roof and the pavement, bit by bit and drop by drop, seeming to tamp down and drown the happiness that had managed to take root these past few weeks.

Later that morning she was sitting on the couch bouncing Dawn on her knee and staring off into space when she heard the doorbell ring, startling her. Katerina was unaccustomed to visitors.

She walked down the hall and lifted the tiniest corner of the curtain, peeking through to see who it could possibly be.

"Oh my." She laughed, racing to unlock the door before throwing it open.

"It's about time. What took you so long? I'm soaked through," Violeta said as she scurried into the house, taking off her plastic rain bonnet as she entered. "I waited, thinking you might come over for coffee. I know how you enjoy the smell of those peppers." She laughed. "And when you didn't, I figured I would come to you. Let the kids kill each other for all I care. I need some quiet and a snuggle from that sweet baby."

And at once, Katerina felt the gray and gloom lift, although outside the rain continued. They sat at the table drinking coffee as Violeta held Dawn and made silly faces that made the baby dissolve into giggles. Violeta glanced over at Katerina and stopped a moment, a wide, bright smile replaced by a laser-focused stare.

"Let me see your arm," Violeta said as she continued bouncing Dawn on her knee. "What's that on your arm?" She reached out and fingered a thin gold bracelet that Katerina wore around her wrist.

"Your mother gave this to me yesterday. When you went in the house to get more olive oil. She said she wanted me to have it. I refused at first, but she insisted. She told me it was her blessing to me and I could not refuse her blessing."

"*Madonna Mia*, dear Mary, mother of God." Violeta lifted her hands to the sky. "This woman. Dear God, what am I to do with this woman?" She looked at Katerina and her face dissolved in an instant from anger and frustration to laughter. "Katerina, I ask you, what am I to do with this woman?"

"I don't understand. I'll give it back, of course. But she insisted. I'm so sorry."

"Oh no, no, no. You have nothing to be sorry about. You did the right thing. A blessing is a blessing." Violeta arched her brow. "Even if it comes from a thief who steals things from her own daughter to give to others." Violeta's entire body shook from laughter.

"What are you talking about?"

"My mother has always been the most generous soul on the planet. Back home, she planted double the size garden she needed for the store and for our family so she always had food to give away. There was nothing she would not do for family, friends, even strangers. She still wants to help and to give, but the problem is, she gives things that are not hers. That bracelet, it's my daughter Louisa's, given to her on her tenth birthday by her godmother."

"You're kidding!" Katerina was horrified and also overcome with laughter. "I'm so sorry, I didn't mean to laugh. It's not funny."

"Oh, but it is." Violeta leaned in, tickling Dawn. "It's quite hysterical when we have friends and family newly arrived from Italy and she tells them she has gifts to welcome them to America. Yes, we have plenty of gifts to welcome you to your new life. My husband's silver pen, the one he saved for weeks to buy, the one he used to sign his name when he bought our house. Well, she took that pen from my husband's desk and gave it to a cousin from Italy who doesn't even know how to write his name. Welcome to America."

"Stop it." Katerina could barely get the words out from laughing so hard.

"Oh, I wish I was kidding."

"How long has she been giving your things away?"

"A few months now. At first it was harmless, a package of peppers, some leftover lasagna. And then one day I couldn't find Louisa's christening cross. I looked everywhere, tearing apart the entire house. Poor Louisa. I screamed at her for days, asking how she could be so careless and lose the one thing of value to her name. And then one day, as I was cleaning Mama's room, I found it."

"What did you do?"

"I told Mama how angry I was with Louisa for losing her cross and that I was going to spank her bottom raw if she didn't find it by the morning. The next day it was back in Louisa's room and we never spoke of it again." Violeta shook her head. She laughed again, only this time it was tinged with sadness and loss.

"What about you?" Violeta asked. "What was your mother like?"

Katerina paused a moment, collecting her thoughts. "She was won-derful. And then she was not. She was loving and kind and damaged, and I see now how she tried to shield me from her heartbreak, her pain. But I think in the end it would have been better for me to know, to understand her better."

"What happened? Why was she so hurt?"

"My father. He would leave us at night. Disappear and come home with the sunrise. He always said he was working, but there were whispers in town that he was having an affair with my best friend's mother, a widow. My grandfather had an affair while my grandmother was on her deathbed and my mother witnessed it. After what happened with her mother, she swore she would never open herself to trust anyone. I was everything to her. I loved her with my whole heart, but sometimes knowing I was her everything . . . it was too much for me. It was too big a responsibility for a young girl, too heavy a weight for me to carry."

"But what about her family, her people? Didn't she have family of her own?"

"No. No one. Her mother's best friend was the one who betrayed her, marrying her father before her mother's body was even cold. My mother left her island, Tinos, as soon as she could. She married my father when she was just sixteen and moved to Corfu. And she never returned to Tinos. She always promised me that we would go back, that we would visit the Church of the Panagia together. It's a beautiful, sacred place, and she promised me that we would pray beside the Virgin Mother and she would keep us safe."

Katerina closed her eyes now, fingering the cross she wore around her neck, picturing her mother, remembering all those times she made that promise as they looked at the treasures in the keepsake box. "But we never went to Tinos. She slipped away from me before we had the chance. She was so hurt and betrayed. I tried. God, how I tried. But in the end I wasn't enough to save her." Katerina opened her eyes to see Violeta staring at her, her eyes glistening. "I still dream that one day I'll make it to Tinos, to

Panagia's church. And I know that when I do, I'll find her again. I know that when I make it there, she'll be beside me."

"Oh, Katerina. Mothers and daughters. How is it that the intensity of our love can both save us and destroy us?"

They said nothing for quite some time after that. The two women, each mothers and daughters themselves, sat silently at the kitchen table, listening as the rain continued to fall.

Thirty-Seven

Bronx, New York

October 1961

"What's that?" Stamati asked as he sipped his coffee while Dawn played with a stuffed bear at his feet.

"I have no idea," Katerina said, closing the refrigerator and going to the door to see who could possibly be knocking.

Violeta burst into the house. "Get your things. Let's go."

"Go? Go where?" Stamati asked, the tone of his voice making it quite clear he was not amused by the neighbor's dramatics.

"Good morning, Stamati," Violeta said as she turned to him and waved. She turned her attention back to Katerina. "It's done. You are I are going on a little adventure. Grab your purse and coat. We're leaving in ten minutes."

"What are you talking about?" Stamati asked. Katerina looked from Violeta to Stamati, reading his face in an instant. It was a look she had grown accustomed to, as if intolerance and indifference coexisted in his eyes.

"Oh, never you mind. I promise to take good care of her. I'll return her in one piece, you'll see."

Shaking his head, Stamati stood and grabbed his hat and coat. "I don't like this." He leaned down and kissed Dawn before walking out the door.

"Bye," Katerina shouted out after him.

"He's in a bad mood today," Violeta said.

"He's in a bad mood every day," Katerina replied. "He's been gambling again. I know it. He's been coming home later and later, smelling of cigarettes and whisky, and the nightly take from the restaurant is smaller and smaller each day."

"Are you worried?"

"I'm always worried. But he won't talk to me about it. He won't even let me finish asking the question before he storms off." Katerina finished clearing the dishes from the table and placed them in the sink. "Now, what are you talking about? What adventure? I can't go anywhere. Have you forgotten I have a small child?"

"It's taken care of. Louisa will watch her for you. We'll bring her next door."

"Violeta, I can't."

"Yes, you can. And you will." Violeta walked right up to Katerina and stood in front of her, nose to nose. "Listen to me, and listen to me right now. Grab your coat and bag. Dawn will be fine in my crazy house for two hours. Trust me. Let's go."

Reluctantly, Katerina did as she was told. They brought Dawn next door, Katerina kissing her on the forehead before placing her in Louisa's arms. Together the women exited the house and walked to the bus stop.

"So you are not going to tell me where we are going?" Katerina asked.

"No," Violeta said as they boarded the bus and she dropped coins in the fare meter, paying for Katerina's trip as well.

The women sat toward the front of the bus, watching out the window as the bus made its way down Allerton Avenue.

"This is us," Violeta said as she pulled the wire above her seat to alert the driver that they would be getting off at the Mace Avenue stop.

They exited the bus and walked east, past the attached homes that looked so very much like the row houses on their own street. Greek and Italian immigrants all along this section of the Bronx cared for their homes with the utmost of pride. Every stoop and front porch was covered in colorful pots of flowers, rosebushes had been planted on even the tiniest patch of front yard, and pristine sidewalks were hosed and scrubbed down with dish soap and a broom at every opportunity. And in many of the driveways, American-made cars—Lincolns and Cadillacs—gleamed from constant washing and waxing, a true testament to their owners' American dream come true.

At last, Violeta stopped.

"We're here," Violeta said, wrapping an arm around Katerina and hugging her tight.

Katerina looked up. She was instantly overwhelmed with emotion. She turned to Violeta, unable to form the words to express her gratitude. But it was more than gratitude, so much more.

Katerina allowed herself to take it all in. The Shrine of Our Lady of Lourdes, right there on the corner of Bronxwood and Mace Avenues, two of the busiest streets in the entire Bronx. She never would have imagined that such a beautiful shrine to Panagia could exist right here in New York, in the Bronx, in their very neighborhood.

Shielding her eyes from the sun with her hand, Katerina looked up at the shrine. It was built from stones, layers and layers placed one upon the other, made to look like a cave carved out from a grotto. Inside the cave, dozens of candles burned in offering to Panagia, the Virgin Mother. To the right of the cave's entrance water flowed from beneath the rocks, a spring of holy water spilling out to the stones below. And above the spring was a statue of Panagia, dressed in a white robe with her arms pressed in prayer, looking down upon the faithful.

Katerina felt the swell in her chest, unexpected and overwhelming. She grabbed Violeta's hand and squeezed.

"When you told me about your mother's island, Tinos, it broke my heart that you were never able to visit with her. I know you'll take Dawn one day, and your mother will be there with you in some way. I'm sure of it. Until then, I wanted to bring you here, to our grotto here in the Bronx. Catholic, Greek Orthodox, what does it matter? She is here too, Katerina. And you can be with her here, when you need to, when you want to. Be with her here until you can visit your mother's island and that beautiful church with the jeweled icon."

"Oh, Violeta," Katerina whispered as tears spilled down her cheeks. She brought Violeta's hands to her lips, kissing them again and again.

Together the women walked farther into the grotto. They lit candles in the cave and then knelt in the shadow of the Blessed Mother. Each of the women prayed in their native tongue and asked Panagia for the same thing. Like mothers through the centuries and generations, Katerina and Violeta each prayed that the Virgin Mother would protect and keep their children safe. But there was one thing more Katerina prayed for. One more person who was never far from her thoughts or her prayers. She thought perhaps that here, in the grotto of Panagia, her private prayer might at last be heard and answered.

"Please," Katerina prayed. "Please, Panagia, help me find Marco. Please, please bring him home."

When they were finished, the women rose, crossing themselves, and began to walk toward the exit.

"Wait a moment." Violeta turned back toward the shrine. "I almost forgot," she said as she pulled two vials from her purse. One by one she filled the jars with holy water from the shrine. "Here." She handed one to Katerina. "Give some to Dawn to drink and bless your home with it as well."

Katerina reached out her arm and squeezed Violeta's hand. "Thank you."

Violeta linked her arm through Katerina's. Together the women walked back down Mace Avenue and to the bus toward home.

Later that afternoon, as Dawn napped, Katerina picked up the phone to call Clotho. It was their weekly routine to catch up every Friday after-noon. Since telephone lines had yet to be installed in the smaller villages of the island, each week Katerina had a taxi pick up Clotho and bring her to and from the periptero in a neighboring town where she could use the phone.

"Clotho!" Katerina shouted into the phone. There was static on the line. "Clotho, how are you?"

"Katerina, my love. Thank God. I am good. Are you all right? You sound different."

"Yes. I'm good. I had the most wonderful day today, Clotho. My neigh-bor surprised me. We took the bus and she took me to a shrine of the Panagia, right here in the Bronx, near my house."

"I knew you sounded different."

"How do you mean?"

"I can hear it in your voice. I haven't heard you like this since those afternoons with Marco in my garden."

"Oh, Clotho . . ." Katerina sighed.

"No, I didn't tell you this to make you sad. Listen to me. Listen to the sound of your own voice. You made a friend, Katerina. You need a friend. Let this person in. I know your mother warned you and that she did her best to protect you. But closing the heart can do more damage than open-ing it sometimes. You need someone to talk to. The loneliness has eaten away at you. I don't need to be next to you to see it. I can see it clearly from here."

"Oh really?" Katerina laughed. "You can see me clearly from there? What am I wearing?"

"Very funny. Very funny." Clotho laughed. "It's time you made a friend, Katerina. Let's learn from the mistakes of the past instead of being para-lyzed by them. Your mother meant well. I know this. But don't allow her damage to be yours any longer. It's been too long and you've been too lonely. It's time to open your heart again, Katerina. It's time you had a friend to share your life with, to share your secrets with."

"I had a friend once who shared my secrets, Clotho. Who shared my everything. And then he was gone."

Before they hung up the phone that afternoon, Clotho said one thing more. "Promise me you'll let her in, even just a bit. Loneliness is a dangerous thing, Katerina. A dangerous, dangerous thing."

Thirty-Eight

Over the years Katerina began to confide in Violeta more and more. She at last opened her heart and let a friend inside, sharing her innermost thoughts and fears about her marriage, motherhood, and even the secret of the cash-filled box hidden away in the back of the closet. But despite it all, there was still someone Katerina could not bring herself to discuss. Many times she tried, his name just a breath away from escaping her lips. But Katerina could not bring herself to say his name out loud.

And then one day Violeta burst into the yard shouting Katerina's name.

"Katerina, hurry up. Quick, come inside. She's on television. You have to see her." Violeta motioned for Katerina to open the gate in the fence that Violeta's husband had recently installed, allowing them to come and go between the yards.

"Come on," Katerina said to Dawn, who was playing with her dolls on the grass as Katerina watered the garden. "Let's see what all the fuss is about." She grabbed Dawn's hand and together they raced into Violeta's yard and down the stairs into the kitchen where Violeta's television blared. The room was chaos, with four of Violeta's five children sprawled across the floor, reading and playing board games. Violeta's mother sat on the sofa knitting and Violeta herself resumed her position at the sink, washing the breakfast dishes and straining her neck to see the television as she finished her work.

The television reporter went on.

"Greece's queen Frederica arrived in New York for the unofficial visit. The queen, accompanied by her daughter, Princess Irene, will spend seventeen days in the United States, first here in New York, where she was presented an honorary degree for preserving Greek heritage and culture by Barnard College. The queen greeted the press as she arrived in New York. Asked what she was most anticipating about her visit, Queen Frederica had a jovial time with reporters saying that she would like to sit in her room at the Waldorf Towers and watch television, even the commercials, adding that there is no television in Greece. Princess Irene said she is most looking forward to visiting the Empire State Building and shopping. After a few days in New York, Queen Frederica and Princess Irene will then travel to Washington, DC, where they will visit with President Johnson. We'll have more on the queen's visit later this week."

Katerina stared at the television, at the image of Frederica. The first images showed her disembarking from the ship that carried her across the Atlantic. She was dressed in a simple coat and hat, holding a dark poodle in her arms as she addressed reporters. And then the images changed to show the queen in her finery, a diamond tiara atop her head and dressed in an elegant floor-length gown as she entered the ballroom to receive her honorary degree.

"She's beautiful, your queen," Violeta said.

"Yes. She always has been beautiful," Katerina said without taking her eyes from the television. "Those eyes, so full of life; those curls, always peeking out from beneath the beautiful hats she wears. And she's just a tiny thing, petite. But, Violeta, that woman is larger than life. She's given so much of herself. I'm happy to see that she's being recognized and honored for it here. She saved so many children during the war."

"From the Germans?"

"No, after the occupation. It wasn't enough that the Germans tried to kill us all; we had to finish the job and kill each other."

"What do you mean?"

"The civil war after the German surrender was even worse than what the Nazis put us through, if you can imagine that. But Queen Frederica mobilized her friends and the wealthiest Greeks and she opened camps across the country. She saved thousands and thousands of children who would have starved or been homeless. She raised an entire generation of children who would have ended up on the streets, or dead." Katerina sighed.

"What are you not telling me?" Violeta inched closer to Katerina, taking her by the elbow. She shouted over her shoulder, "Kids, watch Dawn! Katerina and I are going outside for a moment."

Only when they were safely outside, under the arbor and away from the prying eyes and curious ears of the children, did Violeta speak again. "What are you not telling me?"

Katerina laughed it off. "Don't be silly."

But Violeta would have none of it. "What are you not telling me?" she asked again. "You're hiding something, and that's all right. You don't need to tell me everything, even though I tell you everything. But whatever it is you are holding on to is causing you pain. I can see it in your face. I can see that something, or someone, hurt you. And I'm sorry." She reached her arm out and placed her palm on Katerina's cheek. "You're not alone anymore. You're my family now, Katerina. And I'll always be here for you."

"You're my family now." The words gutted Katerina. Marco had said the very same words to her before he left for the paidopoleis. *"Promise me you'll*

always be my family." She had promised, and she meant it. But then she was left alone, and now another man was her family.

Katerina took a breath, gathering her courage. "His name was Marco. And he was my best friend."

Katerina and Violeta spent the better part of the morning out there, under the arbor. As the bees buzzed all around them and the children laughed and screamed and fought inside the house, Katerina at last opened up to Violeta, sharing with her the story of the boy who had been her first and only friend, and so much more. She told her about the day her world came crashing down, when she and Clotho visited the paidopoleis to find he was gone.

"Are you sure he was there?"

"Yes. I'm sure. I asked my father-in-law about it several times. He brought him there himself. He said they drove up to the gate and walked inside and he personally delivered Marco to the attendants and made them promise to take good care of him."

"Do you think he ran away?"

"I thought so for a long time. I thought he might have gone to Mon Repos. It's a villa belonging to the royal family not far from where my mother and I lived in Corfu Town. Marco's grandmother worked there and his mother spent her early childhood there, and she always told him that they would go back there one day, that the palace would always be his home, if you can believe that." Katerina's head hung low with the weight of empty promises. So many empty promises. "I actually went there, snuck onto the grounds one afternoon. I walked for hours, all along the grounds and down to the water, and called his name. But he wasn't there. I saw Frederica and her family on the beach. I still can't believe that actually happened. I hid behind a tree and watched them swimming." Katerina shrugged her shoulders just a bit. "But Marco was not there."

"You loved this boy?" Violeta leaned in closer, lowering her voice.

"He was my best friend. My only friend."

"You loved this boy." It was not a question.

Thirty-Nine

Bronx, New York
April 1972

Katerina was seated at the kitchen table, nursing a cup of chamomile tea, when she at last heard the door open. It was one a.m.

She smelled him before she saw him, his signature scent of cigarettes and stale liquor and diner grease permeating the air as he stepped through the door and walked down the hall toward her. As he entered the room, he threw his jacket on a chair and opened the refrigerator door to grab a beer. He turned and found her there, waiting for him, startled at the sight of her.

"What are you doing up?"

"You haven't been home in three days."

"I'm home now."

"I see that." She lifted her tea to her lips. It was cold.

"We had a visitor while you were gone."

"Did your Italian friend come over again to fill your ears with gossip?"

"No. This one was Greek. His name was Stavros. He rang the bell at midnight and asked for you. When I told him you were not here, he said to give you a message."

"Is that right?"

"He said you owe him money."

"He did, did he?"

"Yes. And he said now he knows where you work and also where you live." She clutched the teacup tighter, until her knuckles turned white.

"It's fine," he said.

"It's not fine. It's anything but fine."

He ran his fingers through his hair and took another sip of beer. "I have it under control."

"No. You don't. I see it. I see it every day. There's no more money coming in. You disappear for days. And now we have strangers ringing our bell at all hours of the night, threatening you. Us. You are going to lose everything."

"No, I won't."

"You will. Haven't we been through enough? Haven't we lost enough?" she pleaded, her voice now cracking with emotion. "This could ruin us."

"What *us* are you talking about, Katerina? Neither of us wanted this. You know it and I know it. This isn't a marriage. It's an arrangement. Let's not pretend we're something we're not. You got what you wanted, a child, a house, money, and a ticket out of that godforsaken village. I gave you what my father promised you. Don't ask me for anything more. I don't understand what it is about my father, why he felt such an obligation toward you. Why he deemed it his responsibility, my responsibility, to be your savior. But here we are. I'm not out to hurt you, and I don't want for you to be miserable. I just want us to go on leading our separate lives. Be a mother to Dawn, have coffee with your Italians. And leave me to my life. I'll leave you to yours."

He finished his beer and placed it on the counter. He walked past her and up the stairs. There was no gesture between them and no emotion. Not that she expected any. She had learned never to expect anything from him, and in this way, she was never disappointed. The creaky pipes announced to her that he was in the shower and then the quiet again told her he was in bed.

She sat there alone in the dark, fingers clenched around the cold tea. She wanted to hate him. To be outraged. But she was not. Every word he spoke was the truth. Every single one. She was not hurt. She was numb. They had come to coexist and would continue to do so, for the sake of their daughter. But there was one word he mentioned that stayed with her, puzzled her, and hurt her. *Obligation.* Stamati had described his father's interest in her as an obligation.

She often thought back on all those years, all those times the mayor had come to check in on her, offering to help with her mother. *Obligation.* It was nothing of the sort. Katerina and her mother had owed nothing to the mayor, and he in turn owed nothing to them. There was no obligation between them, only genuine kindness and generosity and a desire to be helpful after her father was murdered. Of all the things Stamati said to her that night, this was perhaps what pained Katerina the most. The fact that she was married to a man who did not have the capability to recognize and comprehend simple kindness was the most upsetting of all.

She placed her tea in the sink and started up the stairs. He was snoring by the time she reached the landing.

"Mama?" She heard Dawn's voice, quiet and tentative, coming from her bedroom. The door was cracked open; her light was on, bleeding into the dark hallway.

"Sweetheart. What are you doing up at this hour?" Katerina asked as she climbed in the bed beside Dawn.

Katerina gazed into the face of her daughter. Dawn had Katerina's grandmother's blue eyes. At twelve, Dawn was now the same age Katerina was when she lost both her father and Marco, thrust into a tragic reality and adulthood in an instant. Dawn was still so innocent, still merely a child. She leaned in closer, pulling Dawn into her arms. She would move heaven and earth and sacrifice whatever she needed to ensure Dawn never experienced pain and loss like hers.

"I had a dream and it woke me," Dawn said as she leaned in and snuggled closer to her mother.

"You did? I'm sorry, honey. I'm here and everything is okay now. What did you dream about?"

"I dreamed I was on a swing and there was a woman pushing me. I kept going higher and higher, but I wasn't scared." Dawn turned to her mother, filled with pride. "I wasn't scared, Mama. Not at all. I know she was beautiful, but I never saw her face. I thought I would see her face, but I opened my eyes and I woke up. And she was gone."

"Were you afraid of her?"

"No. That's just it. She didn't scare me. She made me feel safe."

Katerina stroked Dawn's face. "I'm so glad. Because you are safe. Here. With me. I will always keep you safe."

"Tell me again, Mama. The story of Nyx. Like you used to when I was a little girl."

"Yes. Because you are very grown up now. But never too grown up for a story."

And so Katerina snuggled together with Dawn and told her the story of Nyx, feared by gods and men and the protector of children in the night. And as she drifted off to sleep, entangled in the embrace of her daughter, Katerina made note to call Clotho in the morning and ask her the meaning of Dawn's dream, the same dream she herself had when she was a child.

Forty

Bronx, New York
May 1972

Katerina wasn't the one who called the mayor, although nothing she said would convince Stamati otherwise. But gossip traveled quickly through the tight-knit community of recent Greek immigrants. It was only a matter of weeks before news of Stamati's gambling reached Corfu. And it was only a matter of days after that, that Katerina found her father-in-law seated at her kitchen table smoking cigarettes and drinking endless cups of coffee, trying to talk some sense into his self-destructive son.

The mayor had always been a slight man. But as he approached his seventieth birthday, he looked even older to Katerina than his years. Weathered now in the way of someone who had survived the storms but was forever changed by them.

His hair had turned completely white, and his glasses, perpetually perched on his nose, were now substantially thicker. He continued to dabble in politics, serving on several local committees and on the Corfu city council, lobbying for funding to bring the tourist trade to Corfu, understanding that the island's verdant natural beauty and rich history gave Corfu a potential that set her apart from other traditionally visited islands.

Katerina had always felt a special affinity for her father-in-law. She enjoyed their conversations and learning about his latest philanthropic efforts or municipal projects. But above all, it was his efforts in helping Katerina find the answers to Marco's disappearance that cemented their bond. Through the years, he had written letters to Queen Frederica's foundation and the Red Cross, as well as soliciting help from political friends, hoping to find answers. Letter after letter, phone call after phone call, the outcome was always the same. Nothing. Not even the mayor's well-placed and influential friends could find any trace of Marco.

And although their search for Marco had proven heartbreakingly futile, Katerina was grateful for the generosity of the mayor's efforts. Often she wondered how it was that Stamati and his father were so very different. How was it that a cultured and kindhearted man like her father-in-law had raised a man like Stamati? How was it that a man who valued hard work and education, who volunteered to find jobs for children who aged out of the paidopoleis, had a son with no work ethic whatsoever?

"You're lucky your mother is dead," the mayor said as Stamati looked at him from across the table. "Because this would have killed her."

The mayor did not yell. Katerina couldn't remember a single time when the mayor had raised his voice.

"It's not as bad as the rumors. Don't listen to those gossips. They're just jealous," Stamati replied.

"Jealous? Of what?" the mayor challenged. "Of you? Of someone who was given every opportunity, every chance, every gift, and then threw it all away? When will you ever grow up? When will you ever learn?"

Stamati glared at his father. Without another word he stormed out of the room and out of the house.

Katerina stood at the kitchen sink watching them, grateful Dawn was at school and had not witnessed the exchange. The mayor said nothing as his gaze stayed fixed on the empty seat where Stamati had been. He took a final drag from his cigarette and stabbed it several times into the ashtray, which was already overflowing. Ash and cigarette butts spilled over on the table and onto the Greek newspaper that the mayor had been reading earlier in the day. His hand trembled as he reached over to clean up the mess.

"No. Let me," she said as she took his hand in hers and placed it back at his side. She emptied the ashtray and wiped the table and the newspaper clean. She glanced down at the front page of the paper. "Fiscal Crisis in Athens," "Wildfires Raging in Ioannina," "Communist Militants Petition to Be Reunited with Family in Greece," "Municipal Workers Call for General Strike."

"Nothing but bad news at home as well," she said as she sat down next to him at the table. "I'm so sorry. I've tried to talk sense into him, really I have."

The mayor was silent for a few moments, then his shoulders and head sank to his chest.

Stamati had been a difficult man for her to be married to, but he had been a lifetime of frustration for the mayor. Katerina sat silently beside her father-in-law, her hand on his, averting her eyes to give him some measure of privacy in his pain.

She had watched silently over the years, how his disappointment in Stamati weighed heavily on him, taking its toll both emotionally and physically. She had always been fond of the mayor, and he had always been kind and generous to her, and most importantly to Dawn. It had warmed Katerina's heart to see her father-in-law dote on Dawn, lavishing her with love and attention, insisting that he pay for Katerina and Dawn to travel to Corfu for the summer, even when money was tight. He had wanted nothing more than to share the beauty and magic of the island with his granddaughter, and Katerina had been happy to oblige.

She stood to get him a fresh glass of water and then placed her hand once again on his.

After a few moments he lifted his head and looked at her. "I always tried my best with him."

"I know you did."

"I've always tried my best, Katerina."

"I know. You've been a rock for me, for so many. I don't know what I would have done without you all these years. I'm so grateful for everything you've done for me, for us. For all of us."

His shoulders fell again as his chin sank into his chest. Katerina reached her hand out to touch his arm.

He lifted his face to look at her. He seemed to her a shell of the man he once was. Broken and old now.

"It's not your fault."

He winced. Her words, meant to give him a measure of solace, seemed to have the opposite effect. His head collapsed and he sat at Katerina's kitchen table and cried.

After a few moments he lifted his head to face her. "Katerina, I have something to tell you. I waited to tell you in person, knowing I was coming to deal with Stamati. I got a letter just before I left Corfu. A letter about Marco."

∾

"I think in some way not knowing was better," Katerina said as Violeta filled her glass with homemade wine. The friends sat outside in Katerina's yard, under the arbor.

It was a cool night and Katerina wrapped her shawl around her shoulders. Dawn had finally gone to sleep and the mayor had gone out to meet an old friend from Corfu. Stamati was supposed to be at work, but she was not really sure where he was. And in this moment she didn't really care.

"At least then I had hope," Katerina continued. "Hope for him, hope for us . . . But now there's nothing."

"Oh, Katerina." Violeta reached her hand across the table and placed it on Katerina's. "What happened?"

Katerina stood and began to walk around the garden. Violeta did not follow her; she stayed rooted in place, allowing her friend the space and time she needed to share her story.

"He received a letter from a friend, a police sergeant in Athens. For years we've been searching. And now we know . . ." Her voice trailed off for a moment. "They found some records in Athens. A document, and then someone who remembered him. They found his death certificate, Violeta. He's dead." There were no more tears now. Katerina had cried them all in the hours since the mayor shared his news.

"He said Marco ran away from the paidopoleis just a few weeks after arriving there. He stowed away onboard a ferry to Piraeus and lived on the streets of Athens for months, stealing food from outdoor vendors to survive. He was just a boy, Violeta. Just a little boy, and there was no one to take care of him. He died on the streets, in the gutter like a piece of discarded trash. He was only a child. And he died alone."

"Oh, Katerina." Violeta walked over to Katerina and enveloped her in her arms.

"I don't understand why he left, why he went to Athens." Katerina turned to face Violeta. "I don't understand why he would leave Corfu. What could he have possibly been looking for in Athens?"

Suddenly the tears came again and she cried into her friend's shoulder, soft and silent at first and then deeper and stronger, unleashing all of the pain, anger, and confusion she had kept trapped deep inside for so many years.

"I know you feel helpless. But there is something you can do for Marco, Katerina," Violeta said as she stroked Katerina's hair.

Katerina pulled away and looked at her.

"I know it's not the way you intended to, the way he intended to. But you can bring him home. Ask your father-in-law to help you find where he is buried and bring him home."

There, in her garden, crying in the arms of her friend, for the first time in a very long time Katerina felt understood.

Forty-One

Bronx, New York
April 1977

The mayor passed away quietly in his sleep just weeks after sharing the news of Marco's death with Katerina. He'd returned to his apartment in Kanoni with a vow to disown Stamati if he didn't straighten himself out, and to help Katerina find and bring Marco's body home to finally rest. Mr. Andonis found him after the mayor failed to show up for a planned meeting to watch the Corfu Philharmonic in Spianada Square.

Katerina's hopes that Stamati could somehow be brought to his senses had died along with her father-in-law that day. And while initially she'd feared her dream of bringing Marco home to rest in the village had died as well, Violeta insisted they keep trying, that she would help Katerina write as many letters and make as many calls as needed until they found him.

The years passed, and as the divide across the yard between Katerina's and Violeta's homes grew smaller and smaller, the fractures in Katerina's own home and family grew wider.

"Won't you come to Easter lunch with us?" Katerina asked as she dressed. She looked over at Stamati lying still in the bed with his eyes open, staring at the ceiling. She noticed there was no stack of bills beside him on the table. "Would you help me—" She caught herself as she said the words and reached back to zip herself up.

She smoothed out the skirt as she admired herself in the mirror. It had been such a treat to ride the bus with Violeta to Alexander's on Fordham Road and splurge on a new dress to wear for Violeta's Easter lunch. The moment she saw the dress she knew it was the one, cinched at the waist and covered in roses across the skirt. The flowers, blood red and vibrant, reminded her of the flowers in Clotho's garden. She would make sure to have Violeta take a photo of her in the dress so she could send it to Clotho.

"Come to Easter lunch with us?" she asked Stamati again. "Do you remember when you were the one who begged me to go out, to have friends and be more social?"

"It's not Easter."

"It's their Easter," she replied. "And they're our friends."

"They're your friends." He rolled over away from her.

She walked out of the room, knocking on Dawn's door. "Honey, are you ready?"

The door opened and Katerina was overcome at the sight of her.

"Do you like it?" Dawn asked. "Is it okay?" She spun around so Katerina could get a better look at her. She wore platform sandals and a yellow jumpsuit tied at the waist, and her hair was blown straight and feathered like all the fashionable girls did at the time.

"Oh, Dawn." She steadied herself against the doorframe. How had it gone so fast? How was it possible that her little girl, her sweet miracle of a baby, was now seventeen years old? She looked at Dawn and was overcome. She was no longer the gangly girl who played with dolls on the floor and helped Katerina in the garden. She was no longer the nervous young girl who begged to keep the light on at night. She was a lovely young lady. And she looked so much like Katerina's mother, Katerina's heart ached at the sight of her. "You're beautiful."

The afternoon was filled with food and friends and laughter and wine. Violeta's mother had passed away a few years before, and while Violeta no longer made the roasted peppers every day, they were still a staple at every holiday and special occasion. The scent, like the rosemary, basil, roses, and outdoor fires that had perfumed the village when Katerina was a young girl, was comforting to her.

"You look tired," Katerina said to Violeta as she put her arm around her. "Everything was delicious. Perfect. Did you get any sleep last night, or were you up all night cooking?" Katerina rubbed her uncomfortably full belly. Lasagna, chicken cacciatore, burrata, octopus and calamari salad, veal marsala, mussels swimming in savory marinara sauce, and spaghetti with fresh garden tomatoes and basil . . . Katerina had indulged in all of Violeta's dishes, one more delicious than the next.

"I'm exhausted," Violeta admitted. "Yes, I'm tired. But it's a good tired. Nothing makes me happier than to see this." She motioned around the room, filled with family and friends. "It makes the tired worth it."

Just then Violeta's cousin Anita walked up to her and hugged Violeta tight. "May God continue to bless your hands. You make magic in your kitchen." She put her fingers to her lips and kissed them.

As Anita walked away, Violeta leaned into Katerina. "Did you see that comb in her hair, the one covered in pearls?"

"Yes."

"Mine. The thief's memory lingers on." Her mouth twisted into a sideways smile as she cocked her eyebrow, dissolving both women into a fit of laughter. Violeta poured two glasses of limoncello and motioned for Katerina to follow her into the yard. They sat together sipping the pale yellow drink that was at once perfectly sweet and tart.

"Look, I knew it." Violeta nudged Katerina. "I had a feeling when he came by last week. He kept lingering in the kitchen and looking out the window to the yard. I asked him what he was looking for, but I knew all along."

Katerina followed Violeta's gaze to where Dawn was seated on the steps to the second floor. Beside her, hanging on her every word, was Violeta's nephew Fabricio. Tall and slim, with a quick laugh and a smile that Katerina thought could light up the entire borough of the Bronx, Fabricio had arrived with his family from Italy just three years before. He often visited his aunt Violeta's house with his parents. But Katerina had noticed him coming by more often these past few days, chatting with Dawn over the lattice fence between the yards.

Katerina watched her daughter's face, how her eyes brightened at the sight of him, how her entire demeanor changed when he was near. She noticed how Dawn leaned toward him as he spoke, how her hand fluttered to her mouth as she giggled, and how her cheeks flushed as he handed her a flower he had picked from the garden.

Violeta placed her hand on Katerina's. "It's bittersweet, isn't it? Seeing your baby grow into a woman. Watching as someone else becomes the most important thing in her life."

Katerina said nothing. As Dawn smiled at this boy and touched his arm as she laughed, Katerina found nothing bittersweet about it. While other mothers might mourn the end of childhood, Katerina would not allow herself the indulgence. Dawn was happy. And her happiness was Katerina's. That was all that mattered.

It went that way for the next few years. Eventually Fabricio crossed over into Katerina's garden. From the window in the kitchen overlooking the yard, Katerina watched as Dawn fell in love with the handsome young man from Italy among the flowers, herbs, and fruit trees she tended so carefully though the years.

The day Fabricio asked for Dawn's hand was the beginning of a beautiful new chapter in their lives. Katerina cried as Dawn raced into the kitchen, showing off her ring and telling her she was going to be married.

"Absolutely not." Stamati slammed his fist on the table when Dawn and Katerina shared the news with him. "Over my dead body." He blamed Katerina for this disaster, insisting if she were a better mother their daughter would be engaged to a Greek, not running around with a foreign boy.

That night, as Dawn cried into her pillow while Katerina stroked her hair, Katerina knew what she needed to do. In the end, what troubled her most about Stamati and their marriage was not the gambling habit, suspected womanizing, or lack of affection between them. She had come to accept that he could never be more, that he would never be the husband she wanted and needed. But in the end, Katerina could not accept that he would never be the father Dawn deserved.

"Shh . . . It's all right," she insisted as she continued to stroke her daughter's hair. Dawn was silent save for the muffled sobs.

Katerina was filled with a calm and silent resolve. In that moment, as dusk settled and the garden outside was cast in ghostly gray, Katerina walked into the room where Stamati sat smoking cigarettes and reading the newspaper and told him she was leaving him. It was one thing to sacrifice her own happiness for the security of others. But sacrificing her daughter's happiness was a concession Katerina was unwilling to make.

Forty-Two

Bronx, New York
May 1981

Second to the day she became a mother, the day Dawn married Fabricio was the happiest day of Katerina's life. Attempting to ease his future father-in law's hesitation, Fabricio had offered to be married in the Greek Orthodox church, understanding what it meant to his future bride and her family. Despite his initial outbursts and protests, Stamati ultimately did escort his daughter down the aisle to her waiting groom.

The marriage went on as planned.

So did the separation.

It was less contentious than Katerina had anticipated, and divorce was never discussed. Katerina and Stamati simply went their separate ways, lived their separate lives, and found this unconventional arrangement suited everyone best. Their relationship had evolved once Stamati and Katerina stopped pretending.

"Our daughter has grown up. We've done our job." It was as simple as that. *Obligation*. Since the day Stamati used that word, that was how

Katerina had come to view her marriage. They had an obligation to raise their daughter together. And now that obligation was done.

Unburdened by obligation, Stamati was kinder to Katerina than he had been in years. Unburdened by expectations or judgment, Stamati moved out of the house with Katerina's consent and began to make better decisions, at last getting his gambling under control. Unburdened by her disappointment of him, Katerina began to invite Stamati to dinner so he could spend time with their daughter as a family and get to know his new son-in-law.

"Do you hate him?" Violeta had asked her.

"No."

"Do you love him?"

"Not in the way you love your husband. Not in that way at all."

"So, then, what is this?"

"It's life," Katerina had said with a finite resolve. "It might seem messy to others, but it makes sense for us." She smiled at Violeta. Stamati had insisted on giving the house on Eastchester Road to Dawn and Fabricio as a wedding gift. And even before Katerina could think of finding an apartment of her own, Fabricio insisted Katerina stay and live with them in the house she had tended to with such love and care. Katerina protested at first, saying the last thing a newly married couple needed was a mother-in-law hovering over them. But Fabricio wouldn't even entertain the notion. Nothing would make him happier, he'd insisted, than to take down the lattice fence between the yards once and for all so Violeta and Katerina could come and go as they pleased and their families truly could become one.

The first year of Dawn and Fabricio's marriage had been one of happiness unlike any Katerina had known. A year filled with love, laughter, friends, family, and wonderful food.

Just days after their first anniversary, when Dawn had announced she was pregnant, Katerina never imagined it was possible to feel such joy. And weeks after that, when Katerina found her bleeding and crying on the bathroom floor, she never imagined it was possible to feel such pain.

"Keep trying," the doctors told Dawn. "You're young and healthy. It's only a matter of time."

Every day without fail, Katerina boarded the Allerton Avenue bus to pray in the grotto of Our Lady of Lourdes on Mace Avenue. She knelt in the grotto, praying for help, praying for the safe delivery of a child for Dawn.

Two more times Dawn had told her mother she was pregnant. And two more times mother and daughter had mourned for the child who was lost.

When, after months of trying, Dawn again found herself pregnant, Katerina was too nervous to share the news with anyone but Violeta. She was too anxious to celebrate, too numb to feel anything but fear. Week after week she waited for the inevitable. But as the days turned into weeks, and months went by, Dawn and Katerina began to allow themselves a glimmer of hope. Could this pregnancy finally be the one to welcome a baby into their lives?

When Dawn at last reached seven months, the doctor assured her that her child was healthy and it was time to begin preparing the nursery.

Upon hearing the news, Katerina picked up the phone to call Clotho. At Katerina's insistence, Clotho had reluctantly moved to a nursing home in Corfu Town a few months earlier after falling and breaking her hip, finally admitting to Katerina that she was losing her vision. Each week without fail, just as they had for more than twenty years, Katerina called to speak with her old friend and catch up on the news from the village and their friends. And each month Katerina opened the box tucked in the back of the closet and took out just enough money to cover Clotho's expenses for the month. Stamati never knew that he was paying for Clotho's care with the money Katerina had siphoned away and saved over the years.

It had been so difficult keeping the news from Clotho these past few months. But now Katerina, still anxious yet hopeful, could not wait to share the happy news with her dearest and oldest friend.

But that afternoon Clotho had news of her own.

There was silence on the other end when Katerina told Clotho about the baby. Katerina could hear her breathing, slightly labored and raspy.

"Clotho."

Still silence.

"Clotho, are you all right?" Katerina's voice was tinged with concern and agitation.

And then Clotho spoke. "Katerina, I have something to tell you. He's back."

"What do you mean? Who is back?"

"He's alive, Katerina. Marco's alive."

Katerina felt the blood drain from her face. Her fingers tingled, numb. She reached her arm out to steady herself on the counter.

"It's true, Katerina. He's alive. He went back to the village, to Yianna's house. He was stocking up on supplies in Sidari and the storeowner told him I was here, in the nursing home. And he came to see me. At first I could not believe it was him; I was certain my eyes were playing tricks on me. But it was him, Katerina. Like a ghost resurrected from the past. Katerina, he's alive. Marco came back."

Katerina felt her legs could no longer sustain her. Still cradling the phone under her ear, she slid to the floor. *He's alive. Marco came back.*

"Marco's home, Katerina. It's time for you to come too. Come home, Katerina."

Forty-Three

Corfu

May 1981

Katerina gazed out the window as the plane began its descent, coming in for a landing at Corfu International Airport. She crossed herself as the plane flew low over the whitewashed Church of the Vlacherna and the tiny island of Pontikonisi behind it. The sight of the church always stirred something deep inside Katerina. As much as she had grown to love her life in New York, one glimpse of the tiny church and fishing boats bobbing in the water along the walkway always made Katerina feel as if this was where she truly belonged.

She had been a bundle of nerves and anxiety from the moment Clotho announced that Marco had returned. At first Katerina didn't believe her, thinking perhaps it was another one of Clotho's vivid dreams that her old friend had confused with reality. But soon it became clear to Katerina that Clotho was indeed lucid, and by some miracle, Marco was alive.

There were so many emotions to navigate, so much information to sort through and process. It made no sense to Katerina that the Athenian policeman would lie to the mayor. With thousands still displaced and miss-ing after the war, it must have been a misunderstanding, a tragic mistake. One lost child mistaken for another. Another orphaned child left to die in the gutter.

The night she'd learned the news of Marco's return, Katerina sat with Violeta, sipping chamomile tea under the arbor. She explained that however much she wanted to go to him, there was no way she could leave Dawn now.

The next morning Katerina came downstairs to find Violeta and Dawn seated in the kitchen waiting for her. There, on the table, was a round-trip ticket to Corfu in her name.

"You have to go. I won't hear of it," Dawn insisted. "I'm not due for ten weeks. You have to go and find out what happened to him. If you don't, the curiosity and stress of it will eat me alive and this baby will come sooner than any of us would like. So for me, and for your grandchild, please, go, Mama. There's time."

That night Katerina boarded a flight for Corfu. She had been back to the island many times since moving to New York. It had been important to Katerina and Stamati that Dawn spend time with Stamati's parents and grow up with a connection to them, and to Corfu. Something that even in their most difficult years the couple had always agreed on. But in all the times she had returned, all those summers spent strolling the Liston, renting paddleboats to explore the caves of Palaiokastritsa and watching in terror as Dawn jumped from the sun-blanched cliffs of Sidari into the blue Ionian, this would be the first time Katerina would return to Pelekito since the day her father was killed.

Thirty-three years later and Katerina had kept her promise.

And now, as if by some miracle, it seemed Marco had as well.

"*Kalispera*," she said to the taxi driver as she closed her door and settled into the back seat. The dry heat punctuated the taxi's scent—cigarettes and body odor. "Can you take me to Pelekito, please?"

She rolled down the window and lifted her face to the dry breeze.

Hair blowing in the wind, Katerina felt the familiar flutter in her belly as the taxi passed the sealed front gate of Mon Repos and continued along Garitsa bay, past the craggy mountain of the old fort, then headed north along the coast toward the village.

It took a little over an hour for the taxi to carry Katerina up the coast and snake around the mountain roads to the village's entrance. A one-hour taxi ride to transport Katerina three decades into the past. And now as she watched the village fall into view from the back seat of the taxi, she felt the memories rushing back. The reminiscences inched toward her slowly at first, faint and distant, then grew and gained strength and weight as scent, sight, and memory fused together, overtaking and over-whelming her. The emotions and the pain, still so raw, even after all this time.

"Here, please," she said, her voice gravelly and weak.

The driver pulled over just beyond the periptero, now shuttered, a plank of wood nailed across the front, covering the window. On one side of the tiny structure, the terracotta-colored plaster had all but crumbled and fallen away.

Katerina paid the driver and opened the door. She breathed in deeply, filling herself with the village's perfume. Rosemary, basil, thyme, wiste-ria, roses, and sea spray layered together in the fragrance that defined her childhood. Only the smoky scent of an outdoor kitchen fire was missing.

"There's no one here to light the fires." She spoke the words out loud, as if the reality of them was too heavy to keep buttoned up inside as she had done with so many of her thoughts and emotions through the years. She was well aware of how the village had changed, of how she was merely one of many who had stayed away, who would not or could not find their way home after the war. Many of these tiny villages, once so full of life, had simply faded away over time, becoming just another casualty of war, a village of ghosts.

It wasn't just my father they killed. They killed the village too. Seeing it with her own eyes brought new clarity and fresh pain. She closed the car door behind her and watched as the taxi pulled away, leaving her alone in what was once the center of the town.

It was all just as she remembered it. The café where the men played cards, the periptero where her father would buy his cigarettes and the newspaper. And just beyond, the home that had once belonged to her father-in-law, the mayor. The gated garden was overgrown and thick with weeds, the once pristinely painted stucco now cracked and faded. She remembered the afternoons she and Marco would race each other across the property, praying old Thea Olga would not spot them and throw rocks or potatoes at them. Marco had once confided in her that his mother had risked Olga's wrath to borrow eggs when times were especially tight. How they had laughed, doubling over and rolling on the ground until their stomachs ached. Katerina remembered thinking at the time that this was the funniest thing she had ever heard, laughing with Marco until tears ran down her face. Now the memory brought tears to her eyes once again, but for very different reasons.

She looked up at the home she once envied, the home she once dreamed of peeking inside, wondering what marvels existed behind the painted concrete walls and ornate iron gate. And this was her own family's home now. The grandest in the village, the house everyone envied, now shuttered and vacant like all the rest. She took the keys out of her pocket and stepped toward the house.

No, she thought, stopping suddenly. *Not yet.* She placed her bag inside the gate and then turned around, walking instead toward the kafenio. Before she could face the present, she needed to confront the past.

She continued walking the narrow lane behind the kafenio. She followed along the path to the spot where that man, that monster, had taken her father.

She spotted a small cross planted in the ground. She traced her finger across the wood, warped and splintering. It was here where he took his last breath and spoke his last words to her.

"Remember Orpheus."

She had tried to honor him, to remember and heed his words. Through her entire life she had focused on what was in front of her, understanding there was no help and no point in looking behind her. The past held nothing but pain and loss. How could Baba have known this in that moment?

Baba had taught her early in life the importance of love and trust, and perhaps that was a gift as well. For the longest time, for all those early years of her marriage, there had been no love or trust. There had been nothing but obligation and duty and survival. And then God blessed her with Dawn, and she at last had someone to love, and she at last understood the meaning and the message in her father's final words.

She placed her cheek against the cross, taking in the moment, taking in the stillness, praying, hoping, longing to feel his presence, the reassurance of him. But she felt nothing. There was nothing left for her here besides painful memories. Empty, like the village. Empty, like the void within her. Empty, like the grief and loss so deep and dark that she imagined nothing and no one could ever make her whole again. She had been filled with love, satiated in a way she never imagined possible, when Dawn was born. But even so, there was still an emptiness that Katerina had come to terms with. A loneliness and ache she had learned to live with.

Months after her father was killed, while she and her mother were living in Corfu Town and her mother was still well enough to work, the mayor had visited the café with news. He told them that the murderers had been found. They had stolen an old fisherman's *caïque* and were found hiding in an abandoned shed on a mountaintop on the tiny island of Mathraki. All three, in addition to the former schoolteacher, had been arrested and executed at Lazaretto. Katerina remembered how the mayor explained that the men had cowered in their final moments, crying for mercy, implicating others and one another for their crimes, and making false allegations against their political rivals. Their pleas and accusations fell on deaf ears, their bodies dumped in a mass grave. The mayor had thought sharing the details of their arrests and deaths would be a comfort to Katerina and Mama, believing they might find some solace in seeing justice served. She found nothing of the sort. Katerina had just felt empty.

It was the same now.

She stood after a while, brushing the dirt from her skirt with her hand. She kissed the tips of her fingers and then gently touched the cross.

She walked again down the alley, a stray cat following behind, its ribs protruding beneath its fur. She continued to the mayor's house, grabbed her bag, and then wrestled with the lock. Leaning in with the full force of her body, she struggled to turn the key. After a few moments, the door gave way and she was greeted by a wall of hot, stagnant air heavy with the scent of heated cedar. She entered, taking it all in, the home of her childhood dreams. This moment was nothing like she had imagined.

Katerina walked along the home's first floor, from parlor to kitchen to bedroom, pulling sheets from furniture and opening windows to allow the fresh mountain air in. It was by today's standards simple and small. A tiny living room gave way to a U-shaped kitchen. A small table was pushed up against the wall; the vinyl tablecloth, dotted with fruits and vegetables, had yellowed and cracked with the passing of time.

It was a last-minute decision to stay here. Dawn had pressed the keys into her hand at the airport as they said their goodbyes. Although Dawn had never stepped foot in the village, she knew her grandparents had maintained this house in pristine fashion throughout their lives. It was always a dream of the mayor's to see the village come back to life one day, and to see his grandchild running through the garden and across the plateia.

Katerina remembered the first time he'd held Dawn in his arms. For hours he carried her, walking in circles out in the garden on Eastchester Road, whispering to her, telling her that he could not wait to show her the home that would one day be hers, to walk with her to the fresh spring, to take her out on his fishing boat and sit with her for hours in the sun as a lamb roasted slowly over coals on the spit. Each summer as they visited with him on Corfu, the mayor would walk hand in hand with Dawn along the Liston, down along Garitsa bay, and across Spianada Square. He bought her freshly roasted corn from the toothless gypsies along the square and giant ice creams from Caprice topped with sparklers that made her squeal with delight. He swore to God and Saint Spyridon that he would host the greatest party the village had ever seen when the day came at last that they could celebrate and welcome his granddaughter to her ancestral home.

Katerina was not one to deny her father-in-law anything; he had always been good to her. But year after year, this was the one request Katerina could not find in her heart to grant him. Katerina refused, saying simply, "No. I can't go back there." And after some time he'd simply stopped asking.

But through his life, until the very end, the mayor had kept updating his home, adding a full indoor bath, plumbing, and electricity, even as the other homes and buildings sat neglected and vacant, crumbling into ruins over time. The mayor's house stood as it always had, out of place in this provincial village of one-room homes built of stones and mud and crude concrete. When he passed away, he left the home to Dawn, saying nothing would make him happier than to know that she had come home, even if he were not alive to see it.

Katerina turned and walked toward the front door again, glancing at the fireplace and mantel. There, in the center of the mantel, was a large photo of Katerina and Stamati on their wedding day. Katerina looked closer at her own face staring back at her, a smile on her lips and an empty look in her eyes. She remembered it well, mustering the strength to force a smile wide enough to mask her emotions that day. Everyone saw and commented on the misty-eyed bride in her white dress.

"Look at her," they had said. *"That poor girl has been through so much. Look at those tears of long-overdue joy."* Katerina had nodded politely and thanked everyone for their good wishes and blessings that day, but only she knew the true nature of her tears.

As her fingers lingered on the mantel, she reached out and picked up another photo, another familiar image staring back at her. This one also from her wedding day. She studied it closer, the mayor and his wife beaming beside Katerina and Stamati. She remembered this moment so clearly. It was taken just after the mayor gave his speech, welcoming Katerina into the family and promising to care for her as if she were his own daughter.

She could see it all so vividly in her mind. *"We're your family now,"* he had said to her, pulling her close as he wept on her shoulder. She remembered feeling the wetness though the fabric of her wedding dress.

Katerina locked the door behind her and walked out of the house and back again toward the center of town. Hands on her hips, she looked around the square again. She closed her eyes and inhaled, wishing she could once more smell the scent of cigarettes mixing with muddy coffee and whisky. She closed her eyes tighter, wishing she could hear the men again, their voices raised as they talked over one another, arguing about politics. She walked around the table, her finger lingering over the rusted metal frame.

What would they say now, with King Constantine in exile and the monarchy abolished? she wondered. The men who'd argued and believed so vehemently in the leadership of the royal family . . . What would they say now, had they lived long enough to see King Constantine's rule overturned by a military junta? Discarded. Like all of their collective ideals, all of their dreams. Gone. Like the simple yet happy life they all once shared tucked away among the cliffs.

She walked farther along the road, gazing through a veil of cypress trees to the windswept and marbled Ionian in the distance. The breeze had kicked in again, the rattling of leaves filling the air with a soft, consistent hum. It felt to Katerina as if the very trees themselves were welcoming her back with their soft rattle that sounded like a song, comforting her and telling her to be still. As she continued toward the schoolhouse, she picked up a rock and tossed it from the cliff to the sea. The stone sailed away from her and then plummeted just short of the shoreline. She watched it sink, laughing at how woefully out of practice she was.

Katerina continued along until the road curved up toward the schoolhouse and the mountain. She looked up, spotting the yia-yia tree in the distance. Katerina was surprised to see that it was smaller than she remembered and yet still majestic. She closed her eyes, trying to picture in her head the games of tag, the rustic school lunches and picnics on the grass in her canopied shade, and all the times Marco sat waiting for her against the broad, sturdy trunk. But it was no use. Despite the countless joyful memories and moments experienced beneath the tree, one vision obscured the rest. One that defined and defiled this once happy place. It was that moment that changed all of their lives, every last one of them.

No matter how hard she tried, when Katerina looked up at the tree, all she could see was Yianna's lifeless body hanging there, swinging back and forth as her long, unbound hair lifted on the breeze to reveal her face, her blue lips.

She thought back to that moment, when Mr. Andonis read Yianna's note and her father collapsed in tears beside Yianna's body. She recalled how her mother recoiled and then stiffened, and how a collective whisper seemed to pass over everyone in the village as the dark cloud passed over her mother's face. What Katerina had been blind to as a child was impossible to ignore as she grew older and began to understand the ways of the world, and of men and women and marriage and relationships. The devastation unleashed by rumors of her father's infidelity had ruined Katerina as well. Over the years, as she came to terms with the realization that hers would never be more than a marriage of convenience, that she and Stamati would share a child and a house and nothing more between them, Katerina took a certain measure of comfort in knowing she could never be hurt in the way her mother was. When you don't open yourself to love, you don't open yourself up to pain.

She went past the schoolhouse and church, stopping when she reached the fresh spring. The weeds and thicket surrounding the spring were overgrown, covering the stone path that once led the villagers to the water. She stepped carefully, brambles sticking to her skirt, and cupped her hands to take a sip. It was cold and refreshing, just as she remembered.

She walked for another thirty minutes up the mountain, thankful the path was not completely overgrown. At last she reached the summit, where the road divided into three narrow trails. The one to the left would lead her to Marco's house.

She heard the clanging as she approached the house. Her stomach lurched as her legs propelled her forward. Her mind raced and yet her pace slowed. She never imagined she would be here. She had waited forever for this moment, dreaming of it, and yet now she felt anxious and slightly afraid.

They had been merely children all those years ago. Children who shared a past steeped in joyful memories as well as trauma. They were no doubt bound by this. So much time had passed. She would like to think that a piece of her twelve-year-old self still remained intact, yet she was no longer that girl.

What about Marco? Was he still that boy? She realized as she inched closer to him with each step that in all those years, as painful as it was to think he had died, in some ways it was easier than this.

Death was finite. Death was not a choice.

But this . . . learning that he had deliberately stayed away made her feel like a fool.

Clang, clang. The banging got louder.

What am I doing here? What was I thinking? The path seemed to wobble beneath her feet. She felt light-headed and reached into her bag for her water. She walked slowly to the side of the path and pressed her back against a lemon tree as she sipped her water and took deep breaths in and out.

She had a home and a family and a life and a new grandchild to look forward to. She had gone on with her life; she had fought and struggled and sacrificed and suffered, and now she was happy. Her family was happy. And yet she had left them to come here and confront a childhood friend who chose to stay away all these years. For what? What they once had between them was no more than a distant memory now. How could anything more have survived all those lifetimes lived in between?

She thought of turning and leaving and walking to the main road until she could flag a taxi to take her straight to the airport and to home.

Her head was pounding, the curiosity she once had now overshadowed by insecurity and shame. She didn't belong here. It was, like all the others, a village of ghosts. And she was tired, so very tired of being haunted by the past.

And then Clotho's words echoed in her mind. *"Come home, Katerina."*
She closed her eyes and replayed the conversation again. She could hear
Clotho's voice, weak yet resolute in her words.

Her entire life she had put blind faith in Clotho's methods and motives.
She had never doubted Clotho, nor had Clotho ever given her reason to.
Clotho had been her constant, her honest and fiercely loyal friend and
confidant.

"Come home, Katerina."

"There can be no love without faith in one another, without trust."

Perhaps this was the moment her father had foreshadowed when he
spoke those words. In a life filled with uncertainty and turmoil, there was
one thing Katerina understood and trusted without fail and without question: Clotho had a gift of seeing things others could not.

Katerina took another sip of water and steadied herself. Coming here
was not a choice. Clotho had summoned her. Katerina did not know why
yet, but she could feel it in her bones. Knowing this gave her the strength
and conviction she needed.

She steadied herself and walked down the gravel path that led to
the house, a wave of nostalgia washing over her as she spotted the home
perched on the cliff overlooking the sea. Yianna had always joked that
despite being the poorest family in the village, their humble home had the
most beautiful view.

The banging grew louder with each step. The house was similar to
what she remembered, but different as well. Updated, clean, and tidy. Gone
was the stone wall that Katerina recalled was always falling down on
itself. Gone was the ramshackle roof, patched again and again over the
years and made of mismatched stones. Gone was the hardened mud that
Marco's father stuffed into the crevices and cracks between the stones to
keep the cold and wind out best he could.

Instead, Yianna's house was, while still modest, clean and refreshed.
The jagged stone exterior replaced by smooth and painted stucco, whitewashed and pristine. The windows now framed with shutters stained a

deep blue. Katerina caught her breath, her hand fluttering to her mouth when she spotted them. In the window were Yianna's crocheted curtains, bleached and pressed, still dancing on the breeze, even after all these years.

Lifting the iron latch, she opened the gate and stepped inside.

She spotted him from behind, silhouetted against the sun as he raised a sledgehammer above his head. She watched as he paused a moment and then brought it down on a post with such force that her entire body reverberated upon impact. She stood quietly for a few moments more, watching him, grounding herself, taking it all in. The tingle in her eyes gave way to tears, and the flutter in her belly seemed to travel up into her lungs and throat.

He lifted the sledgehammer once more. She took a tentative step toward him. He brought it down again, hard.

He was a man. She should not have been surprised by this. Decades had passed since she had last seen him, since they clung to one another in that terrible, tearful goodbye. But it wasn't until now that she realized in all those years, no matter how much time had gone by, when she pictured him in her mind, she always pictured him as he was. As they were.

Her hands flew to her hair, smoothing out the unruly head of curls, now streaked liberally with gray. She dropped her bag and took another step toward him. He raised the sledgehammer again.

"Marco," she said.

He flinched, startled by the sound of his name, then turned to face her.

"Marco." Her heart swelled in her chest.

In an instant, all those years and miles between them, all the truths and lies, and all the misinformation in between seemed to simply dissolve, disappearing like morning mist. His hair, still dark and curly, was streaked with gray at the temples. A salt-and-pepper beard covered the bottom half of his face. His nose was not the same as she remembered, now slightly crooked and misshapen, appearing to have been broken, perhaps more than once. His eyes were the deep-black olive color she remembered, the ones that twinkled with such mischief and laughter. But they, too, were different.

The way he looked at her reminded her of her own eyes staring back from the wedding photos on the mantel of the mayor's house. Empty. Vacant.

She looked into the face of her childhood friend, who was now a man, and she saw it in an instant. It wasn't just his physical appearance that had changed. It wasn't just life with all of its struggles and disappointments that he carried with him, weighing down his shoulders and spirit. Something had happened to him. Something had changed him.

He stared silently at her, blinking slowly.

"Marco." She ran toward him, enveloping him in her arms. She hugged him tight, losing herself in the moment, then loosened her grip and released him, stepping back to regard him, drinking him in.

He stood there still, arms at his sides.

She stared into his eyes as she reached out and took his hand in both of hers. His skin was rough and calloused and blackened with earth. She lifted his hand to her cheek and leaned into it, pressing her skin against his.

"Katerina." Her name sounded heavy on his lips.

"What happened to you? Who did this to you?"

Forty-Four

Corfu
May 1981

Katerina sat outside on the patio, staring across the channel. The wind kicked up and the cypresses swayed back and forth in rhythmic unison as if in a mournful island dance. The maestro winds intensified, blowing in from the west and whipping the marbled sea into a white-capped frenzy.

He came out of the house carrying two glasses. His clothes hung on his angular frame and he walked with a pronounced limp. He placed the glasses on the table, water for her, whisky for him. There was silence between them as he slid into his chair. He lifted the glass to his lips, his hands trembling as he gulped.

They stayed like that for several minutes, her gaze shifting from the sea, to him, and then out again toward the horizon when she felt uncomfortable and awkward. He was either unfazed or did not notice; he just stared into his glass. Pushing back his chair, he stood to get more.

When he returned, his glass was filled to the rim this time. She placed her hands on the table and leaned toward him.

"What happened to you?" She tried her best to remain emotionless, her voice cracking nonetheless. She dabbed at the wetness in her eyes with her fingertips. "Clotho and I went to the paidopoleis. We went looking for you. We took the bus from Liston to see you. And when we got there, they said you weren't there."

He drained more of the amber liquid and then put the glass back on the table and dropped his head. Chin to chest, he sighed deeply as she watched him.

"My father-in-law . . ." She caught herself, realizing he likely did not know she had married, or that she had married the mayor's son. "The mayor told me that you died." Her voice cracked again, and she stopped a moment to catch her breath and contain her emotions as well as her thoughts. "A policeman in Athens told us you were dead. That you died years ago, in Athens."

More wordless moments passed, the silence between them punctuated by the rustling of leaves and branches and a frenzied symphony of crickets and cicadas.

He stared at her for a moment and then shifted his gaze out across the water.

"I know we were children. But still. You promised to come back." She felt her emotions churning now, like the sea in the distance, swirling and roiling into a dangerous and unpredictable current. "I looked for you. We looked for you. We wrote to the paidopoleis, to the queen's offices. We spoke to police officers and government officials, but no one knew anything. And even after the mayor found out you had died, even then I never stopped looking, Marco. Even if all I could do was bring you home to bury you."

She could no longer control her emotions. She was visibly crying now, her voice shaky as her body convulsed in tears. "I don't understand. Why would you leave the paidopoleis? Why would you leave the queen's care? Your mother sent you there so you would be safe. That was all she wanted. For you to be safe."

She tried to will the tears away, but it did no good. He made no effort to comfort her. His arm never reached out to touch her hand. He offered no napkin to wipe the wetness from her face.

After several moments he spoke at last. "The mayor told you I was dead?"

"Yes." She nodded as she used the hem of her blouse to wipe her cheek.

Katerina could see him ruminating, digesting the information. She watched as a black shadow crossed his face.

"He wanted me dead."

"Who wanted you dead?"

"The mayor." His voice was flat. Emotionless.

"No." She shook her head. "He tried to help you. He brought you to the paidopoleis. He was the one who made sure your mother's wish was fulfilled. And then he tried to help me find you. All those years, he was the one who tried to help me find you."

"No. He lied to you, Katerina." Marco took another long, deep drink from his glass. "He never brought me to Frederica's care. We never made it to Benitses. He lied to you. He lied about everything."

"What do you mean?" She leaned into the table to steady herself.

"He gave me to the partisans, Katerina."

"What?" She held tighter to the table now. "How?"

"The men he was supposed to be protecting me from. He gave me to them knowing they used children in their war, thinking I'd be killed. How could I survive it? And I nearly didn't. He almost got his wish. But somehow I made it out alive, even though thousands like me didn't. I still wonder how and why. For some unknown godforsaken reason, I'm still alive."

"What are you saying?" She stood now, her mind racing as fast and deep and wild as her emotions. His words made no sense. None of it made sense. She paced away from him and then back to the table. She leaned in, hands on the table, eyes wide, afraid of what he might say next.

"Do you remember that day at the cove?" He stared into her eyes now. "When we snuck away and I was going to teach you how to swim?"

"Yes. But what—"

He didn't let her finish. "We saw Mr. Andonis and wondered why he was in the old abandoned house."

She ran through her memory of that day. "Yes."

"He wasn't wrestling, Katerina. It was more than that."

"What do you mean, more than that?"

He went inside the house and brought out the bottle this time. He poured himself another glass, then reached across the table to pour some in Katerina's glass as well.

"He was with the mayor. And they were not wrestling. They were together, Katerina. The mayor and Mr. Andonis, they were together. They had a secret life, together. And I found out his secret. And I was a danger to him because I knew. Even if I was away in the paidopoleis, I still knew. I was still a risk to him. And he couldn't take that chance."

She stared at him in disbelief. She thought of her father-in-law, the man who had been so kind to her, the man who had tried to save her. The man who welcomed her into his family and lavished so much love and affection on Dawn. How could this be?

Obligation. Was this what Stamati meant? *Was saving me some twisted way of atoning for destroying Marco?* She felt light-headed, taking deep breaths in and out. She steadied her hand on the chair and sat back down.

"It's true, Katerina. Every word of it." He drained his glass.

"It's not your fault." Those were the very words she remembered saying to the mayor that day, the day Stamati's failures weighed so heavy on him that he sat in tears at her kitchen table. She said those words to him just before he broke down and told her the news that Marco was dead. But there was something else about that morning, something that gnawed at her. In the recesses of her mind there was an image and a memory, something of importance and value that she struggled to remember.

"Communist Militants Petition to Be Reunited with Family in Greece." She remembered the newspaper from that morning, the paper he had been reading just before the explosion with Stamati. The article said that

thousands of adult Greeks who had been sent to Communist camps as children were still trapped behind the Iron Curtain. But finally, decades after the war, there was a glimmer of hope as the Red Cross and international community were putting pressure on the Greek government to allow their return. The mayor had read the article that morning. They both had. And shortly after, he told Katerina that Marco was dead.

He wanted me to stop asking questions. The guilt and the lies had consumed him, and he wanted me to stop looking. He needed me to stop looking. She felt the bile rise in her throat. The earth seemed to spin, and she closed her eyes and breathed deeply in and out to steady herself. Finally, when she felt she could speak without being sick, she asked again the question that had haunted her for more than thirty years.

"What happened to you?"

Part Six

Forty-Five

"How far is the camp?" Marco asked as he walked with the mayor.

"It's only about an hour. Just south of Corfu Town in Benitses. I'll take you in my car. We'll be there in no time," the mayor assured the boy. His wife, Lina, had always accused him of speaking without thinking. And perhaps this was proof that she was right. He felt sorry for the boy, there was no question of that. And as the mayor, he did feel a certain responsibility to each of the village's citizens. *"Your bravado has gotten the best of you again,"* Lina had said. *"Why do you always have to show off, to be everything to everyone else and have nothing left to give your own wife and child?"*

He could not deny she had a point. Especially now, with reports that the partisan escapees had been spotted in the northern villages. Yes, he did have a responsibility to stay and protect his village and his family, and he would. But now that he had promised to help Marco, he couldn't change his mind because it was inconvenient. Besides, the gesture made him look like a hero, coming to the rescue of a desperate child. He liked that narrative. That narrative would serve him well, personally and professionally.

They climbed into the car. Before he turned on the engine, he faced Marco.

"It will be all right," the mayor assured him. "You'll be in the best hands and you'll have the best of care. The queen's camps are beautifully run, giving children like you every opportunity you wouldn't have otherwise. I know you can't see this now, but your mother wanted the best for you. I hope you'll be able to see it one day," he said, smiling at the child.

The mayor started the engine and gingerly maneuvered the car down the rocky dirt road away from the village and toward the paved road that led down the mountain and south along the shore, with only the car's headlights to illuminate the way.

The moon was full and low that night, casting a silver glow across the sea. In the distance, across the channel, the beaches and cliffs of Albania's shoreline were silhouetted against the moon's pale light. A small cluster of fishing boats bobbed up and down in the water along the rustic concrete marina that hugged the cove.

They rode in silence at first. And then Marco spoke, unknowingly uttering the words that would change the course of his life with devastating consequences.

"I saw you," Marco said as they reached the bottom of the mountain.

The mayor turned toward him, confused. "You saw me?" He smiled at the boy. "Where?"

"At the old fisherman's house. With Mr. Andonis."

The mayor clutched the wheel tighter now, his knuckles white. His cheeks flushed, and he felt his heart beating wildly in his chest.

The mayor pulled over on a grassy patch of land beneath the cliffs overlooking the sea. He took a deep breath and ran both fingers through his hair. "I don't know what you are talking about."

"I saw you near the old house, the one that's fallen down. The one near the cove on the other side of the island."

The mayor wiped the perspiration from his forehead. His eyes narrowed and his lips formed a tight, tense line as he glared at Marco. His breathing became rapid and shallow.

Marco went on. "I saw you the first time when I was with Katerina, but I didn't know it was you. Neither did she. But then I went back alone yesterday, before the storm, when I was looking for barnacles and sea urchin to eat, before my mother . . . And I saw you there, with Mr. Andonis. But I don't understand. Why do you go to the abandoned house to wrestle when the schoolyard has a wrestling pit?"

The mayor stared at Marco silently, not knowing what to say or do. This was what he had feared, what had given him terrible nightmares and anxiety for the past several years. At times the fear was enough to make him stop, to keep him away. But then there were times when the pull was stronger than the fear. It had been that way for both of them. The mayor and the schoolteacher had danced around each other for years like this, like magnets, pulled together by something primal and powerful, and then repelled apart by fear and society's norms. And now this child, this boy he had promised to help, knew the secret that could undo him. Undo them all.

"Marco. It's nothing. Nothing. You saw nothing." He slammed his palm on the steering wheel. Ruined by a child with nothing and no one to his name.

Marco stared at him. "But I don't understand. Are you angry with me?"

Before he could respond, the mayor heard a rattling from the brush beyond the road.

He strained to see in the darkness; leaning closer, he looked again. As the dim silver light of the moon reflected off the still sea, the mayor could barely make out the figure of a man, emaciated, face obscured by filth, emerging from the brush, walking toward the car with purposeful strides.

The mayor's mind raced, unable to keep up with the thoughts in his head and the happenings all around him.

Tap, tap, tap. The man tapped at the window with the blade of his knife. A wave of recognition washed over the mayor.

"Panos." The former schoolteacher. The mayor knew Panos's politics, and by his appearance—filthy, matted hair and torn, dirty clothing—he immediately understood the situation. This was the closest point of Corfu to Albania. The policeman had mentioned the Communist navy being dispatched to bring the escaped partisan prisoners from Lazaretto to safety in Albania.

The mayor looked across to the beach where a few small fishing boats were anchored in the shallow water. The silhouettes of three more boats bobbed in the water between the two countries. This cove, tucked away as if carved out from the mountain and hidden from the cliffs by the thick brush above, was the perfect location where the Communist navy could pick up their comrades undetected.

Tap, tap, tap.

"Roll down the window."

A gun was visible in his waistband. Reason told the mayor to start the car and press on the gas, to flee this place and this man. But he was frozen by fear of this partisan soldier at his window and paralyzed by the reality that his secret life had been discovered. The mayor did as he was told.

"Mr. Mayor." Panos spat the words more than said them.

"Don't hurt us," the mayor said. "We haven't done anything to you and don't mean you any harm."

Panos leaned in and looked at Marco in the front seat. "Give me your money. I know you have some. Give me your ring and watch."

Marco sat silently while the mayor did as he was told.

"Please don't hurt me," the mayor cried. He was shaking now, hands trembling even as he attempted to steady them on the steering wheel.

"I'm not going to hurt you. That would fall too conveniently into the narrative that we are all barbarians. We are not. I am not." He placed his knife in his waistband. "I'm leaving and I have no plans of ever coming back. But if you whisper a word of this to anyone, I will come back and I will find you. Do you understand?"

The mayor nodded. Panos looked at Marco seated silently beside him.

"Why is Marco with you?"

"His family is dead," was all the mayor said, understanding that this encounter could have a very different outcome if he mentioned his intention of delivering Marco to the queen's paidopoleis.

The mayor's mind was a jumble of information and emotions. All of the stories from the northern villages came back to him. All of the warnings about partisans stealing children from villages, using children on the front lines to fight their war. Sacrificing children to further the Communist cause.

"They use children as shields."

"Taken from their families and homes, never to be seen again."

In an instant the mayor realized the very thing he had lived in fear of could be his salvation.

"Take him," the mayor said.

Marco braced himself against the door.

Panos leaned into the car. The stench of body odor and cigarettes made the mayor gag. He looked from Marco to the mayor. "What did you say?"

"His parents are dead. He has no one. No one will ever know." The words rushed from his mouth like a dangerous river current. "Take him. I know you use children in your army. He's healthy. Just take him and we'll never breathe a word of this."

"Why are you doing this?" Panos asked, leaning in closer to the mayor.

The mayor turned to face Marco. Leaning across the boy, he reached for the door handle and opened the car door. "Get out."

Forty-Six

Corfu

October 1948

"Get out," the mayor said again.

"I don't understand. I'm so sorry, Mr. Mayor. I'm sorry if I did anything wrong. I didn't mean to upset you," Marco cried. "Please. Please don't leave me here. Please don't do this. I promise to be good."

At first Marco tried to wipe the wetness away, determined to appear brave even now, even as everything he thought he knew and understood spiraled so terribly out of control. But then the mayor got out of the car, walked over to Marco's side, and tugged his arm, pulling him from his seat and spilling him onto the dirt below. The tears came fast and hot. There was no wiping them, no hiding his fear.

Finally, although his legs felt shaky and unsteady, Marco managed to stand. Panos walked over beside him, and they watched as the mayor maneuvered his car away, tires screeching on the gravel, and drove south along the shore.

296

"Just stay quiet and everything will be fine," Panos said.

Marco felt out of his body, as if he were watching himself from above.

They sat on the sand, staring out across the water. Neither spoke for a while. Only the sound of the waves gently lapping at their feet and cicadas and crickets calling to one another filled the air. Finally, Panos said, "I heard about your father and brother," he said as he turned toward Marco. "Your father was kind to me, even though we disagreed. He was a good man. A hardworking man." Panos looked out across the sea as he spoke.

Marco said nothing. He fell asleep that night curled up on the beach under the stars.

At some point in the night, Marco was woken by the sounds of voices, harsh and hurried.

"What do you mean they're not here yet?"

"They must have gotten lost," Panos said. "The mountain roads are a maze and it's easy to get turned around, especially in the dark. I'll go. I know the villages and their back roads and paths. I'll find them and bring them down."

Marco sat up and looked over to the farthest edge of the cove where the voices came from. He spotted Panos there, at the water's edge, speaking to another dirty and disheveled-looking man. Marco stood, looking up and down the small beach. The main road was not even a kilometer away. If he ran, he might be able to make it there and get back to the village. Or anywhere but here with these men.

Just as he was about to run, Panos walked up. Marco considered running anyway, but he knew his legs were no match for these men.

He stood, facing Panos, trying his best to be strong, to swallow his fear and show how brave he was.

"Here. You must be hungry," Panos said as he pulled a package from the rucksack he wore draped across his body. Marco unwrapped the paper. It was a sandwich made from crusty peasant bread and tomatoes. Marco bit into the sandwich, devouring it within moments. He had not realized how hungry he was.

"Slow down. You'll make yourself sick." Panos handed him a flask of water.

When Marco was finished, Panos led him back to the man waiting in the boat. It was a small blue-hulled fishing boat, sun-bleached and battered, like the countless others belonging to fishermen up and down the island. There was no way to distinguish this caïque from any other across the island, but this boat's cargo was unlike any other.

Panos led Marco into the boat. "Stay here with Yianni," he said. "I'll be back with the others. And we'll go."

"Are you sure about this?" There was agitation in Yianni's voice, bordering on anger. "We should leave now. We can send others for them. It's too risky to wait here another full day."

"We can't leave them behind," Panos insisted. "You stay here with the boy. I'll find them and bring them back after dark and we'll go then."

Marco waited all day on the boat, doing as Yianni ordered, hiding in the small, dark hull that smelled of rotting fish and stale cigarettes. Above deck, Yianni spent the day at the boat's stern, fishing net in his hands, looking as if he were just another fisherman mending a net. As the sun set behind the western mountains, Marco heard Yianni pacing above. Back and forth along the narrow wooden planks he walked, cursing Panos and the idiocy of the other men who were smart enough to escape Lazaretto but had been dumb enough to get lost among the labyrinthine roads and paths of the small mountain villages.

Curled up into a ball on a wooden bench below deck, Marco eventually drifted off to sleep.

He woke with the sun beating down on his face from the doorway, unsure of what time it was or where he was. The smell of rotting fish again filled his nostrils, bringing him back to reality. He could feel the boat rocking gently from side to side as it glided through the water, the engine's hum vibrating through the hull. He rubbed his eyes and walked up the steps, leading to the outside area of the boat. Squinting against the sun, Marco steadied himself in the doorway. Yianni was steering the boat toward a ramshackle marina. Its location was unfamiliar to Marco. He turned and looked behind him, instantly recognizing the shoreline of Corfu in the distance. Scanning the coast, he saw the sun-bleached cliff of Pelekito behind them, the green cliffs of Kassiopi to the south, and to the north he spotted the distinct silhouette of the tiny island of Erikousa. He turned his body forward and looked ahead.

Albania.

The boat was heading to a harbor on the Albanian shore.

None of this made sense. And as he scanned the boat, the bile rose in his throat as he realized he and Yianni were alone. Panos and the other men had not returned.

Marco steadied himself as the boat continued toward the shore. *No, no, no,* he thought. *This is not right. I don't belong here. This is not what my mother wanted.* He turned again and watched as the familiar shoreline of Corfu faded farther into the distance. They were nearly at the dock now. But even so, it wasn't all that far across the channel. He could throw himself overboard and swim home; he would swim across the channel and make his way back to the village, or south to the paidopoleis. He knew he could do it.

He braced himself to jump overboard just as Yianni shouted to the men on the dock. The men pulled the fishing boat in, securing the line as Yianni walked to the doorway where Marco stood. "Let's go."

Marco stood frozen in place.

"Let's go," Yianni repeated, pulling at Marco's arm.

Marco bit his lip, promising himself he would not cry. Promising himself he would be brave, braver than these men would think possible for a boy of his age. The metallic taste of blood filled his mouth as he bit down even harder on his lip. He stepped off the boat and onto the cracked, crumbling dock of the marina. Looking back over his shoulder again, he stole one last look at the shoreline of Corfu in the distance. Beautiful, green, lush Corfu. Home. The only home he had ever known. The only home he had ever imagined. Just across the channel, a world away.

Yianni pushed him forward from the shoulder, forcefully this time. "Walk," he commanded.

Marco did as he was told, taking his first steps toward his new life in Albania in the care of the Communist Party of Greece.

Forty-Seven

Albania
October 1948

Marco's belly ached with hunger. He had eaten nothing since the bread and tomato sandwich Panos gave him on the beach on Corfu. And that had been two and a half days ago.

His head ached from the sun and the stench and the hunger. He sat wedged among other children, almost two dozen of them, packed into the back of the truck so tightly they could barely move or breathe. The trip had taken half the day, over pockmarked roads and through villages, gray and impoverished. The villagers, whose gray pallor matched the vista of stone and crude concrete buildings, averted their eyes as the truck passed. Merely existing was an exhausting and dangerous endeavor. Empathy could not take root here, emotions as barren as the soil among the rot and dirt and gray cinderblock homes.

The boys and girls ranged in age from infants to Marco's age and were dressed in the ragtag peasant attire of the poor northern Greek mountain villages. Two women rode in the truck with the children. Both wore soiled headscarves knotted beneath their chins and stern, exhausted expressions on their faces.

Beside Marco, a young boy named Dino clung to his younger sister, who looked to be no more than five.

"Mother," Dino said to one of the women as he leaned over and pulled at her skirt. "Mother," he said again. "Nina needs to go to the bathroom." Nina wrapped her arms around her brother, leaning into him as if attempting to disappear. "Please, Nina needs to go to the bathroom."

"We stop when they stop. There is nothing we can do until we arrive," the woman said, sounding devoid of emotion or concern.

Dino held his sister as the wetness spread from beneath her skirt and trickled down the floor and onto the other children. Nina began to cry.

"It's all right," Marco said, attempting to comfort them both. He noticed Dino's lip quivering, even as he tried to soothe Nina.

"Do you think your mother has a towel? For your sister?" Marco asked.

"That's not my mother," Dino whispered, the cracking of his voice betraying the bravery he so desperately tried to convey.

"Then why did you call her Mother?"

"They told us to."

"Who did?"

"The men who took us. She's not our mother." He bit his lip as he spat the words.

"They took you?" Marco asked.

"There are twelve of us from Karditsa. We were all outside, playing. Our mothers were working in the fields. We saw the truck, the soldiers standing on top with their guns, and the older children yelled for us to run. They knew right way that the men had come to take us away. They had taken our fathers away weeks ago. They left only the young boys and our grandfathers. They shot our fathers and tossed them off the cliffs. All of them, one by one. When they saw us running, the men jumped from the trucks. Most of the older children got away. But the smaller ones were not as fast. I was almost to the caves when I heard Nina call my name. I turned around and saw she had fallen. I was almost there. I was almost away from them. But I couldn't leave her. I turned around and went to help her. And that's when one of the men grabbed us both and threw us into the truck with the others."

Marco looked around to the children huddled together. They looked like skeletons with their hollow eyes and protruding bones.

"Our mother came running. We saw her . . ." Nina now burrowed herself even deeper into her brother's neck, making herself as tiny as she could. She sobbed silently, her tiny body heaving up and down.

"Our mother ran to us, screaming at them. She begged them to take her and leave us behind. I can still hear her screaming, the sound of her voice. I can still hear her calling our names. And then nothing. There was no more screaming. They shot her. They shot our mother. And then they told us that we were children of the Communist Party now, and that these women are our mothers."

Across from Marco two young girls clung to one another. They had the same wide hazel eyes and pink cheeks that were streaked with mud. Marco thought they must be sisters. "Mother, when will we eat?" one of the girls asked.

"When we reach the camp."

"The man told me there would be jam and sweetcakes and warm milk with sugar. I'm so hungry. I can't wait. He told me I could have two pieces if I wanted. And he said Mama is waiting for us in our new home."

Marco leaned in closer. "Who told you this?"

"The men who brought us here," the older of the two girls said. "A soldier said Mama went ahead to get everything ready. That's what he told us when he found us playing on the mountainside. How much longer do you think it will be? It's been two days already. I miss Mama." She leaned over and placed her head on her sister's shoulder.

The younger of the two women looked over at the sisters. She then turned her attention to Marco, glaring at him. She said nothing, but no words were needed. He understood the warning in her eyes.

As he rode through the Albanian countryside, packed in with the stolen and lost children of war, Marco felt his head spinning with uncertainty. What would happen to him, to them?

As the truck rolled deeper into the night and toward a life his mother had not chosen for him, Marco made a promise and a vow. He promised to do what he could to protect the younger children. And as he stared up toward the night sky, flickering with stars, he vowed that no matter what was said or demanded of him, he would never, ever, under any circumstances, call any of these women Mother. He had a mother, and she had loved him enough to sacrifice herself for him. He knew he would rather die than defile the word that had meant everything to him.

Forty-Eight

Poland

May 1950

Comrade Vouri stood in front of the classroom dressed in his drab green uniform, his gun strapped at the waist, visible to the children. Another building, identical to this one, served as the barracks where the children slept, their beds lined up one after the other with only a thin blanket allotted to each child, even in the harsh winter months. Boys slept on one side of the curtain divider, girls on the other. It was forbidden for the children to use the latrine or get out of their beds no matter how badly they needed to go to the bathroom or how thirsty they were. Only officers and soldiers fed their cravings in the darkness, entering the barracks and slipping into the bed of a boy or girl, depending on their appetite.

The children, about two dozen of them, sat at their desks. They wore the scratchy, gray woolen uniforms of the Communist Party of Greece, their hair closely shorn and haunted looks in their eyes.

"All right, children. I want you all to listen closely and do as I say. Today we are writing letters back home to your families. You will tell them about all of the wonderful things you are learning and how well you are being taken care of by your comrades and teachers."

Marco squirmed in his seat as he listened.

"These letters will come as a great comfort to your parents. They know you are safe here, away from the threat of Frederica and her army that would come and take you away and throw you in her children's jails. Copy this letter I have written on the board and sign your name, and the Red Cross will make certain your families know you are safe and well."

"Marco, you don't—" Nina whispered to Marco.

"Shh, Nina." He shook his head and put his finger to his lips as a warning.

She did as she was told, looking ahead and copying the letter.

Nina, Dino, and Marco had been inseparable since the truck ride. Together they endured endless hours of drills, marching in circles, and lessons about the great commanders of the Communist Party. Marco and Dino took turns sharing their rations with Nina, who cried herself to sleep each night from hunger. When they first arrived at the camp, Marco had shared with his new friends his secret for eating the smells on the breeze, assuring them this was a perfect way to stave off the pains in their bellies. But the children soon learned that only the putrid smell of overflowing latrines could be detected at the camp.

It was Marco who had held Nina as she cried, inconsolable for days, when Dino never returned from fighting the Hellenic Army of the Greek government in the final battle on the mountain of Vitsi. Marco had caught a glimpse of his friend that day as he wedged his body beneath two rocks to shield himself from the gunfire, explosions, and screams erupting around him. The sight of Dino, arms and legs contorted impossibly, entrails and blood spilling from his gut like an Easter lamb, had been seared in his memory from that moment on. There were no tears shed on that mountain by Marco that day. There was no sadness or fear or pain. There was nothing, only numbness and a black hole where his emotions had once dwelled. Marco emerged from his hiding place at dawn and walked back to camp between the blood and bodies all around him. And although he made it to the barracks alive, he left a part of himself on the mountain alongside the body of his friend. Gutted, eviscerated, and emptied.

"You should have seen him," he'd told Nina as she cried in his arms. "He refused to shoot at the Greek soldiers and instead turned his gun on the partisan commander, the one who beat us and forced us to march in the snow for hours with no shoes or coats. He died a hero, Nina. A hero." But no matter how many times he repeated the story of Dino's heroics for Nina, Marco could not forget the sight of Dino crying out for his mother as the soldier lifted him from the ground by the collar and slit him open with his knife. Not long after that, when the fighting was over, the surviving children were brought to this camp in Poland.

"Marco!" Comrade Vouri shouted as he rapped the desk with the stick that he used as a pointer and to beat the children across the knees and knuckles. "Marco. Your assignment." He pointed to the words on the board.

Marco put pencil to paper and copied the words.

Dear Mother and Father,

I am treated very well here in the camp. There is plenty of good food and good friends and I am studying very hard. We are learning lessons about government and the leaders of the Communist party who paved the way for us. I will continue to study hard and make you proud. I hope one day you can join me here.

Your son,
Marco

∞

Winter dragged endlessly. The gray cinderblock walls of the camp matched the gray of the earth and sky. Flu ravaged the barracks, rushing in like a blinding squall, taking two dozen children by the time it was done. Nina woke one morning drenched in sweat, her skin burning to the touch. Three days later she was gone. Marco envied her.

Marco sat in the classroom one spring morning as Comrade Vouri entered. He rapped his stick on the board. "Children, I have an announcement. The Red Cross has distributed letters from your families. When I call your name, come and get your letter. Anna, Nicholas, Christina, Petro, Marco . . ."

Marco walked to the front of the classroom and took his letter from the teacher. He waited until he was seated again to turn the letter over in his hands. On it, in clean, precise handwriting, was his name. The return address read simply "Corfu." He slid his finger below the fold and opened the envelope. Marco looked around him as the other children read their letters. Some hugged the paper to their chest; some had tears in their eyes. All were smiling. Marco unfolded the letter and began to read.

Dear Marco,

It made us very happy to read your letter, son. We are thankful to the Communist Party of Greece for taking such good care of you. We know you are getting a great education and eating good food. Pay attention to your lessons and mind your comrades. We hope we will be fortunate enough to join you one day. Until then it makes us happy to know you are in their care.

Mother and Father

Part Seven

Forty-Nine

Corfu
May 1981

Sleep was an impossibility for Katerina. Restless and fitful, if she slept at all. She rolled over in bed and glanced at her watch. Three a.m. The moon, full and luminous, filtered her gray light through the window that was open to the fresh mountain air.

Katerina grabbed her robe from the foot of the bed and wrapped it around herself. The pink chenille was soft and comforting. She slipped her feet into her slippers. They, too, were chenille and a deeper shade of pink. Dawn had called it bubblegum pink when she presented Katerina with the bow-adorned box on that Mother's Day morning years ago. Katerina smiled to herself recalling how excited Dawn was to see her try on the gift, giggling as she spun around and the robe twirled in the air. Each time she felt the soft fabric against her skin, she was reminded of that morning and her heart swelled with love for her child. So many times through the years, Violeta had laughed as she pointed to Katerina in her tattered pink ensemble, asking if she should take up a collection at church to replace it.

Katerina shuffled to the kitchen and made herself a cup of coffee. She rifled through the drawers but couldn't find a can opener anywhere. Finally, she took a kitchen knife and banged at it with a mallet until she pierced the top of the can of condensed milk that she had tucked in her bag along with the can of Nescafé. She sat at the kitchen table and reached for the phone, which was attached to the wall.

"Hello?"

The mere sound of Dawn's voice brought a smile to her face.

"Hello, sweetheart. How are you feeling? How are both of my babies?"

"Mama." The joy in Dawn's voice matched her mother's. "We are good. Thank God, we are good. I went to the doctor yesterday and everything is great. He said about nine weeks to go and you should be holding your grandchild in your arms."

Katerina felt the tingle in her eyes and exhaled. She took the news in, savoring it. Saying a silent prayer for the healthy delivery of the baby she had prayed for incessantly. Dawn's baby, her grandchild.

"Mama. What happened? Violeta has been over here every hour on the hour asking if I heard from you yet. Did you see him? Did you speak to him? Is he there?"

"Yes. I saw him." She had played the conversation over in her head countless times since yesterday. Her heart and head and soul ached from it. Every moment he recounted, every word from his lips, shattered her heart, from the moment he told her about her father-in-law's betrayal to the pain, abuse, and devastation in the Communist children's camps. But that was just the beginning of his tortured life. So many had hurt Marco along the way, a long list of criminals, abusers, and tormentors. And yet still, although there were many who were culpable, Katerina understood that it all had been at the hands of her father-in-law.

"Mama. Tell me. What happened to him?"

Your grandfather denied a mother her dying wish. Your grandfather destroyed a young boy's life to protect his own. Your grandfather was not the man you thought he was. Your grandfather was a monster. These are all things Katerina could have said, and would have said, had the situation been different. These were all the things that would have slipped effortlessly from her tongue had Dawn not been carrying a child.

"He didn't want to talk much about it. He's had a very hard time. Your grandfather was given the wrong information. Marco didn't go to Athens. He was taken by the partisans, by the Communists, and sent to a children's camp in Albania."

"What? Are you serious? Oh, Mama, that's horrible."

"Yes. Horrible. It was horrible, and so much more. He said the children were starving, and they were beaten, and they were forced to fight in the Communist army against Greece. He lived through things no child should live through, Dawn. And then after the war was over, he was sent to another camp, in Poland. And things there were even worse. The children were literally starving and would sneak out of the camp to steal food, just so they could survive.

"He tried coming back to Greece, but he wasn't allowed across the border. All of those children were taken from their families, stolen. And then there were other children whose parents actually gave them to the soldiers thinking it was the only way to keep them safe. Can you imagine? Those poor parents so desperate to save their babies from the war? They were lied to. They were told their children would be safe. For years those children had no way home, no way for their families to find them. For the past ten years he was living in a small village in Poland, working with an old widower, a carpenter. He said life was difficult, but the old man was kind and he taught him carpentry so he was able to make at least somewhat of a living. And then just months ago he received a letter from the Red Cross telling him he could come home. That the Greek government was allowing them to return. Everything your grandfather told us was wrong. It was all a lie."

"But how?"

"I don't know." It was Katerina's turn to lie.

"That poor man. How . . . I mean, how is he? Is he all right?"

"No, honey. He's not all right. He's a shell of a man. He's not the boy I knew anymore. I don't think there's any of that boy left in him. I think he tried, but year after year, the abuse, the neglect, and the damage just chipped away at him until there was nothing left. Dawn, there's nothing left of my friend."

Even that was more than she wanted to say, had intended to say. There was no need to burden Dawn with the truth right now; the time would come for that.

They hung up the phone with a promise that Dawn would call Katerina with any news.

Katerina was scheduled to stay in Greece for a few more days. She wasn't quite sure yet whether she would stay here in the village or in Corfu Town. It all depended on Marco, and she had learned enough in the few hours they spent together not to press him for any more answers. Last night they sat together until the sun set, conversation fading along with the light. At first he seemed somewhat eager to share his story, but as the light dimmed and the whisky bottle drained, his mood matched the blackened sky.

"Will you come with me to Corfu Town? We can walk along Garitsa and have lunch on the Liston. Remember we used to dream about that as children," she had said. "Let's go. Let's enjoy an afternoon in town."

"No."

"Just come for the afternoon. Keep me company."

"Katerina, there is nothing I want to see."

"But, Marco, you can't just stay here, alone, without leaving your house. There's nothing left here but ghosts."

"Then I'll fit right in," he said as he sank lower into his chair and closed his eyes.

She left him there, asleep on the patio where his own mother would stand, gazing out at the sea, wailing for her husband and son who had been lost, pleading with the current to give up her secret and bring them home. And although he was there, flesh and bone before Katerina's very eyes, she ached to think that Yianna's younger son had been lost across that very same channel as well.

She had turned one last time before walking out the gate and heading down the mountain toward home. "Good night, Marco," she'd whispered into the night.

I don't know how I will ever bring myself to tell Dawn the truth, Katerina thought as she grabbed her bag and walked toward the front door. She glanced at her wedding photos as she passed the mantel. The mayor, her father-in-law, stared back at her, his smile broad, eyes bright and twinkling. She shuddered now to think of what he had done, what he was capable of, the secrets hiding behind those eyes. There was no question the mayor had also done much good in his life, had devoted himself to the community and to helping others. But he had willingly sacrificed a child in order to protect himself. Had everything else been a lie? Had it all been nothing more than penance, an attempt to atone for his sins?

And what about Mr. Andonis? Did he know? She thought back to the last time she saw him before he passed away. It was at the mayor's funeral luncheon. Despite the gray at his temples and the suits now faded with time and age, Mr. Andonis was still an elegant man, in both his appearance and demeanor. They had spent the afternoon reminiscing about life in the village and his admiration for Yianna and her boys, lamenting the loss of lives so innocent and young, laughing at all the futile attempts to get Marco to focus on his work. There was an authenticity and a gentleness to the schoolteacher, just as there had always been. No. There was no way he knew of the mayor's deception. The mayor and Mr. Andonis had shared a lifetime of secrets between them, but not this one.

In the end, it seemed no one truly knew the mayor.

Katerina walked to the mantel and, one by one, lifted the photos and took the images out of their frames. She crumbled the pictures in her hands and tossed them into the fireplace, knowing she would light a fire tonight when she returned home.

Outside the air was crisp and cool. The faint scent of an outdoor fire lingered in the air. Katerina knew it must be from Marco's home, the breeze carrying the smoky scent down the mountain. She walked the path along the beach once more, following along the dirt road overlooking the sea.

She continued along until she saw the house in the distance, stopping as the old stone wall came into view. The memories and emotions washed over her—the love, the loss, what might have been. As she approached the house, her eyes fell on the wooden door, riddled with rot. The stone wall had fallen years ago, weeds and plants having taken root, like a small green mountain formed here on the patio. She walked to the terrace, nostalgia overtaking her as she spotted the old outdoor kitchen where she would steal fried fish to ensure Marco would have something to eat. The house was now no more than a pile of stones. She went to the other end of the patio, where Baba would sit with her and watch the sunrise. She thought back to the morning, just before he was murdered, when she sat with him and watched as dawn's blush washed over him, transforming him before her eyes. He was a tired, poor, and broken man and yet, baptized in the morning sun, he had appeared to Katerina in that moment like a golden king.

She had thought about that moment so many times when she gazed at her daughter or found herself calling Dawn's name. Tradition dictated that her firstborn daughter be named for Stamati's mother, but Katerina had put her foot down and refused. After so many years spent mourning the children she had lost, Katerina knew in the instant she heard Dawn's tiny cries in the delivery room that only one name would befit this tiny miracle.

Katerina walked through the rubble and decay that once was her childhood home. She pictured her mother there, pulling up water from the well and stoking the fire where freshly dug potatoes sizzled and popped in home-pressed olive oil. She could see her father mending his nets by the firelight as she sat beside him, mesmerized by the dancing flames. She could picture herself—curly hair pulled into plaits; scabbed knees, dirty and cracked; wearing a dress two sizes too big, handed down from Calliope, as she listened to her parents' stories of the gods, goddesses, and legends that filled and fueled her imagination.

After about an hour of wandering, Katerina walked down past the beach again and up the mountainside to Clotho's house. Clotho had lived in the nursing home for almost a year now. It pained Katerina to think of Clotho's garden—her flowers, plants, and fruit trees—once so vibrant and alive with color and life, dying slowly over time from neglect.

The climb up the mountain winded Katerina. She remembered hiking up and down these rocky paths so effortlessly in her childhood. It was just one of the many things that had changed.

She reached the top of the mountain and stopped at the familiar bamboo gate to Clotho's home. Unlike her own home, the gate was still intact, unmarred and unmarked by the passing of time.

She shook her head as she took it all in. It was impossible, and yet so very possible; shocking, and yet unsurprising. As Katerina walked through Clotho's garden, everything—every plant, flower, and fruit tree—was in vibrant, luminous bloom. The lemon tree's branches bent with the weight of giant yellow orbs, and the waxy-leaved fig tree burst with plump purple figs whose sweet nectar dripped from the stem. And every pot of fresh herbs—spiky-stemmed rosemary, lush basil, and bushels of thyme—perfumed the air. And the roses . . . Clotho's roses welcomed Katerina back in every glorious color of her childhood: deep blood reds, soft pale pink, and luminous yellow. She crossed over to the other side of the patio, the edge overlooking the sea, and there thriving in the sea air were pots of Clotho's beloved gardenias, their pristine white flowers permeating the air with their sweet, intoxicating scent.

She had always been told that scent was the strongest conduit of memory, and now Katerina could confirm this to be true. As she walked through Clotho's garden, she was transported back to the day Clotho shared with her the tragic story of her own mother and the sacrifices she was willing to make to ensure Clotho's safety and happiness. Katerina remembered sitting under the arbor as Clotho explained the story of Marlena's life, how she chose to hide away in this house, enduring the pain and trauma of an abusive man, so she could watch over and raise Clotho herself. And there, tucked away in the corner of the garden, away from the other flowers and plants, was the source of the sweetest and most powerful scent of all, the deep purple flower that facilitated Marlena's betrayal and cemented her fate.

The villagers had long ago labeled Marlena and Clotho sorceresses. Katerina would never use that word to describe Clotho, but she knew that her dear old friend was in some mystical way charmed. Yes, this home was enchanted, but the villagers and gossips were wrong. The magic in this house, in the soil and even in the air, was not steeped in witchcraft or sorcery. What made this place magical was the lesson Clotho had learned from her mother years before: to pierce the darkness with light and love and color. This was her power, and it was infinite.

Fifty

Corfu
May 1981

By the time Katerina reached Marco's house, she was hot and famished. She found him sanding down a giant slab of olive wood, which he was transforming into a table. He looked up at her as he worked, nodding slightly in her direction. His fingers never lost their grip on the strip of sandpaper; his hands never stopped their movement, back and forth along the bark. A thin layer of dust settled across his hands, clothes, and the patio as he worked.

"I walked to Clotho's," she said. "Marco, you won't believe it. She hasn't been there in nearly a year and it's as if nothing's changed. The garden is exactly as it was when we were children. Like she's still there, every day, watering and caring for her flowers. It's a miracle. Can you believe it?"

"Miracles don't exist, Katerina."

"But they do. Of course they do." She could have said so much more, but then she stopped herself. She wondered how many times Marco must have prayed, asking for a miracle over the years. She wondered if he still believed in anything at all.

"Have you eaten yet?" she asked. "Do you want me to make something?"

"There's bread inside, and tomatoes and cucumbers with olives and feta. There's a leftover fish from last night if you want. It's in the refrigerator."

"You giving *me* fish." She smiled at him. "Isn't that a change?" She thought maybe she saw a small glimmer in his eye.

When she could no longer ignore the rumbling of her belly, she went inside the house and cut a piece of the crusty bread, dipping it into a plate of tomatoes with olive oil, salt, and oregano. She noticed an opened bottle of whisky on the table. And a glass beside it, half drained.

She went back outside and sat with him under the sun. He worked with single-minded focus and attention to detail. At some point during the day, he brought the whisky bottle outside, draining it slowly, glass after glass, as he worked. She watched him like that all afternoon, not bothered by the quiet. She was instead comforted by it. She just wanted to savor being in his company, to watch him, to breathe the same air, to know he was safe. As unsteady as he had seemed yesterday, awkward and unsure of himself as they talked, he was a different man out here today. There was something about his hands, coarse as the sandpaper he worked with, yet his movements so controlled and graceful. He sanded and shaped the wood as he transformed it from a cumbersome slab to an elegantly carved and crafted thing of beauty.

He stopped working only as the light faded. He seemed startled when he looked up and saw her watching him, as if he had forgotten she was there.

"Are you hungry?" she asked him. "I can make you something."

"No. I'm not hungry," he said, the glass at his side.

"Can I get you anything?" Her hand wrung a paper napkin until it was a tight, knotted mess.

He shook his head no. "It's late. You should probably get home before it gets too dark."

"I can stay a bit longer. So you don't have to be alone."

"I'm used to being alone. For years I was surrounded by people, crammed in like animals in cages. Packed in so tightly sometimes it was hard to breathe from the lack of air, from the stench. In all those years in the camps, with all the other children, I never had a moment of solitude. But even so, every moment of every day, I was alone."

"But you don't have to be alone any longer." She reached across the table and placed her hand on his, his skin rough against her palm. "I came back for you, Marco. You're not alone any longer. Don't you remember what you said to me just before you left? You told me that I was your family now. You asked me to promise that I would always be your family. And I am. I'm here. I kept my promise, Marco. Please don't push me away." Her eyes and words pleaded with him. And yet, again she was met with silence.

"Marco. What happened to you was a crime. We can't change the past. I wish I could, but I can't. What I can do is be here for you from this moment on. I can be your family, and I can help you. Marco, Dawn is pregnant. She's going to have a baby. I'm going to be a grandmother. We can be a family. Your family. Just please, let me in. Let us in."

His eyes widened and he sat up in his chair. Leaning in, he looked deep into her eyes with such intensity and focus that she found it unsettling. "You're going to be a grandmother?" he said, running his fingers through his hair.

"Yes." She smiled at him. "Yes, Marco, I'm going to be a grandmother. Can you believe it? I just pray everything is all right and the baby is born healthy. I don't think we can take another heartbreak."

And again he retreated into silence.

He sipped the last of his drink and then pushed his chair back from the table and walked into the house. He came out moments later carrying something in his hands. Katerina felt a swell of emotion when she realized what it was.

"Take this," he said, arms outstretched to her.

It was Stefano's prized school bag, the one his grandmother brought home with her from Mon Repos, the one Yianna caressed and carried with her constantly after his death. She looked up at him, confused.

"Take this back home with you. I found it here in the house. She left it here for me. How could she have known it would take a lifetime for me to come home?"

She took the bag in her hands, the buttery leather soft to her touch. She reached her hand inside and felt something. She pulled it out to find it was a stack of letters, tied together with old fishing twine, the kind that once held Marco's shoes together.

"I don't understand . . ."

"Read them tonight. And then you will. She gave up everything . . . for nothing. I lost my childhood, my life. So many innocent victims. For what?" The words depleted him. He looked frail in that moment, as if he barely had the strength to stand.

She held the bag to her chest and took a step toward him. He shook his head. Katerina stopped and stood there in the moonlight. She watched as he turned and went back in the house, shutting the door behind him as Yianna's lace curtains lifted on the breeze.

Fifty-One

Corfu
May 1981

Katerina sat on the couch and pulled the letters out of the bag. She glanced over at the fire, watching as the flames consumed the crumpled wedding photos. The kindling cracked and popped as the fire slowly began to warm the room from the cool evening air. She wrapped her robe tightly around herself and sipped chamomile tea with honey that had been harvested on the mountaintop years ago and preserved in glass containers in the cabinet.

Each of the letters was addressed to Marco. It looked to Katerina like a child's handwriting, shaky and uncertain.

She pulled the first letter from the pile and began to read.

Dear Marco,

My son. Please don't cry for me. You deserve so much more than I can give you. And I know that in Frederica's care, you can be more. I know that in taking my life, I will give you life.

There is cruelty in this world. We know this. But there is also kindness. I am able to write these letters to you, to say all the things I would have said as I watched you grow into a man, because of one man's act of kindness. At first Laki helped me by writing letters to Princess Alice. We tried so many times, but we never received a reply. Even so, I knew in my heart that one day her promise would somehow be fulfilled.

After your brother and father were taken from us, I asked Laki if he would teach me to read and write. He has been teaching me slowly, and I am so grateful to him. I asked Laki to do this so I could write you letters that you can touch and hold in your hands after I am gone, the way I once held you in my arms when you were a little boy. Press them to your cheek and think of me pressing my own cheek against yours, my lips against your skin as I kiss your face. He did this for no other reason than because he is a good man.

I asked him also to swear to keep my secret, and I know he has. He is a man of faith and a man of his word. He does not know that I will also write down my final wishes and that I will take my own life. I fear Laki would not help me if he knew the truth. I pray he will find it in his heart to forgive me one day. I also pray God does not judge me harshly for this sin of deceit. But if I am to be punished in eternity for what I've done, then that is a sacrifice I am willing to make. For you, my son.

I hope you will read these letters and keep them safe and return to them as you grow. You are a child now, but as you become a man, you may see and understand things with different eyes. And when you become a father, I pray you will finally understand why I left you. There is no greater love than that of a parent for a child. Remember this. Remember that I loved you enough to leave you. I loved you enough to give another woman the blessing of being your mother and watching you grow into a man. Queen Frederica is your mother now. She will protect you and help you in ways I could not. She will make sure your life is filled with love and give you the chance to be a devout and strong Greek Orthodox man. It warms my heart to know that we are surrounded by good people who will ensure that my final wish is carried out and you will be safe.

I will watch over you always.

I love you, my son.

Katerina clutched the letter to her chest. Her head, heart, and soul ached. Yianna's words swirled in her mind. She read the letter again, to ensure it was not a dream. Her tears fell onto the paper, staining the page and blurring the ink. She pulled the letter away to save it from further damage. *Damage.* So much damage had already been done. To all of them. Her cheeks were hot and wet, and now her head pounded with the reality.

I asked him also to swear to keep my secret, and I know he has. He is a man of faith and a man of his word.

All those nights Mama thought Baba slipped away from her bed into Yianna's. All those rumors and whispers. She was mistaken. They were all mistaken. Baba was a man of honor to the very end. And it was ultimately his honor and integrity that had destroyed them all.

And for what? It had all been a waste. All of it.

Katerina pulled the next letter from the pile.

Dear Marco,

I want to tell you the story of our family, so you can remember where you come from and how you were loved. We know what sacrifice is in our family, and we also know the importance of being a godly man.

The villagers still whisper to this day about my mother's mother, your great-grandmother. They say she went mad and threw my mother penniless and helpless out on the street. They say her heart turned black and cold when she was abandoned by her husband and that she lost the ability to love. She let the villagers believe what they wanted to believe, but it was not true, my dear Marco. None of it was true. I finally learned the truth from my mother when I summoned the courage to ask her. I should have talked to her about it sooner. Because while there is heartbreak and tragedy in our family's story, there is also beauty. Your great-grandmother never lost the ability to love. It was love that led her to send my mother away. She had nothing left in this life, only the love of her daughter, and yet she sent her away, in order to save her. Just as I sent you away to save you.

Your great-grandmother saw an omen in her cup and she knew what it meant for our family. It was a giant blackbird with wings outstretched, hovering over our house. She knew the danger. She knew that tragedy stalked our home, so she sent her only child away to keep her safe. That is how and why my mother found herself working and living at Mon Repos. She was happy there. I was happy there, and my mother was blessed with a family and a beautiful friendship with Princess Alice. It was heaven for a while, before our descent into hell.

We can try to hide the ones we love, we can send them away and pray, but the omen only lies in wait. Time went on, but the blackbird of death did not forget. He came back to claim your father and brother.

Sometimes it is beyond our control, what is etched in the grounds of our cups or passed down from the bloodlines that came before us. This is not village folklore or gossip. This is truth. This is our truth.

You are a good boy. Grow to be a good man, a man who keeps his word and a man who lives in faith and honesty. There is nothing more important than this. And I know Queen Frederica will guide you on the right path with faith and love and a pure heart.

I love you, my son.

Katerina's hands trembled. The paper rattled in her fingers. She looked up from the page, staring into the flames of the fireplace. She was tempted to toss the paper into the fire, to incinerate it and make the words disappear as she had done with the face of her father-in-law staring back at her from the photo.

We can try to hide the ones we love, we can send them away and pray, but the omen only lies in wait.

Sometimes it is beyond our control, what is etched in the grounds of our cups or passed down from the bloodlines that came before us.

The horrific truth washed over her in an instant.

"You're going to be a grandmother?" Marco had asked with an intensity that unsettled her.

And then she remembered the silence. Clotho had said nothing when she learned of Dawn's pregnancy before insisting, "Come home, Katerina."

Dear God, no. She jumped from the couch, the papers falling to the floor all around her. Running her fingers through her hair, she paced the floor back and forth. *No, no.* All of those years, all of those lies. All of the tiny lives lost, heartbeats forever dimmed. Dawn's twin, born silent and still. They were all boys. Each of the babies she and Dawn had lost . . . they were all boys.

Katerina threw open the doors and walked out to the terrace. She leaned over the rail, feeling as if she might be sick. Feeling as if her entire world both fell apart and fell into place at the same time. How could she have not realized this the moment Marco told her what happened to him, what her father-in-law had done?

Marco was right. Her father-in-law did have blood on his hands, but not just Marco's. The blackbird had witnessed what the mayor did to Marco and had hovered over their home ever since, lying in wait to settle the debt.

Again and again and again.

She frantically paced back and forth along the patio. She spent hours walking in circles, praying, asking for mercy, for a way to fix this.

Finally, she could stand it no more. She left the house and raced up the mountain to Marco's, desperate to speak with him. She would ask for forgiveness. She would fall on her knees and beg for mercy, wondering if he had the power to forgive and absolve.

When she got to the house, she ran through the gate and onto the terrace. The door was closed. She knocked at first, but there was no movement from the house. All around her the sky was black, the clouds low and heavy, obscuring the stars and allowing only a hazy light filtering through from the moon. She knocked again, louder this time. Again nothing. She pushed open the door and walked inside, placing the bag with Yianna's letters on the table.

She thought it would not be possible to feel any more pain, to have her heart broken any more. But she was wrong. Seeing him there, passed out, his head and shoulders sprawled on the mattress while his torso and stomach were on the floor. The whisky bottle beside him, tipped over and empty. It was more than she could bear.

She walked to him and knelt next to him. "Marco. Please, wake up." She shook his shoulder. "Marco, please."

He rolled over, off of the mattress and onto the floor. She tried again, but it was useless. She sat there, beside him, watching and listening as he slept fitfully. Even sleep provided no relief from his demons.

At last she got up and walked home in the dark. *Clotho.* She would visit Clotho in the morning and tell her what had happened and what she had learned. Clotho would understand and tell her what to do.

She walked down the mountain toward home and replayed the evening in her mind. So much loss, so much devastation. And for what?

She finally reached the house and stepped out on the patio once again. She looked up at the heavens as if expecting to be met by the black-winged bird, waiting, hovering. But she saw nothing. Nothing above but low clouds, obscuring the moon and stars. She stood there a few moments longer, thinking of Dawn and the joy in her voice when they last spoke.

She sank to her knees, and holding her head in her hands, she cried for all the loss and pain. She cried for the babies taken from her. She cried for the unbearable pain of watching her daughter suffer the loss of two pregnancies, and she cried for the fear that this child would be taken from them as well. And she cried for Marco. He had finally found his way home, and yet he remained lost.

She looked in the distance, across to the horizon, and all she could see was black sky, black sea, and the black of the mountains of Albania to the east.

"Please, please, Panagia. I'll do anything," she pleaded. "Please help us.

Please let this child be born healthy. Please bring this child home and help us be a family. I beg of you."

Katerina looked up at the black sky. When she was a child, her parents told her that Nyx heard the prayers of desperate mothers at the brink of dawn and dusk. She closed her eyes and clasped her hands in prayer again, pleading that despite the darkness, Nyx might somehow hear her prayer as well.

Katerina turned and walked back inside the house and climbed into bed. She hoped perhaps she might be able to sleep at least a bit before going to visit Clotho in the nursing home. She said one last silent prayer as she slid between the sheets. "Please help me find a way to make this stop."

As Katerina closed her eyes, there, in the east, undetectable to the naked eye, the first golden sliver of dawn emerged beyond the horizon and pierced the night.

Fifty-Two

Corfu

May 1981

Katerina sat straight up in bed. She tapped her toes along the floor until she found them, sliding her feet into her slippers and wrapping her robe tightly around her shivering body.

She shuffled into the kitchen and began her preparations. Perhaps it was still too early for Hemera's chores, but not for hers. It was never too early for hers. She walked outside to the garden and clipped a bouquet of the most perfect gardenias she could find. The gardenia was a fragrant contradiction, evoking both purity and sensuality. Katerina often felt this way herself, a walking paradox of reason and emotion, of duty and her deepest desires. The garden overflowed with a rainbow of flowers. Like precious Dawn, these flowers were her children. She relished the hours spent nurturing them and watching them grow. The garden was her solace, her escape, and these flowers, her joy.

She placed the flowers in the glass vase beside the handwritten note at the center of the table.

Stepping back, she admired her efforts. Her work was done. It was time to go.

As she read the note again one last time, she began to cry. At first she tried fighting the tears, begging her emotions to cooperate, to be strong. But then she realized that she was alone and it was still dark outside. There was no one to judge her, no one to witness her tears but the goddess of night herself. Throughout the centuries, Nyx had helped countless women hide their secrets and tears in her darkness. And this time would be just once more.

Still in her tattered pink slippers and robe, she stepped outside and closed the door behind her. Without looking back, she crossed the courtyard and started down the dark and deserted road toward the port. She did her best to keep her mind clear, to think only of Dawn—and, of course, him. She would fill these moments thinking of him.

She reached the port and climbed onboard a small caïque. Undoing the knot, she turned on the motor and started out to sea. As the boat sputtered forward, Hemera awoke, hitching her chariot just as Nyx began her descent. The first light of dawn sliced through the night sky as mother and daughter passed each other at the gates of Tartarus. No words were exchanged between the pair, but none were needed. Deities, like mere mortals, speak the silent language of mothers and their daughters.

She cut the motor and stood, watching the light bleed into the black. The goddess of day had begun her journey. It was now time to begin hers.

"I love you, Dawn. My dear and beautiful girl," she said, praying her words might somehow catch a ride on Hemera's chariot and be carried home to her sleeping daughter.

"Oh, and how I love you," she said to him. "I love you more than you will ever know. I love you more than you can imagine. I never dreamed there could be anything, anyone who would tear me away from Dawn." Her voice cracked and grew strained. Then the thought of him helped her find her courage once again. "But then there was you . . ."

She willed the tears away this time. Hemera would bear witness to what she would do next, but not to her tears. She wanted the light to shine only on her strength, her determination, and to know nothing of her fears. Unlike her mother, Hemera was not a keeper of secrets.

She kicked off her slippers and looked up toward the brightening sky. Holding the mast for balance, she stepped onto the boat's railing and kept her gaze on the horizon. Unlike Orpheus, she would not look back.

With one fluid move, she released the mast, stepped off the boat, and plunged into the sea. She felt the shock of cold first. It was colder out here, colder than she thought possible. She had never been fully submerged in the sea, and the sensation was new, strange. She felt herself pulled instantly down. Instinct told her to kick, to resist the pull, to fight. She willed this reflex away. Some urges are stronger than instinct.

As the water filled her nose, her lungs, and poured into her body, she felt the weight carry her down; the weight of the water, of her responsibility, of her disappointments, disillusionment, and long-ago dreams. She knew that all this weight, all these burdens, were enough to make her disappear.

To make it stop, she had to disappear.

With her head tilted up toward the surface, she could barely make out the sun's rays calling to her, reaching down into the depths of the sea and pleading to her from the sky. But Hemera was no match for the mother goddess who came to stake her claim. Even territorial Poseidon and the great god Zeus deferred to the wishes of the night.

She opened her arms in surrender and felt Nyx overtake her, carrying her farther and farther away. Others feared the black, the dark unknown. But she knew better. Where others saw only the unanswerable mysteries of the night, she saw the relief and respite that only darkness can bring. While others waited impatiently for Hemera to illuminate their lives, she counted the hours until she could once again hide under Nyx's dark veil.

As she floated deeper toward the end, she felt the force lunge at her and seize her. With inhuman strength, it grabbed around her waist, yanking her as if it might split her in two. Her insides burned with the weight of the water and now this. The force pulled her up toward the surface. It was dragging her away, away from the dark palace, and bringing her again toward the light.

No, that's the wrong way!

But she didn't have the strength to fight.

She could hear his cries as he pulled and lifted her to the surface and out of the water. "Katerina!" he screamed. "Katerina, what have you done?" Her limp body landed on the boat's deck.

A soft haze infiltrated her darkness. Through impossibly heavy eyelids, she could see his silhouette as he hovered over her. "What have you done?" he cried as he cradled her body against his.

She could not make out his face through the fog, but she knew the voice. It wasn't a divine being of either night or day, but a mortal man, divine nonetheless. It was Marco. He was here with her, holding her now as she had prayed so many times he would. She had dreamed of this moment for years, wondering what her hand would feel like in his, his skin against her own. And finally, he was here.

"Why have you done this?" he sobbed as he held her, folding his body onto hers.

She wanted to tell him, to explain why, to confide in him as she could no other. But sometimes there are no words, even for the man who holds the missing piece of one's heart.

"Katerina, no!" he shouted, shaking her limp body, willing her to expel the water from her lungs. "No."

She could barely hear him now, his cries growing fainter and fainter. She would have loved to stay, even for just a few moments longer. But it was too late for her, too late for them.

This was not the first time she had been bound by duty. This time, just as before, she had already been promised to someone else.

The gates of Tartarus opened once again. The dark goddess emerged. Nyx reached out her hand, beckoning Katerina to come. Without hesitation, Katerina slipped away from the boy she had always loved and gave herself over to the night.

Arm in arm, Nyx and Katerina crossed the threshold of Tartarus and entered the dark palace. They gazed into each other's eyes and nodded in silent agreement, both fluent in the silent language of mothers, both willing to confine themselves to a life in the shadows so their children could walk forever in the light.

Gasping for air, Katerina opened her eyes and sat up in bed. It was still dark out.

She replayed the dream in her mind. Vividly. Frame by frame. This time she didn't need the help of Clotho's dream book to understand.

Katerina went to the kitchen to make coffee. She searched through the house, opening every drawer and cabinet until at last she found what she was looking for. When the coffee was ready, she went outside to the terrace and sat down. Sipping the hot, bitter liquid, she stared out across the water and collected her thoughts. By now the sun had risen, revealing it to be a gloriously bright and sunny day. The sea was calm and glassy, reflecting the few wispy clouds that dotted the sky like puffs of cotton scattered across the heavens. Inspired by the brilliant sunshine and fueled by the coffee, Katerina began to write.

> Dear Dawn,
>
> My dear sweet girl. Please don't cry for me.
>
> If you are reading this letter, you are a mother now. And so I know you will understand . . .

Fifty-Three

"She's been quiet all week. And weak. We've tried getting her to eat, but she will barely take anything." The nurse greeted Katerina as she entered the building, which was tucked away among the cobblestone alleys behind Saint Spyridon Church.

"I brought spanakopita and *bougatsa*. I thought maybe she would like something from the bakery on the corner," Katerina said, fingers wrapped around the pastries. The brown paper wrapping glistened, soaked through with olive oil from the filo dough–encrusted pastries, one savory, one sweet. "I can't tell you how many times she treated me to a pastry when I was young and didn't have even a drachma to spare." She could picture it so clearly, as if it were yesterday. Clotho, in her father's fisherman's cap and mother's apron, holding her hand as they strolled along the winding lanes and alleys.

"She's in here." The nurse motioned to the door. As Katerina passed,

335

the nurse stopped her, placing her arm on Katerina's shoulder. "I want you to prepare yourself. She is declining. I'm not sure how talkative she will be. She sleeps most of the time. She always spoke so highly of you. She loved you as if you were her own daughter."

Katerina nodded, words impossible to find.

"You've taken better care of her than most daughters would. I want you to know that. Even though you were thousands of miles away, you were more present than some of these families who live right here in town, who can't be burdened by the inconvenience and indignity of old age. She knew that. It's important for you to know that too."

Katerina smiled at the nurse, still holding her hand. "Thank you," she said before knocking lightly and opening the door to Clotho's room.

Despite the nurse's warning, Katerina was unprepared for what she saw as she entered. The sight of her, gaunt and pale, translucent skin clinging to angular cheekbones, forced Katerina to confront just how much time had passed. It had been three years since Katerina had been back to Corfu, three years since she had seen Clotho. Every summer Katerina returned with Dawn, and Clotho took a taxi to Corfu Town, where they would spend the afternoon together at Josephine. But these past few years, between the wedding and Dawn's pregnancies, it had been too difficult to get away. And now as she looked at her old friend, Katerina felt a pang of guilt along with the passage of time.

Clotho's eyes were sunken and dark. Her hair—through the years worn long, dark, and braided, covered by her father's faded fisherman's cap—now reduced to a shock of white. She was dressed in a hospital gown, her arms, like two frail twigs dotted with brown spots, at her sides atop the blanket. Her fingernails were ragged and ridged. They, too, were pale, void of the black earth Katerina remembered embedded under her nails from all those hours spent tending the garden. Katerina walked closer and spoke her name.

"Clotho. Clotho. I'm here. It's Katerina. I came home, like you asked me to."

There was no movement or acknowledgment from Clotho, just shallow breathing, slow and rhythmic, the heart and pulse monitor beeping behind the bed.

Katerina pulled a chair over to her bedside. She reached her arm out, taking Clotho's hand in hers. She rubbed her fingers along Clotho's skin, remembering how those very hands had held her all those times when it seemed there was nothing and no one left for Katerina to hold on to.

"Clotho. It's Katerina. I'm here. I came like you asked me to. I saw Marco." Her voice cracked at the mention of his name. "I saw him and I know. I know what happened. I know why you told me I needed to come." She stood up, leaned over, and pressed her cheek against Clotho's chest. Katerina stayed like that for a few moments, focusing on the rhythmic beating of Clotho's heart, then she lifted her head, wiping a stray white tendril from Clotho's forehead.

"Clotho. I know why I lost my babies." Her voice trembled as she reached again for Clotho's hand. "I know why Dawn lost her babies. I have to make it stop. I know what I have to do. I had a dream last night and I saw it. I saw it all clearly in front of me. Remember when I would come to you and you would read my dreams for me? This time I knew even before I saw you." She laid her head on Clotho's chest once again.

I know what I have to do.

It was then that she felt it, the lightest touch like the flutter of a butterfly's wing in flight. At first she was unsure, but she felt it again, the softest touch against her curls, and she lifted her head to see Clotho, eyes open, smiling at her.

"My Katerina. I knew you would come."

Katerina hugged Clotho, careful not to hold her too close or too tight. So many years later and so much had changed, and yet there was still safety in Clotho's arms.

Her voice was soft, even softer than the other day on the telephone. "I had a dream too. It was a wonderful dream." Clotho's eyes lit up, crinkling at the corners.

Katerina sat down again and inched her chair closer. She held Clotho's hand in both of hers.

"Katerina, Yianna came to me."

Katerina sat up straighter.

"Yes. It's all right," Clotho said, patting Katerina's hand. "She came to me in my dream, and together we went home. I was back home, Katerina, among the olive and cypress trees, with my oldest friend." Clotho closed her eyes. A smile unfurled on her lips, as if she was transported back to the mountainside again. "We walked along the old roads and paths together, we tended to my garden, and we even drank from the fresh spring. And then we sat together on her veranda, the house of so many generations, so much love and laughter and also so much sorrow. We were at once young and old, filled with the light and hopefulness of our youth, but also the weight and wisdom of all we have seen and endured in our lives.

"She had so much to tell me, Katerina, so many stories and so much wisdom to share. She told me she tried to do her best for Marco. But she was damaged by her grief. She knows this now. She said she would have given anything she had to give Marco a better life, but she had nothing left. Nothing at all to give, except herself. She gave herself for her child. And then the mayor committed the ultimate betrayal and sin, Katerina. By the laws of God and man, he must pay. And he continues to pay."

A guttural moan escaped Katerina's lips. Her head hung low, the weight of it all, the reality of what he did.

Clotho shifted toward her, placed her fingers beneath Katerina's chin, and lifted her face to meet her eyes. "Look at me, Katerina."

Katerina did as she was told. She looked into Clotho's eyes, clouded over yet kind as ever.

"Marco is home and Yianna can finally rest easy. And now, Katerina, so can you. A mother's place is with her child. She knows this, Katerina. Go home to Dawn and prepare to hold your grandchild in your arms. There will be no more tears."

It took a moment for Clotho's words to sink in. "Clotho. Are you saying . . ."

"Yes. It's finished now. She knows what it is to lose a child, Katerina. And she never wanted you to know this heartbreak. The mayor will suffer for all eternity for what he did. But not you. Not your children. And not their children's children. Not anymore."

"Oh, Clotho." Katerina jumped up and hugged her. The ferocity of a mother's love was indeed powerful and dangerous enough to place a curse, but it was also powerful enough to end one.

"Katerina." Clotho held tight to Katerina. There was something else she needed to say.

"It was more than words, Katerina. She wants you to know. She said you need to know."

"What do you mean, more than words?"

"Everyone in the village would whisper and laugh, and even Yianna's husband and children would laugh at the idea, Katerina. But I believed her. And I still do. And she wants you to believe her as well. It's important that you do."

"I'm not sure I understand. Believe what?"

"The promise Alice made to Vasiliki was more than empty words. It was not just an old family story to share and reminisce about from time to time. It was a sacred vow between two friends, between two mothers. Yianna always knew this. Alice's words still linger in the air, among the clouds, drifting on the breeze, waiting to be fulfilled. A promise like this does not just fade away or disappear with the years or lost memories of a life gone by. A promise like this is timeless and infinite . . ."

"Like a mother's love."

Clotho smiled at her. "Yes, Katerina. Exactly." Her eyes then fluttered shut.

Katerina sat there all afternoon, silently holding her hand, soaking in every moment spent in Clotho's presence and playing their conversation over and over again in her mind. It was past nine o'clock when she kissed a sleeping Clotho goodbye and walked out and onto the cobblestone square. She gazed up at the church's rust-hued bell tower, framed against a cloudless black sky. The stars above looked to Katerina like silver confetti, twinkling and shining against the black. Above the roofs and bell towers of the old town, thousands of swallows raced and danced across the sky in their frenzied evening performance.

Part Eight

Fifty-Four

Athens

February 1981

The Olympic Airways flight from Madrid taxied down the runway and came to a stop on the tarmac. King Constantine appeared in the doorway and looked down at the journalists and crowd gathered below. He descended the stairs, followed by Queen Anne-Marie, wearing a black dress, head covered in a veil. Their children, Crown Prince Pavlos, Prince Nikolaos, and Princess Alexia, followed behind.

Once his feet touched the tarmac, the king bent down on his knees, made the sign of the cross, and kissed the ground.

It was the first time King Constantine had stepped foot on Greek soil in more than a decade.

Frederica had been by her son's side the night they were forced into exile, driven to flee the country in the early-morning hours after the king attempted a countercoup of the military junta that had taken control. Encouraged by his military advisors to press on, the king instead made the impossible decision to flee, insisting he would not see one drop of Greek

343

blood spilled on his behalf. And now, thirteen years later, King Constantine had finally returned home with his mother. Only this time it was to bury her. The government granted him five hours in the country to do so.

The trip from the airport took no more than thirty minutes, the funeral procession winding through the streets of Athens to Tatoi, the former summer palace of the royal family. All along the route, on the narrow streets of the old city and along the broad boulevards leading to Tatoi, as the king and queen and their family looked out the window, they were greeted by crowds and cheers and chants. Despite the government's best efforts and threats against pro-monarchy demonstrations, supporters of the royal family congregated on the sidewalks to pay their respects and welcome Frederica home.

Frederica was buried on the leafy grounds of Tatoi, beside her beloved Paul, and generations of kings and queens before them. Dressed in his funeral robes, the archbishop of Athens waved his censer, smoke and incense filling the air as the family chanted the funeral hymn alongside the priests and bishop. "May her memory be eternal. Amen."

Prince Philip closed his eyes and bowed his head as the prayers were read. Something familiar stirred inside of him that afternoon. The smoke, the incense, the ancient chants kindled a spark within him that time and country and duty could never extinguish. He was just a child when he left Corfu, and yet the glimmers of memories—the sights, sounds, colors, and scents of the island—had lain dormant inside him all this time.

As he stood at the gravesite that afternoon, Prince Philip felt a faint and familiar reminiscence buried deep inside him. Somewhere between a memory, a vision, and a dream, he recalled a moment in a dark incense-filled room, rich jewel-colored icons adorning the wall. He could see and feel it. In a childhood marred by instability and trauma, in that memory, in that moment, in that room dripping with silver lanterns, Prince Philip recalled what it was to feel safe and loved.

Alice had come to live with Philip and Queen Elizabeth in Buckingham Palace just after Constantine went into exile. At first she resisted, saying she could not fathom leaving her beloved Greece or the sisterhood to which she had devoted the last years of her life. But as the political climate in Athens darkened, Queen Elizabeth insisted Alice was welcome to make her home in Buckingham Palace.

For two years, Alice lived in a bright and spacious palace apartment overlooking the grounds. Each day after his lessons, Charles would walk in the gardens with his grandmother, admiring and sketching the various flowers and animals. And each afternoon after her bath, Anne would run to her grandmother's room where Alice would regale her granddaughter with stories of her adventures and travels. And while the queen rather enjoyed her nightly cocktail and game of canasta with Alice, Philip preferred to watch from a distance as he read the newspapers by the evening fire. They were at last, as Philip had always wished for as a child, and as Alice had prayed for year after year, a family. When Alice died after those two years, the funeral took place at St. George's Chapel on the grounds of Windsor Castle.

The day of the funeral, a thick, deep, blinding fog descended on London, grounding flights and making it impossible for many friends and family to attend. Despite the inclement weather, King Constantine found his way to the chapel that day. He stood by Philip's side as Alice's casket was lowered into the ground.

And now, just as they had the day a dense fog swallowed London more than a decade ago, Prince Philip and King Constantine stood shoulder to shoulder as Frederica was laid to rest on Greek soil beside her husband.

"*Zito Vasilefs!* Long live the king!" The crown erupted again in cheers as the funeral procession made its way back to Athens. "May her memory be eternal."

As he gazed out the window watching the scene unfold, Philip recalled one of the final conversations he had with his mother before she died. He'd sat on the edge of her bed as she slept, and when she woke, she'd smiled to see him there.

"*Philip, I had the loveliest dream,*" Alice had said. "*I dreamed we were back on Corfu. I dreamed we were out in the garden, among the olive groves and cypress trees overlooking the sea. You were running and laughing and playing as the sun caught your curls. And there was a woman there with us as well, who came from beyond the mountain. I was so happy to see her, and yet I did not know her name. She came closer to us, and as I took your hand in mine, I reached my other hand out toward her.*" Alice sat up in bed then, a serene smile crossing her lips. "*And just as she was almost upon us, just before I could see her face, I woke up.*"

"*What do you think it means, Mother?*"

"*It's been a long time. And there is so much I no longer remember. But I do know we were happy there, Philip. I've felt this pull for so long, but I was always too busy with my work. We were too busy . . .*" Her voice trailed off. She closed her eyes, taking a few shallow breaths before she spoke again. "*But even so, we finally went home together, Philip, even if it was only in my dream.*"

Philip nodded and placed his hand on hers. Alice smiled.

She closed her eyes again and leaned her head back against her pillow. Her breath was shallow and rapid. The next morning she was gone.

"Zito Vasilefs!" The chants of the crowds at the airport brought Philip back from his memory. "Long live the king!" The chants grew louder as Philip exited the car. He stood on the tarmac and watched as Constantine waved to the crowd and then ascended the stairs of the plane with his family. Philip followed, stopping at the top of the stairs to take one last look around at the crowds and the mountains surrounding Athens in the distance.

As the plane taxied down the runway, Philip replayed the scene at Frederica's grave. The ancient chants of the priests, the jingle of the censer, the smoky scent of incense. The sights and sounds and smells had indeed stirred something dormant in him. He closed his eyes now and could see the images so clearly in his mind. The dark church, the feeling of his hand in his mother's, the assurance of her friend's touch on his arm, kneeling between the women as they whispered their prayers and bowed their veiled heads.

And then another image came to him. He saw himself now, hand in hand with a young girl as they emerged from the dark church, laughing and giggling as they ran into the bright Corfu sun.

Part Nine

Fifty-Five

Four weeks after returning from Greece, Katerina became a grandmother when Dawn gave birth to a beautiful and healthy baby boy. He came into the world with a shock of black hair, chubby pink cheeks, and a strong set of lungs that heralded his arrival with a piercing cry that reverberated down the halls of Montefiore Hospital. Katerina and Violeta, who had spent the entire night pacing the hospital's halls, had jumped into each other's arms when they heard him wail. Stamati's face had erupted into a broad smile as he handed out cigars to anyone who crossed his path.

They named him Spiro, after the patron saint of Corfu, knowing Saint Spyridon would always watch over him.

Life had been happier than Katerina ever could have dreamed. The house she had lived in since the early days of her marriage had at last became a home. Each morning during Spiro's infancy, Katerina and Violeta had met in the garden over coffee where they doted on the baby as Dawn caught a few hours of sleep. Spiro had grown to be a precocious and curious child who loved comic books and dogs and his Nonna Violeta's roasted peppers, which he devoured with crusty bread, fresh olive oil, tomatoes, and fresh basil picked from his yia-yia's garden.

Over the years, the family had welcomed two more children, a boy named Alex and a girl named Katia, short for Katerina. In addition to her name, Katia also inherited her yia-yia's dark curls and Ionian blue eyes.

The yard on Eastchester Road was as Katerina always dreamed it would be, filled with laughter, love, and children. She took great pride in the oasis she created for her grandchildren. It reminded her in so many ways of the wondrous escape Clotho's terrace had provided her and Marco.

Clotho had passed away in her sleep just weeks after Spiro was born. But as Katerina tended to her garden, guiding tiny hands to water the flowers and pick the herbs and vegetables, she could still feel Clotho's hands guiding her own.

Each summer the family returned to Corfu, where the children learned to swim and jump from the scorched cliffs of Sidari into the sea and dive for sea urchin and fish for their dinner. The family stayed in what was once the mayor's house. The house, once sealed shut against curious and prying eyes, was now a hive of activity as children raced in and out, laughter spilling out from every open window and door.

Every summer Katerina found the village infused with new life as more families began to move in and children and grandchildren returned to reclaim the homes of their ancestors. The café once again came alive with political discourse, the church bells once again welcomed worshipers on Sunday mornings, and even the schoolhouse again filled with young voices plotting their next adventure as they dreamed of sailing away to follow Odysseus's journey back home to Ithaka.

And yet, each summer the knot in Katerina's stomach would tighten with each step up the mountain that brought her closer to Marco's house. The anticipation of seeing him mixed with the anxiety and fear of what state she might find him in. Katerina would cross herself and pray that it might be different each time she pulled open the gate to find him. But time after time it was always the same. Marco, gaunt and pale and quiet, so very quiet. Even as the village came slowly back to life all around him, Marco remained a ghost.

Every time she walked through the gate, she was amazed by the transformation of Yianna's once rustic village home. A new terracotta-shingled roof, hand-laid olive wood floors, hand-carved wooden shutters for the windows, and a beautifully laid stone floor on the patio. The house grew more colorful and vibrant each year as Marco slowly faded before her eyes.

The summer Spiro turned ten, she found Marco on the terrace, asleep in his chair, empty glass still clutched viselike in his hand. Her heart sank as she walked closer to him, his shoulders narrow and sharp. She could make out the bones protruding through his shirt. His face was tanned from working in the sun and yet there was still a gray pallor to his skin. And although his face was covered in weeks-old whiskers, mostly gray and wiry with a few remnants of black, there was no camouflaging the haggard, skeletal appearance of his drawn face.

"Marco," she said. "Marco. I'm here. I'm back."

She was met with a guttural sound emanating from his throat. He remained asleep and shifted in his chair slightly, the grip on his glass intact.

"Marco," she said again, shaking his shoulder this time.

He reached his hand up and laid it on hers, eyes still closed. He was quiet and still, save for the rattle and wheeze of each breath in and out. She stayed there, his hand resting on hers, for a while longer. His reptilian hands, rough and scarred and cracked, and yet they were beautiful to her.

How many times had she tried to find a way to help him, to help him create a life away from this veranda, away from the weight and wounds of this house and of this place? Time and again she had offered him a fresh start, begging him to come stay with her in New York, asking if they might open a shop together where they could sell his handcrafted olive wood pieces. When she was in Corfu, she would ask him to take a drive to Corfu Town together, where they could stroll and people-watch and perhaps take in a performance of the philharmonic in the park. At times her pleas were met with the nervous laugh of a man who found her ideas ridiculous; other times she watched as the anger in him simmered and erupted as he slammed his hand on the table and stormed off away from her. And other times she was met with nothing but silence.

As she stood there, his hand on hers, listening to his breathing, Katerina remembered what Clotho told her in the nursing home that day. *"A promise like this does not just fade away or disappear with the years or lost memories of a life gone by. A promise like this is timeless and infinite."* She had believed Clotho and her words. And yet Katerina feared Marco was running out of time.

She went into the house to make him some coffee and toast, hoping he might wake soon and knowing he likely had not eaten anything all day. The house was meticulously cared for, clean and bright. His bed, tucked in the corner as it had been in childhood, was covered with an old quilt that had been crocheted by his grandmother during her time at Mon Repos. The table, carved from a thick and sturdy olive tree, was flanked by four chairs, each delicately carved with rosettes etched into the wooden frames. On the table was a small glass vase holding three pink roses and two pristine white gardenias.

Yianna's curtains hung in every window frame, and Stefano's leather bag, still with Yianna's letters inside, hung from a nail above the bed.

Katerina turned on the burner and waited for the coffee to boil. She glanced around the room again, marveling at every detail. It struck her in that moment what this was, what he had done. The home, the attention to detail, the décor, the flowers . . . it was not for Marco. It was for Yianna. All of it was for Yianna.

Fifty-Six

Corfu
August 1994

"Are you sure you don't mind?" It was just before seven a.m. The children and Fabricio were still sleeping.

"Of course." Katerina waved Dawn away with a flick of her hand. "Of course I don't mind. I want to. I insist. Besides, it's tradition at this point."

"Yes. But it's also a hundred degrees. You'll melt out there."

It was an annual tradition for the family to drive to Corfu Town and celebrate the saint's procession and blessing with a big breakfast at Josephine. But Corfu was in the midst of a historic heat wave. For more than a week now, the temperatures had soared past a hundred degrees daily. Even now, even before daybreak, Katerina's blouse and skirt stuck to her damp skin in the stagnant air.

"Go back inside." Katerina kissed Dawn's forehead and shooed her away.

She started the car and pulled away from the house. But instead of driving south, down the coast toward Corfu Town, she turned along the newly paved road, up the mountain to Marco's house.

She found him outside, drinking coffee and smoking a cigarette.

"Good morning," she announced as she opened the gate. She put effort into sounding upbeat and cheerful as she fully anticipated the conversation that would come next. "It's the *litania* today."

He nodded, lighting another cigarette, the ashtray before him overflowing onto the table. Three gray kittens chased one another on the other side of the patio as their mother lay back on the stone floor watching over them while another kitten nursed.

His shirt was stained, as were his pants. It was clear to Katerina that he had not bathed in days. And perhaps, she thought, as his trembling hands lifted the coffee cup to his lips, he had not eaten either.

"Come with me to town. It's been years since you've gone. Just for today, come so we can receive the saint's blessing." She forced a smile.

"No, Katerina. Please. I know you mean well. But just leave me alone." He turned his head from her.

She went inside the house to get some water. On the table was a box of bread and pastry that she brought him just three days before, hoping they might entice him to ingest something other than coffee, cigarettes, and whisky. Beside the box, a vase held a delicate spray of lavender blossoms. She lifted the lid with her fingertip and looked inside. He had touched none of it, except for a small corner of bread that had been broken off.

"Please, Marco," she said as she walked back outside to the terrace.

"Katerina. Just go. Go to your family. Go to town. Go to your saint. Just go."

"Marco, please. Don't let them win. They took your childhood; don't let them take these years too."

He lit another cigarette.

His words replayed in her mind the entire trip down the mountain and along the coast. *"Just go."* It was the refrain he gave her more and more frequently these past few years. It had been thirteen years since he had returned. As damaged as he was, he had a purpose and a reason to wake up and accomplish something when he came back to the village. But now that the work on his house was nearly finished, Katerina feared what might come next for Marco.

She parked the car in the lot adjacent to the cricket court overlooking the old fort. Stopping at the periptero, she picked up a newspaper, a few comic books, and an assortment of candy, knowing these would help keep the children entertained.

It was just past eight o'clock, and already the best tables, adjacent to the square and affording the best view of the procession, were taken, even in this heat. She kicked herself for not coming earlier. She should have known better.

"Katerina!" She heard her name called from across the square.

"Thanassi." She walked over to him and greeted him with a kiss on each cheek. Thanassi had inherited the café when his father, Manoli, passed away a few years before. He had also inherited his father's kind and generous spirit as well as business acumen. After he'd changed the café's name from Olympia to Josephine and rebranded the menu, the spot was now one of the busiest and most successful on the island.

"Come. I have a table for you." He ushered her to a table up front, one that would provide the best view of the procession no matter how crowded the square became.

"Thank you. I didn't expect you to save me a table."

"Are you kidding me?" He laughed as he snapped a towel into the air. "My father would come back and haunt me if I didn't take care of you."

Katerina settled in as the plateia buzzed around her. Families claimed their seats as they sipped water and juice to stay cool. Vendors sold plastic fans in the square to old ladies dressed head to toe in black, complete with black stockings and tightly knotted headscarves, despite the historic heat of the morning. She sipped her frappé coffee and settled in to read the newspaper as she waited for Dawn, Fabricio, and the children to arrive.

Katerina glossed over the headlines announcing the latest government stalemate and crisis and shook her head at the weather report. The oppressive heat would linger for at least another three days. She dabbed at her forehead with a napkin and held the cool glass of coffee to her neck.

"Yia-yia." She heard her grandchildren call to her as they raced across the plateia into her arms.

"My babies." She hugged and kissed them multiple times before summoning the waiter. After a breakfast of flaky chocolate croissants and custard-filled *galaktoboureko*, the children settled in with the comic books Katerina had bought for them.

"I hear it!" Spiro shouted. His brother and sister followed suit, jumping up and down with excitement. The boys stood on their chairs to get a better view while Katia sat on her yia-yia's shoulders.

They watched as the Corfu Philharmonic shuffled by, keeping time with the mournful melody announcing that the saint's procession would soon follow behind.

A dozen or so priests turned from Spianada Square and into the Liston, some carrying icons, others with incense-filled censers, and four black-robed priests had the honor that day of carrying the remains of Saint Spyridon through the streets in his glass-enclosed crypt. A quiet fell upon the crowd as the saint's procession passed. Everyone came to their feet and made the sign of the cross as the saint went by and the priests filled the air with the clinking jingle and smoky aroma of their censers.

"And next year, with the saint's blessing" was heard again and again as the faithful kissed one another on the cheeks and began to disperse, looking for respite from the oppressive heat of the day.

"And next year again, with the saint's blessing." Katerina kissed Dawn, Fabricio, and the children on both cheeks as she grabbed her things and prepared to head back home.

"Yia-yia, will you take us to the water to see the boats?" Katia asked, tugging at Katerina's skirt.

"Yia-yia is tired and hot. Let's give her a bit of a break, shall we?" Dawn smiled at the children as she tried in vain to herd them from Katerina.

"No, it's fine." Katerina shooed Dawn away with a flick of her hand. "Of course, my darling," she replied to Katia, motioning for the children to come with her as she folded the newspaper and prepared to tuck it in her bag. As she did, a headline caught her eye. She opened the paper, looking closer at the headline and scanning the article. She exhaled deeply and clutched the newspaper to her chest.

"What is it, Yia-yia?" Spiro asked as he fanned himself with the comic book.

"It's a blessing from the saint, my dear. A beautiful blessing from our beloved saint." She made the sign of the cross again as she grabbed Katia's hand and headed toward the old fort marina with the children.

Fifty-Seven

Corfu

August 1994

"Won't you please just go?" The agitation in Marco's voice bordered on anger.

"Marco, I need your help. This time it's not about you. It's about me. And Dawn and my grandchildren. I need your help."

"What could I possibly do to help you?" He stormed out of the house and began pacing the patio, cigarette smoke trailing behind him.

"Come with me to city hall, please. You're the only one left who knows that the property is mine. My parents' house has been abandoned for so many years I need to file paperwork to prove ownership. I thought it wouldn't be necessary, but with so many foreigners snatching up every piece of property they can find, I can't take the chance. I need to secure it. Please. It's for Dawn and the children," Katerina pleaded.

He stomped his cigarette out on the ground.

"You just need to sign the paperwork and we'll come right back. We won't stay long. Just sign the documents for me and we'll go. Please."

Wordless, he went in the house and grabbed his cap and a pack of cigarettes. He sat in the car beside her, slamming the door a little too hard. They drove down the mountain and south along the sea. He spat out the window as they passed the beach where the mayor had forced him out of the car.

They rode in silence for about an hour until they reached the center of town. The streets were teeming with families and tourists, clusters of tour groups dotting the waterfront and park. Katerina drove past the Liston, the old fort, and then headed farther south along Garitsa bay. It was only when they passed the Corfu Palace Hotel, her sentry of international flags flapping in the wind, that Marco paid attention to where they were and the route Katerina chose to take.

"Why did you go this way? City hall is behind us."

"I know," she said, continuing south along the bay and then following as the road turned west.

She drove a bit longer and then turned left into a long, poorly paved driveway that seemed to cut though a dense forest.

"Katerina." He sat up in his seat, looking right and left. "Katerina, what is this?"

She ignored him, continuing silently up the drive, past long-forgotten stone structures, through the dense forest. She drove past the ancient stone arches lining the road until the narrow lane gave way to a large circular driveway, flanked by two rusted gas lanterns beside an oval overgrown with weeds and shrubs. The house, with her curved marble entrance, stately ionic columns, and floor-to-ceiling windows, was at once derelict and majestic; years of neglect, scorching sun, humidity, and rain taking their toll. In the distance, past cypresses and pine trees, beyond the weather-beaten yet still stately marble patio terrace, the Ionian glistened.

Marco's face turned red with rage. "How could you do this to me?" he hissed. "You lie to me and bring me here, for what? To remind me of my wasted life, my mother's wasted death? You have no business and no right. Turn this car around. Let's go." He sat back in the seat, arms folded tightly across his chest.

Katerina stopped in front of the entrance columns, peeling and discolored. Above the entranceway the marble and stone balcony and railing were dotted with rust and decay. And yet the architecture and views were just as sublime as when the villa was home to generations of the royal family. Neither time nor decay could dull the majesty of this place. And just as with the rest of the island, there was an ethereal beauty about it all, the way the light fell upon her, accenting her color and contrasts and even her imperfections. Like Corfu itself, Mon Repos's perceived flaws only served to enhance her magnificence.

Marco turned to her again. "Katerina. Let's go."

Katerina ignored him and got out of the car. She walked to the entrance and knocked on the door.

The door opened, revealing a white-haired gentleman with a bushy mustache to match. "Hello, hello, welcome to Mon Repos." His pants and shirt were white as well, and fastened with red suspenders. "Katerina, it's so nice to see you again." He shook her hand and walked over to the car, where Marco was still seated inside.

The man extended his hand to Marco through the open window. "Hello, Marco. It's such a pleasure to meet you. Katerina has told me so much about you. And I must say, she showed me your work, and it is extraordinary."

Still seated in the car, Marco looked to Katerina, his brows knotted. His lips formed a tight, straight line.

"Marco, this is Petro. Petro is overseeing the renovation of Mon Repos," Katerina said.

"Restoration," Petro corrected.

"Forgive me. Restoration. I read about it in the newspaper the other day. I came here after the litania and was lucky to meet Petro, who was kind enough to show me around himself. I told him about your work. And then I came back with pictures to show him what you've done to your house."

Still seated in the car, Marco shot dagger eyes at Katerina. She looked away before he could catch her eye, knowing the fury simmering beneath the calm exterior he was presenting to Petro.

"Marco, I saw what you did to your ancestral home. And it's beautiful. Your technique with woodwork is extraordinary. And your stonework is excellent, so precise. And by hand, a true artisan. Which is exactly what we've been looking for."

Marco looked from Katerina to Petro. "I don't understand. What does this have to do with me?"

Petro motioned to the door. "Please come inside and let me show you."

"Please," Katerina pleaded.

Marco hesitated a moment, then finally opened the door and stepped out of the car.

"This way." Petro motioned for them to follow him inside.

∞

They walked up the stairs under the portico and back in time as Marco entered Mon Repos. He stood there, in the cavernous entranceway, taking it all in. It was the first time he had stepped foot in the home he had heard so much about, the home his mother had been born in and dreamed of returning to.

Inside, doric columns dotted the welcome hall, mirroring those that greeted them outside. These, too, were cracked and spotted with rot and mold. The floor, a mosaic of brown, tan, and beige marble tiles, was dulled and scuffed. Above, a circular crystal chandelier dripped from the ceiling, long ago burnt-out light bulbs collecting dust in the sockets. And just beyond the columns, a marble staircase lined with a delicate S-shaped iron railing swept and curved elegantly to the second floor. He both smiled and felt crushed inside as he walked over to the staircase, fingering the delicate banister, now discolored and oxidized, bending down to feel the cold stone against his fingertips. His mother had toddled her first steps on these floors and climbed these very steps holding her mother's hand.

And all around, in each of the rooms surrounding the entranceway, huge windows flooded the villa with light, illuminating the grandeur that once had been and the decay that years of neglect had now set in.

"After years of lawsuits, the government has finally settled with King Constantine and his family. Now that the government has purchased the palace from the royal family, I've been assigned the task of overseeing the restoration. We are going to bring her back to life, glorious life, and open Mon Repos as a museum and public park."

Marco turned and faced Petro. "What does this have to do with me?"

"What you did with your family's home . . . that's what we aspire to do here. This was not just a palace, a place for receptions and gowns and jewels and kings and queens. This was a home. People tend to forget that. For generations, this was a home filled with laughter and the sounds of children playing, a home where generations of families lived and loved. The restoration needs to reflect that. I want Mon Repos to be a home again. One that will welcome Corfiots, Greeks, and tourists—where they can wander and explore and experience the history and magic of this place and our island."

Marco was unmoved and undeterred. "Good luck with your project." He turned and began walking toward the front door.

"There's something I'd like to show you before you go," Petro said.

Marco turned, tugging his beard with his hand, his other shoved firmly in the pocket of his jacket.

"Please." Katerina walked to him and placed her hand on his back, motioning for him to follow Petro. "Please."

He looked at her and shook his head, the red flash of anger rising. The frustration now intensifying from a simmer into a full boil threatened to erupt in full view of Petro.

Katerina stepped closer toward him and whispered to him. "I know you are angry with me. And I am sorry. But I am asking you to trust me. I will never ask you another thing in life, and if you choose to walk away from me after this, then so be it. But I'll know I at least tried. Marco, please. Just trust me enough to listen and to come."

They locked eyes. The pain and fear reflected back at one another, a mirror image of each other. She gripped his arm. "Please."

He nodded in reluctant agreement and followed.

They walked past the staircase and through several high-ceilinged and sun-drenched rooms before arriving at the back of the house. They then turned right, entering a rectangular room lined with three oversize windows that looked out on the circular driveway out front.

"This was the kitchen." Petro motioned to an empty room. Like the rest of the house, the paint and plaster on the walls were cracked and peeling. Above, the ceiling was vaulted and arched. A film of black mold had settled across the ceiling and down the walls. The disrepair and distress of this room seemed to magnify and frame the natural beauty of the view beyond the windows, heightening the brilliant blue sky contrasted against the verdant trees and jewel-toned flowers beyond.

Marco stood in the doorway, arms crossed at his chest.

"And over here, we found something in the pantry that I wanted to show you." Petro walked just beyond the kitchen, to an adjacent room that also led outside to the cellar and the maids' quarters above. He pointed. "Come, have a look."

Katerina smiled at him, her eyes crinkling at the corners. Despite his annoyance, Marco followed.

"Here, look on the wall. Look what's written here, beneath the notches in the doorframes. Here, the first one says 'June 1922.' There are two notches down here on the doorframe; one is marked 'Philip,' and the other 'Yianna.'"

Marco blinked rapidly at the sound of his mother's name. He cocked his head slightly to the left and narrowed his eyes, taking a closer look at the markings from where he stood.

"And then here, there's another one. This one says 'October 1922.' See how both children had grown?"

Marco crept closer to the markings.

"October 1922. Prince Philip was eighteen months old. This must have been right before they fled," Petro said.

Marco inched closer still. He reached his hand out to touch the notches in the doorway, his finger lingering over the marking beside Yianna's name.

"It's been a bit of a mystery around here. For quite a few years now we've been trying to sort out who Yianna was. We know it was Prince Philip, of course. But no one in the archives or the historical society could figure out who our little Yianna was. Until the day Katerina came to see me and told me about your family."

"It was your mother's dream to come back here. She was never given the chance. But you have been; you can." Katerina leaned against the wall.

"You have the craftsmanship and history with this house," Petro continued. "Katerina told me about your grandmother and her friendship with Alice. She also told me your mother was born here. It would make the restoration even more meaningful to have you join us. This house has a rich, storied history, and you and your family are part of that history. It would be an honor to have you as part of Mon Repos's future as well."

No one said anything further for a few moments, allowing the offer to settle in and marinate in Marco's mind.

"I'd like to walk around a bit more, if that's all right."

"Of course. Take all the time you'd like."

Marco and Katerina spent hours exploring Mon Repos and her grounds. They walked up the staircase to the second floor, marveling at the domed ceiling and cutout octagon framed by semicircular windows all around that flooded the room with brilliant sunlight. They walked outside to the cellar and up a back staircase to the servants' quarters, lingering in the tiny apartment where Vasiliki and Yianna had lived and known such happiness.

From there they went outside and through the forest, dwarfed beneath towering pine trees, and stepped gingerly over the protruding roots of the ancient olive grove.

"Oh, look, it's still here," Katerina said, quickening her step toward a massive, multitrunked olive tree.

Her fingers traced the sinewy lines of the tree as she spoke. "I came here looking for you, after I learned you were not at the paidopoleis. I thought maybe you ran away and came back to Mon Repos and were hiding in the forest. And then I saw Frederica and her family. They were on the beach, swimming and laughing. I wanted to ask her for help, ask if she knew where you were, if she could help me find you. But then I saw the police officers and I got scared. I thought they might throw me in jail for trespassing." She laughed. "So I hid here, behind this tree. And I watched as they walked away. I was so afraid I would never find you."

"You came looking for me?"

She laughed now, a nervous laugh. "Of course I did. I told you I did." The smile faded from her lips. "I never stopped looking for you."

He lit a cigarette, taking a deep, long drag, and together they continued walking through the forest, past the gardens and patches of wildflowers, until they reached the beach.

"I watched them swimming here. Frederica, Paul, Constantine, and his sisters. I remember thinking how beautiful Frederica was and how lucky they were to be her children. I watched them, wondering what it must be like to have everything they could possibly want in life. How easy life must be for them. And then I watched Constantine lean in and take a drink of water from Kardaki, right over there." He followed her gaze just beyond the shoreline to the freshwater spring, still flowing, almost obscured beneath years of overgrowth and brush.

They climbed down the stone steps toward the sea. Katerina stayed on the beach while Marco walked out along the thin pier.

He stood out there alone for quite some time, taking in the beauty of his surroundings, taking in the meaning of this afternoon and this place. He walked back toward her, and together they sat on an old, carved wooden bench, gazing out across the sea. On either side of them the cliffs of Corfu jutted out, covered in the lush, dense greenery that defined the island and this place.

"It's something, isn't it?" Marco said as he gestured out across the beach to the beauty all around them.

"Yes. It's beautiful here."

"Yes. But it's more than that. All those times I laughed at my mother, made fun of her, joked about buying her a crown like a proper princess. All those times she shook her head at me and told me one day I would believe her, that one day I would understand our connection to this place . . . I laughed at her, Katerina. But I understand now. I finally understand."

"Tell me what you mean."

He took a moment to collect his thoughts, watching as a gull glided along the shore and then disappeared into the water, emerging again with a fish in its beak. It landed on the pier and began to feast as Marco explained.

"No matter how much she tried to convince me, to make me believe in this eternal bond, this connection between our families, I never believed her. No matter how many times she insisted, I never imagined I could possibly have anything in common with Alice's family, with a prince, let alone a king. But I do." He turned to face Katerina.

"And it goes beyond Alice's vow to my grandmother. Like Alice and her family and the king, and the kings who came before him, I know what it is to be adrift, Katerina. I know what it is to want one thing more than anything in life, to just go home."

In the distance, the gull took flight again, joined now by another. Marco and Katerina sat together as the birds dipped and soared and glided together in the cloudless sky above the sea. After a few moments, the birds flew toward the forest, disappearing beyond a cluster of cypress trees standing sentinel above the shoreline.

Katerina placed her palms on Marco's cheeks and leaned in. Unblinking, she stared into his eyes.

"You are home, Marco."

Fifty-Eight

Corfu

April 2001

Petro stood halfway up the staircase, champagne glass in hand, toasting to the crowd gathered in the entranceway below.

"Thank you, friends. We appreciate your endless support and help in restoring Mon Repos. Now, before I end our program and encourage you all to explore this beautiful museum and her grounds, there is one more person I'd like to thank. It took a bit of convincing at first . . ." Petro laughed and lifted his glass toward Marco, who was standing with Katerina, Dawn, and the family, beneath the glimmering chandelier.

"But I want to extend our gratitude to an artist and a craftsman," Petro continued. "Ladies and gentlemen, please join me in thanking Marco Scarapolis. Marco spent years painstakingly working on the restoration. And we are forever in awe of his artistry and in debt to his commitment to Mon Repos and to Corfu."

"Bravo, Bravo!" Violeta cheered, lifting her glass in salute. She had arrived on Corfu earlier that morning, planning to stay for a week before joining Katerina, Dawn, and the children on a long-overdue trip to Tinos.

Katerina leaned in and kissed Marco's cheek, now clean-shaven, as the room erupted into applause. Marco stood there, dressed in slacks, a button-down shirt, and a blazer, looking a bit embarrassed by the attention, but also grateful for the acknowledgment.

He lifted his chin toward Petro, smiling and glancing around the room to the well-wishers, patrons, and friends. The children all clapped wildly and Katia looked up at him. "You're famous," she said. He smiled down at her with a wink.

Katerina wove her arm through his and whispered in his ear. "It's beautiful. Come, show me around. I want to take it all in."

Together they walked around the newly renovated museum of Mon Repos. Marco guided Katerina through each of the rooms, pointing out the projects and details he had crafted and restored over the past seven years.

"Come," he said as he led her by the hand to the second floor. "You have to see this." Pristine white ionic columns formed the base of the exquisitely restored dome. The octagon was painted robin's-egg blue, with a delicate floral relief embellishing the architecture. And from above, sunlight filtered down and filled the room with brilliant light.

"It's beautiful." She took it all in, amazed at the transformation. He led her from room to room as he explained how he spackled and patched the walls, working with the historians to choose just the right paint color for historical accuracy and detail. He told her how he collaborated with the brightest minds from the Corfu Municipal Archives to research and explore period details that he lovingly and carefully carved and crafted to life. He explained how he sanded and power washed the stonework to rid the terraces of discoloration and mold, and how he used pine and olive trees from the forest to handcraft new shutters and doors that he stained and polished to period perfection.

She hung on his every word as he spoke, marveling at the transformation not only in Mon Repos but in him as well. She had watched the change over the years. Each layer of paint and grime and rust and rot that Marco carefully and meticulously removed from Mon Repos seemed to have a reciprocal effect on him. Each project slowly stripping away the layers of sorrow, heaviness, and guilt that had anchored him to the past, preventing him from finding purpose and joy in his life. As Marco had breathed new life into Mon Repos, Mon Repos had breathed new life into Marco.

After the reception, the crowd wandered the halls and grounds of the museum. Taking two glasses of champagne from a passing waiter, Marco led Katerina out the front door and into the forest. Arm in arm they walked, savoring the beauty of the afternoon as sunlight flickered through the trees, forming a swirling kaleidoscope on the forest floor.

They walked through the olive grove and past the meadow alive with tiny yellow wildflowers and followed the path down toward the swimming spot of kings. Marco led her to a carved wooden bench, where they sat and watched the tide gently lap against the sand.

"Cheers to you," she toasted, lifting her glass.

"Thank you," he said, and then he leaned in closer. "I mean it, Katerina. Thank you."

She smiled back at him.

"Thank you for everything. For believing in me, even when I thought there was nothing left to believe in."

She squeezed his hand. "It's beautiful. And you should be proud. You made a difference."

"No, not just to Mon Repos. For bringing *me* back. I have something for you," he said as he stood, taking a final sip from his glass. "It's long overdue, but I wanted you to know that I am a man of my word."

She looked at him suspiciously, unsure where this was going. "I don't need a gift. You didn't need to get me anything."

"It's not a thing. I made a promise to you years ago. I thought about that promise recently, and I knew it was time." He smiled at her, his eyes twinkling as his lips slid over his teeth to reveal a broad smile. He stood before her, backlit by the rust-hued sky, silhouetted in the fading light.

"I dedicate this long-overdue poem to you, my Katerina, my lifelong friend, my family . . . my everything." He stood taller, taking a deep breath. He spoke slowly and precisely, savoring each word.

"As you set out for Ithaka
hope your voyage is a long one,
full of adventure, full of discovery.
Laistrygonians and Cyclops,
angry Poseidon—don't be afraid of them:
you'll never find things like that on your way
as long as you keep your thoughts raised high,
as long as a rare excitement
stirs your spirit and your body.
Laistrygonians and Cyclops,
wild Poseidon—you won't encounter them
unless you bring them along inside your soul,
unless your soul sets them up in front of you.
Hope your voyage is a long one.
May there be many summer mornings when,
with what pleasure, what joy,
you come into harbors seen for the first time;
may you stop at Phoenician trading stations
to buy fine things,
mother of pearl and coral, amber and ebony,
sensual perfume of every kind—
as many sensual perfumes as you can;
and may you visit many Egyptian cities
to gather stories of knowledge from their scholars.
Keep Ithaka always in your mind.
Arriving there is what you're destined for.
But do not hurry the journey at all.
Better if it lasts for years,

so you are old by the time you reach the island,
wealthy with all you've gained on the way,
not expecting Ithaka to make you rich.
Ithaka gave you the marvelous journey.
Without her you wouldn't have set out.
She has nothing left to give you now.
And if you find her poor, Ithaka won't have fooled you.
Wise as you will have become, so full of experience,
you will have understood by then what these Ithakas
      mean.'"

Katerina felt the tingle in her eyes the moment he began to speak. The words filled her in ways she never could have imagined when she first heard Cavafy's poem as a child.

"Bravo. Bravo." She smiled through her tears. "I knew you could do it. It's beautiful, isn't it?"

"Yes. It's beautiful, and so is all of this." He motioned around them, to the sea and the beach and the green cliffs above. "For so long I could only see what was behind me, certain that it defined me, and would for the rest of my life. But somehow you dragged me back to the world of the living. I don't know how, but you did."

"Remember Orpheus." She closed her eyes as Baba's voice whispered to her among the rustling leaves.

Marco sat beside her again and tucked a stray curl behind her ear. "I could have memorized those words years ago, recited them again and again, but they would have been meaningless. And now they mean everything to me, as do you."

She inched closer to him and placed her head on his shoulder. They stayed like that, side by side, savoring this moment and this place.

The journey home had been a long, circuitous, and often torturous one. So many times along the way they had wondered if they would ever find the road back, back to the village, back to a life of meaning, back to each other. And now in this moment, in the twilight of their lives as dusk settled in around them, their long, twisting roads home had at last converged.

The moon was low and full on the horizon, her gray light reflecting on the sea's surface like a layer of molten silver.

"Come with me," Marco said, taking her by the hand.

Katerina stood and turned toward the path leading back up to the forest and to the house.

Marco stood in place. "No. This way." He turned and walked toward the water.

"What are you doing?" She laughed, letting go of his hand.

"Making good on my other promise," he said as he walked farther into the sea.

Katerina stopped at the shoreline, laughing and bringing her hands to her mouth. She wasn't quite sure if she should be worried or amused. In the moment she felt a bit of both.

"I promised you I would teach you to swim," he said. "Come on." He reached his hand out to her, waving his fingers.

"Marco." She laughed, lifting the hem of her dress as if to remind him of the special dress she purchased for the museum opening. "You're crazy."

"Come on, Katerina. I promised, and it's about time you learned how to swim."

"But I can't . . ."

He walked a bit deeper now. The water was now waist-high. "Katerina, come in the water."

She took a few steps closer to him and then stopped again when the water reached her calves, the hem of her dress now soaked through.

He looked back at her. "You trust me, don't you?"

Without hesitation, Katerina walked into the water until she reached him. The water was just past her waist as he took her in his arms and tilted her back. As the sun disappeared behind the western hills of Corfu, Katerina at last experienced the magic of floating weightless in the sea, in the swimming spot of kings.

Epilogue

They sat outside at Josephine, sipping coffee in the shadow of the old fort as schoolchildren played cricket on the grass beside the square. Marco opened the newspaper and showed Katerina the headline.

"Look," he said. "It's true. King Constantine is returning to Greece."

Katerina leaned in to get a closer look as Marco read the article aloud.

"After years of legal wrangling, the government has finally granted Constantine's request. While he maintains his title of king, Constantine will return to Greece a private citizen, with no official government role. Constantine has always maintained that more than anything in life, his dream was to one day return to his homeland and live out the remainder of his days on Greek soil."

"So it's true." She smiled, her eyebrows arched. "Marco, do you think maybe there is something to Kardaki after all?"

Katerina and Marco laughed together as dusk fell across the island. One by one, the lanterns affixed to the Liston flickered on. The gas-fed lamps lining Garitsa bay sputtered to life, and tea lights and candles adorning the café tables in the square flickered on the breeze as Corfu was cast in the ethereal glow of evening.

∾

She watches them from a distance as she always does.

She watches in silence as she always has.

If she were inclined to speak, she would assure them that yes, there is magic to be found here on this enchanted, verdant island. There is magic in the old fresh spring that bonds people to her, just as there is magic in the sleeping saint who rises in the night to help and protect those who kneel beside him in faith. And there is magic in the dark, when we most often feel alone.

But this is more than what she knows. This is who she is.

Some call her by her ancient name, envisioning her as she paints the sky black each evening. Others find her in the stillness of a quiet grotto, or in a majestic church adorned in gold and jewels.

They summon her in the night when they are helpless and afraid. They summon her with their screams, tears, and prayers—and also with their quiet whispers. It is often the whispers that call to her the loudest. They are of different times and worlds, and yet they speak the communal language of mothers, understanding what it means to love a child so deeply and completely that blinding love and searing pain are intertwined. She knows they are one and the same, that one cannot exist without the other.

She watches Katerina and Marco now, so filled with love for one another, so present in this place and moment. Although it took a lifetime, she knows the frantic whispers and prayers of their mothers that summoned her long ago have been answered.

She watches as Marco and Katerina read the story of the king's return.

She remembers those nights, the nightly prayers of a queen as she asked for the strength to be mother enough for all of the children of Greece. She has fulfilled her duty now that the queen's prayers for her own child have been answered.

A rare smile pulls at her lips as she gazes down at Marco. He is holding Katerina's hand. The serpentine smile unfurls a bit wider. Ninety-two years after their frantic goodbye on the grounds of Mon Repos, Alice's promise to Vasiliki has been realized. The sacred vow between mothers has been honored and the circle has closed at last.

As Marco and Katerina linger in the square, thousands of swallows begin their frenzied evening choreography. They dip and soar and glide above the curved arches and bell towers and ancient alleyways of Corfu.

Arm in arm, Marco and Katerina leave their table and walk along the Liston. They wander from Garitsa bay and then back again through the alleyways and lanes of the old town. Leaning on one another, whispering to one another, they walk along centuries-old cobblestones and paths. They walk in the footsteps of the saints and the sinners and the kings and queens and villagers and islanders who all call this place home.

And in that moment, as night settles in across Corfu and the lines between man and myth and legend are blurred, the gates of Tartarus inch slowly open. Draped in her long cloak, black hair flowing behind like a turbulent river, the goddess of the night, mother of sleep and dreams and nightmares, emerges and climbs aboard her golden chariot. Raising her arms to summon the moon and stars, Nyx races across the sky. She passes her daughter at the cusp of day and night and whispers her own prayer into the darkness as the twinkling lights of Corfu flicker below.

Author's Note

"Yvette, meet Nikolaos. He's Greek, like you."

And with those words I met the newest addition to our NYC news-room in the early 1990s where I was a young journalist working my way up the ranks. Nikolaos and I quickly formed a friendship in the broadcast news trenches and in the bars after work where we commiserated with our colleagues about the madness of producing a nightly news program.

I soon learned that while my new friend was Greek, he wasn't exactly Greek like me. Nikolaos was actually Prince Nikolaos of Greece, son of King Constantine and grandson to King Paul and Queen Frederica. It was important to Nikolaos that he be judged on his work ethic and not his pedigree, so he made the decision to keep his true identity secret at first, earning him the title of our undercover prince.

When we weren't chasing down breaking news, Nikolaos and I spent hours discussing our mutual love of Greece. I shared that my family was from Erikousa, a tiny island just off the coast of Corfu, and that I returned to Erikousa and Corfu each summer and considered the islands my home. Nikolaos also shared a deep connection to Corfu, as his family's summer villa, Mon Repos, is located there. But with his father, King Constantine, in exile, the Greek government would not allow Nikolaos and his family to return to Greece. Wouldn't it be wonderful, we dreamed, to meet in the homeland one day and toast the country, culture, and people that meant so much to us both.

He was the grandson of a queen who had everything others would envy, and yet, the one thing he truly wanted was to go home to Greece. I was the granddaughter of a poor, illiterate yia-yia, who had the luxury of returning home to Greece each summer. The irony was not lost on me.

I told him about my yia-yia's love for his grandmother and how she kept a framed photo of King Paul and Queen Frederica in her tiny village home. On the day I gave Nikolaos's parents and his brother a tour of the newsroom, we took a photo together. My yia-yia then proudly placed that photo of me with King Constantine, Queen Anne-Marie, Crown Prince Pavlos, and Prince Nikolaos beside the picture of King Paul and Queen Frederica on her mantel. For weeks on end the entire village streamed in and out of the house to marvel at the photo as yia-yia looked on, nearly bursting with pride.

My yia-yia explained to me that one of the reasons she was so devoted to the royal family was because of how Queen Frederica dedicated herself to saving the children of the Greek Civil War. When I mentioned my interest in learning more about Frederica, Nikolaos gave me a gift: a biography of his grandmother.

Decades passed and we went on with our lives and careers. In 2013 the Greek government allowed King Constantine and his family to return to Greece, where Nikolaos and his wife, Tatiana, settled in Athens. I continued working as a journalist in New York and published my first book, *When the Cypress Whispers*, in 2014. As I struggled to come up with the subject for my next novel, I came across the biography of Queen Frederica that Nikolaos had given me more than twenty years before.

I read once more about Frederica's campaign to save the children of Greece and found myself wondering why history so clearly remembers the Kindertransport of World War II and orphan trains of the American

Depression while stories about the children of the Greek Civil War remain mostly untold. I thought about my old friend and my grandmother's love for his. His family members were born in palaces and mine in poverty, and yet, we shared a bond that transcended it all. We shared a home. I knew these were the themes of the story I wanted to tell.

I hope *Where the Wandering Ends* transports you to Corfu and perhaps inspires you to visit our beautiful island one day. I hope you'll experience the wonder of wandering her cobblestone paths, the serenity of praying beside Saint Spyridon, and the magic of floating in the crystal blue sea as you gaze at the cypress-covered cliffs above.

And of course, I hope you'll visit majestic Mon Repos. Roam her sun-lit halls and explore the forest and gardens. And before you leave, be sure to refresh yourself with a sip from Kardaki, ensuring that you, too, will be destined to return to our magical, sickle-shaped island home in the Ionian Sea.

PHOTO BY YVETTE MANESSIS CORPORON

Left to right: Prince Nikolaos, Yvette Manessis Corporon, Crown Prince Pavlos,
King Constantine, and Queen Anne-Marie

Acknowledgments

Thank you to the friends, family, and colleagues who supported me though every step of this long, circuitous journey—my very own road to Ithaka.

My thanks begin with my old friend, Nikolaos of Greece, who opened my eyes years ago to the power of home. And to his beautiful wife, Tatiana, who through her work with the Hellenic Initiative and Breathe Hellas, has proven that home is not necessarily where you are born; it is where your heart is.

Endless thanks to the incredible team at Harper Muse. To Amanda Bostic, Nekasha Pratt, Margaret Kercher, Julie Breihan, and Jodi Hughes. To Jocelyn Bailey for welcoming me into the Harper Muse family. To my editor, Becky Monds, I'm forever grateful for your insightful suggestions. Collaborating with you is pure joy.

To my agents, the fierce and forever chic Jan Miller and Ali Kominski. Thank you for believing in this story, and in me. My dearest Nena Madonia Oshman, your spirit is etched on every page of this book.

A million thanks to Gigi Howard and SW for the most peaceful and perfect writer's retreat.

To my amazingly supportive and inspirational friends, Bonnie Bernstein,

Jen Cohn, Rachel Cohen, Karen Kelly, and Lark Marie Anton Menchini. My forever friends, Adrianna Nionakis and Olga Makrias. My valued friends and first readers, Marie Hickey, Denise Sheehan, and Michelle Tween. And to my *Extra* family who have supported me beyond my wildest dreams, especially Lisa Gregorisch, Theresa Coffino, and Jeremy Spiegel.

To my dearest Cheslie Kryst, who cheered me on and danced, smiled, and celebrated every moment and milestone leading up to publication with me. Each moment in your presence was a treasured gift.

To my parents, who understood the life-changing value of sending me to Greece each summer, even when times were challenging. And especially my mom, Kiki, a literal goddess, the best person I know, and my best friend in the world.

My husband, Dave. Home is anywhere you are beside me. My children, Christiana and Nico. Nothing makes me happier than watching you soar and chase your dreams. You are the greatest joys of my life.

My Corfu crew, George, Alexia, Aleko, Alexandra, Patty, Niko, and Noli. Here's to our magical summers together and to many more laughs and memories to come. Extra special thanks to Effie Orfanou, forever my Popi.

Heartfelt thanks to Nella Pantazi and everyone at the Municipal Archives of Corfu.

My deepest gratitude to the survivors of the Greek Civil War who have shared their stories and experiences. And to the journalists, educators, and authors who have documented these stories, as well as the history of the Greek royal family. The following books helped me immensely in my research:

- Mazower, Mark, ed. 2000. *After The War Was Over: Reconstructing The Family Nation and State in Greece, 1943–1960*. Princeton, NJ: Princeton University Press.
- Karavasilis, Nick. 2006. *The Abducted Greek Children of the Communists: Paidomazoma*. Pittsburgh: RoseDog Books.

- Danforth, Loring M. and Riki Van Boeschoten. 2012. *Children of the Greek Civil War: Refugees and the Politics of Memory*. Chicago: University of Chicago Press.
- Vickers, Hugo. 2000. *Alice: Princess Andrew of Greece*. New York: St. Martin's Press.
- Queen Frederica of the Hellenes. 1971. *A Measure of Understanding*. New York: St. Martin's Press.
- Papanicolaou, Lilika S. 1994. *Frederica, Queen of the Hellenes: Mission of a Modern Queen*. Malta: Publishers Enterprise Group.

Discussion Questions

1. Best friends Katerina and Marco share a bond that transcends time and place and the many challenges of their lives. What is it about their shared childhood experiences that bonded them to one another in such a way? Do you have a friendship from childhood that has stayed with you and left a lasting impact on you?

2. The power and magic of a mother's love is explored though the little-known myth of the goddess Nyx. While she is traditionally depicted as a dark and dangerous character, Nyx is also revealed to be a benevolent protector of mothers and their children. How is Nyx symbolic of the duality of motherhood and what mothers are capable of?

3. Yianna's and Marlena's stories speak to the depths that a mother would go to save her child. What do you think of Yianna's and Marlena's choices and sacrifices? How are they similar? How are they different?

4. As the rest of the world was celebrating the end of World War II, Greece was plunged into a deadly and dangerous civil war, and

yet, little is known about the war outside of Greece. To this day, many families in Greece do not freely discuss this time, as the memories are too painful. What are your thoughts on the trauma of survivors and the importance of discussing and documenting history, however painful it is to recall? What role does fiction play in bringing these often-forgotten stories to life?

5. The pull of home is one that drives Katerina and Marco as well as members of the Greek royal family. What does home mean to you? Where do you consider home, and why?

6. Marco's journey comes full circle as he recites Cavafy's poem, "Ithaka," to Katerina on the grounds of Mon Repos. How does this poem reflect their relationship? What does the poem mean to you? Has there been a journey in your life, however difficult, that you have learned and grown from?

7. The story of the Greek monarchy is explored and told, starting with the enthronement of King George I in 1864 to the return of exiled King Constantine to Greece in 2013 as a private citizen. What are your thoughts on the monarchy? Do you believe the idea of a monarchy is antiquated or can it be beneficial to a country and how?

8. When Violetta shares her family's tragedy, she explains why her house is always filled with family, friends, and chaos, saying, "Anything is better than the silence." After experiencing so much loss and trauma in her own life, how does Violetta's story affect and change Katerina?

9. Clotho tells Katerina that dreams can, "help you examine what's behind you or to better examine yourself. Sometimes, in the black of night, dreams help us see what we often overlook in the light of day." Katerina and Dawn both see a golden woman in their dreams. Who do you think the golden woman is? Have you ever had a dream you felt was a premonition or a prophecy?

About the Author

Photo by Connie Fernandez

Yvette Manessis Corporon is an internationally bestselling author and Emmy Award–winning producer. To date, her books have been translated into sixteen languages. A first generation Greek-American with deep family roots on Corfu, Yvette studied classical civilization and journalism at New York University. She lives in Brooklyn with her family where she spends her spare time reading, running, and trying to get into yoga.

yvettecorporon.com
Instagram: @yvettecorporon
Twitter: @YvetteNY
Facebook: @YvetteManessisCorporonAuthor